The Times We Fell in Love

By: Kaycee King

Contents

A Quick Note on Nathan's Character

I wanted to take a brief moment before reading to acknowledge that Nathan's experiences and emotions are only one facet of nonbinary representation. Being a nonbinary person isn't a flat, one-dimensional experience, and it isn't fully possible to represent with one, singular character. Some choose to use various pronouns, others do not. Nathan's preferences regarding pronoun usage will unfold throughout the story, and I don't want to spoil it, but I'll offer that this is limited to his character's experience and that should be noted. I will also clarify that, as narrator, the pronoun 'he' is used in regard to Nathan all throughout for continuity. The decision to write as such was with great consideration to the character's accepted pronouns and a desire to make the narration as immersive as possible.

In addition, I'd like to underscore that not all nonbinary people wish to be 'androgynous', nor do they always wish to be more closely presented as the gender opposite the one they've been assigned at birth. Sometimes embodiments of masculinity or femininity will vary from day to day. All this to say, I hope you will enjoy Nathan the way he has been written, but also consider that there are many other ways that nonbinary people exist and express themselves. This has been beta read by nonbinary people, and I myself do not neatly fit the binary.

Thank you for taking a chance on my book. I hope you love it as much as I loved writing it.

Don't Ask Me Why

It started with a selfie of Jackson Mitchell mooning his friends, of all things. Nathan was sitting in the apartment he shared with his childhood best friend, Maverick, when that strange little event happened. He'd been in his room, innocently strumming fingers over steel guitar strings, generally avoiding all the work and deadlines looming above his head. They were college seniors now, finishing up their time in Boise. How Nathan had gotten this far was completely beyond him, but somehow he did. Things were much simpler for Maverick. He was always smart as a whip, and Jackson…well, Jackson tended to get by with smooth talking and a clever smile. It definitely didn't hurt that he was tall, athletic, and bulky in just the right ways.

Jackson wasn't a friend from their youth. This guy, this charismatic guy who looked like he ought to be a football player, actually studied law. He and Maverick met through shared classes, and where Maverick was eagerly, almost rabidly following in the footsteps of his father, Jackson was there more of his own writ. Nathan, from day one, always found the guy to be fairly okay. Kind of annoying and cocky for sure, but he had a good heart, was wickedly hilarious, and pretty sharp, too. In contrast to the historically easygoing nature of things with Nathan, Jackson often seemed to rub Maverick the wrong way. To outsiders it probably felt strange that they kept Jackson around, but Nathan knew Maverick well enough to understand. At some point along the way, Jackson had clearly been identified a rival worth keeping close. It would explain their dynamic, and the motive suited Maverick to a hideous T.

Those two were always bickering and arguing over nothing. In the early days it was all law, then it slowly escalated and flooded into every facet of their lives. They agreed on nothing, they were both right about everything, and it was absolutely imperative that someone admitted fault. Despite Jackson's size and the fact that often times Nathan quietly agreed with him, it was usually Maverick who came out the victor. Nathan always felt Jackson gave that to Mav, like a little unspoken gift extended day, after day, after day.

In the flurry of constant agitation and conflict, it certainly didn't help that Jackson was rooming with an apartment full of beautiful women. Mav bitterly told Nathan when he'd heard of the arrangement that Jackson was probably laying them, each and every one. Nathan didn't doubt it. The vibe was there, and even though Jackson had his shortcomings, he was handsome and smooth enough to exploit it when he wanted. All of this to say, even though Jackson folded into relationships with Nathan and Maverick fast, he was never fully able to penetrate the solid nature of their rooted, childhood bonds.

At least, not at first.

Over their time spent in college, while Nathan and Maverick weathered the tides of growth and change, the things they disagreed on felt a bit larger than before. They remained friends. They often proclaimed one another as best friends even, but it was difficult to deny the fact there were ever increasing places they no longer seemed to click. Perhaps, at this point, it was merely familiarity that held them together. That and Julia, who continued to encourage them whenever things got shaky. She still came by once in a while, not as Nathan's girlfriend anymore, just as a friend. That, and the occasional romp in his bed.

Things weren't the way most would imagine after a split between former high school sweethearts. They didn't make it as a couple in the least dramatic of ways, for example. They grew up together, quite literally, from the days of kinder into something just shy of adults. They changed, and explored, and figured out who and what they were in unison. She was the first to notice the softer things about him, the confusion he carried inside at the time. They were seniors in high school when she'd decided to start pressing him. She was gentle at first. She suggested small things, like putting on lipstick before kissing her, painting his nails, or trying on heels just for kicks when he took her shopping. He indulged her. It opened the door and made him feel more comfortable being honest about who he was. The first time he'd really said it out loud, they'd been laying in bed kissing and getting heated. She asked him, breathless, what he really was. It'd confused him, though not enough to get him to stop touching her body.

2

She'd had to prod him some more, he played ignorant at first, but he did eventually whisper those words against her damp, impatient skin. He wasn't necessarily a man, nor did he feel like a woman, either. He just was. They loved one another ardently that night, and when they were through, they got more serious about what it meant for them; for him. She understood him in ways that he'd been terrified she wouldn't. To assist, she'd confided in him that, sometimes, she wasn't quite certain where her attractions settled. She accepted him, asked about pronouns and the like. He said it was okay to call him 'he' because that was the way he presented himself then.

In the comfort of her presence, he was able to explore parts of himself he'd otherwise pretended weren't there his entire life. This worked for some time, and it bonded them in ways that still remained intimate and tender. Though they were closely tethered from stark honesty, when they'd gotten to college, it wasn't enough to hold them together, and that was okay. It ended between them the day Julia realized she was falling in love with a female friend she'd made in her art class. Nathan didn't mind, he'd fallen out of love by that point, too. Julia was and always would be an incredible friend, and she'd helped him grow into a hint of the person he truly felt like he was. They appreciated one another, and she still came over to sleep with him once in a while. It worked. It was fine. At least, it would be until he met someone who could sweep him off his feet.

He still wanted that.

Which was the thought he was having when that cursed selfie arrived on his phone.

Ding!

Like a bomb, the notification that rang 'round the world had gone off. Nathan set his guitar down and lifted the phone, his eyes wide while he took in the surprising image, in all its pale glory. There it was: Jackson's bare butt for everyone to see. He was in a dressing room somewhere, looking over his shoulder and clearly snapping the picture from the mirror. It was captioned 'think my ass looks nice in these…woops! Forgot the jeans!' with an awkward smiley face at the end.

Dude…what are you up to?

Before Nathan could make any sense of it, he heard Maverick shouting from the living room. Nathan rolled his eyes, annoyed because Mav was bothered by Jackson the way he always was, which was obviously why Jackson had done it in the first place. It occurred to Nathan that the primary source of his contempt had less to do with predictability, and more to do with how juvenile it all was. For God's sake, college graduation was just a few months away. When the hell were they going to grow up?

Nathan rose from the bed and walked into the living room, immediately accosted by Maverick's high-pitched, indignant voice.

"Did you *see* it? Disgusting! Why the hell would he do that? He's such a jerk…why can't he just mind his own business!?"

Nathan shrugged, lacking the energy to deal with any of it. It was all so stupid and mundane. He trudged into the kitchen and pulled out a bag of chips, carelessly munching while Mav droned on, and on, so full of ire. He was clearly answering the group text, which Nathan figured he'd peek at later. He could hear the pinging and dinging, and it was all so terribly conventional. Maverick would continue to be furious, hurling insults about any flaw he could find. Nathan would zone out and ignore it until later when he had the spoons to deal with it. Jackson would be enormously gratified that he'd set Maverick off.

Boring, boring, so damn boring.

Nathan quietly sighed and went back to his bedroom. He fetched his cell phone, not bothering with the group text, and opened his conversations with Julia. He quickly hammered out a text:

Jules…help! Mav's having a fit and I'm bored out of my mind. You free?

He waited and stared at his phone, pleased when she responded quickly.

You want an orgasm, love?

He grinned before responding.

4

Yes please :)

Be right there!

He smiled a little wider before tossing the phone back to the bed. He collected his guitar, put it away, then went back to the living room to wait for Julia. Maverick was settled by then, and Nathan couldn't help but wonder why Jackson's photograph had triggered him so much. He had a hunch, but he'd never have the nerve to accuse him of it. Still, he *was* kind of obsessed with all things Jackson. It wasn't the behavior of a man who didn't carry some tension about his sexuality, at the very least.

Still, he'd never seen Maverick with anyone outside the usual. He slept with women here and there, but not all that often. Honestly, Mav didn't seem especially interested in sex. He was preoccupied with school, and his career, and his goals. He wanted to be a lawyer, like his father, but rather than defending any rando with the cash, Maverick had ideals of defending people who actually deserved it. He had higher ethics and aspirations that went beyond financial gain, which Nathan had to admit he did find admirable. There were still little things here and there he liked about his friend.

Nathan sat down on the couch and flicked the television on, mindlessly watching ESPN for a while. He didn't really care about sports all that much, just enough to keep up with other men in conversation. He still tried his best to pass, to act like he was more of a man's man than he felt like he was. Maybe someday he'd be ready for honesty, but today wasn't that day. He was relieved, though, when he heard Julia's knock at the door.

Nathan hopped up and answered it, then gave her a quick kiss. She and Maverick exchanged hellos before he awkwardly disappeared into his bedroom. Maverick knew whenever Julia came around it was only for a hook-up.

Once they were alone, she didn't hesitate at all, taking Nathan by the arm and leading him to the privacy of his room. They shut the door, then got down to it, kissing and generously letting their hands roam. She shoved him atop the bed, taking charge as she was prone to do. He loved it. He absolutely loved when they got to be like this. The way she took control of him and had her way was the hottest

5

thing in the world to him, and she always delivered. She never disappointed.

They took their time, and they took their turns, each making sure they got what they came for. When it was through, they collapsed into a salty, satisfied mess. He nuzzled up against her, resting his cheek near the top of her chest. She pulled the blankets over them and smoked her vape, holding it to his lips for a puff here and there.

"So, what's the deal...what had Mav's panties in a bunch?" she asked.

Nathan smiled and laughed, "Jackson sent a picture mooning us."

"Ew...let me see!"

Nathan sat up and looked around, trying to locate his phone. An amused expression rested easily on his face while he dug around the sheets, eventually finding it before settling in close to her again. He opened the text and handed it over. She erupted with laughter.

"Why the hell would Mav be mad about this? Who cares? It's funny! Everyone's seen a healthy amount of Jackson's ass by this point, anyway."

Nathan took the phone and set it aside, still not ready to really look at it.

"He's obsessed with Jackson, specifically his ass."

Julia let out another laugh, "Yeah...he really is. Those two need to get it on and get it over with."

Nathan rolled his eyes. He thought the same thing, but again, he couldn't bring himself to say it out loud. He didn't really like the idea of it, truthfully. Something about the thought of those two in a relationship really got beneath his skin, though he wasn't exactly sure why. The subject was dropped, thankfully, while Julia casually moved onto other things.

"You seeing anyone yet?"

Nathan shook his head, "No, just you here and there."

6

She sighed, "Nathan…you've got to at least *try* and put yourself out there. What about the Internet? Maybe that'd be a little bit easier…?"

He shrugged and trailed kisses along the skin of her collarbone. She let him for a while, then nudged him away, "Nathan…come on, I'm serious. You need someone you can love, not just rendezvous with me."

He sighed, facing her with his cheek propped in his hand.

"I know. I'm comfortable with you, though. Where am I going to find a woman who gets me like you? And I'm sure as hell not ready to ask out a man."

"Even if you *knew* he was gay? Like, seriously, Nathan. You could make an online profile…"

He shook his head, "No. What if someone I know saw? I haven't come out yet. I'm not ready. I don't know if I'll ever be."

Julia looked at him sympathetically. She ached for him. She wanted him to feel comfortable with who he was.

"Well, you can't go on like this forever, Nate. At some point, you're going to need more than just this."

He lowered his gaze, "I know."

They didn't talk much further after that. She pulled him close and kissed him tenderly for a while because she knew it made him feel cared for, and she wanted to give him what little she could. It was lovely until it came time for her to leave. She re-dressed, collected her things, gave him a deep kiss goodbye, and then she was gone. Nathan was left lying atop his bed, regarding the ceiling and pondering the things she'd said. It took him a while to remember the text on his phone, but he eventually lifted it and opened up the group chat.

The photo was there, and so were the comments. They were exactly along the lines he'd expected, which made him want to roll his eyes. He considered tossing the phone aside once more, but instead, he scrolled back up to the photo and let himself look at it for a while. It was understandable, really, why Mav was so obsessed.

Jackson was gorgeous, and the view *was* nice.

He looked around the room, feeling as though someone might be watching him, that he'd somehow get caught. Once he was convinced there was no one there, he pressed his finger atop the picture, applied some pressure, and brought up a menu. He touched the button, making a folder and saving it. He labeled it: Jackson. He wasn't sure if another picture would ever come, but just in case it did, he wanted to hang onto them.

He wasn't sure why. He wasn't about to question it. Sometimes things were just better like that.

Terribly Wrong

Jackson strode up to the classroom as confident as ever. At least, that was the way he came off and he knew it. He approached Maverick, his backpack slung over his broad shoulder casually while he greeted his haughty friend unceremoniously.

"'sup, loser?"

He leaned against the wall and took in his surroundings. There were law students everywhere, working hard at becoming something, someone, anyone. Many of them were nearing the end of their undergraduate studies by this point, including Maverick and himself. Three more years of law school were lying in wait just ahead. At times it felt daunting. At others, it was an inexplicable thrill. Life could be like that, though. He just tried to roll with it and go wherever the tide took him.

By the time he stopped looking at everyone else, he could practically feel Mav's hot-and-bothered eyes boring holes in the side of his skull. It was the response he'd wanted, naturally, so it wasn't much of a surprise. Still, he had to psych himself up for it. Round one, so to speak, was about to unfold. Jackson mentally walled himself off and looked toward his frienemy, ready to hear it all: the comments about how pale, or hairy, or out of shape his ass was; the accusations about why he'd do such a thing; the rant about how disgusting and annoying he was. Blah, blah, blah. Maverick always delivered in spades.

"What the hell was that all about last night, Jack? Why'd you do that? For God's sake…like my days aren't crappy enough, do I *really* need to be assaulted with photos of your pasty, white-ass on top of everything else?"

Oh, how it hurt when Maverick would talk to him like that. Still, Jackson would rather endure this than the alternative, which was a total loss of Mav's most valuable attention. Yes, it was true. Jackson would rather be belittled than ignored. Anything was better than a fate such as that.

"What's the matter, Mav? You like what you saw? What's the big deal? It was just a joke, dude…" he taunted, ready to spar.

Play with me, Maverick. Give me your attention. Notice me, notice me, NOTICE ME!

Maverick rolled his eyes and let out a frustrated groan. Jackson smirked and went out of his way to maintain a false air of cockiness. Truthfully, it was embarrassing and difficult to do. Sending out a picture like that, knowing it'd provoke Maverick to fury and insult was far from something easy to undertake. Jackson had opted to do it anyway, and it was fully intentional. He had a motive. He had a plan. It was all going to come to fruition eventually, so he hoped.

Maverick let go of it, checking his watch, "Come on. It's time to get in there."

Jackson silently followed Maverick into class. The two of them, though tense, chose to sit side by side up in the front row. Round one was over, now it was time for round two. As invigorated as Jackson had initially felt, he couldn't help but sigh when he pulled out his laptop, thinking about the endless lengths he consistently went to for any crumb of Maverick's attention. For example, though they already shared an abundance of classes, Jackson typically sniffed out what Maverick's electives would be and signed up for them, too. They'd bicker in every one of them, but their classes on law were by far the worst. Predictably, they had very different ideas of the law and how to best represent it.

Maverick, ever the idealist, was passionate about defense. He had dreams of building a career around social justice. He wanted to defend those who were truly innocent, the ones that society was fanatical to incarcerate. Jackson, on the other hand, didn't posses this rose-colored view of the world. It wasn't that he didn't believe innocent people went to prison. They did. They did all of the time. The fact of the matter was, though, there were monsters out there lurking. There were people who deserved a life in the slammer. That was more where Jackson's passion burned. He wanted to be a prosecutor for the state. He wanted to put the bad guys away. He could do something good there, he knew it. It was just that when it came to Maverick, his ideals were usually scorned.

And so, throughout their classes, whenever there would be any semblance of social or philosophical debate they'd inevitably get into it. Jackson would be calm and collected, intentionally and genuinely pressing Maverick's buttons. Maverick would cap his characteristic rage and opt for maturity in class, but often he'd get to a point where he was bested. It wasn't because he'd run out of arguments, however, nor was it an inability to think of something to say. Rather, the reason Maverick always managed to lose was that temper of his. There was that frustrating point where, if poor Maverick kept going, that vein in the center of his reddened forehead might burst and hemorrhage all over the floor. Jackson had to hand it to him, even if Maverick couldn't eradicate the rage, he was able to shut his mouth when it came down to it. Jackson wanted to keep pushing him, though, but not for mere entertainment (although, admittedly, there *was that*). No, the real reason Jackson pressed Maverick's buttons was a noble one. He wanted to help him grow into the lawyer he had such high hopes of becoming. He'd need a tremendous amount of patience if he was going to accomplish it, particularly if they were ever to show down someday in court.

How delicious that would be.

On this day, however, class easily came and went. There weren't any exceptional debates or altercations, which was kind of a shame, but also a relief. Jackson did have to admit, he had enough on his plate already with that picture he'd sent. It'd been on his mind all day, though he could tell it wasn't affecting Maverick quite like that. In fact, Maverick seemed cold and unapproachable. It was actually starting to make Jackson wonder if something might be wrong.

While the two of them walked beside one another, much the way they always did, Jackson wrung the straps of his backpack and decided to ask about it. He could drop the game for a moment. He was capable of being serious now and then.

"You okay there, Mav? You seem kind of stuck in your head...?"

Maverick narrowed his eyes and glanced at him. He looked guarded and suspicious, like Jackson couldn't possibly be genuinely curious about the state of his affairs. Maverick stayed like that so long it started to get awkward, but before Jackson could make any smart comments about it, he decided to answer.

"It's this girl I've been seeing. She's needy. I like her, we have fun and everything, but I don't have the time to give her what she wants. I don't know. I've been thinking about ending it. It just bums me out, I guess."

Jackson's stomach soured. He was more than aware Maverick was seeing someone.

"Why? Who cares? If you don't like her, dump her. Why waste your time on someone who doesn't do it for you?"

"I just said I *like* her, Jack. That's not the problem!"

Jackson sighed and looked down at the ground. Maverick was already getting pissed. He'd pushed too hard, the same way he always inadvertently did. Dealing with him was like trying to negotiate with a volcano. *Please, just this once, could you not blow your lid?*

"Alright, okay, fine. I'm sorry. I'll be a little more sensitive, or whatever bullshit you need right now. My point is, if you're not feeling happy with her, or you think you're not compatible, it's probably best to just call it a day and move on. That's all I'm saying. There. Is that better?"

Maverick shrugged, "Yeah, alright. A little."

Jackson grinned and playfully nudged Maverick's arm, "Lighten up, man. We're young. It's not like you're gonna marry her. Don't worry about it so much."

Jackson watched with quiet fascination while Maverick's pouty little lips moved into a smile. It made his heart skip more than just a beat. He loved seeing Maverick happy. He'd never admit something like that out loud, but it was true.

The two of them proceeded to talk about things of no consequence. They went through the motions of their days, sometimes separate, sometimes together. By the time classes were done they were tired, and their goodbyes were lackluster and thoughtless. Maverick didn't have to work because his parents made total bank, but Jackson wasn't cut from that cloth, so work was where he had to go next. He made his money over at the mall, at the loathsome weenie stand. He was subjected every shift to that ridiculous, tacky outfit. It drew so much attention it sometimes made him feel jokingly suicidal. All so he could sling a few hot dogs at some teens who were always rude to him. They joked about the outfits. They put down the employees with the confidence of their youth, and their parents' bank accounts, assuming that they'd never be in his shoes. God, it was embarrassing. The only nice part about his job was the fact that Nathan worked there, too. Although, to be fair, Nathan's personality was quickly becoming that of a wet blanket's these days. Something was going on with him, of that Jackson was sure. The thing was, he'd just been too preoccupied with his desperate schemes to properly address it.

He couldn't help thinking now that maybe he ought to. He did care about Nathan. He considered him his best friend, even though he knew Nathan didn't regard him the same way.

"Hey, man…" Jackson sighed, tying his apron while he went behind the counter to clock in, thoroughly humiliated as always about the uniform.

Normally, Jackson was rather polished in his appearance.

"Hey," Nathan listlessly responded, not paying Jackson much mind.

At least, that's how it looked to Jack. The truth was, Nathan had been thinking about him a little throughout the day. That damn picture. He'd never really noticed Jackson like that before, but now that he'd seen more of him than he'd asked to, he was grappling with these tiny little pricks of emotion he didn't quite know what to do with. He was playing it off, though, acting the way he typically did. Although, whenever Jackson turned around, or met his eyes, or smiled, or laughed, or just shot the shit, Nathan kept capturing these glimpses of something ethereal. It was making him feel all kinds of crazy, strange things that he couldn't even begin to parse out.

Their shift carried on like that. It was dreadfully busy and trying for several hours. Teenagers mobbed them. They were rude. They didn't tip. They made fun of their uniforms. Nathan remembered a time, not so long ago, when he and his crew used to do uncouth things like that. He felt both bad for it, and shamefully just a little bit nostalgic. Things were easier back then, on the other side of the counter.

Eventually, the crowds abated and the mall darkened. People trickled away with the sun, and the hour to close arrived. Nathan and Jackson were the closers, and they'd gotten pretty good at doing their thing. They tackled it the same way they always did. Jackson was the shift manager, of course, so he had the keys and he called the shots. He never did boss Nathan around, though, which he appreciated.

The lights went out. The work was done. They walked out to the parking lot and approached their vehicles. They typically parked near each other, both for safety and convenience. Before taking off, however, Nathan spun around and started to fidget with the keys in his hands. He looked like he wanted to say something, and Jackson could tell he was going to need some encouragement. Nathan could be shy like that, especially lately. Something had him really muted these days.

"What's up, Nate? What is it?"

He bit his lower lip and looked away. Jackson started to feel a little short on patience because he still had to study and somehow get a decent amount of sleep. He swallowed it down, though, because this was Nathan and he had a little bit of give when it came to him.

"That picture you sent...uh...why'd you do that?" Nathan finally came out with it.

Jackson couldn't help but let out a hearty laugh in his surprise, "Oh, that!? I was just messing around. It was nothing."

Nathan eyed him doubtfully, and Jackson felt his stomach lurch.

"This wouldn't happen to be about Maverick, would it?" Nathan asked, somewhat boldly.

Jackson sighed and shifted his weight. Shit. He may as well just level with him. If there was anyone in the world Jackson could trust with his secrets, it was Nathan. He turned around and leaned against Nathan's car, looking up at the dark, starry sky. Nathan leaned beside him, looking up as well.

"It is about Maverick," Jackson quietly admitted.

Nathan watched him, carefully taking in the sight of his friend. The moonlight was illuminating his face in this beautiful way. The colors he could see were interesting, and it made him stare perhaps a moment too long. Jackson didn't notice. Nathan wished he could take a picture. Unfortunately, the moment was broken when Jackson sighed and dropped his gaze, carrying on with an explanation for his strange behavior.

"Sorry about sending it to you, too. It just felt easier like that, if it didn't just go to him. I'm just…" he paused and held out his hands, like he was offering up his heart on a platter for consumption, "…I thought if I could get his attention, if I could get him to look at me privately, maybe it'd lighten things between us a little. I'm not stupid, I know one picture isn't going to change the way things are. Actually, I'm planning to send some more, so sorry in advance for that, I guess."

He glanced toward Nathan and shrugged, an apologetic and helpless expression on his face. Nathan nodded before dropping his gaze down to the ground.

Ah, that makes sense. You wanted Maverick to look at you the way I did. Of course.

Nathan folded his arms and crossed one of his ankles over the other. He pondered it for a moment before deciding to chime in.

"You know, maybe I can help you here. Like…look, I know you know Maverick super well and everything, but I don't think this is the way to go about it. For one, from what I can tell, he's not super interested in dating or sex at all, let alone with a man…and for two, even if he *does* have it in him to go there with you, throwing it in his face like that isn't going to work. It's just going to make him dig in his heels harder."

Jackson folded his arms while he thought about it.

"Okay, so, what do you propose I do? I don't know if you've noticed, but I'm pretty freakin' good at directing people. I sent that photo right before dinner for a reason…you ever heard of Pavlov?"

15

Nathan suddenly laughed, knowing exactly where he was going.

"What? You think you're going to Pavlov him into bed with you because dinner makes him think of your ass?"

Jackson shrugged and laughed, "I mean…yeah, that was the idea."

Nathan put his hand to his forehead and kept laughing. Once he quieted, he shook his head and refolded his arms.

"I mean, theoretically, that *could* work, maybe…but I think you'd have better luck being less lewd and more romantic with him. Like I said, from what I've gathered, he's not an especially sexual person."

Jackson was listening, even if he wasn't so sure about it. Nathan was one of the very few people he could trust and drop his guard with. There was no real sense in being anything short of authentic.

"What do you think he'd like?" he asked quietly, side stepping the fact that his own plan was flawed.

Nathan rubbed his chin while he thought for a moment, "Uh…I don't know. What about, like, just taking him to get some ice cream or something? Take him out on a date without calling it one, but you've got to be nice about it, Jack. Don't be an asshole like you usually are."

"Ice cream, Nathan? Really? That's your big master plan?"

Nathan shrugged, "I mean, it's a start, isn't it?"

Jackson shook his head and sighed, "Okay. He's your best bud and all. I guess you'd know him better than me."

They were quiet after that. They looked back up at the stars, lost in their heads. Nathan was just about ready to call it a night when Jackson turned his head and looked at him directly.

"What is it?" Nathan asked.

Jackson swallowed. He actually looked kind of nervous.

"Look, Nathan…no one knows this about me, okay? No one knows the way I feel about Maverick."

16

Nathan squeezed his lips together, "How *do* you feel about Maverick?"

Jackson dropped his eyes, an unmistakable expression of sorrow crossing his face.

"I love him."

Nathan was quiet. The crickets sang. He looked back up at the stars.

"Okay, so, let's give this a shot. What's there to lose?"

Jackson broke out in a wide smile, "You'll help?"

Nathan shrugged, "Yeah, dude. Sure. I'll help."

Nathan pushed away from the car, fully prepared to get in and take off, when Jackson abruptly scooped him up in his arms and hugged him close. So close, in fact, that it was making it difficult for Nathan to breathe.

"Thank you, man…thank you, thank you…" he said happily, squeezing just a little bit harder.

Nathan would've hugged him back, except his arms were firmly pinned. He let the hug pass, entirely relieved when Jackson finally let him go. They each went to their vehicles after. Nathan sat quietly and watched while Jackson took off, realizing that he was feeling even stranger than before. He wanted to help Jackson. He felt good about it. He wasn't surprised at all to hear he was in love with Maverick, and yet, something about it just wasn't quite right. Something about this was terribly wrong.

It's a Date...?

It was Saturday. The room was dark and Maverick felt entirely spent while he tried to force himself to get out of bed. This last push before he moved onto law school was really taking it out of him. Thankfully, he didn't have to juggle his studies with a job like Nathan and Jackson did. Although, Nathan's major wasn't anything exceptionally challenging. He was getting a degree in English, which Maverick did warn him over and over wasn't going to amount to much. The most Nathan would ever do with that was teach, best case edit. It was kind of fitting, though, really. Maverick had become cognizant fairly young that Nathan was just one of those guys who'd never live up to his potential. It wasn't for any lack of intelligence. It was more that Nathan was lazy and depressive, so he never managed to get much done. Maverick looked down on him for that, there was no denying it.

Jackson, on the other hand, was someone Maverick could at least respect because he hustled and worked hard. He was still a scheming, conniving son-of-a-bitch, but he wasn't so bad that it detracted from the good of who he was. Although, perhaps the only real reason Maverick could tolerate Jackson was the fact they were busy beyond belief. After all, the way he saw the law was polar opposite to Maverick. Where he saw injustice, systems in dire need of reform, and a profession starved for people with more integrity, Jackson saw people in want of punishment, a hammer that was essential to come down hard atop the heads of the damned. Neither of them were entirely right or wrong, per se. Maverick was sharp enough to recognize as much. Still. It was just another one of those things they didn't see eye to eye on, and it frustrated him to no end.

Maverick let out a groan and forced himself from the bed. He stretched, causing his neck and back to pop. *Oof.* He felt like he was at least ten years older than he really was. He sighed, looking around the room and noticing a small stream of light leaking through the boundaries of his blackout curtains. He picked up his phone and checked the time. It was already nine! *Shit!* He overslept.

He jumped to his feet and went to the kitchen. He popped in a K-cup, eagerly anticipating the lackluster cup of coffee it'd make. He waited around before waving a dismissive hand and grabbing a box of frozen waffles. He placed two of them in the toaster and resumed waiting. While everything was going, he looked around the apartment through tired eyes. The living room was a mess. Nathan's jacket was carelessly thrown atop the couch, and there were quite a few empty beer bottles on the coffee table. Maverick grumbled beneath his breath while he opened his texts and shot a quick one to Nathan. He didn't really care if he woke him. That lazy slob was always sleeping in too late anyway.

Maverick: NATHAN! You left a big mess in the living room again! Pick it up please! I really don't have time.

It was worded with all the patience he could summon. Despite his plummeting opinion of this person who used to be his best friend, he still didn't really want to upset him. Nathan was kind of sensitive. Sometimes it almost felt like dealing with a girlfriend.

Ugh.

Which reminded Maverick about his current predicament with Kamila, his tall, curvy, drop-dead gorgeous partner. She was an art major, so she wasn't nearly as swamped as Maverick when it came to her studies. It was the predictable, primary conflict in their relationship. Maybe Jackson was right. Maybe Maverick was stressing about this whole thing too much. It was true, they weren't going to be getting married. He probably should just focus on enjoying the sex and the dates, both of which were fine. Maybe he lent too much weight to these matters.

POP!

The waffles jolted him from his head. He grabbed his coffee, picked up the waffles, then settled down at a small desk inside his room. He left the door open so he could talk to Nathan whenever he finally managed to wake up. He munched on plain waffles while he cracked open his books.

***

DING!

Nathan awoke to the sound of an incoming text. He felt groggy and pulled back toward sleep, but he could also tell it was starting to get

19

late. He wanted to wake up and have some time to himself before he had to study. He rolled over, groaning loudly while he picked up his phone and focused his eyes. It was just a pissed off text from Mav. He should've known. When he got home from work last night he wound up getting drunk on the couch. It was a thing he did once in a while when he got exceptionally stressed, which he was. He still didn't exactly know why. Maybe things were starting to catch up with him? The things Julia said about him eventually needing more were definitely on his mind. Maybe coming out wouldn't be such a bad thing? Maybe he'd feel better if he could just be who he was?

No, no, no, no. That's not safe. That's not okay. Mav would never understand. My dad would disown me. My brothers would kick my ass. I don't even know what Jackson would do. Not to mention all the people I don't know…

He felt sick to his stomach and more than a little panicked. His thoughts started to run away from him. He pressed a hand to his chest and closed his eyes, trying to breathe through it. He'd had lots of moments like this before. He could do this. He could get through this. After several, long, drawn breaths his heartbeat settled down and the discomfort in his stomach subsided. Confident the panic attack had been circumvented, he sat up and touched feet to the soft, old carpet. He trudged from the bedroom and started collecting beer bottles from the table. It took him all of ten seconds at best, which annoyed him. Maverick couldn't be bothered to take ten seconds out of his day? Really? Not that Nathan *wanted* him to do it. He never expected that. It was just that Maverick always made such a big deal of the smallest damn things.

"Hey, how're you feeling?" Maverick's voice suddenly interrupted Nathan's impatient thoughts.

Nathan shrugged, putting a K-cup in the Keurig and firing it up, "I'm fine. Why?"

Maverick eyed the now empty table, "Just looked like you put back a few, that's all. Anything going on?"

Nathan shook his head, "Nope. Just cutting loose. Stressed about finals."

Maverick could absolutely tell Nathan wasn't being up front. A lifetime of friendship made that plain as day. He always knew when Nathan was holding something back, and honestly, for years now, it'd felt like there was something really heavy wedged between them. Maverick couldn't for the life of him figure out what it was. For a while there, he'd wondered if he'd done something wrong; something to infuriate Nathan and orient their friendship toward a disastrous crash and burn. These days, though, Maverick's instincts were telling him it was something else. Something bigger than anything he could've possibly done. He wanted to talk about it. He wanted to ask so badly, but the truth of it was he didn't know how. They weren't close like that anymore. They didn't connect the same way that they used to. It hurt. It hurt them both.

"Hey, uh, just a heads up…I talked to Jackson about the weird selfie and I think he's going to knock it off. He was telling me last night he wants to hang out with you, though…" Nathan casually changed the subject.

Maverick cocked a brow, "He wants to hang out with me? We hang out all the time. We have all the same classes."

Nathan shook his head, "No, not like that. I think he just wants to do something fun one on one with you. He's feeling, uh…well, I don't really know. But I do know he'd like to spend some time with you, and he said that he'd be nice about it. I just thought I'd let you know. I think he's going to ask you to do something soon."

Maverick folded his arms, trying to make sense of it. What was the big deal? Why was this being made into a thing? It wasn't like he and Jackson hadn't ever hung out like that before.

"Uh…yeah, okay. That's fine. I don't know that I really needed a heads up. I doubt I'd have thought anything about it if he asked."

Nathan looked at him and shrugged, "Okay."

With that out of the way, awkwardness fell over them. They felt like they wanted to talk, to attempt and fix this fragile, cracked thing they were trying to hold onto. Graduation was coming, and that truth hung heavy. If it wasn't fixed soon, they'd be out of each other's lives permanently. Just when the words were inching toward the tip

21

of Maverick's tongue, *Nathan…what is it? What in the world is going on with you? You can tell me! I'm your best friend, remember? You can tell me anything…*

DING!

Nathan's phone went off, snuffing out the moment. They exchanged an uncertain glance before Maverick dejectedly returned to his room. He resumed his studies feeling sorry and low. Nathan unlocked the screen of his phone and grinned, happy to see it was a text from Julia.

Julia: Hey! You up? Want to get a mani/pedi with me? My treat!

Nathan: Yeah ok. What time?

Julia: We have appointments at 10. I'll come by in a few – be ready!

Nathan ran a hand through his hair. She was the queen of doing things like that, so he wasn't especially surprised. He quickly scurried to his room, grabbed some clothes, then took the fastest shower he could manage. He shaved his face, dried his hair with a towel, and dressed himself in a sweater, jeans, sneakers and coat. He'd just barely had enough time to get ready, because as soon as he'd gotten the keys she was knocking at the door.

"Mav! I'm going out with Jules…I'll be back later!" he hollered, not bothering to listen for a response.

He'd probably just lecture him about the importance of studying or something condescending like that anyway, like Nathan didn't know. He was well aware he was supposed to be prepping for finals. He was only putting it off for a few hours, right? What harm was there in that?

"Heyyyyy!" she greeted him with a warm hug and brief kiss.

"Hey, gorgeous," he responded, linking their arms and heading to the car.

They sat down and started to drive toward the salon. Nathan kicked back in the passenger seat, staring out the window with a breezy expression on his face. It felt so good to see the sun. That apartment was really starting to get him down.

"So, how are things?" Julia started in on him.

He could tell from the tone of her voice she had an agenda. His tenor was cautious, letting her know he was aware.

"Fine…why, Jules…what's up…?"

She shrugged and grinned, her pixie cut shining brilliantly in the sun. She was a vision. There was no denying that.

"No reason…nothing at all…don't worry your pretty little head…" she teased.

Nathan shook his head and grinned. She'd come out with it when she was good and ready. It wasn't long before they were at the salon, and they mostly talked about school and their plans while the techs worked on their nails. It was moments like these where Nathan could gently be who he was, semi-open and out there, and it really did feel good. The thought crossed his mind again that maybe, just maybe, if he were out he'd feel a bit lighter. At least, it seemed that way when he looked down at the black polish on his toes and the clear coat on his fingers. Maybe someday he'd dare to put some color on his hands, but not now. He wondered, though, what might that feel like…?

When they finished Nathan tipped, Julia paid, and they made their way to Starbucks for some lattes and conversation.

"So, what is it…spill it. I know you asked me out because you have something you want to say," Nathan urged her.

Julia sighed and offered him a resigned smile, "Alright, alright. You got me."

"I know you through and through. You can't trick me."

She shook her head and pulled out her phone. Nathan leaned forward curiously while she opened a dating app. He instantly knew what this was all about.

"Jules…no…come on, seriously…" he started to protest.

"Hang on, hang on…hear me out, okay?"

Nathan shut his mouth and sat back, eyeing her, but also not telling her to stop anymore. She took it as permission to explain, so she ran with it.

"Look, this app is *super* old. These platforms are kind of trendy, and hardly anyone uses this one anymore. It could be a good place to start. The risk of seeing anyone you know is pretty minimal, and even if you did, the way the algorithm works, they wouldn't even see you unless you're someone they'd be interested in. It's not searchable on Google or anything like that. You'd only be seen by other people in the app who'd like someone like you. It's really not so bad. I think you should try it, Nate. Dip your toes in the water…" she let her voice trail off while she looked at him hopefully.

He sighed and looked down at his nails, enjoying the shininess and smoothness. He considered it, the thoughts he'd already been having, the way it felt to indulge in the more feminine parts of himself.

"Alright. Okay. Will you help me put it together?"

Julia smiled, broad and mischievous.

"I *kind of* already put one together for you. Don't be mad! Here, take a look…"

Nathan shook his head. He wasn't mad. He trusted her not to do anything that'd get him in any trouble. He looked at the profile, and he had to admit, it was pretty much the way he'd have done it himself. She picked a nice photo of him, a selfie he'd sent her where he looked just as ambiguous as he often felt inside. His profile read:

Name: Nathan

Nickname: Nate

Gender: nonbinary

Pronouns: he/his

Sexuality: bisexual

24

Bio: I'm an easygoing person looking for someone to spend some time with. I love animals, music, and doing just about anything to pass the time.

Hobbies: reading, watching movies, listening to music, playing guitar, eating out and going on adventures.

Nathan smiled, "Okay. This is good. Thanks. How do I work this thing now?"

"Here, give me your phone."

He fetched the phone from his pocket and handed it over. She downloaded the app and logged in. She told him she'd text him the info in case he needed it, then showed him how to look at who was available. This naturally resulted in no shortage of time spent looking at various men and women, deciding who he might be interested in. Amidst the ocean of available people in the area, they suddenly noticed a familiar name. Chris Donahue, the very handsome, very popular quarterback from high school.

"Oh, no…Donahue's on here…" Nathan whined, feeling a little panicked.

"Settle down…like I said, no one should show up here that isn't an option. Let's take a peek at his profile, shall we?" she replied, raising a playful brow.

Nathan sighed, but leaned in for a look nonetheless.

Name: Chris

Gender: male

Sexuality: gay

Bio: Hello world! The name's Chris! I love having fun and hanging out! I'm down to do anything, just hit me up!

Hobbies: parties, movies, dancing, clubbing, EATING, baking, wandering!

Nathan leaned back and let out a laugh, "Dude uses a lot of exclamation points."

"He's very enthusiastic," Julia agreed.

They were quiet while they looked. Nathan had to admit, he'd always thought Chris was pretty cute. He'd never known he was gay. It seemed like, if he was, wouldn't he have had a boyfriend at some point? Maybe he did?

"So, what do you think? You want to send him a message?" Julia pried, trying her best to get something, *anything* going here for her beloved friend.

Nathan looked back down at the profile picture.

Aw, hell...why not?

"Yeah, okay..." he took the phone from her and hit the button to send a message.

He hesitated. What should he say? It took him a moment before he came up with this brilliant little line: *Hello Chris...it's Nathan.* And that was it. That's all he wrote.

Julia looked at it and chuckled, "Um...a person of few words, huh?"

Nathan shrugged, "I don't know what else to say."

"Well," Julia sighed, leaning back in her seat casually, "all you can do now is wait and see."

Nathan nodded. Of that, she was definitely right.

***

Jackson was up and at it by six a.m. He cooked a full on breakfast to share with his roommates. There was bacon, eggs, hash browns and toast. The girls loved him because he kept them well fed, and to boot, he cleaned up afterward. Truthfully, it was more self-serving than that. Cooking and cleaning were simply distractions; something to help alleviate the constant troubles of his mind. He needed to stay busy if he was going to get through this. He was beyond nervous, practically coming out of his skin. He was going to do it. He was going to text Maverick and ask him to get ice cream, which was such an ordinary thing he really shouldn't have been feeling so rattled. It wasn't necessarily the asking him part that was making him tense. It was more the thought of them being alone, without the fall back of intentional aggravation. He wasn't sure how to interact with Maverick outside the safety of their conflicts. What would it be like to just…*be*? The thought made his stomach hollow. He pushed through the morning, and when the hour grew acceptably late, he texted Maverick.

Jackson: Hey, Man! You down to get some ice cream or something? I don't have much going on this afternoon.

Maverick: Yeah, sure. That sounds fine. You know, Nathan was being weird this morning. He told me you were going to ask me to hang out, made a big deal about it. Do you think he's okay? Something seems really off about him lately.

Jackson eyed the text, letting out a deep sigh. Of course Maverick was worrying about Nathan. His mind was always occupied with anything but Jackson.

Jackson: I'm sure he's fine. He was normal at work last night. Don't worry about him. Okay, so…ice cream? Let's say 3 o'clock?

Maverick: 3 is fine.

Jackson sucked a breath between his teeth, held it and released. Well…great. Now he had, what…? Five plus hours before he'd actually see Maverick...? Damn. How was he ever going to survive his nerves for that long?

Studying.

He decided to bunker down and do that. It was kind of a win-win, because he really needed to do it, and he had to keep busy so he wouldn't think about Maverick with his thick head of hair, stupid nice smile, and wicked fine eyes. He most certainly didn't want to think about Maverick's skinny little arms, or the stubble that probably decorated his chin in the soft glow of morning after a night of…

AGH!

He shook his head and forced himself to stuff those thoughts down. He ran off to his bedroom and did what he'd planned. He buried himself in his notes and his books. His obsession with Maverick fell to the wayside, and the time actually did manage to fly. Just about an hour before they were due to hang out, he went into a frenzy getting himself ready. He showered. He shaved. He put on cologne and styled his hair. He checked himself in the mirror. He tried to pump himself up, then he retrieved his wallet and keys before texting Maverick the location of the place. He drove over, his stomach screaming at him all the way. Why was he like this? It was just ice cream! They hung out like this all the time, right? Although, it was generally with Nathan or Julia. It wasn't very often they were alone outside of school.

He pulled into the parking lot, went inside and proceeded to wait. He waited, and waited, and after twenty minutes or so he was starting to feel dejected. More agonizing time passed before he finally saw Maverick's car outside. He smiled while he watched, but it soon faded into a devastated frown. Maverick brought Kamila. There she was, in all her modelesque glory, with her long legs, flowing hair, and sharp heels. Jackson felt sick. He realized in an instant that this wasn't going to be what he'd hoped.

Wait…didn't Nathan tell you I wanted to hang out alone?

He did. Maverick knew, at least vaguely what this was, and he'd deliberately gone and shown up with *her*. Jackson felt heart-sick when Maverick and Kamila came inside. He forced himself to smile and act like everything was normal. Maverick rattled off poor excuses for being late. Jackson could tell from the messiness of Kamila's hair the real reason they'd been untimely, and it only served to injure him further.

I want to make you late to things. I want to be the person who gets to be with you like that.

"Whatever, man. It's cool. I have so much free time you know. I just *love* spending it waiting around for you…" Jackson replied sarcastically, falling into the familiar grooves of their relationship.

Maverick expertly ignored him, probably because he'd just had an orgasm. Life's small irritations were easier to take after that.

28

Jackson quietly stewed in his misery while they ordered ice creams and sat down together. Maverick and Kamila mostly talked to each other, only addressing Jackson a little here and there. Of course, the most conversation he got out of his beloved friend was regarding the ice cream Jackson no longer had the stomach to eat.

"Why aren't you eating that? Aren't you the one who wanted to do this?" Maverick asked, the aggravation in his voice more than just a hint.

"I'm not feeling great," Jackson responded, sounding more pathetic than he'd meant.

Maverick lowered his spoon, actually looking concerned, "Are you okay? Do you need a ride home?"

Jackson shook his head and rose to his feet, his eyes cast toward the ground, "No. It's cool. I'm gonna go lay down. I'll catch you later."

He didn't bother with grabbing his trash. He kept his eyes on the floor and went out to his car, feeling like he wanted to puke, or scream, or cry. Hell, maybe all of it. He couldn't quite decide. He didn't do any of those things, though. He simply gripped the steering wheel and drove back to his apartment. His knuckles turned white, and the little bones in his hands started to ache. He went inside and headed straight for his room. He fought with himself valiantly. He wasn't going to cry. This wasn't something to cry about. So, what? Maverick misread the situation and showed up with his girlfriend. Whatever. It wasn't like Jackson was super up front about it anyway, right? Did it count as a rejection if he didn't really know? Nathan was obviously wrong. Subtlety was a poor choice. Jackson's face felt hot while he struggled with his emotions. He grabbed his phone and texted Nathan.

Jackson: Nice job, asshole. The ice cream date was a bust! I'm going back to sending my selfies.

Jackson stared at his phone angrily, surprised when Nathan responded fast.

Nathan: What? What happened?

Jackson: He showed up with Kamila, that's what.

Nathan: Shit...I'm sorry. Do you want to hang out? Maybe we can think of something else?

Jackson: No. I don't feel good. I didn't even eat my ice cream.

Jackson watched while the dots danced then disappeared. Nathan clearly didn't know what to say, and Jackson couldn't help but think it served him right. He deserved to feel bad. He'd put Jackson in a crap situation and it'd all gone wrong.

Nathan: Do you still want ice cream?

Jackson furrowed his brow, re-reading the text in disbelief. What? What a dumb-ass question. No! Of course he didn't want...well, wait...did he? It *was* kind of a bummer leaving that tasty treat behind...

Jackson: Why?

Nathan: Because, you can get some with me. The sugar might help us come up with a better plan. I'm really sorry. I didn't think he'd do that, I swear.

Jackson: I don't think you know him as well as you think you do. But, I guess I still want ice cream, so fine. Come pick me up.

Nathan: Okay. I'm on my way :)

Jackson sighed and sprawled out on his bed. He stared at the ceiling and pondered his predicament. Nathan didn't know squat. He and Maverick were barely even friends anymore. What was Jackson thinking listening to him? He wasn't going to anymore. He was going to go with his gut and do his own thing. He was good at subtly getting people where he wanted them, and even though Maverick was savvy and difficult to control, Jackson really did know him like the back of his hand. He could do this. He could get Maverick all on his own.

He continued to think about it, how he planned to approach the whole thing, the ways he wanted to steer the course and conquer. He got so lost in his head that it was a total surprise when his phone pinged. It was Nathan letting him know he was out in the parking lot. Jackson rolled from the bed, barely even registering the creaks before slipping on his jacket and shoes. He went out in a huff and got into Nathan's car. While he got comfortable in his seat, Nathan offered him a sympathetic, sorry smile that made Jackson roll his eyes.

"Don't look at me like that. I'm fine," he insisted.

Nathan simply nodded, not bothering to say anything while they silently drove to a different place from before. They wandered inside and looked at the options. It was one of those places where you could pick your ice cream and they'd mix in some toppings for you. Nathan decided first, going with birthday cake flavored ice cream with brownies and cookies mixed in. Jackson thought that sounded pretty good, so he got the same, but had them throw some caramel on it, too. Maverick probably would've made comments at him if they'd gone to a place like this. They were all in plenty fine shape, but Mav was kind of a health nut. He loved condescending when people overindulged. Nathan didn't say anything, though. They sat down and started to eat. Jackson felt calmer than he'd expected, inexplicably soothed by the safe space he now shared with his life's best friend. His anger and resentment dissipated with each delicious, sugar-filled bite.

"I'm really sorry. Maybe the ice cream thing *was* too subtle. He obviously didn't get it," Nathan apologized.

Jackson shook his head, "I don't know. He said you made a big deal about me wanting to spend time with him. Maybe it freaked him out."

"Huh? I didn't make a *big* deal out of it. I was just trying to, like, nudge him."

Jackson shrugged and continued eating. Nathan pulled out his phone and glanced at it. He'd been doing it obsessively ever since he'd sent that message to Chris. He could see whether it'd been read or not, and it hadn't been opened yet. At least he hadn't been rejected. He wasn't so sure why he was worried about it at all.

"What's going on there?" Jackson asked with a lift of his chin.

"Huh? Oh, sorry…um, Julia made me a profile on this old dating app. She says I need to date."

Jackson grinned, "Really? No shit! Can I see?"

Nathan's eyes widened, "Uh…no, dude…no. Just…look, it's bullshit anyway. I was just checking because I sent a message to someone and I wanted to see if it'd been read…"

"Is she hot?" Jackson asked, wanting so badly to get his mind off of Maverick for a while.

Nathan's cheeks flushed, "Um, yeah, she is."

"Come on, show me!"

Nathan shook his head and pocketed the phone. He leaned in close, speaking quiet so no one else would hear, "What do you care? Aren't you, like, gay?"

"Yeah, so? I'm gay, not blind."

Nathan leaned back, "Oh, well…I mean, still. No. You'll meet her if I date her, alright? So, there."

He was hoping that would end the conversation.

"Fine, fine."

Jackson was almost finished with his ice cream already. When he lifted his head, he had some pooled along the side of his mouth. Nathan gestured to let him know, "You've got some on your face…"

"Oh…" Jackson said, wiping and missing.

Nathan smiled and leaned forward, wiping it away with his fingers without thought. Jackson blinked, surprised by the contact, watching uncertainly while Nathan settled back in his seat and went about eating. Jackson was suddenly wary, feeling like that small interaction was kind of strange. What was that? It felt a little too intimate. Maybe it wasn't? Maybe it was…?

"Hey, uh…so, what app are you using? I've got a roommate who's looking to start something like that…" he lied.

"Oh, um, it's this one…" Nathan answered, holding up the phone and flashing him the app.

Jackson nodded, taking note.

"Alright, so…what's plan B then, genius? You have any *good* ideas this time?" he quickly changed the subject.

"Oh! Yeah, so, I was thinking on my way over…what about, like, a camping trip? It's warm enough now. We could go up to the mountains…like…anything could happen, right? Hiking, fishing, drinking…sleeping in tents. If we could get the two of you in the same tent, who knows?"

Jackson leaned against the table in languid thought.

"Hmmm…not bad. Not bad."

Nathan smiled, "Cool, so…I'll arrange it, then. Mav'll just think it's me wanting to bond or whatever, and we'll take it from there. You down for this?"

Jackson beamed before taking the last bite of his ice cream, "Alright, yeah. Let's do it."

Nathan nodded before finishing his, too. They tossed their trash and went to the car, then Nathan dropped off Jackson where they said casual goodbyes. Jackson sauntered into his apartment, feeling a lot calmer and more optimistic than before. He said hello to his roomies, then went to his room. He changed into some pajamas and got comfortable in his bed. He pulled out his phone, however, as soon as he remembered his intention to investigate. There was something about the way Nathan touched his face that made him wonder…

He opened up the app store and downloaded the dating program. He input his information figuring, hell, what can it hurt? Then he started to browse. He was unable to search for a specific name, so it took him some time, but eventually he did find Nathan's profile. He opened it. He read it. He drew in a deep breath once he realized what it was.

Holy shit!

Something *was* going on with Nathan. Something was going on with him, indeed.

***

When Nathan got back, he found an empty apartment. Maverick must've still been out with Kamila, which was fine. Nathan was happy to have the place to himself. He grabbed a beer from the fridge and went to his room, sipping on it while he sat at the desk and pulled out some papers. He needed to study so badly, like, *really*. He forced himself to log a few hours, nursing brews all the while. By the time he was through, he was fairly spent. He settled into the bed, and just when he started to close his eyes and drift, he heard a notification on his phone. He grabbed it, opened it, and was pleasantly surprised once he realized who it was.

Chris: Hey, Nate! I didn't know you were on here! How are you?

Nathan eyed the message, his heart beat rushing. It wasn't that he was especially into Chris or anything like that. It was just the fact that, clearly, Chris had seen his profile, looked at who he was, and messaged him back anyway. He was interested enough to answer, even knowing Nathan's most carefully guarded secret.

Nathan: I'm good...how are you?

Chris: Oh, hanging in there. Sooooooo...you want to hang out sometime? It'd be great to catch up!

Nathan bit his lip and smiled, typing out a response.

Nathan: Yeah, that sounds awesome. I'm out of town this weekend...want to grab a coffee this week?

Chris: I'm totally swamped this week, man. How about the weekend after you get back?

Nathan: Okay – it's a date...?

He waited anxiously. That was far bolder than he typically behaved.

Chris: It's a date ;D

Oh, No.

When Maverick woke up in the morning, Kamila was snoozing soundly in the bed. He looked at her while she slept on her back, her bare chest uncovered and on display. He wasn't aroused, just searching. He wondered what he was doing exactly. She had feelings for him, he knew as much. Was it love? God, he hoped not. It was already enough that it would hurt her when he left. It gave him more pause over the things he said and did. It worried him. It stressed him to virtually no end.

Aside from that, there was also the thing in the ice cream shop with Jackson. He knew, he *knew* Jackson had wanted him to go alone. Maverick had an inkling why that might be, despite the confused show he'd put on for Nathan when he'd mentioned it. He wasn't oblivious to the nature of their relationship; the heat between them, the messed up mixture of aggravation and desire. They'd come close to kissing once. It was at a party when they were both smashed. Maverick threw up before it could happen, his head was spinning and his stomach was acid. Jackson took care of him that night. He brought Maverick home, tucked him into bed, and left without taking a single thing from him.

They never did address it, but that was the night Maverick understood more about the reasons he got so triggered by the person Jackson was. It all boiled down to desire. There'd always been a pull. He was terrified of it, though. There was *no* way in hell he could do something like that. He couldn't go there, not with a man, let alone a man like Jackson, no matter how deeply he may have yearned. His family would never approve. Hell, *he himself didn't approve!* Not because of the same-sex factor. It was a Jackson problem. Why, of all the men on this godforsaken, massive planet, did it have to be *him*? Why, oh why, did it have to be Jackson?

So it was. Even though Maverick was well aware of what they were and what they meant, he'd deliberately chosen to show up with Kamila. He'd crushed Jackson right there in the ice cream shop, and the pain of it was written all over his face. Maverick had known he'd be upset, but he thought he'd just get annoyed. He wasn't prepared to witness such heartbreak. That's what it was. He'd broken Jackson's heart when he did that, and the pain he felt in himself was unexpected and difficult to make sense of. He'd gotten beneath Jackson's skin to the point that, for the tiniest moment, Jackson dropped the façade and was blatantly disappointed. It made Maverick feel low while he covertly slipped from the bed and his room. He went into the kitchen and got his coffee started. He was surprised to find Nathan already awake, a textbook in his lap.

"Wow, look at you. Already at it, huh?"

Nathan had to mindfully stop himself from rolling his eyes. It was early. He wasn't in the mood to be judged.

"Didn't get much in yesterday, making up for it today," he answered, his voice intentionally measured.

Maverick just nodded. He knew the comment bothered him, and he mildly regretted making it. Why was he always doing things like that? Why did he have to pick on Nathan so relentlessly?

Maverick collected his coffee and went about getting ready for his day. Once he was showered, shaved, caffeinated and dressed, he went in to kiss Kamila goodbye and hurried off to class. He had an all too familiar pit in his stomach when he rushed through the halls. He wanted to see Jackson before class started. He had to at least try and make things better. He'd dropped the ball worse than he'd meant to yesterday, and it was steadily chipping away at his conscience. While he approached the classroom, Maverick was instantly relieved to find Jackson leaning against the wall, staring at his phone.

"Jack!" Maverick called, unsurprised when Jackson didn't look up from his phone.

He supposed he couldn't blame him for that.

"Hey," Jackson responded flatly.

Maverick leaned against the wall and looked him over. Jackson was clearly doing his best to ignore him, which wasn't an uncommon way for him to act when he felt slighted. It was okay. Maverick knew just what to do when he got like this. He knew Jackson better than anyone in the world.

"So, uh…look, I'm sorry I showed up with Kamila yesterday. I knew you wanted it to be just us, but…I don't know, I guess I got a little weirded out. We haven't hung out alone like that in a while."

Jackson shrugged, his eyes still down. Maverick sighed and touched his arm. Jackson's stomach instantly fell. He couldn't help it. He looked toward Maverick. He looked into those sorry eyes, the contrast of light skin and dark hair. It melted him. He settled. He decided to listen.

"Really, I am sorry. Why don't we do something else? Me and you…we can hang out, okay?"

Jackson searched his face a moment longer then gave into the conversation.

"Nathan wants to go camping this weekend."

Maverick retracted his hand, an immediate look of distress on his face.

"Oh, Jesus. Of course he does. I don't know how I could possibly swing something like that. Finals are coming. Kamila won't want me taking the whole weekend away from her…"

Jackson rolled his eyes and looked back down at his phone. It made Maverick feel panicked. He grasped Jackson's arm again before starting to ramble.

"Wait, wait…hang on…okay, alright. I'll do it. I can bring my books. It's fine. I can study outside. What's the difference, right?"

"What about Kamila?" Jackson mocked.

Normally that would've jostled Maverick, but he was trying. He sighed long and slow before speaking in a defeated tone.

"I think I need to end it with her anyway. You were right. I'm not going to marry her, so why keep forcing this thing…?"

Maverick watched with satisfaction while the corners of Jackson's mouth raised ever-so-slightly. It gave him a bit of a rush. Jackson liked what he'd just said. He liked the thought of Kamila gone and Maverick being available.

Jackson suddenly moved from the wall and put his phone away, "Glad you came to your senses," he said, patting Maverick's head and walking past him to the classroom.

Maverick wanted to be annoyed, but he simply wasn't. He was something else entirely, in fact. He took in a sharp breath, trying his best to ignore his fluttering stomach and the slight excitement in his veins. A camping trip with Jackson…Maverick newly single. Anything could happen.

Do I want it to, though?

He walked in a slow daze through class, all caught up in his head when he sat down beside Jackson and blatantly stared at him. Time would tell he supposed.

Only time would tell.

***

Nathan had about an hour to kill before class started. He was bored out of his mind, so he wound up going to the mall. He'd be back there later for a shift with Jackson, but for now he was just another patron of this sad, dilapidated place. He wandered around, primarily among teenagers and mall walking moms with babies in strollers. He kind of liked doing this, being around people but not really with them. He looked into the windows of various stores, mostly passing by without thought. Eventually, though, he did stop in front of one, the same one he always did. It was a trendy, whimsical little place with high quality women's clothing inside. He wasn't necessarily interested in that. He didn't feel female, exactly. There were things in there that always caught his eye, though. Particularly, what he saw on one of the manikins in the window just now: a floral headstring, one that just loosely sat atop the head, like a dainty little crown. He'd like to wear something like that. Not every day, just sometimes. Maybe for a special event or something. He'd like to wear it, possibly with a roomy, pastel sweater, some jeans and some boots. He felt like it'd look nice, perhaps a little feminine, but not entirely. That's what he wanted. masculinity with just a hint of female flare.

He wasn't brave enough for that, though. What would people think? What would they say? Wouldn't they stare? Wouldn't they tell him he was strange, or sick, or worse? Probably. Some might have the gall to say it to his face, but he supposed most of them would just whisper behind his back. They'd mock him and judge him. They'd laugh over his natural inclination to break free of the mold, his inability to be the person he'd been told he ought to be. He sighed then begrudgingly forced himself to move on. He walked and he sulked, then drove back to school. He got lost in the work for a while, but that merciful distraction inevitably reached its end. He changed into his stupid uniform. He prepared himself for the teens that would mock him. He went to work and did all the things he knew he had to do. The necessity of it wasn't nearly enough to stop him from feeling low while he trudged behind the counter. Jackson was already there waiting.

"Hey, man…dude…these kids, I'm telling you…they're being epic pains in my ass today…" he instantly started to complain.

Nathan couldn't help but crack a smile as Jackson launched into a string of obscenities that'd impress a proper sailor. Some of the doom and gloom started to leave him. Nathan perked up more and more while they moved through crowds of families and teens who were, indeed, royal pains in the ass. Something must've been in the air. It was okay, though, because the busyness of it made the shift go by fast. Before they knew it, it was closing time again. The mall fell dark and quiet. They finally started to talk while they plowed through their tasks.

"So, I already brought up the camping thing to Mav. He's going. Maybe we should invite someone else? Like, what about that dude you have class with, uh…Greg? I'd hate for you to be a total third wheel…"

Nathan nodded, "Oh, cool. Yeah, I can ask Greg. It'd be nice to have another person in the mix I guess. Was he tough to convince?"

Jackson shook his head, "No. He feels guilty for showing up with that bitch of his yesterday."

Nathan rolled his eyes, "Don't call her that, Jack. Just because she's dating Maverick doesn't mean she's a bad person."

Jackson shrugged. It was true. If anything, he was being the catty one. Still, he could scarcely help it. Initially, he'd said things like that about Julia, too. Especially when he'd learned she still slept with Nathan habitually post-breakup. He warmed up over time, of course. Once he realized their friends with benefits situation really did work he eased up on her. Jackson tended to get this way about women when it came to his friends, even the ones he hadn't fallen in love with. There was a fundamental difference aside from that, however. Whereas Julia had this fantastic capacity to make Nathan smile, Kamila only seemed to drag Maverick down.

"Aaaannnywaaayyy…" Jackson drew out the world and ignored Nathan's chastising, "…what's the plan of attack here? How do I get his attention during this trip?"

Nathan shook his head and laughed, "You don't already have ideas? Come on…I know you better than that."

A sly grin crossed Jackson's face, "Okay, okay. You caught me. I was thinking, we really only have one full day, so I have to make every second count. We should head out as early as we can on Friday, and I was thinking a hike. We could split up, you and Greg go ahead or stay behind, whatever. Just pair up and stay away from us. I'll also need you to come up with a reason to share a tent with that nerd. I'll leave it up to you, but just...make it happen, okay? It has to be you. If I tell Maverick we're sharing a tent he'll just argue against it because I'm the one who came up with it."

Nathan smiled. That was true.

"Okay, so, Friday…hiking and bonding. What about Saturday?"

"Saturday I'm thinking fishing and drinks. We could go to a restaurant for dinner maybe, then polish off some brews back at the camp fire. I want it very chill. Again, try and sit away from us when we're fishing. Just, like, far enough that he and I can talk without worrying about anyone listening in."

Nathan nodded. Neither of them said anything after that for a while. They got caught up in their tasks, then finished up and headed for the parking lot. Nathan, as per usual, was swept up in his thoughts, striding silently beside Jack. He didn't notice that Jackson was looking at him from the corner of his eye. He had no idea whatsoever that Jackson had seen his dating profile, or that he knew about his gender fluidity, nor his interest in men. He didn't notice anything was going on until they'd gotten to their cars. Jackson cleared his throat. His expression was uneasy, and it made Nathan anxious, too.

"You know, Nate…it's okay to be different," he said quietly, hints of discomfort and concern in his voice.

Nathan stared at him, not sure why he would say something like that. Did he know?

"What do you mean?" he asked hesitantly.

Jackson shrugged, "I mean exactly what I said. It's okay to be whatever it is you feel like you are. At least, when it comes to me it is. You're my friend, no matter what, okay? You're my…" he hesitated. He wanted to say it, but it didn't come so easily for a person like him. He drew in a breath and forced himself to say it anyway, "…you're my best friend, and there's nothing you could ever do to change that," he paused while a grin spread across his face, "Whether you like it or not."

Nathan felt a mixture of butterflies and warmth. He was tense about the whole statement. He realized Jackson must've found out, though he couldn't for the life of him figure out how. No matter. Apparently, it was okay because here he was, standing in front of him, telling him so and proclaiming him his best friend. Nathan smiled. He stared. He wasn't sure what to say. Jackson grinned awkwardly and scratched the back of his head.

"Anyway, I'll see you around," Jackson said before walking away.

Nathan watched. Jackson turned toward him and looked, just a moment, another sheepish grin crossing his face. Once the pleasantry had been offered, he got into his car and started driving off. Nathan's stomach continued to flutter. His heart felt pulled. Was it those words? Or was it the person they came from? More of that uneasy feeling washed over him, the sensation that something awful laid just ahead; the concern that something about his emotions, desires, and the repression of who he was, and what he needed, was getting bigger than himself. He noticed with no shortage of fright that these feelings were only happening when he was in the company of Jackson. Jackson who, apparently, considered him his best friend. Jackson, who was obsessively in love with Maverick. Jackson, with his deflective jokes, his cocky smile, and his secretly openhanded heart.

Jackson…Jackson…

…

Jackson…?

Oh, no.

Friday arrived fast, like everything else seemed to for Nathan these days. Finals were just ahead, followed by graduation, moving away from Maverick, looking for tangible work, and starting his real adult life. It was scary, much in the way high school graduation had been. Transitional phases reliably gave him a steady dose of anxiety, though he was feeling worse than he had when he'd gone off to college. Back then he was still figuring it all out, his identity and such. Now he knew and was hiding it from the world. Each and every day he continued to keep it secret left him shouldering a heavier emotional burden. He wanted to come out with it so, so badly. If only he weren't so terribly afraid.

He shook off the thought when he heard Maverick approaching his bedroom.

"You ready, Nate? Jackson's going to be here any minute."

Nathan nodded and zipped up his gym bag, "Yeah, I'm all set."

Maverick hung by the door until Nathan approached, then the two of them went to the living room to wait for their ride. Nathan rested against the couch and pulled out his phone, figuring he'd check his dating profile rather than try to force small talk. Neither of them really knew what to say to each other anymore. When he opened the app, he was shocked to see he had quite a few messages from various people. It was mostly men, although a few women had reached out to him, too. He started opening them to see what they said, quickly realizing it was by and large just sexual advances. The women sent friendlier messages, but he wasn't sure that was exactly what he was after. He didn't want to get involved with another female just yet. He wanted to at least have some experiences with a man before settling down, that much he was sure of.

While Nathan went through his messages, Maverick stood awkwardly. His travel bag was down on the floor beside his feet, and his hands were stuffed deep in the pockets of his coat. He kept fiddling with the lining because his nerves were running wild. His stomach was riddled with butterflies and his heart was beating just a hair faster than usual. This trip, he wanted it so badly, and yet at the same time he didn't. He was eager and terrified while he considered the possibilities, which felt so vast it only worried him more. What if they held hands…or kissed…or…?

His cheeks ran hot. His stomach continued to trouble him. These thoughts weren't anything new. Jackson had been occupying his headspace from the moment they'd met. Sometimes, even, when Maverick had sex with his girlfriends, he'd shut his eyes and imagine it was Jackson. Admittedly, the task required quite a bit of imagination. Still, he could get to that place in his mind if he tried. Now, however, he might actually, physically get to experience him. He might finally get to lay hands on his tall, charismatic friend. The thought gave him a rush in all the worst kinds of ways. It was right around then a group text arrived. Nathan read it first.

"He got Greg already. They're down there," he said, pushing away and walking toward the door.

They collected their bags and went downstairs, still not talking to each other while they got into the back of Jackson's car. Greg was already up front in the passenger seat. He turned around to greet them, all glasses and teeth. Nathan and Maverick returned the sentiment, easily falling into conversation and banter. It wasn't often the four of them hung out, but whenever they did it was typically pretty light. After some time spent driving, Maverick couldn't help but notice Nathan was glued to his phone, lost much the way he tended to be. He was such a dreamer, that one. He was almost never fully engaged. Maverick briefly considered teasing him for it, maybe even trying to get a peek at what he was doing, but he ultimately decided against it. Things were already bad enough between them. The last thing he should do was pick on Nate again.

Jackson, naturally, took the reins and guided conversation all the way to the mountains. He had a way of doing that, keeping things going, interconnected and engaged. He even managed to draw Nathan out of the little world on his phone here and there. Jackson didn't think much of it because, quite honestly, he'd always been able to draw out Nathan whenever he wanted. Not to mention, his mind was heavily preoccupied with Maverick and the things that might happen on this trip. He could multitask like that, guiding conversation, listening, yet also calculating and scheming. He had his plans: the hike, the fishing, the dinner and the booze. It was so well thought out he'd all but decided he had this thing fully under control. Nothing could go wrong, not with Nathan by his side helping orchestrate the whole thing. By the end of this weekend, he was altogether convinced Maverick would finally be his. He knew it. He could feel it in his bones.

The drive up to the mountains wasn't terribly long, and luckily Greg knew a place they could camp for free. They did a lap around the area, trying to pick the most secluded site they could. There was some bickering over which campsite ought to be chosen, particularly between Jackson and Maverick, but eventually a decision was made. They chose one way in the back, nice and isolated. It was small, but that was fine.

They went about setting up their tents, and once they were through it became obvious they needed to decide where they'd sleep. Nathan didn't make much fuss about it. He simply grabbed Greg's bag and his, tossing them both into one of the tents. It made it clear that Maverick and Jackson would be sharing for the duration of the trip, and it made easy sense because Greg was more his friend than theirs. The gesture wasn't unnoticed by Maverick while he collected his bag and went to put it in the tent. Why did Nathan do that? Were things really that bad between them? He'd rather share a tent with that weirdo Greg than him? Not that he was complaining. He *did* want to share a tent with Jackson. It was more the fact that, not so many years ago, it would've been a given he and Nathan would share. It cut Maverick deeper than he'd thought it could in that moment. It was yet another sign of how demolished their friendship was.

The harsh truth of it instantly put Maverick in a mood. He retreated into himself while Jackson started insisting they all go on a hike. Maverick really didn't want to. They'd only just gotten there, and now they had to load up in the car again and drive off to a trail. He was too forlorn to protest, though. Nathan and Greg both seemed pretty into the idea, so he let it go and just followed along for once. Jackson drove. The seating arrangements were the same. Nathan promptly got onto his phone again.

Why are you even here if you're going to be so checked out?

Maverick felt all the more peeved. Nathan was getting under his skin. Maverick forced himself to shut his eyes and take in some deep breaths. He needed to stop this wallowing before it got the best of him. So what if Nathan wasn't his best friend anymore? This kind of thing happened all the time, right? People grew and changed over time. He and Nathan were no exception to the rule. They'd diverged too much somewhere along the line, and now they were just these adults all of a sudden, trying to hold onto the withering strings of an old childhood bond. It was stupid, honestly. It wasn't worth a moment of his time.

At least, that's what he'd convinced himself by the time they'd arrived at the trailhead. The group exited the vehicle. Nathan finally put his phone away. He started to engage some, which was fine. At first they were all together on the trail, but eventually Nathan and Greg separated and fell behind. They kept looking at plants, or whatever. Who even knew when it came to those two? Their conversations and interests felt so dull to Maverick. No matter, them being outrageous nerds left Maverick alone with Jackson, which was a position he absolutely wanted to be in. His anxiety did start to increase, though, as things got quieter and the sense of privacy grew. He no longer heard Greg and Nathan. Soon, it was just the crunching of their feet and belabored breath in the air.

"You seem like something's on your mind, Mav?"

He shrugged, "Just thinking about things. Nothing major."

Jackson grinned. Maverick. Always thinking Jackson couldn't tell when he was feeding him a lie.

"Come on, man. I know you. Spill it."

Maverick grinned as well. He wasn't aggravated. Honestly, he kind of liked the way Jackson could read him like that.

"It's me and Nate. Things are basically done between us. We hang on, but once he graduates and moves out, I'm pretty sure it's over."

Jackson's face looked solemn while he let those words settle. He wasn't blind. He'd noticed the steady erosion of their friendship, which was already starting to strain when they'd met. In a way, it was sad. He found himself wondering how he might juggle that if he actually got into a relationship with Maverick. Nathan was his best friend. He treasured them both. He treasured all of his friends; the girls he lived with, the ones from his youth, and even acquaintances like Greg that he'd met through closer pals. All the people who'd touched his life mattered, at least to a degree. He wasn't the sort of person who just let those connections go.

"Okay, so, what? Is it such a big deal? You've grown apart. Let it happen. Let it be what it is, and if you two somehow stay in touch, you know, like through me, just let it be whatever it is. You can be casual friends. It might even feel like acquaintances sometimes, but does it really matter? It's not like you're super invested in the friendship anymore either."

Maverick sighed and shrugged, "Yeah, I guess. It's just, no one ever prepares you for something like this, you know? Growing up is so weird. It's like, when you're a kid, you think you have it all figured out…what you want to do, who you want to be, the people you're going to spend your life with…all of it. But then one day, you're an adult, and when you stop to look around nothing's the way you thought it would be. One day, you wake up and realize you're pursuing a career you thought you'd never want, you're behaving like a person you never thought you'd be, and you're no longer interested in the people you thought you loved most. I don't know. It's just, well…it's depressing."

Jackson nodded. He took a while to answer, nothing but footsteps on dry dirt.

"Maybe it is, but isn't it kind of exciting, too? You know, the possibility of things you'd never expect? It keeps life interesting if you ask me. I mean, you never know what's going to come at you next."

Something about that statement made Maverick's stomach roll. That was true. He couldn't help but let his eyes roam Jackson while he thought, *you're a little unexpected at times. You're exciting. You seem fresh and new.* Jackson felt his eyes on him, so he glanced. Maverick quickly cleared his throat and awkwardly looked away. Jackson smiled. That was a good sign. The two of them pushed onward. After a few steps this little clearing caught Jackson's eye.

"Hey, come on…let's get off the trail and ditch those losers…"

"What? They're already…"

Before Maverick could protest further, Jackson grabbed his hand and led him through dense trees. He drug him to the clearing, full of foliage and light. Jackson tucked their bodies behind a tree, pressing a finger to his smiling mouth. They stayed there in silence, listening for Nathan and Greg. It took a while, but eventually they heard them come and go. They either didn't notice them in the clearing, or Nathan had kept it moving along like Jackson had asked. He was being such a killer wingman. Jackson figured he'd have to buy him a case of beer or something when this was all through.

"See, Mav? Unexpected, right?" Jackson finally said, nudging him playfully.

Maverick smiled brightly and looked around. It was nice. It was warm and sunny. So warm in fact, that he wanted to shed some layers. He undid his coat and let it drop to the ground. He stretched his arms above his head, lifting his shirt just enough that it caught Jackson's eye. It made Jackson blush, and he had to force himself to look away if he was going to avoid being a total, hot mess. When it came to Maverick, he didn't want it to be some weird, rushed hook up. He wanted to romance him. He wanted to take his time.

"I'm tired," Jackson yawned while he sat on the ground, taking a gander at the plants all around him.

There was a good variety, which got him wondering what they were. Nathan probably would've known. Greg definitely would've. They were both interested in stuff like that. Normally, Jackson wasn't, but right now it felt like he was in a dream, so he noticed.

"Yeah, me, too. Everything's been wearing me out lately," Maverick agreed, taking a seat, his eyes looking out on the clearing and trees.

"Especially Kamila, I bet…" Jackson quietly commented.

Maverick pulled his knees to his chest and trailed one of his fingers along the soil. Jackson could tell from the muted response he still hadn't left her.

48

"Haven't ended it yet, huh?"

Maverick shook his head, "No. I want to. It's just hard. I know she's going to be hurt…agh…I hate doing that to people."

"It's only going to hurt worse the longer you drag it on, you know…"

Maverick sighed, "I know."

They were quiet for a long time before Jackson decided to lighten things and tease. He suddenly wanted to rile Maverick up.

"If anything, actually, you're being kind of a dick, you know…stringing her along like that…"

Maverick immediately understood Jackson wanted to play. He decided to indulge. Why not? This was just the way things were, after all.

"Jackson, I swear…"

"No, no…I'm serious…you're doing the same thing you always do, man…putting yourself before everyone else. It's why you have issues with your girlfriends, your friends…Nathan…"

Maverick's cheeks were suddenly fire. *God!* Why did Jackson always have to hit him where it hurt?

"Damn it, Jackson! Did you really drag me all the way out here for this!? All that bullshit about wanting to spend time with me, and you have to go and be a dick about Nate!?"

Jackson shrugged, "The truth hurts."

Maverick's skin started to itch while his body ran hotter. *The truth…ha!*

"God, you're so fucking impossible, Jack…!" he suddenly spat out, further ramped by the itching on his skin.

He couldn't help it. He was hurt. He was confused. He was starting to slip into rage. He grabbed Jackson by the collar and shoved him to the ground. Jackson was smiling, which infuriated Maverick more. He hopped on top of him and straddled his hips. They were both breathing heavy, Maverick with anger, Jackson with thrill. Maverick gripped the fabric of Jackson's hoodie and glared. *God! His skin was so itchy!* Jackson's expression changed, shifting from a smile into something Maverick didn't quite recognize. What was that look? What was going on? His own glare softened as he felt Jackson's hands gently touching the small of his back. His stomach hit the floor while it dawned on him what this was. Another shot at a kiss, and this time he wasn't drunk. He felt consumed with this sick, nauseated feeling of irrefutable desire while they stared at one another. He'd have done it then. He'd have given in, leaned down, and finally, finally, *finally* taken a taste of that mouth…it was just that…the itching…!!!

"I feel like my skin's on fire," he suddenly complained.

"You do? I thought that was just me," Jackson said, faintly winded.

Maverick released him and sat up straight, taking a closer look at the greenery around them.

"Oh, God…Jack, what are these plants? Is this Poison Ivy!?" he hollered, abruptly standing and scratching his uncovered arms.

Jackson panicked while he stood up, too. He looked around and suddenly realized that, yes, it absolutely was.

"Oh, shit…" he grumbled.

Maverick instantly lost it. Jackson winced. *Damn it, damn it, damn it!*

"Oh my God it is!!! Jackson!!! You did this on purpose!!!" he screamed, grabbing his jacket and storming off.

Jackson felt more dread seizing his chest.

"What!? Maverick! Wait! Come on…do you really think I did that on purpose!? It got me, too!" he protested while he followed.

They got back on the trail. Maverick was visibly livid. He headed back in the direction they'd come, wanting to leave. He pulled out his phone, then texted Nathan and Greg. He let them know briefly what happened.

50

"Maverick! Really, I mean…why would I do that!?"

"I should've known you were up to something," Maverick grumbled, "You let me take off my jacket! Look at my arms!"

Jackson looked. They were red, and welted, and it looked exceptionally horrible. Jackson's lower back was itching like crazy…and his ankles, and hands, and neck were, too.

"I was laying on my back in it!"

"Fuck you, Jackson!" Maverick shouted, effectively ending the altercation.

Jackson looked at his feet, shoving shaking hands into the pockets of his hoodie. He walked along, forlorn and defeated. Now this weekend was obviously ruined. Maverick was convinced Jackson asked him up there just to screw with him. Which, like, yeah…maybe he wanted to poke a little fun at him, get him riled up, but that wasn't the overall goal. He felt like he wanted to cry, but his pride was entirely too much for softness like that. When they arrived at the car, Jackson unlocked it and fished out some water bottles. They silently rinsed the injured skin, then angrily settled in to wait for their friends. Maverick sat in the back, even though the front was now open for the taking.

"Oh, come on, Mav…you don't have to be such a bitch about it…"

"Shut up!"

Jackson felt his face run hot with humiliation. He started up the car, then slammed his palm against the radio, turning it on in a discernible huff. Maverick didn't care. Well, he did, a little. He was just too mad to give it much thought. They sat in fuming silence while they waited for Nathan and Greg. Thankfully, they were quick. Greg sat in the back. Nathan took the open seat up front.

"Holy shit, dude…your arms!" Greg gasped and gawked.

"No shit," Maverick quipped.

Nathan glanced back, taking note of the situation. He looked toward Jackson and saw the welts on his neck and the tops of his hands. The heartbreak on his face didn't escape Nathan either. Maverick was furious. He could tell they'd had a fight.

"Let's stop by the gas station and get you guys some meds," Nathan said, trying his best to bring some calm to the situation.

God, he was tired of mediating between those two.

Jackson didn't say anything. He miserably shifted into reverse and backed out. He drove into the small town they'd passed on their way to the trail. There was a drug store on the corner, which they opted for in lieu of a gas station. Nathan was the one who went inside, gathering up various creams and a big pack of antihistamines. He purchased the goods, quiet and calm all the while. When he returned to the vehicle, he handed some cream and pills back to Maverick, who instantly started slathering it on his arms. The rest of his body would have to wait for the privacy of a tent.

Jackson toughed it out while they drove back to the site. He parked, then Maverick practically launched himself from the car. He went directly to the tent he was supposed to sleep in, grabbed his bag, and huffed over to Nathan and Greg's.

"I don't give a shit which one of you sleeps with him, but it sure as hell isn't going to be me!" he shouted.

Greg was wide-eyed, not nearly as familiar with Maverick's capacity to tantrum as the other two were. Nathan, of course, was well acquainted and unimpressed. He quietly rolled his eyes and went to grab his bag. He walked it over to Jackson's tent and threw it in, catching his sorry friend's eyes along the way. Jackson looked so sad, it made Nathan feel sick. In his eyes, all he could see was Maverick being the little brat he so often tended to be. Overreacting, making a big fuss when one didn't need to be made. The thing Nathan couldn't know, of course, was that Maverick wasn't only combative about the uncertainty of Jackson's motives. He was also terribly embarrassed about the rash. It was getting worse very fast, and there was no way he felt like he could share a tent with Jackson like that. This thing they were dancing around would have to wait until he was better. He didn't want to be a red, welted, itchy disaster when they kissed, or touched, or…

He forced the thought down again while he slathered lotion all over his body and dropped into his sleeping bag. He was done and he was sad. He was checking out for the day.

Nathan folded his arms and looked around. He hated seeing Jackson so down, and he also didn't want the entire trip to be a bust. The whole thing was really burning him up. Maverick. He was always doing this, not seeing what was right there in front of him. Not seeing someone so loving and giving, someone loyal and willing to bring the moon down to earth if it'd make him happy. Someone that Nathan would've been more than grateful to take for himself.

His stomach rolled. He'd been grappling with it all week, ever since that moment in the car when he'd realized what he'd actually been feeling. It was a crush, a strong one. It was emotional and deep because the friendship was close. It was occupying more and more of his thoughts, and it was starting to infect his heart. Watching Jackson pursue Maverick was difficult enough, but watching Jackson get rejected was worse.

Nathan went to the car. He asked Jackson to pop the trunk, then he pulled out a case of beer and approached the other two. Greg smirked. Jackson didn't change at all. Nathan handed out the beers anyway, and then he and Greg got a fire going. Jackson grabbed some lotion from the grocery bag Nathan left in the car. He applied it to the troubled areas, then downed a pill with his beer. He sat atop a log in front of the fire. He drank in silence, listening while Nathan and Greg talked about school. It went on for about an hour before Jackson excused himself to the tent. It was still fairly light out, but it was late enough to sleep. Nathan watched him from the corner of his eye while he sipped his beer and tried to figure out what to do.

"Those two," Greg shook his head and whistled between his teeth.

Nathan nodded in agreement, "Yeah, those two."

Nothing else was said about that. He and Greg talked a while longer about nothing of consequence, but Nathan was entirely preoccupied with his concern over Jackson. He eventually excused himself and went to the tent. It was starting to get dark while he zipped it behind him. He could see the flicker of the fire, and he could hear the comforting pops of burning wood. It was light enough he could see Jackson was still awake. He was lying on his back, staring up at the top of the tent, looking just about as miserable as ever.

Nathan stripped from his shoes and pants, then pulled on some pajama bottoms and settled into his sleeping bag. They were close enough to talk without being overheard. Nathan positioned himself on his side so he could look at Jackson while they spoke.

"Are you okay?"

Jackson looked on the verge of tears, and when he answered he sounded like it, too.

"This weekend's a bust. I screwed it all up. He thinks I did it on purpose."

Nathan sighed, "He doesn't really think that. He's just throwing a fit. You know how he gets."

Jackson swallowed and looked down. He fiddled with his hands atop his belly.

"I know. That makes it worse. He's pushing me away. We barely just got here and he's already pushing me away."

Nathan kept his eyes focused on Jackson, watching with surprise while a few tears escaped him. Jackson kept wiping them away, clearly embarrassed.

"Why do you love someone who treats you like this?" Nathan finally asked.

Jackson's face looked pained while he tried to explain. It was difficult. How could he possibly begin to articulate the fact that he was *so* desperate for Maverick that even the terrible things felt good? When he'd pinned him down like that, all violent, clearly wanting to hit him, it gave Jackson a rush. He wanted that attention. He'd even have taken a punch. He'd have gone wild for it, actually. A hit, then a kiss, and maybe something more. There wasn't a snowball's chance in hell of that happening now, though. Not now. Maybe not ever.

"I can't explain it," he finally answered, his voice shaky and low.

Jackson continued to quietly lose his grip on his emotions. Tears kept streaming. He sniffled and wiped them away. His face was all twisted up with sorrow. Nathan just quietly watched. He watched and he wondered how the hell someone could be so caught up in a relationship like that. He tried to comprehend how Maverick was this massive, all consuming force in Jackson's life when there were so many other options out there. Most of all, though, he wondered what this would mean for their friendship while the situation progressed.

Nathan's stomach hurt. His emotions and thoughts started to creep up on him. He wanted to reach out and touch Jackson's hand, to hold it tenderly and tell him all about the people who'd be gentle and kind to him. People like himself. He didn't, though. He didn't take his hand. He didn't dare speak the feelings perched upon the tip of his tongue. He did, however, decide to say something a bit more subtle.

"There are people out there who'd love you better."

Jackson turned his head and looked at Nathan with aching eyes.

"I don't want better, Nathan. I just want Mav."

The following morning Maverick woke before the rest of them. He stayed tucked into his sleeping bag. It was exceptionally chilly and damp. He continued to feel itching and burning on his arms, and when he pulled one out he was mortified to see how welted and bad it had gotten. This was going to take a while to heal. He slipped his arm back inside the sleeping bag, trying to ignore the physical and psychological discomfort he was in. There was a deep sense of regret now that morning had arrived, his outrage waxed and waned. He'd overreacted yet again and he knew it. Jackson was crushed, he could see that. He'd considered coming out of the tent, apologizing, and maybe even moving back over to sleep with Jackson last night. By the time he'd mustered up the courage, though, Greg was already coming to the tent. Maverick had pretended to be asleep, listening to see if Nathan and Jackson were still awake. They weren't, so he'd lain there itching and remorseful until sleep finally came.

He pulled the sleeping bag to his chin and miserably stressed. They'd almost kissed, again, and Maverick ruined it…again. They were so tantalizingly close there for a moment. The way Jackson's large, firm hands felt on his back lingered in a way that made his chest ache. His eyebrows knit together while he reeled, carrying the tension, that need to go back and experience the moment better. He knew he couldn't, though. Hell, he couldn't even manage to create a different situation now, not with his arms in a ravaged state like this. It was vain, and shallow, and he knew it, but still. It just wasn't the way he pictured things going down when they did.

Maverick's fretful thoughts were abruptly interrupted when he heard the tent unzip. Greg stirred, then sat up and looked. It was Jackson popping his head in, offering them an ill at ease smile.

"Nathan's making breakfast."

Greg stretched his arms and yawned. He knew Jackson was trying to get him out of the tent. Nathan told him all about Jackson's scheme to nab Maverick while they were walking yesterday. He was privy to the situation at hand, so he stepped out and made himself scarce while Jackson cautiously entered the tent and zipped it shut. Maverick stared at him, feeling that familiar pit in his gut. He was silent while Jackson sat down, resting his elbows on his knees. Though careless in posture, Maverick could tell he was on edge.

"I'm sorry about yesterday. I really didn't know…"

"No. I'm sorry. I know you didn't know, obviously…shit like that just really freaks me out. I overreacted."

Jackson nodded and looked at his hands, fiddling aimlessly to occupy his eyes. Maverick glanced down at his skin, realizing he had a rash, too. It wasn't nearly as brutal as his own. No surprise there. As a child, Maverick had always been predisposed to reactions and illnesses. His body was sensitive. Yet another reason he tried to justify completely going nuts.

"Is it bothering you much?" Maverick asked, nodding toward Jackson's hands.

"I put lotion on. It's okay. What about you?"

"It's really bad," he admitted, looking ashamed.

Jackson sighed, "Where's your lotion?"

Maverick nodded toward his gym bag. Jackson followed his eyes and leaned over, retrieving the soothing pink treatment.

"Give me your arms," he instructed, doing his best to sound confident.

Maverick hesitated. Jackson watched with a blank face. It was awkward, and neither one of them was certain how to behave.

"I don't want you to see them," Maverick admitted, "That's why I moved over here last night."

Jackson blinked, entirely caught off guard. That was why Maverick acted like that? Because he was feeling insecure? Jackson let out a laugh because he really didn't know what else to do. Maverick looked hurt by it, though, so he quickly walked it back.

"Mav, I don't care. I know what you normally look like. Besides, even if your skin was always a red mess, do you really think that would bother me?"

Maverick quietly considered his words. They were nice and comforting, and not entirely outside the realm of Jackson's personality. Still, there was that *little* part of him that was constantly suspicious of Jackson's motives. Maverick was always searching for danger when it came to him. He was constantly on high alert. He forced himself to ignore the sirens in his head, though, and timidly pulled his arms from the sleeping bag. He exposed them to his enemy, the object of his constant, irate desire.

Jackson took note of the particularly bad state of his arms, but he didn't react. He could tell Maverick was feeling sensitive about it, and under any other circumstances he definitely would have ripped on him for a rise, but the situation was as raw and tender as his skin. He needed to drop the act and just be real if there was any hope of salvaging the weekend, so he softened himself. He poured some lotion into his hands. It was cold, so he rubbed his palms together briefly to warm it, then tentatively took Maverick's arm and carefully applied it. While he did, Maverick stared at him, not bothering to conceal his curiosity. It was fascinating to him, this affectionate gesture, this moment of vulnerability. Things like this had happened here and there between them over the years, but typically it was Maverick who initiated. Never before had Jackson dropped his walls and gotten intimate like this.

Unfortunately, though intense, the moment was over entirely too soon. Jackson eventually had the skin covered on both arms, and there was simply no excuse to keep touching like that. He let Maverick go, and the places his hands had just been felt cold. Maverick wanted Jackson to keep touching him, and not just on his arms. They stared into each other's eyes, both of them illuminating how afraid they really felt. The moment went on just a breath too long. Maverick cleared his throat. Jackson dropped his eyes. It was over. Neither of them said a word before Jackson left and Maverick was alone again.

He stayed there for a while, but eventually decided to venture out and join the rest of them. Nathan was cooking breakfast. He had bacon, potatoes and eggs going on a cast iron skillet. He offered Maverick a muted, apathetic smile. It was just enough to acknowledge him, but fell short of making Maverick feel like he was happy to see him. So it seemed like it would forever be between

58

them. Another pang of sadness seized Maverick while he sat and tried to join the morning's banter.

As per usual, Jackson kept everyone talking. Everyone except Nathan, of course, who simply fixated on the fire and food, looking zoned out as always. Normally, it would've ticked Maverick off. Nathan's self-indulgent melancholy got on his nerves, but for whatever reason he felt more concerned than anything else. Granted, Nathan was prone to depression, of that there was no doubt. However, the degree to which he'd been checking out was starting to grow, exponentially snuffing out the person he'd once been. Something was wrong.

Maverick did his best to try and juggle all the tensions he was holding while the morning wore on. He ate his breakfast, sitting closely beside Jackson. Nathan recognized the way Maverick's ferocity had cooled, predictably replaced with remorse driven offerings of peace. It was difficult because, while he sat there eating his breakfast and watching his friends, his insides felt knotted up and confused. On the one hand, he could clearly see that Maverick's tempered down mood this morning left Jackson feeling happier. Jackson was smiling and joking, goofing around the same way he always did. That part made Nathan feel good about it, the way he was trying to help set the two of them up. There was the other part of it, though, the part that hurt; the part that was watching Jackson cozy up to Maverick when *he* longed for that affection. He hated this crush for slamming down on him from nowhere. It was terribly unfair. What cruel, awful forces were making him feel this needless way? Why did it have to be Jackson his heart latched onto, his brain couldn't let go of, his stomach ached and longed for with more vehemence every day?

He alternated between staring down at his food, or his feet, or the trees, anything but them…but also, them. He snuck glances, sometimes long ones. He looked at Jackson's relaxed, smiling face. He wondered what happened in the tent this morning when they were alone. Did they kiss? Did they touch? Did they exchange romantic nothings? It made Nathan queasy to the point he couldn't eat any breakfast. He sighed to himself and threw it in the trash. He wasn't sure if anyone noticed. He wasn't entirely certain he cared. He went in the tent and grabbed a change of clothes. He excused himself and walked to the bathrooms. Upon arrival, he glanced inside a shower stall and assessed the situation. It was one that needed to be fed coins, which he had in his pocket. He gave it enough to get a seven minute shower. He washed in a hurry, then spent the remainder beneath hot water while he let himself fret.

Everything in his life felt so out of place. The way he dreamt of dressing different, of wearing his hair a bit longer, of painting his nails…anything, *anything* to outwardly feel like who he inwardly was. It made his stomach hurt, this desperation to just be, this need to feel loved and accepted for it, too. Those words Jackson had said crept into his mind again.

It's okay to be different…

His heartbeat slowed while he repeated that phrase over and over in his mind, hearing Jackson's voice saying it. His stomach stopped hurting. His breathing quieted down.

It's okay to be different. It's okay, it's okay.

He put his hand to his head and breathed slow and steady. That's what it was, really. That was the thing that took the little, confused feelings he'd been having around Jackson and shoved them right in front of his face. He was grateful for them, because obviously there in that moment they were soothing and calming. They made him feel like it was actually true. In another sense, though, he wished Jackson had never said it because, if he hadn't, then Nathan wouldn't even have considered the things he was wanting from him now; his attention, his touch, the idea of Jackson being that missing piece of the puzzle, in a sense. It was there, though. The thought had already been soundly planted in his mind. Jackson was someone he could picture himself with. Jackson was someone who understood.

Before he could examine it further, the water stopped and he had to get out. He was instantly cold, so he dried off fast in an effort to warm up. He dressed in his usual dull clothes. He looked in the mirror, taking note of how typically male he actually looked. His dark hair was short and his face had a bit of shadow where his scruff was growing in. He sighed and got out his things to shave it away. At least that was something. He could erase the shadow from his jaw and get rid of that ruggedness.

60

He stepped back and looked a bit longer. His shape was classically male, too; broad shoulders, small waist. He could deal with all of that, though. He was so thin he could crush it out with an oversized sweater if he wanted. Sometimes he did, although even then it felt like people would somehow know. Nonetheless, he did enjoy wearing a massive sweater on occasion. He loved pulling his knees to his chest on the couch and sipping hot tea while he played with his phone. He only did that when he was alone. The body language was too soft. He'd never, ever let Maverick see him like that.

Just then, Nathan heard the bathroom door opening. He immediately quit looking in the mirror and stepped forward to grab his things from the counter. He heard Jackson, Greg and Maverick's voices while they filed into the bathroom and stole away the peace. Nathan offered them a soft smile, an acknowledgment of their presence. Jackson's eyes lingered, and Maverick's did, too. It made Nathan feel light and nervous, and he quickly excused himself. He didn't want to hang out. He scurried back to the campsite and put his things away. He sat down on one of the logs near the fizzled out fire and checked his phone. He smiled when he realized he had a message from Chris, opening it without delay.

Chris: Hey-o! Sorry if this is weird, but I'm kind of excited to catch up with you! I just wanted to say hello. You mentioned you were out of town. What are you doing?

Nathan suddenly felt lightheaded while he typed up a response. Maybe it was the attention. Maybe it was simply the fact that Chris knew.

Nathan: Hey! It's not weird! I'm excited to catch up with you, too. What should we do next weekend anyway? I'm camping in the mountains with some of my friends. So far it's been kind of boring. I think I need a drink to get through the rest of it! XD

Nathan eyed the screen, waiting eagerly for a response. He was pleasantly surprised to see it come fast. Chris was online.

Chris: How about we eat somewhere nice? I haven't gotten anything besides friggin' fast food in forever. I'd love to split a bottle of wine and eat something with nutrients O_O ha! Depending how it goes, maybe we could dance at a club or something after…? I love to dance!!

Nathan: I think that sounds really nice. I never eat anywhere good either…too broke XD I'm not a very good dancer, but I guess if I had enough wine I might be down.

Chris: Okay, I'll pick out a place. Let's do a rideshare so we can get tipsy and see where the night takes us, yeah?? ;) Sorry to hear your trip's been a drag. I hope you're able to have a little fun before it's over!

Nathan: Ok :) Cool! Ha – Like I said, I'm going to get smashed tonight. I'll have fun! I have a feeling next weekend's going to be better, though.

Chris: I have a feeling it's going to be, too.

Nathan bit his lip and smiled wide before shaking his head and shutting off the screen. He put it away, and while he did he heard his friends coming back to camp. They were all so loud. He was in higher spirits now, though, so he rose and genuinely smirked at them. He decided to engage. They fell into conversation easily and made plans for their day. Jackson basically told them all what was going to happen, and though Nathan half-expected Maverick to protest, he didn't. He seemed more easygoing than his typical posture, which tugged on Nathan again. Things were softer this morning and it hurt.

Nathan forced himself to ignore the tension. They piled into the car and headed out toward town. It was a touristy location just starting to open now that things had gotten warm enough. They walked around, browsing the shops. Maverick split off with Greg, disappearing into an eclectic little gift shop. Nathan somehow wound up walking the street beside Jackson.

"Do you think I should get him a gift or something? Like, a peace offering for yesterday's disaster?" Jackson suddenly asked.

Nathan came out of his head. His stomach was in knots while he tried to play along, ignoring the ways he didn't want things to really work out when it came to them. It was selfish and he knew it. He really didn't want to be that person, so he decided he wouldn't. At least not externally.

"Sure, yeah…a gift can't hurt."

"Okay, help me pick something out…come on…" Jackson insisted, grabbing Nathan's arm and leading him to a store that'd caught his eye.

It made Nathan's stomach hurt worse. Jackson's hand felt so nice on his arm. He released him as soon as they were inside, though, and it made Nathan feel a mixture of relief and want. They wandered a while, Jackson commenting on little things here and there. Maverick was kind of difficult to buy for. He wasn't really interested in much outside of his studies and aspirations. He wasn't much for sweets, either, so chocolates and the like were automatically out. He wouldn't be into a shot glass with his name or anything like that.

"Damn, there's nothing here that feels right to me," Jackson complained.

Nathan had to agree.

"Let's just keep looking. There has to be something."

They walked along and then, in the corner of the store, Nathan noticed an array of cheap trinkets. In it, there were these mood rings with fancy wooden borders. They were actually pretty nice, and it would be kind of funny to give him something like that.

"Jack…over here," Nathan called, looking up and gesturing.

Jackson walked over and took a glance, instantly letting out an endearing, snorty laugh.

"A mood ring? Oh, my God…that's hilarious," he commented, picking one up.

"They're kind of nice with the wood along the edges," Nathan explained.

Jackson kept grinning while he looked them over.

"You know, Nate, it's perfect. It's like, I can give him a ring, which I'd obviously love to, but if he's weird about it I can play it off like a joke. I like it. Very sneaky, dude. I didn't know you were capable of being so sly!"

Nathan shrugged, "I'm capable of a lot of things."

The words were casual, but they inadvertently came out flirtatious. Jackson glanced at him, clearly surprised. Nathan's stomach lurched while he cleared his throat and walked away, ending the uncomfortable interaction in a snap. Jackson watched him leave. The thought occurred to him, then. It was brief, but it was there.

Nah. No way.

He shrugged it off and went to pay. He put the ring in his pocket so Maverick wouldn't know he'd bought something, then he and Nathan went out to meet up with the others. The group wandered around for hours, stopping to take in the view of a sizeable lake outside the town. Evening eventually fell and hunger settled in. They selected a restaurant overlooking the water. They were given a table outside on the patio, and Nathan was faced with yet another moment where he felt like he wanted to do something he couldn't. They needed to order drinks, and of course they all wanted beers. Everyone except Nathan. What he really would've liked to do was order some wine because he liked it better, but somehow that felt too feminine so he went along with the group. He silently drank his beer like the rest.

While the night wore on Nathan wound up ordering more alcohol than his friends. This habit of Nate's didn't escape Maverick. He was always doing that, drinking himself into oblivion and avoiding conversation. By the time dinner was through, Maverick was a mixture of concerned and annoyed over the sloppiness of his friend. It caused more pressure in the group while Jackson drove back to the site. That strain only increased when Nathan drank more back at camp. Not that the rest of them didn't. They did. They gathered around the fire and they indulged, but Nathan was definitely hitting it the hardest.

It was difficult to be mad at him, though. He wasn't loud or obnoxious. He didn't cry or say anything stupid. He was a little looser than usual, but that was about it. The thing that made his friends feel tense was the fact that, lately, every single one of them

64

had noticed he wasn't right. Even Greg, who wasn't especially close. They were worried he was drinking to suppress or forget something rather than have fun. No one said anything, though. When the hour grew late, Maverick took Jackson to the side. Greg and Nathan were talking politics, taking no notice whatsoever. Maverick touched Jackson's arm, then leaned in close and spoke soft, his breath sending a shiver down Jack's spine.

"Listen, I'm going to level with you here. I'm worried about him. I'd like to share a tent with him tonight because he clearly needs someone to talk to but…" Maverick drew in a breath and let it out, "…I think it should be you. You guys get along better these days. Can you look after him? Can you do that for me? Try and figure out what's going on with him, okay? I know something's wrong. I *know* it."

Jackson eyed him. He felt tremendously disappointed because he wanted nothing more than to get in that tent with Maverick. It was the entire point of the weekend, that moment, that chance. Unfortunately, he was just as concerned about Nathan as Mav was. He sighed and nodded.

"I have an idea what it is. I'll try and talk to him."

Maverick tilted his head and looked at him curiously. Jackson shook his head, indicating he had no plans of sharing what he did or didn't know. Maverick nodded, accepting it for once.

"Okay."

Jackson moved to step away from him, but Maverick grabbed his arm again.

"Thank you," he said in a rare show of affection.

Jackson blinked. His stomach rolled. He smiled, despite his best efforts not to.

"You're welcome."

Maverick held his arm a moment longer before they reluctantly separated. Jackson felt bright while he walked over to Nathan and coaxed him into lying down. He wasn't difficult. He didn't put up any fight at all. He said goodnight to Maverick and Greg, then stumbled into the tent, dizzy and off balance.

"You okay there? Can you handle yourself?" Jackson asked while he zipped up behind them.

"Yeah, yeah...sorry..." he said, realizing even in his drunken stupor that he was kind of screwing things up.

"It's okay. He and I are fine," Jackson replied.

Nathan nodded and stumbled to his gym bag. He pulled out some pajamas and clumsily changed. Jackson kept his eyes to himself for the most part, though he did catch a glimpse of Nathan here and there out of curiosity. It was innocent but, he had to admit, as much as he was obsessed with Maverick, Nathan was way beyond cute. He just was. Jackson found himself grinning and laughing while Nathan got into his sleeping bag. Nathan looked up at him and smiled wide, laughing some, too.

"I'm sorry, God..." he chuckled.

Jackson shook his head and laid down, "Don't be. None of this went the way I wanted it to, but it's still been good. I'll give him the ring tomorrow. It'll all be just fine."

Nathan stared at him, clearly feeling chatty. The alcohol had him all loosened up.

"Jack?"

"Hmmm?"

"Did you mean it, when you said it was okay if I was different?"

He nodded, his full attention on Nathan while he felt the sudden urge to hold his breath.

"Yeah, of course."

Nathan eyed him, clearly anxious. He sat up and scooted his sleeping bag closer, close enough that when he got back into it, Jackson could feel his body against his own. It made him a little nervous, though it was obvious Nathan was off on something else.

66

"How did you find out?"

"Your dating profile. You showed it to me, remember? So I made a profile and looked you up."

Nathan's eyes widened, then he laughed and put his hand to his forehead.

"Oh, God…right…"

Jackson smiled and looked away. They were quiet for a moment before he gently prodded.

"You want to talk about it?"

Nathan looked at him, then he let out this enormous, relieved sigh.

"Yeah…so, so badly."

"Okay, so, tell me."

"It's like…okay, listen…it's like I'm…I don't feel, like, tied to a gender. I don't feel like a man, and I don't feel like a woman. I know it's tough, but…okay…so…" he looked at Jackson like he wanted to make sure he was following along. He was so drunk. Jackson nodded, trying to encourage him to keep talking. Nathan drew in a deep breath before letting it all out, "…when Julia and I have sex…and you can*not* make fun of me for this, I'm serious…this is hard for me to say…"

"I won't, Nathan."

"Okay, okay. She, um…well, sometimes she…have you ever heard of…shit, I can't say this. Um, look, sometimes I'm like, her bottom, okay? And it feels good, and I like it and…God, I'm sorry, this is…I've *never* told *anyone* this stuff. But it's not just that, okay? Like…my sexuality is *all* over. I've never been with a man, but I want to be…I like women, too. I was so in love with Jules for a while there, you know that, but, yeah. *So*, anyway…there's that. But also, I kind of want to look different. Inside I feel, not like a woman exactly, just…softer I guess? Does that make sense?"

Jackson stared at him, trying his best to follow along. He was kind of stuck on the whole 'bottom' thing, but he did figure that one out.

67

The other stuff, though, he wasn't sure he understood. He felt entirely male, of that there was no doubt. Still, he was trying to take it in. He nodded. Nathan watched him while he went on.

"There's this store in the mall…the fancy one next to that Goth store. I keep going there. I don't go inside, I just stand out front. Going in is, like, *way* too scary, but I stand there and I look inside. Right now they have this floral headstring, kind of like a crown but small and light. I want it. I want to wear it for special occasions, and I want to put on a big pastel sweater, like baby blue or pink, and that's it. I want to wear my hair like, have you ever seen those haircuts women get? Like the longer pixie cuts I guess? A man could wear it for sure and no one would think anything about it, but that's what I want. I want to look like that. I'd still wear men's clothes, but just…you know…kind of ambiguous, I guess? I'm too scared, though. I mean, people are so mean…" his voice trailed off there; his face looked painfully sad.

Jackson stared at him, and when he spoke he was careful to keep his voice down.

"You seem like you think about this a lot?"

Nathan looked down. He felt tears pooling up in his eyes. He sniffled and, when he spoke, his voice was a gasp.

"I think about it all the time."

Jackson waited, letting Nathan collect himself. He was struggling not to lose it, teetering along the edge of the things that cracked his heart.

"I just want to be who I feel like I am, but I can't. I just can't."

Jackson wasn't sure what he could say, so instead, he grabbed onto Nathan and pulled him close. Nathan broke down. He started to cry as quietly as he could. He cried into Jackson's chest, his hands clutching the fabric of his shirt. Jackson rested his hand on the back of Nathan's head while he thought about everything he'd just learned about his friend. It took some time for Nathan to calm down, but when he did, he stayed there. Jackson wasn't sure how to end it, so he didn't.

"I'm sorry," Nathan whispered.

"It's okay," Jackson whispered back.

Nathan sniffled while he clung to Jackson's shirt.

"Do you still like me? Am I still your best friend?"

Jackson pulled away. He looked down at Nathan's watery eyes. He felt more empathy than he was accustomed to in that moment. He understood what it was like to be fearful and insecure like that, even if it was over different things.

"Nathan...of course. I still like you, and you're still my best friend. I meant what I said. There's *nothing* you could do that would ever change that. I'd literally kill people for my friends, you know that."

Nathan stared at him. Jackson sighed and touched his hand to the back of his head, commanding his attention.

"It's okay to be who you are. You're a good person, one of the best I've ever met. I'm sorry you're feeling so scared, and I'm sorry you're not able to express who you are. No one should ever have to feel something like that."

Nathan's eyes wavered.

"Why are you so nice to me? You're such a jerk to everyone else," he asked, trying to lighten the mood.

Jackson shrugged, "Because, I like you."

Nathan held his breath for a moment.

Oh, God, Jackson...I really like you, too.

They quieted down after that. They drifted off to sleep. Their sleeping bags were close, and they remained so, too. They didn't touch. They stayed separate and apart, and while Nathan fell into a deep, dreamless sleep, he couldn't help but wonder if it would always be like that. He hoped it wouldn't, but he had this horrible feeling it would.

Oh well. It's just your heart screwing with you, Nathan. Try to ignore it. Try and let him go.

When the morning came, Nathan was hung over with a headache. He took stock of where he was, slowly coming to and squeezing his eyes shut. Pain slammed against the backs of his eyes, and when he looked beside him he quickly realized how close he'd scooted toward Jackson in his drunken state. It made his stomach flutter, but he was terrified to move. He didn't want to wake him and draw even more attention to the way they'd slept. Although, in a world where Nathan didn't feel anything for Jackson, would it really be all that big a deal? Probably not, so he laid there in silence and let his eyes linger.

This hurt in its own way, too. Just taking in the sight of him, having a moment to really look at and examine the contours of his face, the little details Nathan was etching into his brain. Jackson looked young, fresh and striking. He was an undeniably attractive guy. The way he was built suited him perfectly, particularly how tall he was. He had a delightful face, the kind that felt welcoming and warm, despite how abrasive he could often times be. He wasn't ever like that with Nathan, though. He was different. When they were alone, Jackson was calm and thoughtful. He was few with his words and gentle in his mannerisms. There was always a lot going on in his mind. Though he never divulged many of those thoughts, it was easy to see how comfortable Jackson was in the company of Nathan.

While he covertly took in the details of Jackson's face, he started to recall some of their conversation from last night. God, he'd been so open. At the time it'd felt like a tremendous weight lifting from his chest. Now, however, he felt ill at ease and far too sober to face it. Jackson had seemed like he was more than okay with the things Nathan told him, but what if it was all a show? What if he actually thought less of him now? What if he thought he was weird, or something to be repulsed by? Nathan lowered his eyes and pulled the sleeping bag to his chin. He wanted to cry, and he suddenly wished he were alone.

It's just the hangover. You always feel like this when the buzz wears off.

Nathan's movement must've been noisier than he'd meant, because Jackson stirred as soon as he did. Nathan held his breath for a moment. Jackson was slow to wake, kind of like a bear coming out of hibernation. It was charming to Nathan, who was prone to behaving much the same in the morning. Not like Mav. Maverick popped out of bed like a spring. Once Jackson was sufficiently awake, he looked beside him and offered Nathan a warm, confident smile that instantly put him at ease. Things were fine. Things were most definitely fine.

"Well, I guess it's time to go back home. You have a shift tonight?"

Nathan shook his head, "No. I scored the whole weekend off."

Jackson huffed, "Lucky you. Damn manager wouldn't hear it when I tried."

"You're a supervisor. I'm just a weenie-peddler," Nathan joked.

Jackson snorted in that cute way of his when he chuckled. Nathan felt fuzzy and eager to make him do it again, but he wasn't good at joking the way Jackson was. He'd have to settle for little moments when they came, however fleeting they were. This one was particularly transitory while Jackson got out of his sleeping bag and stretched. Nathan could tell he was eager to get on with his day. He was probably excited to give Mav that ring.

Nathan hung back in his sleeping bag for a while after Jackson went outside. He could hear the other two were awake because they all started talking. Nathan clutched his sleeping bag around him, hoping it might pacify him but it didn't. He felt off and unstable. He felt downtrodden and lost. Talking with Jackson did help last night, but he needed something more than that. He needed to actually act on and do these things. He needed to go ahead and wear the big sweaters, paint his nails, and grow out his hair. He *needed* to hit the mall and buy that flower crown he couldn't put out of his mind. Jackson was good, and acceptance felt nice, but what Nathan really wanted was to start expressing himself. Perhaps he'd start with something small…?

Eventually he grew tired of lying along with his thoughts. He got out of bed and joined his friends outside. He mostly listened, though he did chime in occasionally. They wolfed down some breakfast.

72

Jackson cooked over the fire this time. Once that was all through, they showered, packed, and got back into the car where more mindless blather was indulged. Jackson kept the banter going. Nathan felt like he was falling in love while he listened. He didn't pay much attention to his phone. He was enthralled with Jackson. He barely looked away from him. Maverick noticed from the back, though he wasn't sure what to make of it.

The first person to get dropped off was Greg, then Jackson drove Nathan and Maverick home. When they moved to get out of the car, Jackson killed the engine and exited, too. He explained that he had his uniform in the trunk, and he wanted to hang out until he had to go to work. Maverick agreed. Nathan felt heartbroken. He knew Jackson wanted to stay, give Maverick that ring, maybe see if they might finally get physical. Nathan swallowed down his yearning while they entered the apartment, then disappeared into his room. He couldn't stand to watch it. He didn't want to know. He flopped atop his bed and texted Julia.

Nathan: Please come over…I'm a mess, Jules.

***

While Nathan waited for a response from Julia, Maverick and Jackson stood gracelessly in the living room. It was really difficult, especially for Maverick, because he knew what was happening on some level. He understood when Jackson took him out into the clearing it was because he wanted to kiss him. They'd been dancing around this tension for years, expertly so. In a sense, Maverick felt entirely consumed with the details of their relationship. Jackson was captivating in both the best and worst kinds of ways. It left Maverick feeling acutely conflicted, frightened, and unsure. He felt timid and anxious about himself the more he contemplated dropping his guard and letting it happen. What kind of person must he have been to be so entranced with someone who'd gone so far out of his way to torment him so? Not that he didn't dish it back, or even at times provoke it. He did. But, still…what the hell did that say about him?

Maverick cleared his throat and glanced at Jackson before going to his room to set his bag down. He felt sick with desire and anticipation when he heard Jackson follow him. The door remained open, but it still felt very private. Maverick turned to face him, watching nervously while Jackson approached, pulling something small from his pocket.

"I got this for you…" he said, clearly feeling out of his element, too.

Maverick tilted his head while he looked at the large palm of his enemy's hand. There sat this ring with wooden trim and a colorful center. He instantly recognized the material. He immediately understood it was kind of a joke. He also understood that, in a small persistent way, it was serious. He smiled softly and took the ring from Jackson's hand, looking at it with amusement.

"I know you're making fun of me," he quipped with a grin, slipping it on his finger nonetheless, "but the joke's on you, because it's actually kind of nice. You should've gotten me a crappier one."

Jackson's heart felt like it was beating up to his throat. Maverick was accepting the gift in a real kind of way. Wow. That was something. That was definitely something.

"Well, you know, you're kind of fussy. Thought this might help you out…give you a little warning when you're about to lose your shit," Jackson teased, trying his best to be laid-back.

Of course, he was anything but.

"What's the occasion?" Maverick prodded, taking it a step further than Jackson had anticipated.

They stared, their eyes flickering between one another's. Jackson swallowed hard while he tried to think of something witty to say. He didn't have anything, so instead he answered, low and sincere.

"I just wanted to."

Maverick felt crippled by the pit in his stomach. He tried to figure out what he should say next, but he had nothing. Nothing felt right. Before he could find a way to either get out of it or push it further, his phone rang from his pocket. It broke the eye contact and shattered the moment. Neither one of them was sure whether it was a relief or disappointment. Maverick glanced at Jackson before answering the phone and putting it to his ear.

"Hey babe…!"

Jackson couldn't help but roll his eyes. Obviously it was Kamila. He sighed to himself and went to have a seat on Maverick's bed, resting his hands in the pockets of his sweater. He looked around the room, taking note of how quintessentially Maverick it was; neat, orderly, full of study materials and books. He was a smart person, which Jackson admired. Maverick was on the same level as himself. Being in law school together with opposing views and smarts like theirs was well beyond exciting. He looked forward to sparring with Maverick over the next three years. He hoped, at some point, to spar with him in more intimate kinds of ways. Jackson refocused on Maverick as his conversation came to a close.

"Sorry, I know…I know what you're going to say. I'll end it, I swear I will…"

Jackson shrugged, "It's your life, Mav. Do whatever you want."

Maverick eyed him and scratched the back of his neck. He dropped his hand, then folded his arms and stepped closer to Jackson, speaking unusually quiet.

"Did you find out what's going on with Nate?"

Jackson nodded, "Yeah. We talked. I think he'll be fine. He's just going through some personal stuff."

Maverick eyed him expectantly. Jackson shifted uncomfortably.

"I can't tell you. He'd have to tell you himself," Jackson clarified.

Maverick glanced toward the living room just to make sure Nathan wasn't there. He turned his focus back on Jackson and continued speaking in hushed tones.

"Does it have to do with Julia? They're kind of strange, you know? She comes over here to hook up with him, and I know she's got a girlfriend and everything…and she always has this massive purse and…this sounds kind of weird and everything, and I could totally be off base, but…I've heard them in there…and I mostly hear *him*…isn't that kind of odd?"

Jackson looked away. He knew now, of course. It wasn't his place to say, though. He had to get out of this conversation, and fast. He glanced at his watch. He still had about an hour before work, but this was all getting complicated fast.

"Maybe he's just one of those guys that makes a lot of noise. Listen, I've got to get going…sorry. Do you mind if I change in your bathroom?"

Maverick blinked, surprised Jackson was ending the conversation just like that. It made him feel like he was onto something, and whatever it was, Jackson knew. Jackson stood and grabbed the uniform he'd brought. He started to walk past Maverick, but Jackson felt his hand on his arm and he stopped. He looked toward him, and his stomach fluttered at the sight. Maverick's eyes were wide and staring.

"Promise me he's okay?"

Jackson nodded, "I'll make sure he is."

They regarded each other a moment longer before Jackson decided to offer up a nugget of advice. He could do that without giving away too much.

"Listen, Mav…if you really want to be there for Nathan, all I can say is, you need to settle down about him and keep an open mind. He needs acceptance right now. I can't tell you why, but that's what he needs from you. Get yourself there. Don't be a judgmental dick like you usually are."

Normally Maverick would've gotten fired up about the insult, except Jackson didn't look like he was joking at all. He looked serious. He was calling him out. He was being confrontational in a way he rarely was. Maverick swallowed hard, unsure what to say. He never knew what to do when Jackson threw his flaws in his face like that. He wasn't sure if he was annoyed or appreciative. Before he could decide, Jackson peeled away from him and went to get changed. Maverick stood there, confused and frustrated. Eventually, he shook it off and walked out of his room. He made a cup of coffee and sat down before the television. Jackson emerged, looking hilarious in his uniform. Maverick couldn't help but grin, and Jackson instinctively rolled his eyes.

"Yeah, yeah...I know, shut up," he grumbled, fiddling with his keys.

Nathan emerged from his room then. He glanced at the two of them, then opened the front door. He leaned outside and said hello. Maverick and Jackson watched as Julia entered the apartment, looking winded and eager. Maverick felt deeply uncomfortable now that he knew *something* relevant was going on there. Jackson felt unsure because he knew *exactly* what was happening. Nathan couldn't bring himself to look at either one as he took Julia's hand and led her to his bedroom. He didn't want to explain or justify anything. It definitely felt uncomfortable for him that Jackson was there and knew what they did. He didn't want to deal with it. He tried to shut it out while he closed the door behind them. They didn't talk. He just fell into her. They kissed passionately, first against the door, then down on the floor.

She was on top of him as usual, and for whatever reason it lit a fire inside him. Maybe it was because Jackson knew, and he wanted Jackson, and he didn't want Jackson to think he was...well, he wasn't exactly sure. He just felt pent up.

"Let me have you this time..." he whispered between kisses.

Julia didn't say anything. She just rolled off him, slipped from her clothes, and stared up at him. She let him do as requested, and it'd been so long it wound up feeling more emotional than they'd meant. It wasn't lengthy, but it was considerate. He made love to her, not sex. It was reminiscent of a time when he was simpler in her eyes. When it was over, they were left winded and confused. They stared at one another, trying to make sense of it. This wasn't the way things went between them anymore. It just wasn't.

"Nathan...I thought...I mean...?"

He brushed some hair from her face, "Sometimes I just need to..." he didn't finish. It was too difficult to explain.

Julia's eyes were watching him with concern. She could tell he was emotional. She touched his face and he met her gaze.

"Are you okay?" she asked.

He looked thoughtful before he answered.

"I'm falling in love…and I know he'll never love me back," he admitted.

"Oh…Oh, Nathan…I'm so sorry."

He didn't say anything. He just pressed his forehead against hers and tried to catch his breath. What could he say? There was nothing more to it. There wasn't anything else to be done.

***

Jackson stepped into the mall, which was low grade humiliating in that stupid uniform. Teens eyed him, made fun and laughed. Whatever. He forced himself not to care about it. He couldn't. It wasn't worth his time. Besides, he had something else on his mind, something he'd decided to do on the way over. He kept his eyes forward and confidently strode toward his destination. It didn't take him long. He instantly recognized the store Nathan had mentioned. He stopped in front of it, taking a long hard look at the manikin in the window. That must've been it, the flower crown thing Nathan had been talking about. Jackson didn't really get it, that was for damn sure, but if Nathan wanted it, well, then Nathan should have it as far as he was concerned. He drew in a breath, trying to build up his cocky persona, then stepped inside.

There were two young, very pretty women working inside. They instantly took notice of him. How could they not? He was tall, husky, and in a red and yellow hotdog uniform. He stuck out like the sorest of thumbs. Still, they were gracious when they approached him.

"Can we help you find something?"

"Uh, yeah. So, I'm here for my friend. He has a thing for that flower crown you have on that manikin there…and he mentioned wanting, like, a pastel sweater…do you have something like that? Is the crown for sale?"

The shorter one with the prettier face looked over at the manikin.

"That's our last floral string…I can get it for you."

The taller one gestured, "Come over here. I'll show you our sweaters."

Jackson followed her to a rack of high end looking clothes. He felt a little overwhelmed while he watched. The woman smiled at him sweetly and tried to put him at ease.

"So, your friend's a man?"

Jackson nodded, "Yeah. Well, sort of. Yes, he is for, uh, size purposes or whatever."

"How big is he? What size do you think he'll need?"

"He's small. I'm not really sure about his size, uh…he's average height, but really skinny."

The woman nodded and started browsing through the sweaters.

"Oh, um…I think, if this helps, he'd like it pretty big."

She nodded, "Yes, that helps. Okay, let's go over here then," she said, walking a little further down.

Jackson watched with bewilderment while she browsed a different set of sweaters.

"These are the plus-sized ones. Should be a loose fit on a small man. What about this?" she pulled out a large, baby pink sweater.

Jackson wasn't exactly sure, but it felt like that was the sort of thing Nathan had described.

"Does it match the flowers?" he suddenly asked.

"Come on, let's see," she said, walking to the register.

The shorter woman was digging out a small box with tissue paper to wrap the items in.

"They match, very complimentary," the taller one responded.

Jackson peeked at them. They looked fine together. He wasn't exactly super great at color coordination or fashion, but they didn't obviously clash.

"Okay, great. I'll take those then."

The shorter one packed them up, carefully wrapping them and setting them in a box. Everything was so elegant and feminine, Jackson felt like it'd appeal to that part of Nathan nicely.

"So, uh…when do you work together next?" Jackson pried.

"Oh, hmmm…I think Thursday. We work together a lot."

"Yeah, Thursday," the taller one agreed.

Jackson nodded, "Could you hang onto this until then? I want to bring him in here, and you two seem pretty nice. He told me he stands out there looking all the time. I just think it'd be good for him to come in and look around."

The shorter one instantly perked up, "You mean that really cute guy with the dark hair?"

Jackson grinned, "Sounds like him."

"Oh, we've always wondered what was going on with him. We've seen him out there…gosh, he's *so* handsome, like a prince…"

The taller one nodded her head in agreement, "He is…and he just has one of those faces that makes you think he's really sweet, too."

Jackson beamed, "He is. He's a really good person."

The young women exchanged glances before the shorter one looked back toward Jackson.

"Well, we'll hang onto this until Thursday then."

Jackson nodded and finished paying for the goods.

"Thanks, I'll be back."

He felt like he was walking on sunshine while he exited that place and headed for work. He was excited about this. He was eager to do this nice thing for Nate.

A Complicated Turn

Monday came and went without incident. Tuesday did, too. It wasn't like things were really bad in any way. It was more like they were stagnant and neutral. The way Maverick had accepted the ring felt like this moment of hope and opportunity for Jackson, but now they were back in their routines and it was as though it never happened. The ring was on his finger, but their interactions remained the same. Maverick was still dating Kamila. Jackson was still quietly pining and too nervous to make any further advances. As far as he was concerned, it really felt like the ball was in Maverick's court, but he was just standing there holding it, unwilling to score any points for the team.

Nonetheless, things were carrying on. They clashed pretty good in their final class for the day, then met in the halls to talk about nothing on their way out. Jackson clutched the straps of his backpack and chewed on his lip while he considered his approach. Should he be aggressive and provocative? Should he fire Maverick up and gain his attention like that? Or should he tap into something more mature for his favor? Jackson decided on the latter as they stepped out of the building and headed for their cars.

"So, uh…how are things?"

Maverick glanced at him, a bewildered look on his face. Jackson felt self-loathing over his awkwardness. It was difficult to communicate with Mav when he wasn't pressing buttons.

"You know, with Kamila and everything?" he clarified, the last bit trailing off as though he were completely humiliated to say it.

Maverick knew what it was, though. The question soured his gut. The truth was, he wasn't moving at all on anything because he was scared. He knew he was at this pivotal, consequential crossroads in his life. One that would ultimately decide who and what he would become. He could stick with Kamila. Maybe it'd work, maybe it wouldn't. It'd be the easier way to go. He could become a respected defense lawyer with nothing to hide, so to speak. He could be the hot-shot guy with a smokin' trophy wife and two kids, a boy and a girl. He'd be lying to himself if he didn't admit there was a sizeable part of him that wanted to adhere to convention.

Of course, there was that other nagging part that refused to quiet down. The part that wanted to take the road less traveled. The pieces of him that wanted so persistently to give in and take what he knew he really wanted, the person his heart undeniably beat for. He could be open about it. He didn't necessarily have to hide it. People were more understanding than they'd been in the past about such things. Even so, there was stigma attached, and supposing he wanted to be the successful lawyer he pictured in his mind, what would it be like to have Jackson on his arm?

Although, he did have to admit, he knew Jack was going to be one hell of a lawyer someday, too. Maybe it would still be just as appealing as the trophy wife in a way? He could be Maverick's trophy husband: the most infamous prosecutor in Idaho. Who knew? Not that they'd be well tolerated in this place. That was the thing, though, wasn't it? He simply couldn't know. He couldn't know which path, if any, would bring him the kind of happiness and contentedness he was hoping for. Kamila, some other woman, or Jackson? Sometimes he just wanted to throw in the towel and let himself die wealthy and alone.

He sighed when they reached their vehicles. He let Jackson wait in a very long, fraught silence. He leaned against the car and folded his arms, looking earnestly at Jack while he spoke.

"I know what you're asking me."

Jackson was standing a little too close for comfort. Maverick didn't budge. He was far too stubborn for that.

"Oh, and what's that, Mav? What am I asking you?"

Maverick stared at him. He wasn't going to say it, not out loud. There was no way in hell he'd actually vocalize it because, if he did, the floodgates would open.

"I don't know," he finally said flatly.

"You don't know the answer, or you don't know the question?" Jackson pushed.

Maverick kept on staring. He longed and he fought with himself. His cheeks felt hot. His frustration grew. He finally shook his head, rolled his eyes, and let out a long, perturbed groan before pushing from the car. He shoved Jackson aside then dropped into the driver's seat. He hesitated with his white-knuckled hands upon the wheel. Jackson was watching him, arms folded, all calm and collected. It drove Maverick absolutely nuts the way he could be like that about something so big as this…so big as *them*. He gritted his teeth and started up the car, speeding away without bothering to look back. Jackson watched while he faded into the distance. His face was stoic. His heart was not.

***

Nathan and Julia were entangled in his bed, sweaty and out of breath. Once more, he'd taken charge of the intimate situation at hand. Neither one of them were entirely sure where it was coming from, but Julia wasn't about to complain. As much as she liked 'topping' him, she definitely enjoyed it when he handled her like this. She also savored the way they cuddled when they were through. She closed her eyes and rubbed the hair atop his chest, yet another thing about his body that got on his nerves. Of course he had to be one of those guys with a bunch of hair. He knew waxing was an option, but he didn't have the money to keep up with it. Maybe someday when he had a better job he would. For now, though, this was the way he was; masculine, hairy, hidden and sad.

He held Julia close while his mind wandered. They were both tired and listless in the wake of satisfaction, drifting in and out of consciousness for some time. It wasn't until they heard Maverick come home that they made any attempt to rise from the bed.

"Don't you have work today?" she asked, sitting up straight.

She was clearly looking around for her shirt.

"No, not today. Tomorrow."

She found it and put it on, pausing while she thought about it, "Oh…today's Wednesday, right? That's nice. No school or work today, lucky you! I've got night classes. Shit. I've really got to go. I need to eat and study…ugh…"

She started roaming the room, gathering her clothes and slipping them on. They'd gotten kind of crazy, doing it all over and leaving a

84

trail of fabric behind. He watched her fondly. He did still love her, even if it was platonic. He never thought in a million years a 'friends with benefits' situation could work, but as it turned out, with Julia it did. Quite easily, in fact.

Once she was finished dressing, she went back to the bed and sat beside Nathan. She touched his arm and looked down, a gentle expression resting on her face, "How are you doing with it…this person you're falling for?"

She hadn't asked since he'd told her. She'd been too afraid to bring it up. Nathan was so fragile, sometimes she worried questions like that might break him. He lowered his gaze and touched her arm, rubbing her skin lightly with his fingers.

"It hurts. I've been trying to see him less."

She glanced at the door, then she leaned in close and spoke as quietly as she could.

"It's not Maverick, is it?"

Nathan let out an amused laugh, "Hell, no. He drives me nuts."

She smiled, "Okay. Fair enough. Who is it then? Can you tell me?"

His smile faded. His eyes dimmed. She waited patiently for his answer.

"It's Jackson."

Her reaction was almost comical. She was clearly stunned. Nathan plainly shrugged.

"I know. I didn't expect it to happen. It just did. He's been…well, he accepts me. I told him all of it. I told him who I am, and what I want, and he's been nice about it. It got me, you know? He, like…he knows me now, and he isn't scared or weirded out. He told me it's okay, and when he said that, I just…it's like my heart cracked open. I don't know. It's horrible, Jules, because on the one hand it feels so, *so* good…like a drug. Being around him is like the very best buzz. But, damn it hurts because I'm watching him, and I know it, and I can see it…he loves Maverick. He actually loves him. I don't stand a chance against that."

Julia's face fell. She slid her hand down to Nathan's. She grasped him, and he held onto her. She wasn't sure what to say because any fool could see Jackson and Maverick were infatuated with each other. Nathan was right. He definitely didn't stand a chance when it came to that.

"You still going out with Chris this weekend?" she asked, trying to offer a glimmer of hope.

Nathan let out a heavy sigh and nodded, "Yeah. I'm trying to focus on that."

"That's good. You should let this thing with Jackson go. Focus on Chris. He wants to go out with you. Who knows, hon…he might catch you by surprise."

Nathan smiled. The thought of it was nice, he had to admit. He felt a little more settled while he looked at her appreciatively.

"Thanks, gorgeous. You always know how to cheer me up."

She offered him a warm smile before releasing his hand and brushing the side of his face.

"Anytime, handsome."

At that, Julia really did have to go. She collected her things. Nathan walked her out, giving her a long kiss at the door before closing it. Maverick was in the living room, and they caught each other's eyes when Nathan turned around. It was awkward, that much was certain. Nathan placed his hands into the pockets of his jeans while he looked around. He tried to decide what he wanted to do. He considered going to sit beside Maverick. He considered trying to connect, but just when he'd determined it wasn't such a bad idea, his phone went off. He pulled it out and opened the text, his heart skipping a beat and his stomach hitting the floor. It was from Jackson.

Jackson: Hey, man. I'm bored. You want to hang out tonight?

Nathan instantly felt messy and confused. Of course he wanted to hang out. He wanted it more than anything! But, didn't he *just* tell Julia he'd been trying to stay away? Didn't he *just* make up his mind to try and focus on Chris instead? Yes, but the chance to hang out with Jackson alone…God, he wanted it. He knew he shouldn't, but he did it anyway.

Nathan: Hey! Yeah, sure. I'm not doing anything.

Nathan felt sick while he stared at his phone, waiting for a response.

Jackson: Killer. I'll come by and pick you up. Let's hit a bar. I need to cut loose. This week's been shit.

Nathan: Okay, awesome. See you in a few. Maybe just text me when you're in the parking lot? Mav might get weird…

Jackson: I was going to say the same.

Nathan nodded to himself and put the phone back into his pocket. He looked toward Maverick, who was staring at him without bothering to conceal it. Nathan cleared his throat.

"I'm going out. I'll see you later…"

"What's going on, Nathan? What's happening here, with you…with me?" Maverick suddenly interrupted, rising from the couch and walking toward him.

Nathan felt even sicker while he watched his former best friend approaching like that. Damn it. He did *not* want to have this conversation right now.

"Nothing, dude. What are you talking about?"

Maverick rolled his eyes and stood before him with arms folded. He looked rigid and indignant, which wasn't surprising. Nathan always felt like a child in trouble when Maverick got like this. It was one of the reasons he didn't care for their friendship so much anymore. Maverick made him feel small.

"Come on, Nate. Cut the shit, please? For once?" Maverick's voice sounded pleading, which was different.

It got Nathan's attention. He held Maverick's gaze for a moment before sighing.

"Look, I don't have a lot of time to talk about this right now, but..." Maverick eyed him expectantly. Nathan scratched the back of his head before shrugging, "...Okay, I'll admit it, things totally suck between us. It's not good, and I don't think this is coming as a surprise."

Maverick nodded, "I agree."

Nathan's eyes were roaming. It was too difficult for him to look Maverick in the face.

"I'm still your friend, okay? And it's not all you. I'm going through some difficult things right now..."

"So tell me! If we're still friends, tell me! Let me help you..."

Nathan shifted uncomfortably. He considered leveling with him. However, as he took in the familiar face of this person he'd once trusted with every piece of his heart, he knew he couldn't trust him like that anymore. There was no guarantee Maverick would handle it with care. He'd probably be confused. He wouldn't understand, and if there was anything Nathan knew about Maverick, it was that he tended to judge the things he couldn't understand harshly. Maverick would only hurt him if he knew. He'd only manage to make it that much worse.

"I can't, Mav. Just...look...I'll be okay, alright? I will. I just have to figure this one out on my own."

Maverick shook his head, terribly wounded.

"You're full of shit, Nathan. You're not handling it alone. I know you told Jack. He's keeping your secret, but it just goes to show...you trust him more than you trust me. I know it."

Nathan felt his phone buzz in his pocket. He knew Jackson was waiting out front. He stared at Maverick helplessly before shrugging. He responded with a cracked, sorry tone.

"He's nicer than you, Mav. He has been for a long, long time."

Maverick felt sick and full of disbelief while he watched Nathan slip away from him.

What the hell? Are you serious? How can you possibly say that to me?

Nathan kept his eyes on the ground and disappeared from the apartment. He had to get away from Maverick. He couldn't face the aftermath of that heavy statement. Still, even if it was true, it didn't feel good to say such a thing. His heart was pounding from his nerves while he practically ran to Jackson's car and dropped into the passenger seat. He must've looked as rattled as he felt, because Jackson immediately looked concerned.

"You okay?"

Nathan nodded, "Yeah…let's just go."

Jackson eyed him a moment longer before deciding not to push the issue. They drove in silence to the notorious downtown area just a few miles from the college. They had to pay for parking in a garage, which they decided to split, then walked out onto the street side by side. The air was only slightly crisp, mostly warm. It felt good, and it settled Nathan down. They continued this way for a while before Jackson pointed out a bar. Nathan didn't really care where they drank, so he readily agreed. They stepped inside, went straight to the bartender, ordered a couple of drinks, and found a high rise table near some large windows. They drank in silence and looked out at the crowds of young college students crawling the streets. Eventually, though, Jackson shifted his gaze toward Nathan. He watched him watching the crowds. He could see something was wrong, and he supposed it was likely an entire pile of things. He wondered then, as he searched Nathan's lovely face, what it must've been like to carry the things that he did.

"How does it feel?" the words came tumbling from Jackson's mouth.

Nathan looked toward him, his expression soft.

"What?"

"Your gender…being nonbinary…I don't really understand…?"

"Oh..." Nathan said, touching the side of his glass of wine. He'd decided to order it since he was only with Jackson, "...um, well, it's kind of tough to explain. I mean, I told you in the tent..."

"Yeah, you told me what it was. I guess, what I'm asking is...like...are you okay? Are you able to handle it on your own?"

Nathan took a sip of his drink. He understood what Jackson was really asking now.

"I mean, right now it doesn't feel very good. It's fucking painful, really...all the hiding."

Jackson regarded him attentively. Nathan looked up, brave enough to hold his gaze while he went on. Jackson respected the hell out of him for it. He knew it wasn't easy.

"I'd imagine, though, that if I ever do come out with it, I'll feel pretty good. I just have to find a way to do it, that's all."

"You know..." Jackson started, resting his elbows on the table while he leaned forward.

Nathan couldn't help but stare at him. He looked great. He had on a gray sweater and plaid scarf. His hair was done nice, as it typically was. He smelled pretty good in the car on the way there, too. He definitely had cologne on. He usually did. Jackson was kind of elegant like that.

"...if you wanted some help with coming out, I can do that for you. I'm here for you, however I can be. It's the least I can do with all the help you've been giving me with Maverick."

Nathan felt like his heart was suddenly in his throat while those words passed through him. God, it was so sweet and so painful all at once, the way he was there for him, but also, the way he loved Maverick. Nathan did his best to hide the heartache and tried to steer the conversation away from himself.

"Thanks. Although, I don't know how much help I've been for you. So far it's been kind of a disaster..."

Nathan laughed, "Not entirely. I mean, he liked the ring. He wears it. We don't *talk* about it of course, but he does wear it."

90

Nathan tilted his head, "Oh…?"

Jackson sighed before taking a mouthful of beer.

"Yeah. Literally nothing's happened since. He's still with Kamila. We don't ever acknowledge what's between us, even though I know that he knows, and he knows that I know. It's beyond frustrating."

"Why don't you just, like, kiss him and get it over with?" Nathan asked, genuinely curious.

Jackson rolled his eyes and groaned, dropping his head into his arms. He spoke downward, his voice muffled by the table.

"I can't! I can't."

Nathan grinned, despite how difficult the conversation was for him. Jackson was cute. Nathan was charmed. He sipped his wine and waited for Jackson to lift his head. Eventually he did, looking at Nathan helplessly.

"Okay, look…there's this thing coming up this weekend. Maybe we could hit that. It's a free music festival in the park. There's supposed to be food vendors and stuff like that. Maybe we go, have some drinks, cut loose and see what happens, huh?" Nathan offered.

Jackson drank some more before listlessly answering, "Yeah, yeah…let's try that."

"You don't look very enthusiastic…?"

He shrugged, "He'll show up with Kamila."

Nathan dropped his eyes to the table and scratched the surface with his finger, "Yeah…I know."

They were quiet for a while after that. They finished their drinks and ordered another round. Jackson fetched the refills, then settled back at the table and dove into his beer. He was only going to have two. He still had to drive back.

"I've got a date on Sunday," Nathan suddenly said, grabbing Jackson's attention.

"No shit…really? That's great, Nate! Anyone I know?"

Nathan squeezed his lips together before looking off to the side, "No, but his name's Chris. He was this hot-shot football player back in high school..."

Jackson raised his eyebrows, "Oh...?"

Nathan's face flushed while he nodded.

Jackson smirked and leaned against his seat, slinging an arm over the back of it casually, "Well, shit...that's great! Sounds like he's probably a hottie, eh...?"

Nathan shrugged with a grin and a tilt of his head, "He was...his profile pic looks good."

"Yeah, I'll bet...show me!" Jackson demanded.

Nathan was blushing furiously while he pulled out his phone and brought up Chris's profile. He handed it over and Jackson took a look, pressing his tongue against the side of his cheek while he judged the photo.

"Nice, my friend...nice," he said, handing it back.

Nathan took the phone and laughed, "Yeah, yeah...alright. Settle down."

They shared a quick laugh and quieted. They were like that for a moment, the room abuzz around them, before Jackson leaned forward, speaking quietly so no one would overhear.

"You said you've never been with a man before...are you nervous? Do you think you might, you know...hook up?"

Nathan's face reddened even further, and the thought that he looked cute drifted in and out of Jackson's mind. He just was, with that hair, and those pretty blue eyes. He was striking. He always had been. Maybe it was just because Jackson was buzzed, but for whatever reason, he was really taking notice of Nathan. It was like he was seeing him for the very first time.

"I don't know. I mean...I'm not ruling it out."

Jackson was quiet while he thought about it. Damn, he was getting pretty tipsy already. He hadn't eaten a thing all day. That was probably why.

"You shouldn't give it up just because you can," Jackson found himself saying without thought.

Nathan got an awkward expression on his face. He tilted his head. Jackson's cheeks started to flush. Why was he feeling so nervous all of a sudden? It was just Nathan…

"What I mean is, like, don't rush into it just to do it. You're the kind of person, and you can deny this all you want, but I know it, so you aren't fooling me…but you're the kind of person who needs someone to love you first. Don't lose sight of that…or whatever…you know. Shit. That was sappy. I'm not like that, by the way…*I* can fool around, alright? I don't need love…"

GOD JACKSON SHUT UP YOU SOUND SO AWKWARD!

Nathan shook his head and laughed, "Yes you do, Jack."

"No, I don't. I don't *need* it…"

"You want it, though," Nathan interrupted, his eyes fixed. There was something really intense there.

Something…something…something…

Jackson hesitated. He breathed. His heart skipped a beat and he didn't understand why.

"Okay, fine. Yeah, I want it. Obviously. Who doesn't? Hence all the bullshit with Mav."

Nathan shook his head. He could tell Jackson felt like he needed to be defensive. Nathan decided to back off and let it go. After that, they ordered a plate of wings and split it so Jackson would be good to drive home. They discussed the concert in the park. It was on Saturday, and it started early afternoon. The plan was to let Nathan organize it all, do the inviting, and make the suggestions. Jackson was just supposed to be an attendee, having nothing to do with their plotting at all; an innocent bystander with yet another accidental shot at making Maverick his own. It was friendly and casual, much the way things always were with Nathan…except…something wasn't. Jackson found himself looking at Nathan more. His eyes lingered, his brain flirted with the notion of him and their friendship, their closeness and how refreshingly easy it was. The thought of what potential existed between them, the idea of a future with someone like that instead of someone as fussy and difficult as Maverick. He loved Maverick, he was absolutely, one-thousand-percent infatuated with him. But Nathan…? With those eyes, and that face…the sadness, the beauty, the disaster. The idea was just there, suddenly, out of nowhere, sitting in a way that made Jackson want to pay attention to it.

They paid their bills. They walked along the sidewalk and got into the car. They talked about nothing on the way to Nate's apartment. Jackson parked the car, and just before Nathan could move to step out, Jackson touched his arm. Nathan looked bewildered and attentive. Jackson wasn't sure what he wanted to say or do. He stared. He wondered. He considered. Then, while Nathan drew in a breath and looked somewhere between desperate and afraid, Jackson touched his face, brushing his thumb tenderly along his cheek.

"I meant what I said. I'll help you, if you want," he offered, his voice low and nervous.

Nathan's eyes flickered between Jackson's. He looked terrified, yet also, he looked…eager?

"You'd look nice in that crown. I think you'd look really, really nice," Jackson continued.

Nathan smiled, and it just about wrecked Jackson. What was this? What was happening?

"Thank you," Nathan said.

Jackson dropped his hand. The moment was through. Nathan left the vehicle and started to walk off. Jackson watched and, just before he reached the stairs, Nathan turned around. Jackson kept his eyes on him while Nathan timidly waved. He continued to gaze while Nathan ran up the stairs and disappeared into the apartment he shared with Maverick. Jackson let out a deep, long, shaky breath, relieved to be alone.

"Damn, Jackson…what the hell are you thinking?" he whispered before shifting into drive and leaving it all behind.

He didn't want to think about it anymore. He didn't want to acknowledge the complicated turn his heart was stubbornly trying to make him take.

Honest

Jackson had trouble sleeping the night before. So many thoughts were running through his mind he could scarcely catch them. He let himself ruminate in the feelings he was experiencing with no lack of indulgence. He understood the little sensation lingering in the back of his ever-active mind was the start of something new, perhaps even monumental. Maverick obviously dominated the forefront of his thoughts. He fantasized about him in just about every manner possible. He wondered what it'd be like to 'just kiss him' like Nathan suggested, or even more simply, what it'd be like to say the words they both knew needed to be said out loud. If only he were brave enough to actually confront it, to come out with it, to acknowledge it at all. But no, he wasn't, and apparently neither was Maverick. Jackson couldn't help but wonder how much longer they could continue with this dance, their hands hovering so close they could feel each other's heat, but never skin itself. That's what it was like between them. That's what it was always like.

Nathan, though…now there was someone else entirely. Where Maverick was harsh and abrasive, Nathan was soft and easy. Where Maverick was walled off and defensive, Nathan was holding out opened, loving arms. Where Maverick was afraid, Nathan was needy. Everything Maverick was, Nathan was practically the opposite. It intrigued Jackson. It'd caught his attention without a doubt. It left him anxious and apprehensive in more than one way. For starters, the idea of letting this thing with Maverick go flitted in and out of his brain like a hummingbird. It made it difficult to sort his emotions properly, how quickly it eluded any platform for examination. Even so, it was there, and it was recognizable. He understood that he was, in some capacity, interested in the idea. He could step away from Maverick. He could pursue the way Nathan was starting to make him feel.

Which brought up another facet of Jackson's anxiety, the events he knew would be unfolding later that day. He had classes with Maverick this morning, as per usual, but then he had an afternoon shift with Nathan. They weren't the closers, which was perfect. It was Thursday, the day those friendly girls would be working. The day he was going to coax Nathan into that store. He was nervous about that, too. What if he couldn't convince him? Or worse yet,

96

what if he *did* and then Nathan was embarrassed? The thought made his stomach lurch because it was the last thing he wanted. All Jackson was trying to do was give Nathan a boost. He wanted to take his hand and gently lead him to the shallows, help him get his feet wet, and leave the rest up to him.

God, he *really* hoped this went off well.

He couldn't let himself think about that too much yet, though. He had classes to focus on. He could see Maverick coming up the hall, fast approaching. When he reached him, Maverick barely even looked at him. Jackson glanced at his hand. The ring was still there. At the very least, the ring was still there.

"Mav," he acknowledged, lifting his chin slightly.

"Jack," Maverick replied with cautious eyes.

Something felt off and it left Jackson uneasy. He wanted to ask if he was alright, but there wasn't enough time. They filed into the classroom, took their seats, and proceeded to go about their usual routines. Class felt eternal, and once it was over things continued to feel strained. Jackson considered being tender and sweet, but that just wasn't the way things were between them. He gave in, for once, to the frustration he felt welling inside his chest while he walked beside his stubborn, beloved friend. Just as they were passing the restrooms, he grabbed Maverick's arm and yanked him inside.

"Hey! What the hell, man!?" Maverick obstinately demanded.

Jackson ignored him and drug him into the handicapped stall. There was no one inside, and even if there had been, Jackson frankly didn't give a damn at this point. He shut the door behind them, locked it, then pushed Maverick's back against the wall. It wasn't hard, just enough to have him where he wanted. Jackson pressed his palms flat against the wall on either side of Maverick, watching while his friend regarded him with a mixture of outrage and uncertainty.

"What!? What is this!?" Maverick demanded once more, though his voice was shaky and hushed.

He was breathing really hard. Was it because Jackson was so close to him? Did he really affect him like that? He couldn't be sure. Nothing felt solid when it came to Maverick anymore.

"Why haven't you left her?" Jackson asked, not bothering to hide it.

"I told you, I will…!"

"When!?"

Maverick shut his mouth abruptly and stared. Both of their eyes were strained, their bellies aching over the closeness of their bodies. Why did it always have to be like this? Why!? They continued eyeing one another, anxious breaths filling the air. Jackson leaned closer. Maverick felt like he could die right then and there.

"What's it matter to you?" Maverick whispered.

He reached up and grabbed Jackson's shirt. Jackson felt such a sudden, violent drop in his stomach he actually had to shut his mouth to keep from throwing up. He knew if he were to pull his hands from the wall they'd be trembling.

"What's it matter to *you*?" Jackson pushed, not wanting to be the first one to budge.

He'd done enough. Maverick needed to do this. Damn it, it *had* to be Mav!

He wasn't moving, though. He simply held onto Jackson's shirt and stared and stared. Jackson felt this intense mixture of frustration and desire. It was so strong he could hardly stop himself from giving in. Despite how badly he didn't want to be the one to make any more advances, he was helpless. He was entirely at the mercy of the parts of himself he'd always done his best to tame and control, the urges he did his absolute best to ignore. He leaned forward a bit further. He pressed his forehead against Maverick's. He held it there, shutting his eyes and furrowing his brow. He let out the smallest, most desperate little whimper over the deep well of disappointment he was trying to destroy.

Maverick released his shirt. He pressed his hands against Jackson's face. He didn't move. He was frozen. They both were. A moment passed, then another, and another, until Maverick drew in a sharp breath and took away his hands. Jackson's stomach sank in the saddest of ways. He shut his mouth and pulled away from Maverick. He removed his shaking hands from the wall and put them in his pockets. He stepped away further. He watched and waited for what Maverick would do next.

There was this moment, just a moment where a look of regret danced across Maverick's face. He blinked it away, though. He blinked and shook his head, then abruptly opened the stall and ran. Jackson dropped disappointed eyes to the floor and bit his lip.

God, Mav…why can't you just do this thing with me?

He let himself stay inside the comfort of the stall for a while, quietly doing his best to get collected. He was yet again on the edge of tears and he wasn't about to let anyone see. He eventually settled down and walked over to the sink, washing his hands and splashing some water across his face. He looked in the mirror. He knew that Maverick loved him. He just knew it. Why couldn't he say it? Was it really that embarrassing? Jackson lowered his gaze. It probably was. At least, it would be to someone like Maverick.

He dried off his hands and face with a rough, brown paper towel before tossing it in the trash and leaving the restroom. He went to the second class he shared with Maverick, this time taking care to sit in the back, away from his 'friend'. Maverick never so much as glanced. Maverick just pretended he wasn't there at all.

Jackson did his best to shut off his emotions and focus on their lesson. He was somewhat able to, though he knew he'd have to review his notes later to really soak it in. He didn't have much time to wallow, though, because as soon as class was over he needed to get ready for his shift. He didn't bother walking with Maverick to their cars. He just went, then headed home and ate a quick lunch before dressing into his uniform and driving to the mall. His stomach was in knots and his mind was a mess until he got to work. Nathan was already there and his presence immediately settled Jackson down. It was the strangest thing, but it was true.

They didn't have much chance to talk, unfortunately. There was already a rush of people there for their lunch breaks. Jackson got into a groove, and though he couldn't exactly talk with Nathan, he did find himself looking at him far more than usual. In those moments, Jackson was surprised at how much of Nathan he found pleasant. His face, obviously, but also, the rest of him was nice, too. He was charming in his entirety, and though Jackson had never noticed it before Nathan told him he was nonbinary, he could see it now. Nathan was soft in his movements, slow and careful. He did, in a way, carry himself a bit more feminine than most of the men Jackson knew. It wasn't flamboyant or anything like that. It was just softness. Nathan was very muted and gentle. How had Jackson never noticed this before? Hell, how had he not taken notice of Nathan before?

It felt kind of absurd while they moved through their work day. It went by fast, and Nathan was set to clock out thirty minutes before him. Jackson had to keep him around, though, so he pretended like he needed Nathan to stay, even after his replacement showed up. Nathan looked confused because the rush had died down, but he listened and stuck around nonetheless. The time went by slower after that, mostly because Jackson was incredibly anxious about how Nathan was going to react to the situation he planned to put him in. Jackson second guessed himself. Then third, fourth, and fifth guessed…agh!

He was so nervous. He really hoped he'd gotten this thing right.

By the time he was set to clock out there was nothing left beyond apprehension, but he forced himself to get through it. Nathan started to head in the direction of the parking lot while they walked. Jackson grasped his arm, and when Nathan turned to look at him there was this expression on his face that made Jackson wonder if he felt something about him, too. His heart skipped a beat in the most involuntary, strange kind of way while he forced himself to speak.

"Come with me…there's something I want to do…"

Nathan looked bewildered, but he followed Jackson anyway. His hands were folded across his chest while they passed various stores.

He kept them like that when they stopped in front of the store with the flower crown inside.

"It's gone," Nathan sighed, looking up at the manikin, "Someone must've bought it."

"Let's go in," Jackson insisted, though his tone was careful.

He didn't want to scare Nathan. He wanted to walk him through this.

"Oh, no...no. I couldn't do that. Besides, it's gone. There's no point..."

Jackson reached out and took Nathan's hand. He drew in a sharp breath, looking at Jackson with beautiful, wide eyes.

"Trust me."

Nathan regarded him a moment before hesitantly nodding.

"Okay..."

Jackson released his hand and walked inside, the two cashiers from before were instantly aware what was happening. They hung back behind the counter, watching while Nathan timidly stepped inside.

"So...um...what now?" Nathan asked, glancing at the two women so blatantly staring.

He folded his arms tighter and hunched forward some, his body language betraying how vulnerable he felt. Jackson smiled and Nathan followed him to the girls despite his glaring reservations. He kept his arms squeezed while he watched the shorter cashier pull out a small, white box. Nathan assumed she was handing it to Jackson, but after it sat on the counter for a moment Jackson looked at him and gestured toward it.

"Open it."

Nathan hesitated. His stomach fluttered. He timidly unfolded his arms and touched the little box. He glanced at the girls, then Jackson, before opening it up and moving the tissue paper aside. Jackson felt like his heart was stuck in his throat while he watched, waiting to see how Nathan would react. He was just staring into the box, looking stunned.

"I, uh…well…um…" Jackson started to stammer.

Nathan looked up at him, his face full of surprise.

"This is for me?"

Jackson cleared his throat and nodded, "Yeah, it's for you."

Nathan couldn't help staring at Jackson while he spoke, "You got this for me?"

Jackson nodded again, "Yeah…yeah, I got it for you."

Just when Jackson was certain Nathan would run off, he didn't. Instead, he set the box down and threw his arms around Jackson's neck, hugging him close. Jackson was thoroughly surprised, glancing nervously toward the women behind the counter. They were smiling at him reassuringly. He gently wrapped his arms around Nathan, embracing him back and letting the moment happen. Nathan held onto him tightly for so long it would've made Jackson feel awkward, except that it was nice and he felt exceptionally good about making him so happy. When he did finally let go, Nathan had visible tears in his eyes. Jackson had to fight the urge to wipe them away, instead grinning at his friend sympathetically while he wiped them away on his own.

"Thank you," was all he could manage.

"You're welcome…really."

Nathan looked at the ground and sniffled, wiping his face again before looking at the cashiers and smiling kindly. They were both looking emotional while he took the box, thanking them as well. After that, Jackson led Nathan from the store, falling into stride while he clutched the box to his chest like it was going to run away from him. They didn't talk at first, but once they stepped outside and started approaching their cars, Jackson felt like he needed to.

"You should wear it to the concert Saturday…it might be a good way to, you know, come out?"

Nathan approached his car and turned around, still holding the box against his chest while he looked at Jackson.

"I don't know. Maverick would see me…"

Jackson reached out and gave Nathan's shoulder a squeeze.

"Maverick will be fine, Nate. He might be uncomfortable or whatever at first, but he does care about you. I can guarantee you, he won't be the monster you think he'll be."

Nathan bit his lip and looked off to the side while he considered it. He honestly couldn't be sure about Mav, but he did trust Jack. He'd handled this whole thing better than Nathan ever could've hoped for. He looked back toward Jackson and forced a smile.

"I'll think about it."

Jackson nodded and placed his hands into his pockets. Nathan regarded him another moment before hugging him again and stepping back.

"Thank you, Jack. This is probably the nicest thing anyone's ever done for me in my whole life."

Something about that statement pulled on Jackson's heart. He nodded, "Yeah, of course. I want you to be happy, Nate. I want you to be yourself."

Nathan nodded before saying a brief goodbye. He got into the car and sat in the driver's seat for a moment, setting the box down and watching while Jackson got into his car, too. They caught each other's eyes again. Nathan smiled brightly, his stomach feeling heavy while he waved. Jackson returned the sentiment, then started up his car and drove away. Nathan felt light and optimistic in ways he wasn't accustomed to when he drove back home and entered the apartment. Maverick was away at Kamila's for the night, so he had the entire place to himself. He quickly went into the bathroom and took off his shirt. He put on the giant, cozy, pastel sweater Jackson had gotten him. He didn't look in the mirror yet, though. He wanted to get the crown on first, so he reached inside the box, lifted it up and stared at it in his hands. He could hardly believe he was actually holding it. It didn't feel real. He felt dazed, as though he were in a dream, when he lifted it up and situated it atop his fluffy, dark hair.

There. Now he could look.

His eyes raised slowly, meeting themselves in the mirror. He breathed in and bit his lip while he took in the sight. He loved it. He absolutely loved the person he saw looking back at him for the first time in his life. He felt tears pooling up in his eyes again, which he promptly wiped away. He smiled wide and stared a little longer, letting the honesty of what he saw wash over him in wave after delightful wave. Eventually, he decided to remove the crown, not wanting to ruin it. He set it back in the box and closed it up before carrying it to his room and carefully tucking it away. He decided to keep the sweater on for a little while longer.

He went into the kitchen next, brewing up a hot cup of tea. He topped it off with some cream and sugar before walking to the couch, settling in, and pulling his knees up to his chest to feel small.

God, this felt good. Being who he really was felt so, so good.

What about Nathan...?

When Saturday arrived, Maverick was already in a bad mood. Nathan had only just informed him of the concert yesterday, which annoyed him to start. He hated last minute plans, particularly when he was trying to study as often as possible. Even so, Nathan had managed to convince him. He'd pleaded with Maverick in that way of his, making it impossible to say no. That way that made Maverick feel so much pity for him, even if it was often times veiled with contempt. He'd given in and agreed, which was bad enough, but then to top all of that off, Kamila stayed over last night and things got awkward. Normally, having her over would've been great. The thing was, though, that interaction he'd had in the restroom with Jackson had shaken him tremendously. He couldn't get it out of his head, the way his face felt in Jackson's hands, the way his heart pounded the closer Jackson got, the way he could feel the heat radiating from Jackson's body against his. How he longed for that warmth. How badly he wanted to make it his own.

It was completely dominating every thought in his head, which became abundantly clear last night when Kamila got physical. He'd done all the usual things, touching her, kissing her, licking the salt from her skin. It wasn't that he didn't enjoy it. It was that, while he did all those things, he couldn't shake the thought of what it might be like to do them to Jackson. It thrilled him at first. He was able to get going with her, no issue. The thing was, he could only fall *so* deep into that fantasy while he had her like that. Even with his eyes closed and mind focused on Jackson, when he touched her it obviously wasn't him. Maverick got hung up on the soft, feminine curves of her body and it eventually rendered him miserably inadequate. He couldn't finish the job.

Kamila did what she could for him, trying to bring him back into the moment. Nothing she tried worked, though. Out of kindness, and on some level shame, he made sure she was taken care of, but he could tell the whole thing left her anxious. How could it not? He was too young to have problems like that, right? What warm-blooded college guy couldn't keep it up with a beautiful woman like her? Maverick couldn't. That's who. Because he'd rather have been sleeping with his enemy than her.

*Oh, God, Mav! What the hell is **wrong** with you!?*

He squeezed his eyes shut and sat on the couch with a cup of coffee and some textbooks. He was trying his best to study rather than focus on the epic failure from the night before. It was difficult, though, because he knew they were leaving soon and Nathan was moving all over the place, which was kind of unusual and kept snagging Mav's attention. Nate was in the kitchen at the moment, munching on snacks and brewing up what must've been his fifth cup of coffee. Maverick couldn't help it. His agitation was high. He looked over his shoulder, sounding exceptionally snippy when he spoke.

"Dude, what the hell's up with you? Why are you so worked up?"

Nathan stopped in his tracks and looked at Maverick, his pathetic blue eyes wide. He looked confused, and Maverick instantly regretted the tone he'd taken. He sighed and rose from the couch, walking over to his friend and deciding to give that another shot.

"Sorry…seriously, though, what's going on? You seem nervous?"

Nathan blinked and regarded the countertop. It felt impossible to say. How could he even begin to explain that he was planning to do something life changing today? That he was actually considering taking Jackson's advice and getting into that getup for the concert? He couldn't. There was no proper way to express it without coming out in advance, and that felt like something he couldn't do. Hell, he wasn't even sure he was going to go through with the outfit.

"I'm gonna take a shower," Nathan spat out, quickly walking away from Maverick to his room.

Maverick stood there a moment before sighing and rolling his eyes. Nathan wasn't going to budge. They were never going to work out the tension between them. He trudged back over to the couch and did his best to focus on his studies. Kamila came out and sat on the couch beside him, quietly browsing through pointless nonsense on her phone. Maverick felt a deep well of aggravation threatening to overtake him. God, he was *so* close to the edge.

While Maverick quietly grappled with his temper, Nathan was trying his best to handle an onslaught of fright. He grabbed some regular clothes from the dresser, then walked off to the shower. He'd already taken one earlier in the morning, but he was seriously considering wearing the sweater. It was warm, though, so he knew he'd have to roll up the sleeves to his elbows, and if he was going to do that, he was going to have to do something about all the hair on his arms.

He stepped into the bathroom, closing and securely locking the door behind him. He turned on the water and waited for it to get warm, stopping to look in the mirror while he did. He took in the sight of his face. He'd shaved already, so it was smooth and soft, which he liked. His hair was starting to grow out some, too. He'd already let it go about three weeks past when he'd normally get it cut. He was starting to get a hint of bangs, though he planned to throw some product in to brush them aside and out of the way. He drew in a deep breath, shaking out his hands when he let it out, trembling and slow.

Okay…this is it. Just do it, Nathan. You can do this!

He turned from the mirror, stripped from his clothes, and grabbed a razor from the medicine cabinet. He felt terribly uncertain while he carefully stepped into the shower, instantly covered in warm, soothing water. He tipped his head back, letting it run over him while he tried to settle down. He breathed deeply, trying to envision what he'd look like later on. It was terrifying to go much further, though. He wasn't quite ready to consider the reactions of the people who'd see him. That part made his stomach really hurt, so he forced himself to push those thoughts away. The only person he really wanted to see him was Jackson. He knew that Jackson would be safe and okay.

That thought made Nathan grin. He couldn't help it. He smiled wide for a long time before tipping his head forward and opening up his eyes. He hugged himself for a moment, trying to imagine the positive aspects of what he planned to do.

It's okay to be different. It's okay to be you.

He hesitated a moment before reaching over and grabbing some soap. He slid it over his arms, then collected his razor and started shaving the hair away. He felt entranced while he pulled the blade

107

along his skin, cutting it from his arms with ease. He fell into a rhythm, swiping a strip gone, rinsing it off, and doing it again. Swipe, rinse, swipe, rinse…he carried on so effortlessly that once he was through, he could hardly believe how fast it'd actually been. He set the razor down and touched each of his forearms, marveling at the smooth feel of his skin. It felt like touching Julia. Oh, wow! He'd actually done it! He smiled again before washing the rest of himself off. He wanted to be fresh and nice for the concert.

Once finished, he left the shower, dried off and dressed in his usual clothes. His sleeves were pulled down, so when he went to the living room neither Kamila nor Maverick noticed anything about him. They weren't paying attention beyond what they were doing in their laps anyway. They were preoccupied and, if he wasn't mistaken, feuding. Nathan shook his head and grinned while he retreated to his room, shutting himself safely inside. He pulled out the little box from the mall, staring down at his beautiful things.

You can do this, Nathan. You can totally do this.

***

Jackson's morning had felt like an eternity. He kept himself busy to try and calm his anxiety, but he was simply a wreck no matter what he tried to alleviate it. He was excited about the concert, obviously planning to put the moves on Maverick. He knew Kamila was going, but that didn't mean he couldn't steal moments alone with him; moments like they'd shared in the restroom the other day. The thought gave him goose bumps.

Of course, that wasn't the only thing eating him. There was also the thing with Nathan, and as difficult as it was to admit, Jackson was kind of excited about him, too. He wondered if Nathan was going to follow through with the outfit. They'd texted about it some last night. Jackson hoped he did it. He knew it'd be good for him. He knew it'd be a relief in more ways than one. He wanted to see Nathan through it. He wanted to be there for him. He wanted, more than anything, to make Nathan smile.

Despite the lengthy feel of the whole morning, the afternoon did eventually come. Jackson readied himself, taking time to spray on cologne and adorn a nice outfit. He styled his hair, then bid his roommates goodbye before driving to Maverick's place. Jackson was set to chauffeur everyone again. He was always the driver. Thankfully, the journey wasn't long, though it managed to feel like an eternity, too. Jackson's stomach was in a state of constant fight-or-flight, despite how hard he was trying to ignore it. He couldn't, though. There wasn't very much point in fighting biology, so while he strode toward the apartment and knocked on the door, he did his best to accept the perpetual nausea. He sighed, surprised when Kamila answered the door. He felt further disoriented when he entered the room, quickly realizing Maverick was standing in front of Nathan's door with his arms all folded and cross. Maverick looked like he was in a hell of a huff.

"What's going on?" Jackson asked while he approached.

"He won't come out. God, I swear…he's acting like a child!" Maverick complained.

"Jackson…?" Nathan's muffled voice floated through the door.

Jackson's heart sank. He knew exactly what was going on. He shook his head and touched Maverick's arm, giving him a warning look while he spoke low.

"Back up, okay? I know what this is. Let me handle it."

Maverick looked miffed, but he stepped back anyway. He rolled his eyes and scoffed, of course, but he did listen. Jackson focused his attention on Nathan's door. He leaned close to it and spoke loud enough for him to hear.

"Yeah, Nate…it's just me. Can I come in? Maverick stepped away."

It was quiet. Kamila and Maverick were standing side by side, looking thoroughly confused. The door cracked open, just enough for Jackson to see Nathan's terrified eyes.

"Can I come in?" Jackson asked again, his voice intentionally warm.

Nathan nodded and stepped back behind the door so no one would see him. Jackson was fast while he slipped in, shutting the door quickly before facing Nathan. He was immediately rendered breathless when he took in the sight. Nathan was standing there, looking anxious and small. He was wearing the pink sweater and floral headstring. His sleeves were rolled up, and Jackson noticed the hair on his forearms was gone. They were folded the way they'd been at the mall, and he was timidly hunched forward. He was trying to disappear.

"Nathan…" Jackson quietly said, bending down and touching his arms.

He looked up at him, and it was painfully obvious he was barely holding it together. He stared at Jackson, and while Jackson peered back, he couldn't help seeing in Nathan's eyes a vast ocean of diffidence and need. He rubbed Nathan's arms while he spoke in hushed whispers, trying his best to say the right things.

"Nathan, it's okay…"

He unfolded his arms. Jackson slid his down, and Nathan responded by grasping them with urgency. It was then Jackson felt how powerfully Nathan's body was trembling.

"I'm scared," he admitted.

Jackson felt sorry to hear the shiver in his voice. He gently moved and Nathan let go. He slipped his hands into those quivering palms and grasped them firmly.

"You look beautiful, and handsome, all at once," Jackson whispered with a kind, sincere smile.

Nathan let out a relieved laugh, though he was still shaking and nervous.

"That's exactly what I want."

Before Jackson even really knew what he was doing, he released one of Nathan's hands and brushed the back of his own against his cheek.

"That's exactly what you are."

Jackson kept his hand against Nathan's face. Nathan kept his eyes locked on Jackson. The moment felt eternal. Jackson knew he had to break it, because if he didn't, he'd fall in love right then and there. He knew it. He absolutely knew it.

"Come on, let's do this. I've got you," he insisted, stepping back and taking his hands from Nathan.

Nathan nodded, re-folding his arms and dropping his eyes. Jackson slowly opened the door and stepped out, looking at a very confused Maverick and Kamila.

"Nathan has something he needs to tell you," he said calmly, stepping out and away.

Nathan took a moment longer to come out of the bedroom, but eventually he did. He walked slowly with eyes on the ground. He was biting his lip so hard it felt like it might bleed, but he couldn't think of anything else to do. He just stood there in front of them, for Maverick and Kamila to see. He prepared himself for insults, for outrage or shock. Instead, while he listened, he was surprised to hear Maverick's voice, wary and considerate.

"Nathan…are you…uh…is there a different pronoun I should be using…?"

Nathan raised his eyes and met Maverick's, realizing they were as wide as his own. Maverick didn't look offended, or pissed off, or even frustrated. He was none of the things that Nathan had expected. For a moment there, Maverick really felt like a friend.

"No…no. I mean, you can…they might be fine, but he's okay, too. Whatever is comfortable is okay with me for now. I'm, um…nonbinary, though, you know? Do you know what that means?"

Maverick nodded, "Yeah…yeah, Nate. I know what it means."

They stared at each other awkwardly before Maverick decided to try some more.

"Is this what's been upsetting you? Is this why we stopped talking?"

111

Nathan nodded slowly.

Maverick sighed and shook his head, "Well…damn…I wish you would've told me sooner. This doesn't bother me. You're still my friend, no matter what you are, okay?"

Nathan sucked in a breath and threw himself at Maverick. He hugged him hard, his heart still pounding from all of the tension and fear he'd been carrying around for so long. Maverick hugged him tightly and looked fondly toward Jackson. The two of them exchanged a smile. So many things finally made sense. Things felt clearer than they'd been in ages. Nathan pulled back and wiped his eyes, getting teary and emotional again. Kamila surprised him next, stepping forward and embracing him sweetly. She didn't say anything about it, but she clearly didn't mind either.

"Alright, alright…enough of this sappy bullshit…let's go…!" Jackson teased, trying to corral everyone.

Nathan laughed and followed. Maverick grasped Kamila's hand and followed, too. They piled into Jackson's car, Nathan sitting up front so Maverick could be in the back with his girlfriend. Normally, Jackson would've tried to get some conversation flowing, but he was too mixed up to facilitate just then. He felt incredibly torn, like he was ripping in half. He kept glancing at Nathan from the corner of his eye, surprised how attracted he felt now that he was 'out'. Nathan really was gorgeous. He was something to behold. Of course, Jackson also kept checking the rearview mirror here and there, catching glimpses of Maverick where he could. Just before they arrived, in fact, Jackson looked and accidentally caught Maverick's attention. Mav didn't even blink, he just stared. He stared at him in a manner that made him feel panicked and seen. Jackson forced himself to shake it off and parked the car. They got out and made their way into the bustling venue.

The place was lively and the energy felt endless. There was already a local band on stage, and there were food vendors everywhere filling the air with enticing scents and bright sounds. Jackson got preoccupied browsing the culinary options while the rest of them got caught up in conflicts of their own. Nathan's body language was much as it'd been when he'd emerged from his room earlier. He was

112

folded and small, feeling especially vulnerable before all of these people. Maverick was holding hands with Kamila, absent-mindedly talking to her while his eyes were locked on Jackson. He was checked out in some fantasy land where Kamila wasn't there, all while he was speaking with her and touching her skin. It carried on like this for a good, long while until the trio eventually lost track of one another. Kamila pulled Maverick away, and once Jackson was gone he was finally able to pay her some attention.

"Let's find somewhere to fool around, huh? Could be exciting, all of these people around...?" she teased, raising her eyebrows playfully.

It made his stomach roll. It did sound like fun, but also, Maverick had a sneaking suspicion he wouldn't be able to perform again. Was she testing him? Was she trying to figure him out? He couldn't be certain, but something about it made him want to prove himself.

"Let's watch some bands and drink a little first," he suggested, not entirely prepared to accept the challenge just yet.

She grinned at him mischievously, "Okay, that's fine."

He grasped her hand a little tighter and led her away, off to find a place to get some brews.

***

Once Jackson lost track of Maverick and Nathan, he felt like he could breathe. All of that anticipation to see them both, and here he was relieved to be alone. He decided to take the opportunity to grab a beer and eat some food. He wandered the vendors, being choosy about where he wanted to eat. He was a hell of a foodie, but he wasn't about to eat just any old trash. It took him some time, but eventually he settled on a spot that heaped piles of sweet crab over a mound of fries with some special house sauce. He picked at it some while he waited in an eternal line for a beer, then he found a clearing on the grass and sat down. The food was amazing and the beer was refreshing. It settled him down, though he knew damn well he was stress eating and drinking. He simply didn't have it in him to care. Honestly, this moment was the most peaceful he'd felt all day, and he wasn't about to ruin it with introspection.

Once he was finished, he decided to stay there and vibe on the music, even if it kind of sucked. It drew him in for a while, before he suddenly heard a familiar voice interrupting him.

"Hey, man! How goes it! You here by yourself?" Greg asked, taking a seat in the grass while he nursed a beer of his own.

"Huh? Oh! Hey, dude. No, no…Maverick's somewhere with Kamila…I have no idea where Nate is."

Greg nodded, taking a gander at the stage. They were in between bands now, so it suddenly quieted down.

"Hey, I should warn you…Nathan's not going to look how you expect," Jackson said.

Greg tilted his head, "What do you mean? Did something happen to him?"

"No, no…listen, he's coming out. He's nonbinary and he's dressed kind of feminine. You can still call him 'him', but I just wanted to give you a heads up. It'd be nice if you, like, reassured him. He's feeling pretty insecure about it."

Greg blinked and grinned, "Oh! Well, hell yeah, okay! I'll let him know he's fine by me."

Jackson smiled, ready to pay Greg a bit more of his attention now. He didn't know the guy too well, but he was Nathan's friend, and he was easily able to take the truth about him so he must've been okay so far as Jackson was concerned.

***

When Nathan lost his group of friends he mildly panicked. He was hoping to be glued to someone's side the entire event, but obviously that wasn't going to happen. He wandered around aimlessly for a while, his body still folded up and small. It felt endless and depressing until he heard a light voice by his side. He looked, not recognizing the face at all. The guy was thin, dressed kind of delicately, and he had a head full of nice blonde hair.

"Hey! Great outfit…what's your name?" he asked, extending his hand.

Nathan hesitated. He wasn't sure if this guy was about to rip on him, but his voice sounded soft and a little flamboyant so Nathan decided he was likely in good company.

"Uh…Nathan…you?" he asked, accepting the handshake.

It was gentle and over quickly.

"Jason. You here alone?"

"Oh, no…I just lost track of my friends. I'm sure I'll find them eventually…" his voice trailed off.

Jason nodded, "Hmmm…well, if you want to hang with me and my buds for a while you can. We're sitting just over there."

He pointed toward an area with a bunch of blankets on the grass. Nathan still felt a little guarded, but once he looked the group over he could tell they'd be safe. There were two girls who looked like they were together, as well as two other men with paint on their faces. Nathan smiled and looked at Jason, "Yeah, okay. Thanks!"

He followed Jason over to his friends. Jason introduced him, and Nathan tried his very hardest to remember all of their names. Alley, Damon, Christian and Tina. Jason sat down with them and patted the empty space beside him, indicating Nathan should sit, too. He complied, pulling his knees up to his chest and wrapping them in his arms. The conversation flowed between friends rather easily, and Nathan was quickly fascinated. He liked the vibe. It was warm, welcoming, and obviously everyone was different in their own kind of way. He liked it, the uniqueness of the group. He liked how at home it made him feel. While time drifted past, he eventually decided to join their discussions. They talked politics, school, love and life. Nathan admitted to the group that he was in love with one of his friends, which was honestly the first time he'd said he was actually *in* love out loud. It was true, though. He was in love. It wasn't just falling anymore. He'd decided it this morning when Jackson's hand brushed his face like that. Nathan also went ahead and shared the fact that the person he was in love with had feelings for someone else. The group responded to that, the women in particular.

"You should just kiss him!" Tina said.

"Yeah! Do it here! It's the perfect setting! Who cares if he has a thing for your friend…who knows? Maybe you'll turn his world upside down!" Alley chimed in.

Jason smiled gently. Nathan caught it from the corner of his eye, but he wasn't sure what to make of it so he didn't say anything. Jason cleared his throat and decided to offer another perspective.

"Or, you know…if he doesn't see what he's got right in front of him, you could always have a fling with someone else…?"

Nathan looked at him with flushed cheeks. He understood now why Jason had singled him out. He clearly thought he was cute, or something. Nathan offered him a coy smile. It wasn't a bad thought, he had to admit.

"Well, I have a date tomorrow with a friend from high school. I'm not trying to chase after Jackson forever," he explained.

"That doesn't sound like a fling, love. That sounds like an option," Jason teased and sat back, lighting up a cigarette and taking a long drag.

Nathan's face grew hotter as he realized this guy was probably trying to bring him home. He considered it for a moment, he really did, but then he remembered what Jackson said to him at the bar the other day.

Don't just do it because you can…I know you…

It was true. Nathan wasn't a one night stand kind of person. Even so, he hung around and chatted, and when Jason took his phone and put his number in, Nathan let him. When Jason handed it back, he winked at Nathan and whispered, "You have my number now…call me any time."

Nathan smiled timidly and nodded, "I'll keep you in mind."

Jason grinned wide and returned his attention to his friends. Nathan hung around a while longer, but eventually excused himself. They all booed him playfully, and he thanked them profusely for the company. He really did need to go, though. He wanted to spend some time with Jackson if he could.

***

Jackson and Greg separated to grab some more beers. Jackson decided in advance it was going to be his last if he was going to drive home. Still, he wanted to ride the buzz because he was having a relatively good time, even if Maverick was off doing whatever with Kamila. The sun was starting to lower, and the sky was all pretty in pink.

Kind of like Nathan...Oh, shit, Jackson! What the hell? Stop!

He stood in line, and just then Nathan found him. Jackson felt his hand touching his arm, and he heard his familiar, comforting voice.

"Hey! Where are Mav and Kamila?"

Jackson shrugged, "Meh...I dunno. I ran into Greg, we chilled for a minute, but he went to get a drink somewhere else. You want a beer?"

Nathan smiled and stepped into line.

"Sure. I got sucked into this big group...the guy gave me his number. Apparently, I'm kind of a catch," he joked, mostly trying to reassure himself that he was okay being dressed the way he was.

Jackson looked at him, buzzed and far less cautious than usual.

"You are. Obviously. It's about time you see that."

Nathan looked at him, surprised with the boldness of his statement. Jackson glanced at him from the corner of his eye and smiled. He didn't care by this point about appearances. He was going to flirt with Nathan. Maverick was obviously busy with Kamila anyway. That guy would never get over himself enough to take a chance on what they had, it was easy to see now.

Nathan cleared his throat and looked ahead, trying to ignore the tension he felt happening between them. They moved through the line, ordered their drinks, then walked over to a railing along the outskirts of the event. The band was playing, but over there it wasn't so loud. Plus, there was a gorgeous view of the sunset happening just above the mountains. The two of them quietly drank and looked out at the range.

"You know, I think this thing with Maverick's done. I just…how long can I keep chasing him, right? I'm tired of it. I'm tired of feeling like this," Jackson suddenly confessed.

Nathan looked at him, trying his best to ignore the flutters those words gave him.

"It's painful, loving someone who doesn't love you back," Nathan replied, a defeated tone to his voice.

Jackson looked at him then. He *really* looked at him. He wanted to ask him if he knew that pain. He wanted to question him about the things he was fairly certain he felt. He was too scared, though. He was just so terrified when it came to those things. Jackson forced himself to look away and drank some more. Nathan did the same. They polished them off, and by the time they were done, the sun was nearly down. The stringed lights all across the venue switched on. The band finished up, and it was suddenly so much quieter. Jackson took their red cups and tossed them in the trash. He walked back to Nathan and leaned against the rail, this time angling his body toward his friend. Nathan did the same. Jackson's eyes were trailing all over him, and Nathan could feel it in the warmest of ways. Nathan was nervous, and anxious, but also very hopeful just then. He stepped forward some, closing the gap between them. It was bold, and Jackson didn't move away. He stayed put. That was something, wasn't it? Jackson swallowed. He reached out his hand and lightly touched Nathan's face again.

"You really are beautiful," he said quietly.

Nathan's stomach ached so badly. He shut his eyes and furrowed his brow, leaning his cheek against Jackson's hand. He wanted to say something, but he couldn't. He felt powerless. Then, he felt Jackson's other hand touching his cheek. Nathan fluttered his eyes open and focused on Jackson's. His breathing picked up and his stomach really fell. He stepped closer once more. He wrapped his arms around Jackson's neck. He slowly let his eyes close one more time.

Breathe…breathe…just breathe…

And then he felt it. He felt Jackson's lips against his own. The pain in Nathan's belly grew with the rapid beating of his heart. He quietly, carefully opened his mouth, breathing loud and shaky as Jackson did the same. Nathan wrapped his arms around Jackson's neck tighter then lifted his weight to his toes. Jackson's arms were around Nathan's waist, and he pulled him in closer. Jackson kissed him deeply. He kissed Nathan like he wanted him. They did this for a while, though it felt like the most fleeting, desperate thing. They parted their lips. They stared into each other's eyes, frightened and uncertain while they held one another.

What does this mean, Jack? What does something like this do to us?

They didn't say a word. They held each other and kissed again, easily melting into whatever this fragile thing was. It felt good. They wanted to hold onto that emotion. They wanted to embrace the safety of what they'd always had together for a while.

***

Maverick had Kamila against the wall of a makeshift row of restrooms. There were people all over, but they were secluded enough most couldn't see them. They'd been trying for a while. She'd been pushing her hips against him, kissing with all she had, biting his lip, performing just about any sexy little movement that might get him in the mood. None of it was working. She just wasn't what he wanted. It got to the point where embarrassment became resentment.

"What the hell is up with you?" she angrily whispered.

He glared at her and pushed away, quickly fixing his pants.

"Fuck off, Kamila…" was all he could manage, humiliated as he was.

He stormed off and left her there, partially nude, angry, and entirely confused. He didn't care. He couldn't deal with her, and her neediness, and her pressure for sex right now. He didn't have it in him. He irritably pushed through the crowd. He wasn't sure where he was going exactly, but he did know one thing. He had to find Jackson. Maverick needed to be near him, so he continued to ram through hoards of people until he emerged. The lights were on overhead, and there was this serene, orange glow blanketing everything. He looked around. Maverick spotted that pink sweater. He blinked. He gasped. His mouth fell open with shock.

WHAT!?

Jackson…his mouth was on Nathan's…his hands were on Nathan…he was *kissing* Nathan! Maverick instantly felt ill. He abruptly spun and ran to the nearest trashcan, vomiting brutally into it. He dry heaved and panted, then wiped his mouth with his sleeve when he was certain it was over.

No, no, no, no, no! This is wrong! What the hell? What the hell!!??

Maverick's head got fuzzy. Time started to feel wobbly and strange. The rest of the night blurred and dulled along with his perception. The bands finished. Jackson and Nathan left their spot, hand in hand, like they were a thing. Maverick never did budge from the trashcan. He was thoroughly in shock. He had no strength to do a thing. Eventually Jackson and Nathan found him. They acted like nothing was wrong, like nothing had changed. They didn't hold hands in front of Maverick, but they were standing close and they looked giddy and fond. They asked about Kamila. Maverick insisted they leave without her, and they leave right now. They went along with it because the behavior wasn't out of the ordinary. They probably assumed he'd gotten into a fight with her. There was no way they could know he'd seen them and his heart was shattered.

They got into the car. Maverick sat alone in the back. Nathan went up front again. Maverick watched the rearview mirror intently, hoping to catch Jackson's eyes. He never did look, though. Oh God, he wasn't even looking at him anymore!

Maverick suppressed the urge to vomit again. They made it home, and it was clearly awkward when Nathan got out. It looked like Jackson wanted to follow him, and it occurred to Maverick that, if he hadn't been there, they'd probably be having sex in Nathan's bedroom tonight. It made Jackson furious and jealous in ways he never knew he could be. He didn't say a word while he trudged into the apartment, straight to his room. He didn't care anymore about what Nathan was doing, or thinking. All he could focus on was the way his entire world had suddenly split in half.

I always thought you'd wait for me. What's changed? Why aren't you waiting for me anymore!?

Maverick pulled out his phone and texted Kamila.

Maverick: I can't be with you. Don't call me. We're done.

It was cruel and cold, but he really didn't care. Nothing in the world mattered to him now, not outside of Jackson. His chest felt tight with panic, and he suddenly leapt from his bed and went to the living room. Nathan was already holed up in his bedroom, probably fantasizing about some kind of life, a future, with the man Maverick loved.

No...it's not going to happen. I'm not going to lose him to you...especially not you!

Maverick grabbed his keys from the counter and stormed out to his car. He dropped inside and sped off. He could scarcely breathe, he couldn't think, and when he knocked on Jackson's door and watched it open, Maverick suddenly found it difficult to speak.

"Mav?"

A moment passed while his breath returned.

"I need to talk to you!" he demanded, shoving his way inside.

He looked around, quickly assessing the situation. No one was there.

"My roommates are out clubbing..." Jackson explained, a bewildered expression on his face.

Maverick turned then. He turned and his eyes...oh, his eyes. Jackson instantly felt nauseous in the most hellish of ways.

"Maverick...?"

"Shut up..." he breathed, literally falling forward right into Jackson.

Maverick threw his arms around his neck. He kissed him. He kissed him frantically, far more desperate than Nathan had been. Everything was soft and careful with Nate. Now, in this unexpected moment with Maverick, years of pent up frustration were bleeding out.

But, wait…what about…

"Mav…"

"Shut up!"

He unzipped Jackson's sweatshirt and that was it. Jackson knew what was happening. There was no stopping it. It was like lighting the fuse to a stick of dynamite. It was sudden and far beyond their control. And so, clumsy, fast, and frantic they did the thing that'd been thickening up the air between them since the day they'd met their freshman year of college. They left a trail of clothes behind them, collapsed atop Jackson's bed, and had sex for the first time. It was burning. It was obsessive. It was absolutely everything they'd both dreamt it would be. It felt good, all of it, but then when it was through, something else loomed.

Jackson laid flat on his back with Maverick settled against his chest. The fan above them was whirring, a little squeak rhythmically interrupting every so often. It was like it was telling them something, that creak; the little hitch in an otherwise perfect rotation. It was hitting them both, the guilt of what they'd done. Neither of them said it, but as Jackson kissed the top of Maverick's head, the thought might as well have been screamed.

"I saw you…" Maverick suddenly whispered through the dark.

Jackson felt sick while he motionlessly watched the imperfect blades, the echoes of those unspoken words ricocheting over and over again in his mind...

What about Nathan?

Oh, God, Mav…

…what did we just do?

Oh.

Jackson found himself lying awake early in the morning, Maverick resting sound asleep against his chest. They'd clung together all night long, just the way he'd always hoped they would. If things had been different it would've been perfect. Of course, that wasn't the case. Instead of basking in the relief of finally knowing Maverick, his stomach felt sick with guilt. Nathan. Damn it. Why did he have to go and kiss Nate? He knew there were feelings there. He wasn't sure how strong they were, but he knew. He'd have been lying if he didn't admit that, on some level, he had some pretty strong affection for him, too. He wasn't exactly in love, but damn was he ever close. He could've chosen Nathan without a doubt. But he didn't, and now he was going to have to face the consequences of the rapid-fire decisions he'd made.

His gut continued to churn while he laid in silence, watching dust float through soft dawn light. Maverick stirred and Jackson instinctively pulled him closer. Maverick smiled in a way that made his face look peaceful, a quality he rarely exuded. He wrapped his gangly arms around Jackson's frame, pressing his cheek firmer to his chest.

"Morning," he said through a voice weakened by night's sleep.

"Morning," Jackson responded, kissing the top of his head and running his fingers through his hair.

They were quiet for some time, more than aware of the fragility between them. Maverick decided to ignore it, focusing instead on the peace found in flesh.

"I can't believe we're actually here like this," he mused.

Jackson smiled, still caressing the back of Maverick's head. He felt exactly the same. It was like living in a dream, a dream he'd been having night, after night, after night since he'd met Maverick on their first day of college. From that moment on, he'd wanted to touch Maverick like this. He'd always wanted Maverick to be his own, and now, so it seemed, he was. Although, maybe it'd be prudent to confirm…?

"Mav?"

The hesitant tone of Jackson's voice grabbed his attention. He pulled back just enough to look him in the eyes, settling his head against the pillow comfortably.

"Jack?"

He looked dreadfully uncertain while he squeezed his lips together. Maverick watched patiently, giving him a chance to come out with it.

"This is real, right? Like...this isn't a one-night stand?"

Maverick's face melted. He smiled and reached over, gently trailing the edge of Jackson's jaw.

"This is real. I love you. I've loved you for ages."

Jackson took Maverick's hand into his own, holding it tightly. His eyes searched while he continued to do his best to make sure they were clear on things.

"So, are we official then? It's not like we need to get to know each other...are we boyfriends? Can we do things in public, like, you know, holding hands and stuff like that? Are you okay with it? I don't really want to hide. We're not kids. I just want to be with you, all of you...all the time."

Maverick grinned a little wider, leaned forward, and planted a loving kiss on Jackson's mouth. He took his hand away from Jackson's and pressed it against his cheek, looking him in the eyes with a sincere expression on his face.

"You bet your ass we're official. I don't want to share you, or hide you. I want the same things you do, okay? I want to be with you, all of you, all the time."

Jackson let out a relieved sigh and kissed him. They carried on like that for a while, stopping before it got too heated. They held each other and marveled at the sight of one another, so intimate and bare to see. All of that time spent pretending drifted away, disappearing as though it'd never been like that. All that mattered now was the fact they were doing this. They'd finally gotten over themselves. They'd finally torn down those stubborn, thick walls.

124

Unfortunately, that was when Jackson started remembering some of the things Maverick said in their frenzy last night. He'd spat out words between kisses, words that desperately claimed Jackson was his. The fact that he'd told him he'd seen him kissing Nate. Jackson's face fell and his heart sank. He looked at Maverick anxiously again.

"Mav...this is really going to hurt Nathan..."

Maverick swallowed, a deep pit in his gut.

"What the hell was that anyway? Why'd you kiss him? If you love me, why would you ever do something like that?"

Jackson felt nauseous, realizing this conversation was both necessary and difficult. He wanted to have a real shot with Maverick, though, so he knew it was going to require some transparency about that kiss.

"It's complicated, Mav. I do love you, I love you more than I've ever loved anyone, or anything in the entire world...but, I care about Nathan, too. I care about him a lot, and we've gotten pretty close since he told me about his identity and all. I've been helping him through it...I don't know, it's just been this really personal thing between us and it's made me feel things for him. I'm not in love with him, okay? Please, don't freak out...please, don't be hurt or scared. I'm not going to be with him, obviously, but...shit, Mav...I'm not looking forward to telling him. I wish you and I could've figured this out before I kissed him, but we didn't, and I kissed him because I knew you were off with Kamila and I was starting to lose hope. I knew you loved me, I just thought you were too embarrassed about me to admit it."

Maverick lowered his brows. It was a lot to take in. It hurt. It absolutely cut to hear that Jackson had feelings for Nathan. It also hurt knowing they were both about to rip Nathan's heart out when this information came to light. As strained as their friendship had been over the years, Maverick didn't relish the idea of hurting Nathan either. He wasn't sure how strongly his oldest friend in the world felt for his supposed enemy, but if there was anything he knew about Nathan, it was that he fell in love with the entirety of his heart. This was going to tear him apart. This was going to crash and

125

burn. Maverick sighed and touched Jackson's face, rubbing his thumb along his cheek.

"I'm not embarrassed by you. I was just scared. It's going to be a thing, you know? Like, my sister's so perfect. My parents are squeaky clean. I've always been the odd one out in the family. It's going to disappoint them…not that it's you, just that you're a man. I know they'll come around, but it shatters the image my mom and dad have been trying to create our entire lives…and, if I'm honest, it does destroy the image I've created for myself, too. I always pictured growing into this lawyer, a really strong, notable one with a hot wife and a handful of kids. Not that you're not hot…" Maverick grabbed Jackson's arm and looked at him with wide, pleading eyes, "…you are. I mean, to me you're like…I mean, come on…but, you know. It's just a different path. Does that make sense?"

Jackson smiled, surprising Maverick. He waited, holding his breath, then laughed with relief when Jackson started to tease him.

"You think I'm seeexxxyyyy, you want my booooodddyyy, you want to touuuucchhh me, you really looovvveee me…" he sang.

Maverick's face got bright red as he pulled Jackson closer.

"Shut the hell up," he whispered fondly before kissing him.

Thoughts of Nathan slipped away from them as they got tangled up in the sheets yet again.

***

Nathan woke early. He felt like he was floating after the kiss he'd shared with Jackson. Sure, it'd been awkward on the way home with Maverick, and he'd heard him leave the apartment. As far as Nathan knew, though, Maverick was blissfully unaware of what happened between the two of them. He'd assumed Maverick went off to Kamila's to try and fix whatever they were fighting about. He didn't trouble himself with it when he'd flopped atop his bed, pulled out his phone, and sent a big, long text to Julia telling her about the night. She was shocked, but encouraging. She was happy for him, which left him grappling with whether or not he should cancel his date with Chris. He decided against it, because he still wasn't entirely sure where things stood with Jackson. He did have a feeling

Chris wasn't the person he was going to wind up with, though. It felt like, with Jackson, he had a real chance. He really thought he did.

And so, once he'd risen from the bed he promptly ran around, frantic and excited. He hummed to himself while he got a K-cup brewing, then showered, shaved, and dressed himself in a large, black sweater and skinny jeans. He sipped his coffee and browsed social media until he couldn't take it anymore. He didn't even finish his drink. He hopped from the couch, fetched his wallet and keys, then hurried to his car.

Screw it…I'm doing this. I'm going to tell you how I feel! Why not? Why should I waste my time leading you on the way Mav does? No. I don't want that. I just want us to be together.

He chewed his lip anxiously, started up the car and drove to Jackson's place. It wasn't far, but he was so filled with anticipation it felt like an eternity. He was so consumed with his thoughts, in fact, that when he parked in front of Jackson's apartment he didn't even register Maverick's car on the other end of the lot. He was barely aware of his surroundings at all when he got out, strode quickly to the front door, and knocked three times, just loud enough to hear. He stepped back, drew in an apprehensive breath, and waited. Only a moment passed before one of Jackson's short, adorable roommates opened up the door.

"Oh! Nathan! Hey! We were just having some breakfast, come in…" she said with a bright smile.

"Thanks," he responded before graciously stepping in.

It felt like slow motion while his brain struggled to make sense of the unexpected scene.

"Mav…?" he asked, his heart pounding while his eyes roamed.

Two of Jackson's roommates were sitting at the kitchen bar eating pancakes. Jackson and Maverick were on the couch. At first, Jackson's arm had been around Mav's shoulders. Now, he'd pulled away, and his eyes were wide with panic while they focused on Nathan.

"Oh…" the word clumsily fell from Nathan's mouth, soft and pained.

Jackson stood. Maverick did, too. Nathan openly stared at them, then he looked toward Maverick. He wasn't angry when he spoke. He was muted. He was shredded into a million, small pieces.

"Now you want him?"

Maverick swallowed hard. He wanted to say something, anything to make it better, but he couldn't think of a single word. How could he? There was no way to make this situation feel good. There was nothing he could say that could stop it from hurting.

"Nate…" Jackson said, stepping forward, "…Nathan, I'm so sorry…"

Nathan focused his big, blue eyes on Jackson's. He opened his mouth like he was going to say something. He stayed like that for a moment, and then he dropped his eyes, turned around and walked fast from the apartment. Jackson ran after him, not bothering to shut the door. Nathan was halfway to the parking lot before Jackson caught up to him. He grabbed Nathan by the arm gently, and it made him spin around to face him. Jackson halted and looked down at him, his face twisted with shame.

"Nathan…I'm really sorry, I shouldn't have kissed you…"

Nathan shook his head, his voice soft.

"No. Don't be. I…look…" he hesitated. He had tears in his eyes and it made Jackson feel heartsick for him. Nathan sniffled and wiped his face, briefly regarding his feet before sighing and looking back up, "I knew you loved Maverick. It's not like I didn't know that."

Jackson just stood there staring. He had nothing to say. There were no platitudes he could offer. Nathan's eyes searched him a moment longer.

"Do you think he'll make you happy?"

Jackson paused then nodded with hesitance.

"Yeah…I do."

Nathan swallowed and looked down.

"Then I'm happy for you. I want you to be happy."

In a way, it was true. He did want that for him, but also…*God*…his heart.

Jackson stared at him, hands in pockets. He could tell Nathan wanted to leave, but he had a question of his own to ask.

"Nathan…were you…are you in love with me?"

Nathan smiled miserably.

"Does that really matter now?" he answered quietly before turning and walking away.

Jackson felt like his heart had a sinker on it, watching with something akin to panic while Nathan got into his car and drove away. Even though Jackson knew he'd deliberately chosen Maverick, this person who'd occupied his heart for years, the person he'd pined for day after endless day, he couldn't help but feel like something really monumental and life-altering had just slipped through his fingers.

He couldn't help but wonder if he should've chosen Nathan.

***

The rest of Nathan's day was a total mess. He'd gone straight home to cry and wallow. He sprawled out on the couch with a box of tissues and sobbed until he felt like he was thoroughly dehydrated and void of anymore tears. His message box dinged. Chris wanted to see him. Nathan was in no state to be going out, so he tried his best to reject him with kindness.

Nathan: I'm sorry. I fell in love with someone. They just decided to be with someone else. I'm a wreck. I can't do this. It's not fair to you or me.

Of course, much to his chagrin, Chris was more than understanding and still wanted to see him.

Chris: If you don't want to come out tonight I can respect that, but if you're worried about leading me on or something, don't. You want to get a drink and tell me about it? We don't have to be a thing. I can just be your friend.

Nathan laughed at the absurd amount of kindliness he felt from the message. He considered it, what he really wanted to do, and then responded.

Nathan: I want to get annihilated tonight. If you're good with that, then I guess you can come pick me up.

Chris: Alright...let's do it! Send me your address.

Nathan bit his lip and sent over his information. He tossed the phone atop the coffee table and decided he ought to go look in the mirror and see how bad he was. Of course, his eyes were all puffy. It was obvious he'd been crying, but otherwise, he looked alright.

*Fuck it...*he thought, striding to his room. He grabbed the floral string and put it atop his head. He felt kind of anxious about seeing Chris, so he decided to pregame while he waited. He fished out an old bottle of vodka that technically belonged to Maverick from the cabinet. Whatever. If Maverick was going to take Jackson, then Nathan was going to take his booze. He took two sizeable gulps of it then set it back where it belonged. It didn't do much, but it did put him a little at ease while he waited. Eventually, there was a knock at the door. He grabbed his phone, keys and wallet before answering. He tried to force a smile, but he simply couldn't do it.

"Hey," he offered.

Chris smiled at him, a look of genuine amusement on his face.

"Nice flowers," he said, eyeing the top of Nathan's head.

Nathan touched it lightly, having forgotten it was there.

"Oh, yeah...thanks."

An awkward moment of silence passed between them before Chris shrugged, "Alright, well...let's go get shitfaced!"

Nathan managed to smile at that. He followed Chris, making sure to lock the apartment. He slipped into the passenger seat, immediately impressed. It was a Cadillac, and it was beyond nice inside.

"Damn…how'd you get the money for this?"

Chris started the car and got driving while he answered.

"My dad. We got a bunch of money after my mom died…you remember the accident? Anyway…um, I'm pretty much set for life, but I still wanted a degree and all that. I don't particularly love the idea of being one of those rich, spoiled brats who doesn't do shit."

Nathan grinned, not sure what to say. It seemed like a touchy subject, bringing up his dead mom. Thankfully, the rest of the drive was short, and before he knew it they were parked and walking the same streets he'd wandered with Jackson not so long ago, the day they'd grabbed a drink. That little memory tugged at his heart, throwing him right back into all the pain he was stuck in. He grew dark and miserable walking beside Chris, which made him feel even worse because Chris was ridiculously gorgeous. He was a little shorter than Nathan, stocky, with one of the more handsome faces he'd seen in a while. Not to mention, as far as Nathan could see, he'd grown into a fairly charismatic, bubbly sort of person. He was charming, and if Nathan weren't so hung up on Jackson, he definitely would have been trying to get laid by him tonight. He didn't want that right now, though. Everything hurt far too much.

They chose a bar, a different one thank God, from the one he'd been to with Jackson. It was dark inside, and kind of classy. Apparently, there was going to be a dueling pianos situation a little later that night, which sounded fun. Nathan wasn't sure he wouldn't be hammered by that point, though. He wanted nothing more than to forget about his life.

They sat on some stools at the bar and ordered their drinks. Chris got a lemon drop martini, which Nathan thought was cute. He got himself a glass of red wine. Once they'd gotten their drinks, Chris sipped and Nathan gulped. Chris's eyes were on him all the while. Once Nathan had downed his first glass and ordered another, Chris decided to try and figure out what the hell went down with Nathan.

"So, tell me about it at least?" he pried.

Nathan eagerly took his second glass, embarrassed over how fast he'd crushed it. He decided to sip a little slower while he got drawn into conversation.

"I'm an idiot. I'm a fucking idiot, that's what happened."

Chris leaned his elbow against the bar and rested his chin in hand, obviously giving him his full attention. Nathan decided to go ahead and oblige him. Why the hell not? What could it really hurt at this point?

"It was my friend Jackson…a guy Maverick has classes with. I fell in love with him, and I knew he was in love with Maverick…I mean…it was so obvious, *everyone* knows they love each other…but I went ahead and let myself fall for him anyway, and I got burned…bad. I told him things…I told him *everything* about my gender, how it feels to be so mixed up and hidden. He told me I was beautiful…he kissed me last night…he kissed me like I mattered to him, and then this morning, when I went over to his apartment to tell him I loved him, Maverick was there. Maverick, now, after *all* of those years leading Jackson on, pretending like they were nothing, *now* he wants Jackson to be his…!? He must've seen us. He had to have. The timing is just too much for a coincidence…and it makes me feel like I hate him…and that tears me up, too, because he used to be my best friend. He used to be someone I could trust with everything…and now…? Now I can't trust him with anything."

Chris regarded him sympathetically. Nathan took a long swallow of his wine before setting down the glass and staring at it.

"I've lost everyone…I've lost the two people who always mattered the most."

Chris dropped his hand and adjusted himself. He leaned forward a bit, and Nathan looked at him while he spoke.

"There's no chance you could salvage the friendships?"

Nathan shook his head, "I don't see how I could do that."

Chris sighed before sipping his beer. He shrugged then, speaking as though it were the easiest thing in the world.

"Well, then, fuck 'em! Be my friend...I'll take you in! Hang out with me and my crew. I still chill with the guys. I'm still pretty tight with Melissa, Dave and Craig. They never minded you...well, David might a little, but if I tell him you're cool he'll be good with it."

Nathan let out a laugh, surprising even himself. He took another swig then eyed Chris. He was feeling buzzed and his inhibitions were starting to drop.

"So...I *never* would've pegged you as gay...you hung out with all those jocks...aren't those guys all, like, college football players now?"

Chris laughed heartily, and Nathan simply watched him, curious about his response. Once he settled down he explained it.

"Yeah, well...it wasn't easy coming out, let me tell you...but, at the end of the day, they were all pretty cool about it. I mean, sure, some of the guys on the team felt some kind of way about it, yeah, but not my ride or dies. Dave and Craig always had my back, and Melissa didn't give a damn. They're all fixing to graduate now, just like you. You never hit the games, or what? Of course the guys are football players, damn! My girl got married, though. Missie lives in the burbs with this old dude now. He's loaded and she's living fat and happy. No kids yet, but I'm pretty sure they're working on it plenty..." he let out a laugh and shook his head.

Nathan smiled, feeling a little uncertain, and looked down. They quietly drank for a few before Chris decided to talk a little more.

"So...Maverick, huh? I wouldn't have pegged *him* as gay. He always dated the finest women back in the day...I remember."

Nathan looked grim while he shrugged, "Yeah, well...apparently he's bi or something. I don't know. We haven't talked about it. Maybe it's just Jackson. Maybe he can't stand the thought of me being happy with someone of my own."

Chris whistled between his teeth, "Damn, dude…for real? You think he'd do you like that?"

Nathan shrugged again, "I mean…he is, isn't he? Like, Jackson's been after him since day one…like, *day one* of freshman year…and now…now that Jackson's decided he's interested in me, *now* Maverick's suddenly ready to take the leap? I don't know. It just doesn't feel like I don't have *something* to do with it. He's always been like that with me. He has to be in charge, you know? He has to be the one who's all put together, and perfect…the star of some bullshit show…and I'm just his inept, loser sidekick…the one with bad grades, too much beer and a fucked up sense of self. He likes me under his foot. He likes it when he feels better than me."

Chris shook his head and took a drink, "Damn…*damn*. I never knew…you two always seemed thick as thieves back in the day."

Nathan took a miserable gulp of wine, "Yeah…well…I guess I didn't really get it 'til now, either."

Chris picked up the small red straw from his drink and chewed it like a boy. He stayed that way before flagging down the bartender. He ordered a round of shots, and Nathan ordered another glass of wine. Once the shots arrived, Chris decided to do a toast.

"To the things we know now," he announced, holding it up.

Nathan raised his shot, clinked it, and swallowed it. It burned their throats taking liquor like that, making them wince and breathe out with invigoration. Chris finished off his martini. Nathan polished off his wine. By the time that was through, the pianos had started. More people were funneling in, and the energy picked up in the room.

"Darling, you should dance with me…let's forget about all those tears for now," Chris said smoothly, taking Nathan's hand and winking at him.

Nathan laughed, accepted Chris's hand, and followed him to the center of the bar. There were a few people dancing already, so they didn't stick out all that much. It was silly, and had Nathan been sober he would've been embarrassed about how poorly he danced. The thing was, though, he was inebriated and Chris was a terrible dancer, too. They laughed and lost their breath, then alternated

134

between going to the bar for drinks, and going back out to dance. The night wore on like this. Nathan got just as hammered as he'd set out to, but Chris watched himself. At some point, Nathan tipped beyond drunk into blackout territory. He ran off to the bathroom and vomited. Chris came in, his hands rubbing Nathan's back while he heaved. Nathan's memories went from there, lost in darkness, in the blackout, in the void.

Which was how he found himself waking up with a headache slamming repeatedly against the back of closed lids. The light that flooded the room felt merciless and cruel when he opened his eyes and took stock.

Wait...where the hell am I?

He forced himself to sit up, whimpering when the headache moved with him. He squeezed his eyes closed again, then blinked and squinted. He looked around, quickly realizing he was in someone's apartment. It was fancy and nice, immaculate and clean.

"Hey, there...you're probably going to need this..." Chris's voice grabbed his attention.

Nathan looked in his direction, immediately embarrassed. Chris was showered, dressed, and looked regrettably amazing. He didn't look hung over like Nathan. Nathan was sure he looked like total shit. He felt like he was sweating liquor from his pores.

"Thank you," he said, accepting some Ibuprofen and a bottle of water.

He knocked them back then downed all the water. He wiped his mouth, realizing he was on the couch beneath a blanket. He glanced back at Chris, his cheeks running hot.

"Did we, uh...you know...?"

Chris shook his head, "No, no. Don't worry. You were *really* fucked up last night, I just got you on the couch. The only things I took off were your shoes and crown, I promise!" he crossed his heart with his finger.

Nathan nodded, visibly relieved, "Thank you."

Chris tapped his thigh and Nathan adjusted his legs to make room for him. Chris settled on the couch and regarded him, "You want to grab a greasy breakfast and some java?"

Nathan smiled, "That sounds awesome...can I take a shower, though?"

Chris nodded, "Yeah, come on. I'll show you where it is."

Nathan stood up, wincing again at the ferocity of his headache. He noted the floral crown resting atop Chris's coffee table, grateful he'd taken care to keep that safe from getting smashed and ruined. He grinned to himself at the kindness and ease of it. He listened to the rundown of how to make the shower work before Chris left him to it. Nathan showered and used a throw-away razor to shave. He brushed his teeth with a fresh toothbrush, then went back to the living room to meet up with Chris, a little taken when Chris smiled at him charismatically.

"Come on," he said, grabbing his keys.

Nathan followed, then they drove over to a diner. Nathan was skeptical at first because it was a total dive, but once they were seated and ordering he saw the food on other people's plates and felt more optimistic. They nursed some coffees while they waited for their breakfast. At first, they didn't talk. Chris just stared at him, a goofy grin resting on his face.

"What?" Nathan finally asked, feeling on the spot.

Chris shrugged, "Nothing. You're just really cute, that's all."

Nathan's cheeks reddened.

"That's pretty forward of you."

Chris waved him off, "Nah. I can think a friend is cute."

Nathan sighed. Their breakfasts arrived and, while he ate, he realized a greasy plate of diner food was exactly what his stomach needed. His headache subsided. His hangover settled down.

"You know, I'm serious. I'm pretty fucked up about Jack right now. I want to be really clear about that with you," Nathan finally said, wanting to address it head on.

Chris nodded, finishing up a bite of potatoes and swallowing it down. He looked directly at Nathan, giving him his full attention.

"Look, Nathan…I know. I'm not necessarily looking to settle down anyway. I'm young, I'm free…I just want a good time. I think you're hot, and the fact that you're sad makes me want to comfort you and take you out to do fun things. We can be friends, or we can be more…that's really your call, but I'm going to be fine either way. I'm not in love, and I'm not looking to be in love. I just want to have good sex, and good fun…or, if you'd prefer to be just friends, we can at least tear some shit up and have a good time doing it. You just let me know, okay?"

Nathan took a moment to process before he broke out in a smile. He wasn't sure what he wanted with Chris, but at least he could tell he was casual about it. They glanced at each other fondly here and there while they ate. Chris laughed some. They talked a little more about trivial, safe things and, despite how badly Nathan's heart ached for Jackson, he had to admit he was really glad he'd decided to go to the bar with Chris. This, so it seemed, had the potential to be something effortless and good.

There is One Thing

Chris took Nathan home after breakfast and they exchanged friendly goodbyes that temporarily made him feel good. Of course, that feeling was painfully fleeting because once Chris was gone reality was there, practically screaming in his face. He looked around the parking lot and saw that Maverick's car was there. His roommate, his former best friend, the guy who'd essentially stabbed him in the back and gone after the person he was tragically in love with was home. Nathan did his best to ignore the sick feeling permeating nearly every atom of his body while he trudged up the stairs and unlocked the door. He kept his eyes down on the ground and entered, locking up securely behind him. He swallowed and drew in a centering breath before turning and looking around. Mav must've been in his room. The living space was empty and quiet.

Nathan set his keys atop the counter, grabbed a beer from the fridge, and proceeded to disappear into his bedroom. He knew that Maverick heard him and made the conscious decision to avoid coming out to face him. He was glad to stave off the confrontation they'd inevitably have, and he was double glad to know that Maverick clearly didn't feel good about what he'd done. Still, as Nathan cracked open the beer and sprawled out on his bed, he couldn't help but wonder what Maverick thought if he was home alone last night. Was he worried? Did he care about what happened to Nathan at all? Or were things really so cracked between them that he didn't?

Hell, Nathan wasn't exactly sure what he, himself felt about Maverick now. Did he care anymore? Did he worry about Maverick? Want happiness for him? Want peace, calm, and perhaps even reconciliation someday? He didn't want to confront those uncertainties just yet. Things were too raw. It was entirely too soon. So, instead of thinking about it, he opened up his phone, put on a sad playlist, cried, and drank until sleep mercifully came.

***

Unbeknownst to Nathan, Maverick did come home the night before, and he did worry about him. He'd decided to go back to the apartment rather than spend another night with Jackson for two reasons. One, he knew Nathan was going to get hammered and he didn't want him alone in case he fell asleep and choked on his vomit or something. Two, he felt such a tremendous amount of guilt, the thought of spending a second night with Jackson while Nathan wallowed at home by himself felt cruel. Of course, Nathan never came back from wherever he'd gone. Once it got really late, somewhere around one in the morning, Maverick started sending out texts to everyone he'd ever known. That was when Chris Donahue got back to him. He let Maverick know Nathan was there, albeit passed out. He assured Maverick he'd gotten him to sleep safe and off his back. He let Maverick know Nathan was going to be okay. Maverick went to sleep after that, though it was plagued with unusual nightmares he couldn't remember upon waking. He was carrying so much tension. He was juggling so many fears.

When he awoke in the morning, intrusive thoughts about what his family was going to think about his relationship with Jackson ate at his nerves. He fretted over what he would say, how he would say it, and what the likely response was going to be. Those thoughts hammered down on him in waves, and when they receded from the shore, his other stresses were left shifted, soaked, and clinging to his skin. This thing with Jackson, it felt good, but also heavy and serious. How could it not? There was nothing casual about anything when it came to them, so naturally, now that they were intimate and doing this thing, it was intense. There was already a momentous sense of obligation, a necessity to establish trust, love, and understanding. *Whew*. Understanding. That word felt weighted considering who he was applying it to. Still, it needed to be done because this romance was real and it was happening. It wasn't a fling. It was the sort of thing that resulted in marriage, a soul mate, a confidant and a friend. This was family, not just late nights of sex in the sheets.

On the flip side, there was the baggage with Nathan. Maverick felt like he was kicking himself over it because he knew damn well what he'd done. He'd seen Jackson feeling for Nathan. He'd seen Jackson holding him with care and kissing him with affection. Maverick had erupted like a volcano inside, running straight into the storm he always thought Jackson was because, well, how could he *not*? Even so, he didn't feel proud of it. He felt guilt ridden and awful. He tried to soothe himself with the reassurance that there was no way he could've known, but in the end, he knew that was only a platitude because, on that day back when they'd driven home from their camping trip, he'd detected a hint of it. Nathan wasn't lost in his phone like usual on that day. Nathan's eyes had stayed on Jackson all the way home.

Maverick locked himself in his room with his meddling thoughts all morning. He heard when Nathan got home, and he was simultaneously relieved and sickened by it. He considered going out, facing him, dealing with the situation at hand. In the end, though, he couldn't bring himself to do it.

You're such a coward, Mav.

***

When the following day arrived, all three of them had to deal with it. There was no avoiding each other forever, not with the living situation being what it was. Maverick felt sheepish and hesitant upon waking. He heard Nathan moving about the apartment, getting ready for school as he usually did. Maverick laid there for some time, staring at the ceiling and pressing the fabric of the comforter between his anxious fingers. He chewed on his lip and wished there were some way he could avoid being in the same room as Nathan, but there wasn't any other option. He had to get to class on time, so he drew in a deep breath and moved through his shaking nerves. He exited the bedroom and entered their shared living space. Nathan looked directly at him, blank and mysterious. Maverick held his gaze, anxious and culpable. They stayed that way for a moment before Maverick carefully lifted his hand and offered a gentle wave.

"Hey…" he said, feeling stupid as soon as the ridiculous word left his sorry mouth.

Nathan looked at him…or through him. Maverick felt like Nathan hated him as the silence permeated the room. He eventually caved and disrupted their eye contact. He lowered his gaze and sulked off to the bathroom to ready himself for the day. He felt defeated and self-loathing. By the time he was finished, Nathan was already gone.

Well, that was it…at least, for now.

140

He finished getting ready and eating his breakfast, then jetted off to class. Despite his unpleasant run-in with Nathan, the knowledge that he'd soon be with Jackson did lighten the load. He practically floated while he walked, and when he saw Jackson leaning against the wall in the hall his heart skipped a beat. Jackson wasn't staring at his phone while he waited like usual. He was watching, and as soon as he saw Maverick the warmest smile crossed his face.

Who knew you could look at me like that?

When Maverick reached him, however, he wasn't sure what to do. They'd agreed to be open, but there *were* people everywhere. What was an appropriate level of affection here? What was okay, and what wasn't in such close proximity to all of these familiar classmates? Before Maverick could decide, Jackson took his hand and planted a soft, quick kiss on his cheek. Maverick grinned, blushed, and squeezed Jackson's hand reassuringly.

Okay, that feels right. That feels just right.

People definitely took notice of it, which both Jackson and Maverick found amusing to a degree. Here they were, still well known enemies by all of their peers, shocking the hell out of everyone. It was comical and beautiful all at once, which honestly felt fitting. What were they if not comical and beautiful themselves?

They funneled into the classroom with the other students when the time arrived. They sat in their usual seats, bickered the same way they always did, and when class was through they decided to take advantage of their free time. Well, Jackson did anyway. Maverick was bewildered once more when Jackson grabbed his hand and pulled him into the restroom again. He watched quizzically while Jackson checked to see if they were alone, then he pulled Maverick into the same oversized stall they'd been in that day; the day Maverick chickened out and refused to kiss him. Jackson locked the door behind them and pressed Maverick against the wall, this time holding his hands on his hips with confidence, and if Maverick wasn't mistaken, no shortage of desire.

"Let's get it right this time…" Jackson whispered, sending tingles up Maverick's spine.

And so they fooled around, right there, in the bathroom. At one point a couple of guys came in, and Jackson ran with it, taking full advantage of how risky the situation was. They somewhat waited and teased until the intruders left, then finished up the flirty thing they'd started. When they were through, they were all smiles.

"God...that was...uh..." Maverick whispered, unable to finish his sentence.

"I know," Jackson happily replied.

They redressed then held each other's hands while they moved through the rest of the day, both of them knowing they'd stumbled upon something miraculous. It wasn't ephemeral, or fleeting, or fake. This was real. This was consumption, a feverish dip inside forever. This was the thing they'd both been searching for every moment of their tension fueled lives.

"I love you," Maverick whispered before departing that day.

"God, Mav...I love you, too."

A kiss.

A hug.

A torturous goodbye.

It needed to be done, though, because Jackson had a shift over at the mall. As lovely as things had been with Maverick, he felt stressed as soon as they separated. He was trying his best to mentally prepare for the next moment he needed to get through. He was going to see Nathan at work. He was going to have to try and salvage whatever he could with his beloved best friend. He hoped that he could. He hoped with every fiber of his being that things weren't so messed up they couldn't be fixed. After all, it was *only* a kiss, and like Nathan said, he *did* know Jackson was in love with Maverick. Which was true, he was! Clearly he was.

There was that thing, though. The little spark Jackson felt when he was around Nathan. The surprising intimacy of the kiss they'd shared. As sexy as things were with Maverick, and really things were full of all the heat Jackson craved, it wasn't like that when he'd shared that moment with Nathan. That was something tender and soft. That was the sort of thing a person could get completely broken inside of, and that vulnerability was tempting. Maverick was all heat, and fire, and interesting stress. Jackson knew a life with him would never be dull. They'd never be ordinary, or predictable, or safe, which appealed to him in no shortage of ways.

However, he was also well aware of the kind of thing he'd brushed up against with Nathan. He understood that, if he'd decided on Nathan, things would've been emotional and raw, because unlike Maverick, Nathan wasn't an element of destruction. He was more like water. He was a running river, thoughtfully shaping the shores; a vast, endless ocean sustaining mystery and life, tenderly caring for a beautiful, unknown deep; a delicate rain falling from the clouds, soaking a person through and through, clinging to them with understanding and devotion.

Though Nathan had always been soft, he still had the capacity to effectively shape someone he loved, breaking down the uglier parts and drawing out something better and new. Jackson was aware of the truth that a relationship with Nathan would bend him and form him, lead him into a person so honest and fresh he'd be difficult to recognize, yet still the same at his core. Jackson also understood that, physically, it would've been more like making love than a pent up fight. It would've been muted and tender, yet beautiful in an explosive kind of way, too, because even if Nathan was gentle like rain, he was also terrifying like thunder, and he could strike you like lighting, too.

Even though Jackson knew all of these things down to his very bones, he still chose Maverick and intended to keep things going along that path. The guilt from it was tearing at him, though, particularly as he walked toward work. He felt highly torn about the opportunity he was missing and the way things had suddenly, tremendously shifted. There'd never been a time where Jackson found himself uncomfortable or anxious with Nathan. In fact, if anything, the moments between them generally served to turn the volume down on those things. It'd always been easy. It'd always been safe. Today, however, it wasn't. Now, while Jackson moved about his workspace, trying to stay focused on customers, he felt a merciless, pounding sensation of insurmountable stress. He could scarcely bring himself to look at Nathan, and he could tell the feeling was mutual. It was devastating. It was heartbreaking, and painful, and they never did say much beyond what they needed to get through their shift.

They closed up the store in silence, and when they left, Nathan walked a few paces ahead of Jackson. They reached their cars and Nathan headed toward his own without so much as looking back. Jackson couldn't take it. He picked up the pace, grabbed Nathan's shoulder and spun him around. He stared at Nathan helplessly, entirely at a loss for words.

"Nate..."

He hesitated while Nathan peered straight into his eyes, down into his very conflicted soul. Jackson swallowed as the pathetic question he knew was pointless to ask came falling out anyway.

"Are you still my best friend?"

Nathan's eyes watered. He didn't blink. He didn't cry. He spoke quietly in response, his voice struggling to remain steady while his emotions clearly swelled.

"You said there was nothing I could do to change that..."

Jackson nodded, "I meant it."

Nathan shook his head and lowered his eyes. A tear fell down his cheek.

"You were wrong. There was one thing I could do."

Jackson stared with confusion, "I don't understand...what do you mean? You didn't do anything?"

Nathan blinked, more tears falling from his eyes. He sniffled and lifted his gaze. His brows were pressed together in anguish while he shrugged, his voice trembling when he spoke.

"I did, though, Jack. I fell in love with you."

Jackson stared at him, his mouth hanging open.

"Nathan...I..."

144

More tears fell while he shook his head, "So, you see? I can't be your best friend anymore. How could I? But it isn't because you mean less to me. It's because you mean so much more."

Jackson felt sick as Nathan abruptly turned and walked away. He got into his car and drove off, not looking back. Jackson took a step toward his car, and when he did an overwhelming wave of frustration rushed through him. He screamed and kicked the side of the car hard. He punched the door, over and over, until his knuckles were red and a little bit bloodied. He pressed his forearm along the top of the vehicle and rested his face into it, suddenly falling into shoulder heaving cries.

Don't Feel it Baby, Just Touch Me and Forget

When Nathan got home from work, after confessing the way he really felt to Jackson, he was a total wreck. He went straight to the fridge, pulled out a beer and started going to town on it. He sat on the couch, just to spite Maverick. He wanted that asshole to come out of his room again, to face him and deal with him. Maverick was stubborn and cowardly, though, because he never came out, not even to use the bathroom.

Whatever. Fine. Stay in there forever. See if I care…

Except that he did care. He cared entirely too much. He cared about Maverick, and he cared about Jackson, and he cared about the stunt he'd just pulled being so honest about it. The first time Jackson asked him, the day he felt so shocked over the thing he'd just walked in on, Nathan didn't want to say. He didn't want to rock the boat or do further harm. He'd resolved in that moment he wasn't ever going to tell Jackson how he felt, but his emotions were messy and all over the place. He alternated between longing, hurt, anger and despair. He felt both good about the soft coming-out he'd done, and simultaneously terrible because maybe Jackson would've chosen him if he weren't so feminine and blurred? He wondered if, had he been a traditional man, maybe Jackson would've wanted him over Maverick?

Of course, better heads prevailed at times. There were glimpses of the truth present when he really started to spiral. Jackson's choice of Maverick had nothing to do with being nonbinary. It had absolutely nothing to do with that at all. Jackson had been supportive. Hell, he'd been *more* than supportive. There were moments where it felt like that part of Nathan actually appealed to him. That was never the problem. The issue at hand was the same old thing it'd been since they'd met: obsession. Jackson and Maverick were fanatical about each other. They were infatuated and intoxicated, neither one of them ever fully able to leave the other one alone. There was no contest with a relationship like that. There simply wasn't. There'd never been any space for Nathan when it came to those two. They'd always been too set on each other for anyone else to penetrate that bond.

Nathan whimpered pitifully to himself as he fell into those thoughts. He grabbed another beer, downed it, wallowed, then succumbed to another fit of bawling on the couch. He hugged himself while sobs poured from his body, physically tugging him along with them. He didn't notice at first when Maverick came out. He only realized Maverick was there when he sat down on the couch and affectionately started to rub Nathan's quivering arm. Nathan put his hands over his face to hide. He didn't like being seen like this, but he couldn't stop. He wailed into his palms, and Maverick eventually laid down atop Nathan's side and wrapped him in his arms. It made the pain of it worse because it reminded Nathan how much he cared about Maverick. He uncovered his eyes. He threw his arms around Maverick and sobbed against his shoulder. Maverick never moved. He held steady and firm while Nathan fell apart. When he finally did calm, Maverick continued to hold him then, too.

"I'm so sorry, Nathan. I never meant to hurt you like this," he whispered, and it felt genuine.

"I know," he quietly answered, clinging to his friend like the child he once was.

They held each other a little while longer before Nathan started to let truths tumble from his mouth. He couldn't stop it. He had to talk to someone, and he didn't want to lay it on too thick with Chris because he still fancied the idea of pursuing something there when his heart felt better.

"I'm so lost, Mav. I don't know who I am, or what I want...I can't...I can't have any of the things I need. I can't dress like I did at that concert again...what the hell was I thinking, acting like that was something people will accept!? I can't have Jackson...and I love him...I'm in love with him and this hurts too fucking bad...I don't want to lose him, or you, but I can't see my way out of this in a way where I don't..." he whimpered.

Maverick pulled away gently and looked down at him, trying so hard to calmly take it in. He wasn't exactly surprised, but it was still difficult to hear. It made him feel territorial and jealous over Jackson, and yet, at the same time, he wanted to protect and soothe

Nathan. He continued rubbing Nathan's arm, watching while his friend rested on his back and tried to better explain.

"I screwed up tonight. I told Jackson how I feel. I shouldn't have. I wasn't going to. I was going to be the bigger person and walk away from it, you know? But I let my emotions get the best of me and I told him that I love him. I know it messed him up, and I swear I'm not trying to interfere with your relationship…I guess…I guess I really just wanted to hurt him. I wanted him to hurt at least a *little* like I do. God, I'm so sorry, Mav. I'm so, so sorry."

Maverick sighed and reached up, brushing Nathan's bangs from his forehead. It was strange he had so much hair now. Maverick hadn't seen him with hair that long since they were little boys. Briefly, it reminded him of those simpler days, the days when they'd been innocent and inseparable. The days they'd both been certain nothing would ever shake the friendship they had.

"I wish I'd gotten the nerve to be honest with him before all this happened," Maverick said quietly.

Nathan sniffled, "I wish I'd paid attention to my instincts and accepted what was there. I always knew about you two. I knew I was playing with fire."

Maverick quietly regarded his life's oldest friend. He felt a sharp pain in his chest while he struggled to figure it out.

"What does this mean for us, Nathan?"

Nathan's eyes were watered and wide while he earnestly answered.

"I don't know. It's really, *really* hard for me to be around you guys. Graduation's only a couple of weeks away…our lease is up soon…I should probably move out. I don't know where I'll go, but I know I can't stay here. It's just too hard. It's just too fucking hard."

Maverick rubbed his thumb along Nathan's shoulder as tears started to pool in his own eyes now. He sniffled and wiped his face before dropping his hands to his lap with a nod.

"I understand. I'll try and give you some space, if that's what you want."

Nathan reached over and took Maverick's hand. Maverick looked back up at him, listening attentively while Nathan spoke.

"I don't know if it's forever, but yeah…I really do need some space right now."

Maverick nodded before squeezing Nathan's hand and releasing it. He stood up, looked down at him for a moment with so much pain and uncertainty on his face, before disappearing into his room. Nathan pulled the throw blanket from the back of the couch and wrapped it around himself, rolling to his side. He was just going to sleep there for now. He didn't have the will to move.

***

The following day went by rather quickly, despite how worn and conflicted Nathan felt. He moved through his classes, knocked out some studying in his room, and then when he was starting to find himself bored and thinking about Julia, his phone lit up with a text from Chris. He'd invited Nathan to come get baked at his place and watch a movie together, and Nathan figured he didn't have anything else going on, so why not? He said a brief, hurried goodbye to Maverick on his way out, trying his hardest to at least be cordial. He breathed a sigh of relief once he'd left the apartment, though, and drove over to Chris's swanky residence. He was surprised at how immediately warm he felt when he entered that place, pleased when Chris greeted him with a friendly hug.

"It smells awesome in here. Did you cook something?" Nathan asked, slipping from his shoes and sliding them beneath the couch.

"Yeah! I made some nachos, you want some? I haven't eaten yet."

"Yeah, okay…that sounds good, thanks," Nathan agreed while he followed him into the kitchen.

Chris pulled a large tray from the oven, complete with chips, cheese, jalapenos, ground beef and onions all cooked together. Nathan watched, suddenly aware of his hunger, while Chris got some sour cream and hot sauce from the fridge and placed them on the counter. He dug out two plates and loaded them up, then handed one to Nathan before they walked into the living room.

"Okay, don't eat yet...we gotta get faded first..." he insisted, setting his plate on the coffee table.

Nathan set his down and grinned.

"You know...I've, uh...I've actually never smoked weed before. My dad was kind of a pot-head and a drinker, really checked out and all that. I always stayed away from it because I thought he was a prick."

Chris raised his brows and pulled a vape pen from his pocket, "And yet, you drink?"

Nathan pulled his shoulders in and shrugged, "Yeah...I guess I do."

Chris let out a laugh, "Dude, I can't believe you haven't even *tried* it. It's way more chill than getting smashed. I mean, if you don't want to you don't have to. Don't feel pressured, alright? It is a lot more mellow, though...if you're down."

"No, no...I don't feel pressured, it's cool. I mean, I've always been a little curious. It's just that Maverick and Julia don't really do it, either, so I've never had anyone around to smoke with."

Chris nodded, leaning back further into the couch and taking a hit from his pen. Nathan watched while he held the smoke in his lungs, then slowly released it, the smell instantly filling the air between them.

"Weed makes everything better, man. Food, sex, TV...it tastes better, it feels better, everything you watch is fucking hysterical...or sad, or exciting, depends what you're watching, I guess."

Nathan nodded, gingerly taking the vape from Chris. He looked toward his friend for some reassurance, finding an amused expression on his face. Nathan took a hit, then coughed really hard. It made Chris laugh and smile, so Nathan didn't mind it so much.

"Try it again...do your best to hold it in...that's what'll get you lifted," he raised his voice for the last bit.

Nathan coughed a few more times before deciding to give it another go. This time, he was better prepared to hold it in, though he did cough some more when he released it. They exchanged the vape a handful of times, then Chris set it down on the coffee table and fully leaned against the cushions of the couch.

"So, you're still in touch with Julia then, huh?"

Nathan nodded, leaning back and waiting to feel high.

"Yeah, we, uh…we have a pretty nice friends with benefits situation going on."

Chris's eyes got wide, obviously intrigued.

"No shit? Damn…I've *always* wanted to have something like that. It's hard, though. Most people can't do it."

Nathan grinned, "Yeah, I know. It's easy with her, though. You know, we were together forever, and then when we split it wasn't bad or anything. We just fell out of love, but the sex was always really good, so we decided to keep it going."

Chris cocked a brow while he thought about it, "Wait, doesn't she have a girlfriend? I'm pretty sure I've seen her hanging around campus with this curvy little thing…"

"Yeah, she does. They're chill, though. They both see other people sometimes."

Chris blew out a puff of air, "Damn…y'all livin' the *life*! Makin' shit happen!"

Nathan chuckled, "What, you don't think you could do something like that?"

He looked toward Nathan, both of them starting to feel pleasantly high.

"Be with someone and let them sleep with someone else? Nah…hell no. I'm way too jealous for that. No way. When I'm with a guy, I want to be the center of his universe. I return the favor, of course, but I straight up need that. No way I could share. Friends with benefits I might be able to pull off, but not an open relationship. No way, no how."

Nathan laughed again, looking up at the ceiling while he thought about it, "You know…I think I'm the same. I could never share. I fall way too hard for people to do something like that."

They were quiet for a while before Chris leaned forward to eat his food. Nathan followed suit, and while he ate he couldn't believe how incredible it tasted.

"Oh my *God*. This is the best thing I've ever eaten in my entire life!"

Chris couldn't help but laugh because he knew it was just the weed talking. He wasn't about to correct Nathan, though. He'd take the compliment. They both ate until they were stuffed, then they went into the kitchen and pulled out even more because it felt like they needed to eat and eat until they could no longer move. Once they were finished, they went back to the living room and put on a movie. It was just some generic romantic comedy, which Nathan alternated between fascination and indifference toward. He mostly wanted to chat with Chris, but he didn't want to be one of those people that talked through a film. He was also starting to get kind of sleepy. Before he could drift, though, Chris started talking to him.

"So, tell me, what degree are you getting? What do you want to do?"

"English. I want to write a novel. I don't know what the hell I'd ever write about, but you know, I figure I'll probably just end up teaching. Maybe editing for a while if I'm lucky."

Chris nodded, "That sounds pretty cool. I could see you doing something like that."

Nathan smiled, "What about you?"

Chris shrugged, "Oh, you know…just a run of the mill business degree. Look, college has been kind of a grind for me, if I'm real with you. I'm not, like, super smart when it comes to academics. I'm functional and all that, but it's tough. I basically just wanted to earn something, and I also wanted to know what I'm doing, because the plan is to take over this bakery my dad bought after mom died. I make a mean cupcake, and I've been practicing my craft. It's been my dream basically forever, and that's what I do when I'm not busy with class."

Nathan looked at him curiously, "Wait, your dad bought a bakery?"

Chris nodded, "Yeah, it's for me. He knew that's what I wanted to do, and he wanted to help me get the business running while I got my degree. I assume ownership as soon as I graduate. I'll be a full-fledged bakery owner, and we do pretty good. I'm excited about it."

"Wow, dude...that's really great. I'm happy for you."

Chris looked at him fondly, smiling warm and lighting up his face. For a moment there, Nathan couldn't help but think he was one of the most handsome men he'd laid eyes on in ages. He was no Jackson, that was for sure, be he was pretty damn cute.

"Thanks."

Nathan watched him a moment longer before sighing and looking down at his lap.

"I wish I could quit my job. I don't mind the work, it's whatever, but I almost always have shifts with Jack. It sucks. Not to mention how shitty it is having to face Maverick at home, too."

Chris regarded him sympathetically. Nathan kept his eyes glued to his lap.

"Sometimes I wish I could just disappear...run away from my disastrous life, you know?"

Chris nodded, "I think we all feel that way sometimes."

Nathan couldn't help it when his eyes started watering again. God. It was probably because he still felt a little high. Why couldn't he knock this off? He hated how vulnerable he felt...how raw he was.

"I'm sorry," he quickly apologized through tears.

Chris shook his head and quickly wrapped Nathan in his arms.

"Don't be. I understand. I've been burned before, too. Love is...well...love's a real pain in the ass."

Nathan laughed, even while tears fell.

"Yeah, it really is, isn't it?"

Chris held him and rubbed his back. Nathan got control of his emotions before they completely ran away from him. He never did pull away, though. The two of them leaned against the back of the couch. Chris kept his arms around Nathan while they watched the movie. Nathan rested comfortably against his chest. He felt Chris's fingers trailing the sides of his arm, and it made him feel warm and tingly. He may well have been in love with Jackson, head over heels in fact, but he wasn't about to complain about being in the arms of a handsome, old friend. It was pretty nice. He didn't want this lovely feeling to go away.

***

While Nathan took comfort in time away with Chris, Maverick took full advantage of the empty apartment, inviting Jackson over. Of course, being as fresh and new as things were, they immediately went for each other without any caution about how, or when, or where. They were all over the living room, then all over Maverick's room. They finished up on the bed, then laid there in each other's arms, cuddling and breathing, feeling infatuated and satiated all at once. Jackson held Maverick close, trailing his fingers along his light skin. At first, it felt like bliss, but eventually the afterglow wore off and the reality of their situation grew heavy.

"Nathan told me what he said to you…" Maverick cautiously admitted.

He didn't want to fight about it, but he didn't want to ignore it either. Jackson didn't say anything at first. He was pensive and careful before he responded.

"I don't feel good about it, but you don't have to worry. I'm committed to you. I want what we have."

Maverick squeezed his lips together, letting himself feel all the worry and doubt.

"Are you sure? Because I don't want to go through with this, telling everyone about us, coming out, if you're just going to end up with him."

Jackson pulled away and stared at Maverick with disbelief. Their eye contact was intense, and it made both of their bellies ache.

"I'd never, *ever* betray you like that, Mav. I'm not that kind of person. I know the thing that happened with Nathan was crazy, but you have to believe me, I thought you weren't an option. I was sure you'd never make a move."

"So…that's all it was? He was an afterthought? You don't love him…and you don't think you would've?"

Jackson swallowed. What the hell did this line of questioning even matter? He didn't want to lie, but he didn't want to tell the entire truth about it either. It would only serve to feed Maverick's paranoia.

"I don't love him, I love you," he answered, ignoring the nuance enveloping the rest of it, the fact that there was no way Nathan could ever be described as an afterthought; the truth that, though he didn't love him, he absolutely could've and would've.

Maverick didn't need to know all of that, though.

"Is this wrong, what we've done here?" Maverick asked, more insecurities creeping from his mouth.

Jackson's eyes wavered while he considered it.

"No, of course not. We didn't do anything wrong. It just happened, that's all."

It wasn't entirely true or false, though. Even as Jackson reassured them that in a black and white situation of right or wrong they were clean, he knew better. The situation was gray at best, slightly nearer to black at worst. There were layers of innocence, the unknown aspects of the way they came to one another in love. Nonetheless, those layers didn't exist on their own. They were mixed with a full cocktail of frustrating truths, lies, and indifferences. Sure, they'd unknowingly come together under fraught circumstances, but there were also the buried parts of them that knew. Maverick had seen it in the car. Jackson had tasted it on Nathan's lips. Poisonous fruit, culpable or wrong, they weren't innocent in any sense. They'd both hurt Nathan. They'd both chosen to pursue their own wants at the expense of another's heart. It wasn't 'fifty shades of gray'; it was a million shades of fucked.

Jackson kissed Maverick then because he didn't know what else to do. Maverick kissed him back, and they shared their bodies and skin once more, perhaps as reassurance; maybe for distraction. The thought crept into Jackson's head that, though it was normal to be hot and heavy, they were already establishing a pattern that might prove difficult to break.

Don't feel it, baby. Just touch me and forget the awful things that we've done.

Going Through the Motions

A week went by, and before Nathan knew it, graduation was only another week away. The finals had been taken, the projects had all been finished. Normally, it would've been a celebratory time with friends, but given the fact he was in love with one and fallen out with the other that didn't seem like such a great idea. He couldn't be sure what they did. He knew they'd invited him to hit downtown with them, Greg included. He'd politely declined, staying in that night instead. While he spent that evening in his apartment alone, he realized he hadn't heard from Julia in several days. He texted her and asked if she'd get some coffee with him the following morning, to which she agreed.

When the time came to meet, Nathan arrived first and grabbed them a table. He bought her a London Fog Latte and a coffee with lots of cream for himself. When she finally arrived, she greeted him with a hug and kiss on the cheek, thanking him for getting her favorite drink. He smiled and said 'you're welcome' before they settled and dove into it.

"I haven't heard from you in a while…you been okay?" he asked, no lack of concern in his voice.

She sighed, trailing her finger along the edge of her cup. She looked troubled and it made Nathan anxious.

"I don't know. I've been so tired. I haven't been feeling well. I got through my finals and everything, but it was hard. Ginny's been mad at me, too. Like, out of *nowhere* she's suddenly very jealous of you," she admitted.

"What? Why?"

Julia shrugged, keeping her eyes down in her lap, "I *may* have mentioned that you and I had, like, proper sex…you know? She didn't like it. She told me she was cool with me, you know, doing the things we usually do, but apparently I crossed a line when I let you do that. I didn't know, I mean, I obviously would've said something to you if I'd known. I wasn't trying to betray her or anything like that."

157

Nathan leaned back and stared, his eyes wide and filled with worry.

"Oh no, Jules…I'm so sorry. I wouldn't have done it if I'd known either."

Julia nodded before wiping her eyes, crying some. Nathan quickly pulled his seat around the table to sit beside her, wrapping her in his arms and doing his best to give some comfort. She never fully gave into it, and eventually pulled away to look at him directly. He swallowed, trying to figure out exactly where this left them.

"Do you want to stop? We don't have to have sex, you know?"

She licked her lips before cautiously answering. The conversation felt delicate.

"I think it'd be best for my relationship. Ginny wants to close things off now. I told her I'd talk to you, but I've been avoiding it, obviously…"

Nathan reached up and gave her arm a reassuring squeeze.

"Jules, don't ever be afraid to talk to me about anything, okay? I understand. It's alright, really. You're my forever best friend, whether we're doing that or not. She doesn't want us to stop talking, though, does she?"

Julia let out an uncomfortable laugh before shaking her head and looking at him earnestly.

"I don't know. She hasn't said. But it doesn't matter. You're my best friend, too, and even if she wants us to stop talking, I won't. That's just something she's going to have to find a way to live with."

Nathan let out a relieved sigh, "Okay, good."

They regarded each other a moment before Nathan decided to try and bandage the subject.

"It's good timing anyway. I've been spending some time with Chris."

Julia raised her brows, a look of obvious intrigue on her face.

158

"Oh…? And how's that going!?"

He smiled and she instantly recognized the look he got when he was talking about someone he liked.

"Good. I've hung out at his place a few times. He took me to the movies the other night. He's really easy to talk to. I feel like we're getting close pretty fast. We're just friends for now, but…well, I think he'd like to be more. I'm not exactly sure I'm ready for a relationship, I'm still kind of a mess over Jackson, but…I don't know, it seems possible that I'm going to be sometime soon and I really do like him."

She smiled wide, "Nathan! That's great! I think this could be really good for you!"

He grinned softly, "I do, too. I just want to be careful. I don't want to hurt him."

"Well, the nice thing about Jack is the relationship didn't go anywhere. I think the fact that you never really had him might make it easier to move past. Honestly, I can't imagine how hard it must be to try and get over someone after years of intimacy. Like, with us it was easy because we fell into a friendship before things ended. I kind of got a taste of it with Ginny now, though. I thought she was going to leave me, the way she reacted. I know Jackson hurt you, and I know it's real and it feels like it won't go away, but it will, and I think it'll be sooner than you've got yourself convinced."

He thought about it. She did have a point there. In a way, the pain was already starting to lessen. He still felt longing, particularly on the rare occasion he saw Jackson and Maverick together. Yet, the more time he spent on his own or with Chris, the better he was able to take it. The pain was starting to subside, if only a little.

"Thanks, Jules. I think you might be right about that," he conceded.

She grinned and tilted her head, "Of course I am. I'm always right."

He laughed. The two of them finished up their drinks and chatted about things that felt lighter, very eager to catch up. When the time came to depart, they shared a friendly hug and went their separate ways. When Nathan arrived back at the apartment he got a text from Chris asking to hang out. Nathan told him to come over and they could figure it out from there. Chris agreed with excitement. He was over at Nathan's apartment within minutes, which thankfully was empty because Maverick was out, presumably with Jackson.

"Hey!" Chris said when Nathan opened the door.

He threw his arms around him and embraced him tightly.

"Hi," Nathan laughed, hugging him back.

They separated and Chris put his hands in the pockets of his jeans, taking a gander at the apartment. They typically spent time at his place because it was big and he didn't have a roommate, but he'd been around a time or two by now.

"So, how you been?"

Nathan shrugged, "Okay. Mostly been in the apartment. I'm relieved to be done with my classes."

"Shit, dude…me, too. Look at us, though, huh? We did it! We're officially owners of legitimate degrees! We're on our way to the American Dream, my friend!"

Nathan chuckled. Chris was so enthusiastic about everything, it was kind of charming.

"Anyway, what do you want to do then?" Chris asked, hopping to the counter and sitting with casually swinging feet.

"Uh, I don't know. Did you have anything in mind?"

"Come here, let me see something," Chris responded, gesturing for Nathan to approach.

Nathan was confused, but he obliged anyway. He walked up close, and felt his heartbeat quicken as Chris took his hand and started looking it over.

"I see you have some clear polish on your nails…want to touch it up with some color?"

Nathan's face flushed while he retracted his hand, "Oh…uh…I don't know. I mean, maybe another clear coat. Jules and I go to the salon sometimes. I don't ever go on my own."

Chris folded his arms and looked Nathan over. Nathan felt terribly insecure and scrutinized, but not in the same way Maverick made him feel. It didn't have an air of judgment. It felt more like curiosity than anything.

"You know, your profile said you were nonbinary, but so far the only thing I've seen you do is wear that little crown the first time we hung out…you know, when you were all heartbroken and shit-faced."

Nathan looked at the ground, a little hunched.

"Yeah, I know. I don't know. I mean, this isn't how I *want* to be, but…" he sighed and forced himself to look at Chris while he explained, "…the thing is, Jackson convinced me to dress how I wanted the day he kissed me. He got me this pretty, pink sweater and I wore it with the crown. I shaved my arms and I felt, like, *so* good. But then everything happened with Maverick and I guess it got under my skin. Like, I understand it's probably got nothing to do with why he chose Mav, but I also can't help but wonder if maybe it did? Does that make sense? I just…I think it's just easier on everyone if I suck it up and dress like a man."

Chris's eyes were wide while he stared, and when he finally did speak, his voice was low and careful.

"Let me see your arm…"

Nathan quietly obliged him again, and he felt butterflies in his stomach as Chris rolled up the sleeve of his sweater. He ran his fingers along smooth skin.

"You've kept it shaved," he commented.

Nathan nodded, "Yeah…I have."

He rubbed his fingers along Nathan's arm a moment longer before stopping and holding on gently. He looked into Nathan's eyes while he spoke to him with intensity.

"You know what I think?"

Nathan shook his head.

"I think it doesn't matter whether or not it had anything to do with Jackson's choice. I also think it doesn't matter what anyone else has to say about who you are and how you present yourself. Now, maybe in some ways it'd be easier to suck it up or whatever, but I happen to know a thing or two about hiding who you are and it sucks. It'll tear you up inside, even if it earns you all the praise in the world. I can't tell you what to do, but here's my two cents. I think you'd be happier if you just let it go and be yourself, and if it means anything, I'd love to see what that looks like for you, because I can promise you this, Nathan...I won't kiss you and tell you I think you're beautiful then walk away and leave you behind."

Nathan felt like his heart was in his throat. His eyes wavered. He started to tremble because the kindness behind those words wasn't the sort of thing he was used to.

"So, what do you think?" Chris continued, "Do you want a proper manicure or what? My treat."

Nathan stared in disbelief then broke out into a wide, beaming smile and let out a laugh.

"Um...yeah, yeah...okay. I do. I've wanted to put some color on my nails for years."

"Great," Chris said, releasing Nathan's arm and hopping down from the counter. He put his arm around Nathan's shoulders, and it made him feel fuzzy and warm, "Let's go then."

Nathan didn't say anything. He just let Chris lead him from the apartment to his nice car. Along the way, Nathan decided he might as well let him know about the development with Julia.

"So, um...something happened with Jules, you know, the whole friends with benefits thing?"

"Oh?"

Nathan cleared his throat, "Uh, yeah. I guess her girlfriend's finally gotten a little jealous about it and wants us to stop, so, that's done. I'm really hoping it doesn't affect our friendship, but I have to admit, I'm a little worried Ginny's going to insist I go away. I don't know. But, uh…I guess you were right, about the whole thing being kind of impossible."

Chris looked over at him and smiled, "I don't know…that sounds about as best case scenario as I can imagine. What'd Julia say about the friendship?"

"She said we're fine. She said Ginny'll have to deal if she's got hang ups about it."

"Well, then I say don't worry about it. You and Julia have been tight for a long time, I doubt this is going to blow up in your face."

Nathan nodded and looked out the window.

"Maybe. I hope not."

Chris drove along, glancing at Nathan here and there with an amused expression on his face. Nathan eventually met his gaze.

"What? Why do you keep looking at me like that?"

Chris smiled a bit wider and shrugged, "You're a real worrier, you know that? You need to smoke more weed and learn how to chill."

Nathan laughed, "Ha! That's easy for you to say! That's all you do, isn't it?"

Chris was still smiling, thoroughly enjoying their conversation.

"Hell, yeah that's all I do! I smoke, I chill and I bake. It's a fuckin' *life* my friend. You should try it sometime. I mean, maybe not the baking…but whatever your thing is. Blaze, chill and write maybe. Work on that book of yours, or whatever."

Nathan grinned and shook his head, "You make life sound so easy, Donahue."

Chris shrugged again, "I mean…life can be whatever you make of it."

Nathan glanced at him, tickled with the intentional suggestion in his response. He felt another wave of fondness move through him. Chris. What a unique, lovely person he was, albeit foul-mouthed.

Nathan wasn't able to think on it much longer, though, because all too soon they were at the salon. They got out and went in. Chris was as charismatic as ever. He ingratiated himself with the women inside right away, explaining that he wanted to treat his 'friend' to a manicure. They all chatted with him and laughed, and eventually the woman who was set to work on Nathan took him to the polishes to pick out a color. He felt a little overwhelmed while he browsed, but he also settled down almost immediately when Chris came to his side and put his arm around him.

"It's summer…maybe something bright?" he suggested, clearly trying to help.

Nathan bit his lip and continued letting his eyes roam the colors. Something bright sounded nice, and he was especially fond of pastels. He thought about the sweater, the one he hadn't bothered to take out since the night of the concert. He'd like it to match that because, who knew, maybe he'd end up wearing it for graduation or something? He searched around a little longer before his eyes landed on a nice shade of baby pink. He moved away from Chris and picked it out, feeling anxious and hot when he handed it to the woman who was going to do his nails. He forced himself to look at Chris, and he felt more relief once he realized Chris was smiling at him with kindness.

"Cool, that'll look nice," he reassured him.

Nathan smiled wide and followed his nail tech over to her station. Chris plopped into the seat before the empty station next to hers. He talked with her casually, regaling the mostly empty salon with entertaining anecdotes and stories while Nathan got his nails painted. They couldn't really talk about anything that mattered in such a public setting, but Nathan was relieved to have something to listen to while he watched his nails get decorated. Most of the routine he'd been through before, but when the moment came for the actual color to be painted, he quickly became fascinated. He stared down, taking it all in while the paint was applied to his nails, two coats on each hand. Once that was done, he had to put his hands inside a machine with a drying light. He was then instructed not to touch them as he pulled them out and looked. He couldn't even stop himself while he beamed. He glanced over at Chris with a broad grin.

"Thank you," he said, almost involuntarily.

Chris smiled at him with affection, "You're welcome. It suits you."

Nathan bit his lip and quietly followed while Chris went ahead and paid up for him. They got back to the car. Nathan kept staring down at his hands, totally enraptured with them. He couldn't believe he'd actually done it!

"Well, where to now?" Chris asked.

Nathan forced himself to tear his eyes from his hands, thoroughly taken with the view when they rested on Chris.

"Do you maybe just want to hang out in my room with me? I want to show you something."

Chris smiled, "Okay, sure. Sounds great to me!"

Nathan bit his lip again while Chris started up the car and headed for his place. Nathan went back to staring at his nails, and Chris turned on some music, well aware Nathan needed to process for a while. When they got back, Nathan was careful with his hands while he unbuckled and handled the door. They walked side by side up the stairs, then Nathan touched the nails to make sure they were dry before grabbing his keys from his pocket. He was all good to go, they were dry and secure, so he opened the door and they went inside, instantly a little uneasy when they found Jackson and Maverick watching television on the couch.

"Oh, uh…hey!" Maverick said, quickly moving away from Jackson.

Clearly they'd been cuddling. Nathan swallowed and looked down.

"Hey, dudes. Haven't seen you in ages, Mav…how goes it? And you're Jackson, I presume?" Chris asked, though his voice wasn't nearly as friendly as Nathan was accustomed to.

Nathan looked up, briefly watching Jackson and Maverick exchanging greetings with Chris. He shook hands with them, then everyone was left standing, awkward and waiting for someone to make a move. Nathan wasn't sure what to do, so he just stood there, blank and uncomfortable. Chris looked between them all and decided to take charge of the situation. He put his arm around Nathan's shoulder, and it made Nathan blush.

"Well, we won't be in your hair. Go back to your movie," he said, expertly guiding Nathan away from them, leading him to his bedroom.

Chris closed the door quietly behind them and placed his hands into his pockets while he looked Nathan over.

"You okay?"

Nathan looked at the ground a moment longer before lifting his eyes to meet Chris's.

"You know…I think I am."

Chris smiled, obviously relieved to hear it.

"Good. Well, let's forget about that shady shit then. What was it you wanted to show me?"

"Come here," Nathan insisted, going to have a seat on the bed and patting the empty space beside him.

Chris smiled and sat down. He watched attentively while Nathan pulled out his phone and opened the Pinterest app.

"I have a board on here. It's got lots of ideas for ways I'd like to look. Do you want to see?"

"Yeah! Absolutely!" he responded sincerely.

Nathan chewed on his lip, looking Chris over with amazement. He was so open and accepting. He didn't seem hesitant at all.

"Okay, um…let's lay down," Nathan insisted, scooting closer to the head of the bed.

Chris looked completely thrilled with the idea as he followed suit. They each settled on their backs beside one another, resting their heads atop pillows. The bed was only a twin, so they were exceptionally close while Nathan held up the phone and selected his 'ideas' board. It was private, so there was no way anyone else could see unless they were in a situation like this. Nathan glanced over at Chris and started to point things out.

"So, I really like big sweaters and skinny jeans. I like cute boots and scarves. I'm not really into the idea of makeup or anything, and I don't want to do my eyebrows either. Like I said, there are still parts of me I'm okay with, but just, like…dressing like this, you know? And my hair…I want it like this. I'm growing it out now, and I really need to cut the back…it's getting kind of crazy. But this, here…" he pulled up a picture of an actress with a long pixie cut, which was basically the sort of thing a young boy might have with a bit more elegance, "…I'd really like my hair like this. That's all I want. I do like having painted nails. I like the way this feels, a lot…like, I've wanted to do that forever, you have no idea."

Chris was smiling softly, and Nathan was surprised when he slowly took the phone.

"I think all of these things would look great on you…" he said, holding it up and scrolling through the rest.

Nathan watched the phone at first, then he found himself watching Chris's face. He found himself wanting things he wasn't so sure he should be, and it put him in another mixed up state of worry and desire. Why did he always have to feel like this? Why couldn't there just be desire on its own?

"It wouldn't bother you…you know, like, I mean, I know we're just friends, but…as a gay man, you'd be okay dating someone like me?"

Chris shut off the screen and set it aside. He rolled over and looked Nathan square in the eyes while he answered.

"I'd be more than okay with it, Nathan. I'd honestly be really, really into it."

Nathan rolled to his side as well, his arms pressed close to his chest while he looked Chris over. They gazed at each other a little while before Chris spoke softly, sounding insecure for the first time since Nathan had started spending time with him.

"So, um…you have a vacancy now, you know, with Julia being out of the picture. Any chance you're looking to fill that position?"

Nathan bit his lip and stifled a laugh, "It's not a job."

Chris laughed nervously, "Yeah, I know, but…uh…I mean…"

He wasn't sure what else he could say, so he simply fell quiet and watched Nathan.

"I don't want to hurt you," Nathan insisted, "I'm still mixed up. I'm obviously, like, my whole life is *so* confusing and awkward right now. But, uh, damn Chris…I do like you. I really like spending time with you, and I'd be lying if I didn't admit I've thought about it…being like that with you."

Chris smiled softly and touched Nathan's arm, rubbing it gently while he stared into his eyes, "I like you, too. Like I said, don't worry about hurting me. I just float around, Nate. I do what feels right on a moment to moment basis, and right now, you feel pretty right to me."

Nathan's stomach rolled.

"I've only been with Julia," he admitted.

Chris rubbed Nathan's arm gently, "I've had casual flings with three other people, and a serious thing with one. No one you know. I'm clean. I used protection with all of the casuals. What are you comfortable with here? We don't have to go all the way…I'm down for whatever you want."

Nathan's cheeks felt warm as they moved through the practical side of it, the getting to know one another, the considerations for safety and comfort.

"Um…Julia used to, uh…she'd top me with a, uh…ha. I'm, like, good to go in that department. I'm okay. I don't know what you like…if you top or bottom or what…but, if I have a choice here, I think I'd prefer the bottom…at least for now."

Chris looked tender as he lifted his hand up to Nathan's face, trailing his fingers along his cheek lightly.

"I'm okay with whatever makes you happy. I'm good either way."

Nathan nodded, feeling breathless and anxious all at once.

"Okay…uh…well…" he stammered.

Chris grinned sweetly and kissed him, bottomless and slow. Nathan got pulled into it and lost while they went through it together, the first time with new bodies, and hearts, and souls. Chris was considerate, and deep. He never did stop kissing Nathan while they did the things they did, and once they were through they just held one another. Chris remained atop Nathan, pressing their foreheads together while they caught their breath. Once they'd done that, they kissed a while longer before laying down more comfortably, cuddling and quiet. A considerable amount of placid time passed before Nathan finally spoke above a whisper.

"Thank you for today. It's the best day I've had in a while."

Chris rubbed the skin of Nathan's back with the tips of his fingers. He kept his eyes closed while he smiled.

"Right back at you. This is the best day I've had in forever."

Nathan smiled, too. He felt sleep starting to overtake his fuzzy, satisfied mind. The idea of love touched the tip of his tongue. Could it be? Was it possible? They say the only way you can really get over someone is to fall for someone else. Is that what was happening here? Could this thing actually be real, and fulfilling, and good? He couldn't be certain, but there was one thing Nathan knew for sure, and it was big. Chris was right. It didn't matter if being nonbinary was responsible for Jackson's choice, because even if it was, it was also responsible for this in a way. And this…?

Damn, this was something good.

It Feels Like Forever

The following morning Nathan woke before Chris. He took stock of where he was and what had happened, and for the briefest moment he felt peaceful. He took in the sight of Chris's face, noting how lovely he looked in morning's light. He grinned, marveling at his good fortune. Sure, things had been awful since that day at the concert, but at least this was happening, and with such good timing, too, considering everything that happened with Julia. He realized, on some level, he wasn't being as independent as he probably should be, but didn't especially care. These days were strange ones, and it definitely felt better to conquer them beside a friend, even better now that he was a friend with some perks.

He yawned before carefully tiptoeing from the bed. Chris didn't stir, which Nathan also found endearing. It made sense he was the type to sleep solid and heavy. How could he not be? Chris was just about the most relaxed person he'd ever met in his life. Of course, some of that might've had something to do with the weed.

Nathan slipped into a sweater and some joggers before sneaking from the room and shutting the door quietly behind him. He planned to go to the kitchen for some coffee, which he was still going to do, but he was admittedly disappointed to see Jackson already awake doing the same.

"Oh...hey, Nathan..." he said, scratching the back of his head with discomfort.

"Hey," Nathan responded, his voice low, almost inaudible.

Jackson watched him enter the kitchen. He already had a cup of coffee resting in the nook of the machine, just finished brewing. He took it away and stepped back to make room for Nathan. He watched while his friend fished out two cups and got one of them going. At first, Nathan kept his body angled toward the counter. Once the second cup was loaded, he forced himself to turn around. Jackson felt at a loss while he looked at him. He wanted to connect, to bridge the ever-growing divide between them, but he had no clue how. They'd barely even seen each other since Nathan had confessed his true feelings. All of his shifts at work had been changed. He had to have spoken with the manager about avoiding

Jackson, which cut. Before Jack could conjure up anything to say, Nathan's second cup finished brewing. He turned to fetch it, but just then Jackson managed to choke out a few words.

"Can I talk to you, like...maybe out on the patio?"

Nathan held still. His shoulders looked stiff, like he was frozen in ice. It tugged at Jackson's heart because never in a million years did he ever think he'd make Nathan so uncomfortable. They'd always been so close. Their relationship had always felt effortless and smooth. It was one of the few dependable bonds in Jackson's life, and he could feel it slipping away from him more and more every day.

"Yeah, okay," Nathan finally agreed.

He turned around and looked at Jackson again. Jackson nodded, sucking in a breath and walking with his cup toward the patio. Nathan brought his, too, leaving the one he'd brewed for Chris. When he stepped outside, the morning air was fresh and chilly against his skin. He immediately went to the left corner of the patio, leaning against the rail and looking out at the other apartments. Jackson leaned in a more central zone of the space, his eyes locked on Nathan. He waited, and it took several moments before Nathan finally looked back. His eyes, they still looked so terribly wounded. It made Jackson want to crawl under a rock for a while.

"How was Chris?" he awkwardly spat out, acknowledging the fact that he knew things were getting physical.

Nathan might've felt chummy if he weren't so heartbroken. As good and fuzzy as he'd felt waking next to Chris, being face to face with Jackson was hard. It felt like a stab to his chest.

"How was Maverick?" he retorted, pointing out the absurdity of the question.

Jackson cleared his throat and looked down.

"That wasn't exactly what I meant...I guess, what I'm asking is...is he helping?"

Nathan turned, angling his body more toward Jackson. He waited for Jackson to meet his eyes before he responded.

"Is he helping me with what, Jack? Getting over you?"

Jackson swallowed, forcing himself to keep looking at Nathan. He at least owed him that much, looking him in the face while he listened to all the different ways he'd cracked open his heart.

"Yeah, that."

Nathan blinked and swallowed before setting his coffee down.

"Chris is a friend. Being around him feels good. He makes me laugh and smile, and it does feel easier to handle it when I'm with him. But, does it make it easier getting over you...?" he stopped and shook his head.

Jackson felt nauseous as Nathan stepped a little closer. He watched, uncertain of what he was going to do. Nathan took Jackson's cup from his hand and set it beside his own. He stayed close, holding out both of his hands for Jackson to see, as though he wanted him to take them.

"Look..." he continued, "...look at me...I shake when I'm around you. My body feels light. My stomach hurts. I feel hopeless and afraid, and then when you leave, when I watch you walk away from me and go to him...I feel like I'm going to die. I actually feel like that, Jack. I'm not exaggerating."

Jackson looked down at Nathan's hands, taking note of the truth. They were trembling, and when he looked back at Nathan's eyes he could see the hurt behind them, too. Nathan held his gaze, and while he did, it made Jackson feel like he was getting everything wrong.

"I'll never get over you, Jack. Julia said I should, that it'd be easier to forget you because I never had you in the first place, but she's wrong. I can't, and I won't, and I know it because you're the kind of person that sticks. I'll never be able to shake you or forget you, and even if this thing pans out with Chris...and God, I hope it does...he'll never be you. And you know what, Jackson? Maverick will never be me either. He'll never see the pieces of you that I do, the parts that are soft and good. It won't matter how much you give

172

him, I promise you Jackson…he'll never, *ever* love you the way I would if you'd have given me the chance."

Jackson's hands started to tremble and even though both of them knew it was going nowhere, Nathan took them into his own. He took them, and held them, and for a moment Jackson felt like he could die, too. He felt a glimpse of that pain Nathan was trying to shoulder, to bury, to leave behind and find safety in someone new.

"You've changed your shifts…I never see you anymore," Jackson commented, though he understood why, "Maverick says you're moving out after graduation…he wants us to move in together. He's happy about it, I think."

Nathan nodded, looking numb.

"He is. We haven't been good for years now. This was the final nail in the coffin. He and I are through, and you and I have to be, too. I'll never move forward if we aren't. I need you to give me some space, Jackson. If you care about me at all, I need you to let me go."

Jackson blinked out a frustrated tear.

"So, that's it then? I just lose you forever?"

Nathan started to cry as well, offering a light shrug.

"You can't lose what you never really had, right?"

Jackson squeezed his eyes shut in an effort to stop himself from sobbing. He couldn't, though. This was tough. God, this was really hard. He felt Nathan wrap his arms around his torso, and he instinctively did the same, burying his face in Nathan's hair and holding him close. They cried as quietly as they could for a while, then collected themselves and separated. They wiped their faces and regarded one another. Jackson sniffled before nodding, realizing then what he needed to do.

"Okay, this is it then. I'll leave. Maverick can see me at my place. What about work, though?"

"I'm quitting. I have enough saved to finish out my lease. I don't know what I'll do from there, I figure I can always go home if I need to. I'm done with this life, though. I'm leaving it behind."

Jackson nodded. Nathan looked back up at him, and it took Jackson's breath away in a manner it shouldn't have. He was *so* tempted, if only for a moment, to say forget it and go for it. He couldn't, of course. He loved Maverick, he cared about him and viscerally wanted that relationship he'd pined after for so many years. And yet, the idea of what he was missing out on here, not to mention the hurt he was inflicting, was difficult to ignore. The what if's, the would-a, could-a, should-a's, so to speak.

What if...I touched you? Kissed you? Loved you? What would you be like? Is the rest of your skin as soft as your lips were that night? Would you wrap your legs around me and breathe in the ways I want you to? Would you look at me like I'm the only person in the room, the way that you do now, for the rest of our days? Would we find ourselves waking up together on Christmas morning in a warm house scented like cinnamon, filled up with kids, and love, and family?

I think that we would, you and I. I really think we would.

He wouldn't go there, though, even though he could feel it deep in his bones, these things he could have with Nathan. These emotional, raw, real, tender things were not his to take, nor were they things that Maverick could reasonably give. He was a different person, a darker one in ways. There'd never be softness and warmth anywhere near the caliber Nathan could offer. Still, Maverick was Jackson's choice; a choice that'd almost regrettably been made.

He felt a small, panicked pit forming in his gut. It moved up into his throat and settled comfortably in the back of his mouth as Nathan simply, quietly walked away from him without fanfare, grabbing his coffee along the way.

That was it. Jackson stepped into the apartment and lingered near the patio door, watching while Nathan grabbed Chris's cup and disappeared into the bedroom with it. It was over now. It was done for good. He could sense Maverick's eyes on him then, so he glanced toward his room. He was leaning against the frame, his arms folded while he looked Jackson over. The jealousy on his face was apparent, and there was no way for Jackson to know how much of that conversation with Nathan he'd seen or heard. It didn't really matter. It was enough that Jackson could see Maverick was feeling hurt, maybe doubt. He sighed and walked over, pulling him close and rubbing the back of his head.

"Don't worry, I was only saying goodbye."

***

Even though graduation was only another week from that day, time moved gracelessly slow for Jackson. Things with Maverick felt off. It wasn't exactly talked about, but that morning with Nathan had clearly had an effect; a lasting one, at that. They bickered frequently, but never directly over Nathan. It was far more insidious than that. Rather than coming out with it and saying what he felt, Maverick nitpicked Jackson. He made mean-spirited comments about anything and everything, and their dates were a string of humiliating disasters. Miniature golf would start out fun and deteriorate along the way, with disputes over who hit what where. Movies were great because they didn't talk, but they eventually came to an end and there was always something to argue about afterward. Dinners were like this. Walks in the park were like this. It didn't matter what it was, it was always like this.

Truthfully, it wasn't so different from the way things were before they'd gotten together, when they'd pretended they were just friends. Unlike those days, however, they had this new tool in their arsenal for casing wounds. Now, every time that they'd bicker and fight, they'd have sex with such intensity it wiped the slate clean. It was like they channeled all of their pain, their hatred, their fraught love and frustration into each other, forcing the rage straight out of tense bodies. As emotional as it was, it came with aggravations. Sometimes, even, they argued about sex itself. Mostly battles of who would be doing what. Jackson wasn't keen on being completely subjugated by Maverick, and Maverick wasn't into giving on it at all. They always managed to work it out, violently or not, which was so burning and screwed up Jackson sometimes couldn't decide if it was cruelty or kink. Most things felt like that, he was beginning to appreciate, walking that fuzzy little line between malice and love.

The two of them were dangerous, explosive, painful and beautiful in all of the ways Jackson dreamt of and craved. He'd been conditioned over the course of their acquaintance and a childhood full of trauma to want something like this. He'd learned somewhere along the way, between a string of stepfathers and a mother's veins flushed with drugs, that love meant submission, performance, and adulation. It felt natural to accept Maverick's unobtainable standards. It echoed of his mother and the men she kept close. As he'd done in his youth, when he fell short of the things he couldn't possibly hope to give, he would shoulder the blame for their relationship's failures. He'd discharge any ounce of culpability Mav might have, and even then the deference was never adequate or seen. Nine times out of ten there'd be a predictable outburst, like he'd done when they'd camped, and so many times before. Sometimes, when those eruptions poured searing words upon his head, Jackson felt certain there was something more ominous behind them, something worse than the emotional pain he carried now; something that felt more sadistic than scorched words. There'd been no overt sign of it just yet, but something about Maverick's miserable countenance made it feel terribly inevitable. Love had always been an endless cycle of brutality and shame. It only felt natural to participate the way he did, the way he accepted the put-downs and offered up sex for a quick fix. Yet still, sometimes when he had a quiet moment to himself, he wondered what it would've been like to be calm in love with Nathan.

Of course, it was far too late for something like that now, even as he laid eyes on his former best friend from the audience. They were graduating. Nathan was finished, so even though it'd felt good for Maverick and Jackson to collect their false diplomas and take their pictures on the stage, it must've felt even better for him. He was actually done, no law school looming around the corner. Nathan was ready to start his real, adult life. It ached deep down, and Jackson felt so pulled to go and hug him, to congratulate him and be there for him in all the ways he would've been if only they hadn't kissed on that night. It wasn't meant to be that way, though. Neither of them had played their hand right, and now they were no more than a deck with missing cards. You couldn't play with that. It was the sort of thing you put away and forgot, maybe even threw out.

They were useless together. There was nothing left about them that made a lick of sense.

Even so, Jackson watched him walking from the stage. Nathan caught his eyes and quickly tore them away. Jackson kept looking, though, drinking in the sight as he went over to Chris and hugged him, celebrating with someone new.

"Stop fucking looking at him," Maverick insisted, his voice gravelly between clenched teeth.

"Why? Who cares?"

Maverick rolled his eyes and folded his arms. Great. Just great. They were going to go at it again. Jackson sighed and folded his arms, too.

Well...at least I'll get a decent lay after this, I guess.

They waited and watched the rest of the students walk. They met up with Maverick's family when it was done. Jackson and Maverick had called them ahead of time, letting them know about their relationship so they didn't have to hide. It was obvious, of course, that it made them uncomfortable, which Jackson actually took some spiteful pleasure from. Unlike Mav and his sour relatives, Jackson's family wasn't there. That was predictable, though. Last he'd heard his mother had lost the house, and Jackson truthfully didn't know who his father was. Given such, he probably should've wanted to fit in with Maverick's kin, but he'd found them distasteful from the first time they'd spoke.

Nonetheless, the air was dripping with false pleasance once they were all together. It continued in that vein while they left for a big event, planned months in advance. It'd been looming large over both of their heads, particularly now that it was set to take place. They weren't sure if Nathan would show, but he was supposed to. It was big, after all. The white-collar parents from their home town had rented an entire restaurant to celebrate their kids. Everyone that'd gone to Maverick's high school and opted for in-state education was set to be there.

Even though Jackson and Maverick were feeling anxious, neither one of them could discuss it because they were stuck in the car with

Mav's family. Jackson was wedged against the window, with Maverick occupying the center beside his small sister. She looked just as uptight and rigid as he was, which made Jackson wonder more about his past. For all the years they'd known each other now, he really wasn't privy to much about Maverick's roots. Something about the thought made him feel sentimental, so he reached for Maverick's hand, which he promptly yanked away.

Jackson's stomach sank, and Maverick must've detected something a little more wounded than usual because, in a moment of rare consideration, he hesitantly gave the hand back. Jackson looked at him with surprise. Maverick squeezed his thin lips together, rubbing his fingers along the skin atop Jackson's hand. Jackson grasped onto him then, swallowing and feeling like he might cry from the small gesture. It was already so rare, even though their relationship was rather young. It was a relief to hold each other's hands, and it made the drive to the venue just a little bit more bearable.

Upon arrival, it was fairly calm and quiet. The volume quickly grew, of course, as families trickled in. Maverick and Jackson sat beside one another at a tremendous, long table. Maverick's family sat nearby, his sister serving as a buffer between disappointed parents and wayward son. A few other families Jackson wasn't acquainted with, but clearly knew Maverick's, arrived. An abundance of small talk ensued. The first person Jackson recognized was Julia, alone, which was strange. Soon after, a group sat down and started inquiring about the whereabouts of Chris, which Jackson assumed was the one belonging to Nathan. Enough time passed, however, that Jackson and Maverick started to think they were in the clear when it came to those two. It wasn't until the Donahue Dad arrived with another family that Maverick grumbled.

"Shit..." he ducked his head down.

"What?" Jackson asked, leaning close and eyeing the people who'd just come.

"That's Nathan's family and Chris's dad."

Jackson raised his eyes and took in the sight. It was obvious who Chris's father was. His son was the spitting image of him. He wasn't sure what happened to the mother, but it didn't seem like one was there. Nathan's family was fascinating to Jackson. He'd never met them before, and he was a little taken aback while he watched them settle. Unlike Chris, Nathan wasn't a dead ringer for his father. Instead, his face bore a much stronger resemblance to his mom. He also had a couple of teenaged brothers. They looked like twins, and more strongly took after the father.

While Jackson got caught up in Nathan's family and their resemblances, he completely missed it when Nathan actually arrived, side by side with Chris. It wasn't until Maverick's family started making a big fuss over Nathan that he finally noticed. They leapt up to hug him and fret about how long it'd been since they'd seen him. He sheepishly accepted the affection, knowing damn well they were oblivious to the painful drama that had played out between him and their son during recent weeks. They insisted he sit down beside them. Nathan and Chris settled diagonally across from Jackson and Maverick, just beside Julia. The families were cozy and close. Jackson kept his eyes down on the table, fearful to even so much as glance at Nathan. He didn't want to set off a fight worse than he and Mav were already poised to have. Maverick, on the other hand, stared at Nathan and Chris without any reservation. Nathan did his best to focus on Julia. Chris openly, calmly stared back at Maverick. Jackson could see there was a storm quietly brewing between them, and he hoped it stayed far away from Nathan and himself. While Chris was staring, he was also listening in on the conversation between Julia and Nathan.

"Where's Ginny?"

Chris glanced over, taking in the sight of her. She didn't look well, not at all.

"She left me," she quietly answered, her voice low and shaking.

"What? Oh my God…why?" Nathan whispered, grasping her arm.

Julia shook her head, "I'll tell you about it later. Let's just try and have a nice meal."

Nathan looked up, realizing her parents were right there. She clearly didn't want to talk about it in front of them. He felt sick. He could tell it was something major by the way she was carrying herself. He sat back and did his best to respect her space and ignore it for now. Dinner, miraculously, went by fast, awkward moments and all. They ordered their food, and Nathan covertly held hands with Chris beneath the table because he hadn't come out yet. He was dressed like a typical man at the moment, and he'd been doing his best to hide the paint on his nails. His mother had noticed at one point, but said nothing. Thankfully, his brothers and father were oblivious.

Despite the situation, having Maverick and Jackson right there and Julia in obvious distress, the night went off mostly without a hitch. They ate their meals and answered a lot of eager questions from their families. They laughed and joked, and took great care to avoid directly engaging Jackson or Maverick. It wasn't until dessert when Julia abruptly left the table that anything felt off. Nathan knew something serious was wrong. He excused himself and went after her. Chris did the same, only going after him. Nathan followed Julia all the way to the restrooms then waited patiently for her to come out. Chris leaned against the wall beside him and they exchanged hesitant glances. When Julia finally emerged, she held up her hand and wiped her mouth.

"Don't ask me. I'll tell you."

Nathan eyed her. Chris did, too. She drew in a shaky breath, a sorrowful expression resting on her pretty face while she explained.

"Ginny left me because I'm pregnant," she kept her eyes locked on Nathan, "It's yours. You're the only man I've been with."

Nathan's stomach just about hit the floor. His eyes were wide and his mouth was hanging open. He felt unwell and unstable. He felt absolutely terrified.

"I thought you were on birth control...?"

"I was, I just...I missed a few pills because I was so overwhelmed with studying for finals and everything. It happened so fast, you know? We never had sex like that, so I didn't really think about it, and then we just did, and I guess I got caught up in the moment

180

and...Oh, God...I'm so stupid...I'm so, so stupid..." she started to sob.

Nathan softened and pulled her close, holding her and shushing her.

"No, you're not...you're not...I am. Julia, I'm so sorry. This is my fault."

He held her and rubbed her back while she cried as quietly as she could manage. She didn't let herself carry on for long. She couldn't. It wasn't the time or the place for it. Once she'd settled down, she stepped away from him and spoke firmly, and for a moment it gave Nathan a glimpse of the mother she might be.

"We'll talk about this later. I haven't decided what I'm going to do yet. I expect you'll want some input..."

She was being so practical and logical. He'd always admired her ability to do that, particularly under pressure. He was driven almost entirely by his emotions most days. She was on a level all her own.

"It's not up to me," he insisted.

"No, it isn't...but, I still want to talk about it," she clarified.

He nodded. She wiped her face before nodding back.

"Okay. Later. We'll talk about this later," she said one more time before walking off and returning to the table.

Nathan dropped back and leaned against the wall, feeling kind of dazed. He looked at Chris, who instantly took his hand and held it tightly.

"Shit...are you okay?"

"I don't know," Nathan confessed, staring at the blank wall before them.

They stayed like that, holding hands and gazing out, for only a few moments. They really needed to get back to the table, so they stuffed it down and returned. They forced themselves to carry on as though everything were normal, and fine, and good. It felt like an eternity with the knowledge they had now, but the night eventually came to an end. Nathan went with his family and Chris went with his father. They spent some time with them, and once they'd departed, Nathan went straight to Chris's for the night. He was practically living there anymore. He was hardly ever at his shared place with Maverick.

When he stepped inside, Chris instantly pulled him close and held him. Nathan had no words, so he didn't offer any. Rather, he kissed Chris deep, which resulted in some time lost, distracted with sex on the living room floor. When that was through, Chris held Nathan tight, running pensive fingers up and down his back.

"What are you gonna do, Nate?"

"About Julia?"

"About everything. Your lease is up, you're not working, you might have a baby on the way. Where will you go?"

Nathan was quiet, trying desperately to locate a point of comfort.

"I don't know. I have no idea at all."

Chris smiled softly, his eyes closed while he rested his chin atop Nathan's messy hair.

"Stay here with me. I have room for you. I'm taking over the bakery now. I need someone to peddle pastries. You can do that, if you'd like. At least until you find the kind of job you're looking for. Let me help you. If Julia decides to have that baby, you're going to need to be responsible, you know? You have to have your life together. A child demands that, and Julia's going to need that from you, too."

Nathan felt anxious and sick, but also deeply moved. It was sweet, and kind, and so very thoughtful. He didn't move while he tried to sort it out. He simply rested against Chris, enjoying the way his fingers felt along his back.

"Won't that complicate things? We're trying to pull of the impossible here already, being friends who do the things we do. If I move in, what does that mean? And this stuff with Jules, it doesn't bother you? Doesn't it freak you out, the thought of me being a dad...or...whatever I'd be?"

182

Chris placed his hand against Nathan's chin and gently nudged upward. Nathan tilted his head and met Chris's eyes, an abundance of timidity clear upon his face.

"One thing at a time, beautiful," he insisted before kissing him. He pulled back and rubbed Nathan's scalp, regarding him as though he were a rare, shining gem, "You don't know what Julia's going to do, so let's just worry about what you do know for now. You know you need a place, and I've got one here waiting. You know you need some money and a job, and I can give you that, too. Let me help you. I mean, yeah, sure, maybe it makes our arrangement a little more complicated, but I'm confident we can handle it. What about you?"

Nathan's eyes wavered as he looked at Chris. He felt sick and afraid, but he also kind of wanted this. He wanted to live with Chris. He wanted that safety and security, and even if it was looking a little too far ahead, he understood the things Chris said about parenthood were true. He had to get his life together. It was time for him to finally grow up.

"Okay. I'll do it. I'll move in with you, and I'll take the job."

Chris smiled and kissed him again.

"Good, that's great…"

They settled against each other. They quietly wondered who and what they were to one another, though neither one of them could bring themselves to say it out loud. They were friends with benefits for now, the kind who lived together, and shared their lives with one another. Perhaps that meant they were something else. Nathan supposed with time he'd eventually learn what that something was.

***

While Nathan and Chris took comfort in one another, Jackson and Maverick had a very different kind of night. They'd held it in, all bottled up and concealed, until Maverick's family left them for the night. Jackson was over at Maverick's since Nathan wasn't hanging around there anymore. He'd found himself wishing he'd gone to his place, though, because at least there were roommates there. Maverick never fought him in that toxic, merciless way when there

183

were other people around. That wasn't the case tonight. Tonight, they were alone, and the full fury of Maverick came out, ugly and loud.

"I don't understand what your fixation on him is…" it began.

"I've told you, Mav, I'm sad about losing the friendship. I've told you a million times, it's not romantic, alright? I chose you…I keep choosing you over and over, why can't you just accept it and let it be? I mean, really, after tonight we'll probably never even see him again. Doesn't that make you sad? He used to be your best friend! How come you don't feel something about this?"

"I fucking do, Jack! Obviously I do, but I'm not about to sit around staring at him and whining about it! What good does that do? Does it make you feel any better when you sit around wishing things were different? Just move on already! Let him go! Put him behind you! It's what he wants, anyway."

Jackson shook his head with frustration. There was no escaping this argument. There was no way to just put it away and have a decent night. How the hell were they already this bad just a few months in? How had it deteriorated so quickly after that discussion on the patio, in a mere week's time?

"I can't just put people behind me like that. I'm not like you. It takes me some time. That doesn't mean I want him, or I'm in love with him, or whatever bullshit you've convinced yourself it is…"

"I heard you on the balcony last week! I heard the things he said to you!" Maverick suddenly shouted, his fists balled up and trembling at his sides.

Jackson shut his mouth. He sighed deeply. He shrugged and looked up at the ceiling, an enormous amount of tension filling him up.

"Maverick! Jesus, stop, alright!? I can't control what he says or how he feels! I didn't say anything to him that should make you feel scared! I heard him out and then I went straight to you! What more can I do? Huh!? You want me to rub it in his face? You want me to send him pictures of us being happy? You want me to tell him to fuck off, or that he doesn't mean anything to me at all!? What, Maverick!? *What!?*"

184

"I don't know!" he shouted, silencing them both.

Jackson stared at him expectantly. Maverick's eyes darted around the room while he struggled to bottle his temper. It looked like it was about to boil over, but then his shoulders suddenly dropped. He spoke quietly. He spoke defeated.

"I don't know."

Jackson softened at the change in his tone. Maverick easily got under his skin when he showed deference like that. It might've been manipulative, or it might've been genuine. Jackson couldn't be certain. Either way, it got him. He unfolded his arms and stepped forward. He took Maverick's hands into his own and held them while he listened.

"I'm sorry, alright?" Maverick insisted, "I am. I don't know what's wrong with me. I just..." he looked off to the side, struggling to explain his toxic, irrational feelings. He finally sighed and met Jackson's gaze in the most pathetic, seemingly resigned sort of way, "I've waited for you a long time, and sometimes it feels like this can't possibly be true. I'm afraid that I'll lose you. I'm really scared that you'll leave..."

Maverick put one of his hands over his face, deeply ashamed with how needy he truly was. Jackson gently took the hand and pulled it away. He knelt down so he was eye level with Maverick, and he spoke softly and lovingly.

"I'm not going to leave you. I love you. I love you more than anyone, you jealous moron," he grinned.

Maverick cracked a smile. He sighed and shrugged.

"Okay, I believe you."

It was true. In that moment, he did. Jackson put a hand to the side of Maverick's head, rubbing with affection.

"Then stop giving me shit, Mav," he playfully warned, still smiling.

Maverick rolled his eyes without malice.

"Alright, alright. I'm sorry."

Jackson regarded him a moment then kissed him, relieved to have escaped another fight. They had sex on the couch, and for the first time in a while, it wasn't full of loathing and hurt. It was thoughtful and patient. It was romantic. It was sweet. It was gentle.

It might've even, conceivably been safe.

Let's Stop Pretending

The following day Julia reached out to Nathan almost as soon as she'd woken up. He showered, shaved, and dressed as quickly as he could, eager to get over to her apartment so they could talk about this enormous, life-altering thing. By the time he was cleaned up, Chris was awake, sitting in bed and rubbing his eyes.

"I'm going to talk with Jules," Nathan explained, sitting beside him.

Chris's eyes instantly focused, "Okay…do you need anything?"

Nathan shook his head, "No, no. I mean, maybe when I get back, but I'm okay for now."

Chris yawned and stretched, "Okay. Let me know. I'm going by the bakery. I'll be taking it from my dad later this week, so I've got to start prepping. You want to come by and see it when you're done? I'll fill you up with coffee and sweets!"

"Yeah, okay. Text me the address. I'll come by when I'm done."

Chris nodded before they exchanged a kiss. He watched in silence while Nathan left to try and solve his problems. Once he was gone, Chris couldn't help but feel just a little bit empty and wanting. He was growing accustomed to having Nathan around, and though he realized it wasn't wise to acknowledge or indulge the emotions stirring in his heart, he really couldn't do much to stop. He was in the beginning stages of falling, his heart dangerously close to beating for only this one, beautiful person. He sighed and did his best to let those emotions go while he lazed about the apartment. He brewed some coffee and took a few hits of his vape while he waited.

Once he was pleasantly high, he mixed up some batter and started frying pancakes. He poured coffee and sipped, then devoured breakfast. He followed it up with a hasty shower. It was true what he'd said to Nathan about having to go to the bakery. He did, but not right away. He had a little time to kill and he also had an idea of how he planned to spend it. Nathan needed a little nudge in the right direction, and today Chris was going to provide that. He finished up his shower, dressed nicely, and hopped into his car toward his destination. He felt a little nervous, but he was confident it was the right thing to do.

***

While Chris got started on his little venture, Nathan made for Julia's. She texted him along the way asking him to buy her some salt and vinegar chips, which he happily obliged. He swung by a gas station, grabbed a family sized bag as well as a coffee and pastry for himself. He anxiously sipped and ate while he resumed driving to her place. Upon arrival, he killed the engine and sat in restless quiet for a while. This was about to be one of the most decisive, consequential moments of his life. He needed to get centered and take some long, deep breaths. While he did, it suddenly occurred to him that he wasn't sure which scenario frightened him most. What if she kept it? What if she *didn't*? He wanted both things, and he didn't want either. He supposed he'd figure out what felt best through conversation. At least, that's what he hoped.

Once he was as collected as he figured he could be, he stepped from the vehicle and approached her front door. He knocked, promptly greeted by her exceptionally handsome, and very straight roommate. While Nathan awkwardly stumbled inside, the friendly guy informed him she was holed up in her room. Apparently, she'd only been coming out to eat and throw up. Nathan thanked him before padding over and lightly knocking on the door, that massive bag of chips comically scrunched in his free hand.

"Come in," she called.

He opened the door a small crack first, "It's me…"

He peeked inside and saw her nodding, waving him over. He let out a puff of air before stepping in and shutting the door. She was sprawled out on her bed, buried beneath a pile of covers and nuzzled up in an impressive nest of pillows. He handed her the chips and sat in the chair beside her computer desk, only a foot or so between them.

"Thank you…God! I've been craving these *so* bad. I've been putting vinegar on *everything* but this is what I wanted…" she explained, opening the bag with enthusiasm.

Nathan smiled awkwardly. He obviously knew women got cravings when they were in such a state, but the only woman he'd ever been around pregnant was his mother, and he was far too young to remember anything about it. Julia was the first person in his adult life to be pregnant, and it was something that felt really intimidating to him.

"Glad I could bring you something, at least," he replied.

Julia ate a few more chips before setting the bag down and wiping her hands carelessly on her pajamas. She pulled the covers back up to her neck before looking at him directly.

"I don't know what to do," she admitted, "I mean, on the one hand, I want this baby, you know? What if it's the only time I ever get pregnant? What if this is my one shot to be a mom? But also, *God*, I'm *just* getting started on my life here. How am I supposed to get a job if my employer knows I'm about to pop out a spawn? How will I ever afford childcare with an entry-level position? I have to work, I can't move back home...well, I *could*, but I won't. I don't want to do that."

She stopped there, her voice trailing off while she continued staring helplessly at Nathan. He wasn't sure what to say, but he cleared his throat and rolled the chair closer to her anyway. She poked one of her hands out from beneath the covers. He held it, rubbing his thumb along her skin while he spoke.

"I don't know what you should do either. I feel just as mixed up as you. Like, I kind of want you to keep it, too. Obviously I'm in the same boat...although, Chris *did* offer me a job at his bakery for now. Maybe I can do that for a while? Chris could help me with my schedule and everything. Maybe I could watch the baby while you start your career? Mine can wait...and I wanted to write a book anyway, so maybe I'll focus on that?"

Julia's eyes started to water while gave his hand a squeeze.

"You'd do that for me?"

"Of course I would. I mean, I'm not sure if keeping it is what you want, but if you do, I'm here. I'll be involved. We can raise it

189

together. I mean, we can't *be* together, obviously…I don't think that's the right thing, but we can do this as a team outside all that."

Julia's face crinkled as she started to cry. She didn't bother wiping away the tears. She just kept looking at Nathan while they did their best to move through the conversation, literally hand in hand.

"What about Chris? What does he think about all this?"

"Chris? Um…I'm not sure. I mean, I don't think he minds. He asked me to move in with him and work for him last night, so…I guess it's okay? I'm not sure it really matters. He's not my boyfriend. We're just doing the same thing you and I did, friends with benefits, you know."

Julia finally wiped her eyes. She sniffled and shook her head at him.

"You're kidding yourself. I see the way he looks at you, and I see the way you look at him. You're not just friends."

Nathan looked tripped up for a moment. She wasn't wrong, but she wasn't entirely right either.

"I don't know what we are," he admitted, "but I'm not in love with him. Not yet, anyway. I'm still deep in it with Jack. I can't even be around him, it hurts too much."

Julia sighed before taking her hand away and scooting over. She lifted the blanket, inviting him to slip inside the cozy little refuge she'd made for herself. He removed his shoes and obliged, lying on his side and pulling the covers to his chin. He rested his hand on her arm while they looked at one another.

"Look, Nathan. Jackson might have your heart right now, maybe he always will in a way, but you have to keep pushing forward. Chris is a good guy…like, a *really* good guy. Don't blow it by pretending it's nothing when it's obviously not."

Nathan eyed her before he started rubbing her arm lightly.

"Love is so weird. I've felt it before with you, and it was really intense when we were young. Then Jackson had to go and get under my skin, and now it feels like he lives there. Don't get me wrong, I

190

loved you. I still do in a lot of ways. But Jackson…like…" he stopped and tried his hardest to find the right words, "…I just know I'll never shake him. Not completely. I'll never be able to get him out of my head. It's not like it was with you. It hurts more. It makes me feel like I can hardly breathe sometimes. It feels like it's absolutely everything I have."

Julia looked sympathetic. She grabbed Nathan's arm, trying her best to reassure him with touch.

"And what about Chris?"

"I don't know yet. I feel things for him, there's no doubt about it. I think I'm falling, and I want that. It's just that I know it won't feel the same as it does with Jack. I could love Chris. I could be really, really happy with him, and it wouldn't be settling or anything like that, because he's a catch and I know it. It'd just be less is all, you know? It'd be lovely and beautiful, but Jackson's the love of my life. He's my soul mate. I know it. I feel it. I can't have him, though, and you're right. I need to move on. I know."

Julia stared at him sorrowfully.

"There's nothing wrong with loving Chris as best you can, as long as you really love him. It'd be unfair if you didn't."

Nathan nodded, "I know. I can love him. I already do, in a way. It just isn't the same."

"Maybe that's okay?"

Nathan shrugged, "Yeah. Maybe it is."

They silently regarded one another before Julia spoke again.

"I think I'd like to keep this baby. The thought of ending the pregnancy's been eating me alive. I don't think I can do it."

Nathan hugged her close and held her there. He rested his chin atop her head, realizing while he answered he was telling her the truth.

"I want you to keep it, too. I want us to have this baby together."

191

Julia clutched onto him tightly, waves of fear and excitement washing over them both. They stayed that way for a long while before deciding to relax. They put a movie on, munched on chips, and when it was all through Nathan gave her a long, heartfelt hug goodbye. Reluctantly, he left her, though they both felt more at peace. He got into his car and took off for Chris's bakery. Upon arrival, he was charmed to find Chris with a platter of cupcakes and a cup of much better coffee waiting. Nathan gave him a hug and quick kiss before Chris led him to the back of the shop. His father was there, and Nathan sat down. Chris eagerly waited for him to try his specialty cupcake.

"Oh, man…this is good…" he sighed, genuinely taken with the treat.

Chris beamed, "Eat up then!"

Nathan didn't hesitate to indulge. He watched while Chris and his father went over some business jargon while he ate. Customers started to funnel in, so Chris went out front and handled them while Richard Donahue focused on Nathan. He wasn't critical or nosy. Rather, Mr. Donahue simply expressed his excitement for the business's future in his son's capable hands. Nathan listened, eating a second cupcake even though he knew he shouldn't. He didn't really comprehend most of what Richard was saying, but he could appreciate the fact that he was proud of Chris and welcoming of whatever Nathan meant to him, too. It felt warm and kind, and it made it easy for Nathan to settle in and get comfortable. He liked Chris. He liked his father. He really enjoyed being folded into their small, sweet family.

Once the bakery's rush was through, Chris returned.

"Hey, since you're going to be working here, how do you feel about some on-the-job training? I'll show you the ropes. We can worry about your schedule and stuff later."

Nathan smiled and agreed, despite how full of chips and cupcakes he was. He glanced at Richard timidly before following Chris to the front. It moved fast, but he was competent and managed to keep up. It wasn't difficult work by any means, but it sure felt a hell of a lot better than working at that god-forsaken weenie hut in the mall. This

192

was a family business, and it was run by this wonderful, handsome, stocky little man Nathan felt increasingly drawn to. It was kinder, and certainly more familiar, despite the newness. Nathan easily got lost in the work, laughing and joking with Chris all the while. Before he knew it, it was already time for them to finish. They said goodbye to Richard, and Nathan was surprised to see father and son embrace before they split. Nathan *never* hugged his father. Not ever. Chris and Richard had an intimacy to their relationship that Nathan had never known. It broke his heart in some ways. In others it made it swell. He kept it to himself, though. They got into their respective cars and drove over to Chris's place, soon to be Nathan's, too. They went inside, and as soon as they did, Nathan could tell something was up.

"What is it?" he asked, an inquisitive smile crossing his face.

"Come here," Chris insisted, motioning him to follow while he rambled, "I did a little prep for when you move in. I'm sorry I don't have a second bedroom for you, but I divided the room at least. So, check it out…I've got this big blow up mattress here. It's like a real bed, I figured you could use it if you wanted, or we could share my bed…I just wanted you to have a choice."

"Oh, that's cool, thanks."

Chris smiled, "No problem. That's not what I wanted to show you, though…Here, this is it…"

Chris walked to his closet and stood before half of it. Nathan stepped inside of the large, well organized space. It took him a moment to process, but once he did, he let out a gasp. He stepped forward, his fingers gently running along the fabrics.

"These are like what I showed you…" he marveled, taking it all in.

There were about ten sweaters hanging there, soft, oversized and in a variety of colors. Some were black and grey, some were vibrant and pastel. It was a perfect mix of feminine and masculine for his whims. As if that weren't enough, when he looked at the ground there were two pairs of lovely boots. One looked similar to Uggs, the other more sturdy for hiking, yet still with some style. They were tasteful and slightly feminine exactly like his pins. It was precisely what he'd been imagining for himself.

"I booked you an appointment, too. I hope it's not too much. I really just wanted to do something nice for you, and I know you've been afraid to do it for yourself," Chris tried to explain.

Nathan turned, a huge smile shining unlike any Chris had yet to see. It made his heart feel like it was wedged in his throat. Nathan was so fetching with all that joy on his face.

"Chris...you did this for me? This is so much...can I repay you? What appointment are you talking about? Oh...wow...I just...thank you!" he rambled, lunging forward and hugging Chris tight.

It took Chris a moment to process, but he quickly wrapped Nathan up and relished the feeling. His stomach was suddenly full of butterflies. God, it'd been a long time since someone made him feel like that.

"It's nothing. It really didn't cost as much as you'd think. I've got a friend who works over at this chill little boutique. She gave me a pretty killer discount. Anyway, you've got an appointment in about an hour to fix up your hair the way you want. I think it's long enough to do what you showed me," he said, pulling back and touching Nathan's hair.

Nathan's face softened while he looked Chris over. It only made Chris's stomach ache all the more.

"You really don't mind if this is who I am? It doesn't, like, turn you off?"

"No, Nate. It doesn't turn me off. Not at all. Um...it's pretty much the opposite, actually..." he blushed.

Nathan blinked in disbelief as Chris tried his best to shake an onslaught of emotion. He cleared his throat, slipped his hands along the skin of Nathan's waist, then gently lifted his shirt away. Nathan thought he was going to have sex with him, but he surprised when Chris pulled a light, baby blue sweater from the hanger. He tenderly slipped it over Nathan's head, and somehow the intimacy of letting Chris dress him was so much more than sex ever could've been in

194

that moment. Nathan smiled. Chris brushed some of the hair from his eyes and openly adored his appearance.

"You look great," he said softly.

Nathan blushed before wrapping his arms around Chris's neck to give him a kiss.

"Thank you. I can't tell you how much this means to me."

"You don't have to. I know."

Nathan looked like he was choking back a mountain of emotion while he slowly shook his head.

"No, you don't."

He kissed him again. He hugged Chris firmly, resting his head against his shoulder and neck. Chris clutched him, struggling to control the blossoming love in his chest. They stayed like that for a while, holding on, neither of them willing to let go. When they finally were able, they let out timid laughs. Nathan got into the hiking boots while he kept his eyes down. They left the closet and talked about lighter things for a while, as if they were dancing around something so bright they couldn't directly look. It stayed like that until the time came to go to the salon. Chris drove there, and when they arrived he behaved much the same as he had back when Nathan's nails were painted. He smooth talked the room full of women with ease. He was casual, all slung over the vacant seat by Nathan's side.

Nathan watched his own reflection intently while his hair was sculpted, ever so slightly stacked in the back, bangs swept to the side. He grinned from ear to ear when it was done, highly pleased with the person he saw looking back from the mirror, perhaps for the first time since the night Jackson kissed him. Chris wanted to pay, but Nathan wouldn't let him. He knew even with a discount Chris had spent a lot on clothes. Nathan paid for his services and then, once they were back in the car, he insisted on treating Chris to a nice dinner. They decided to go on a long, unhurried walk around the park first. They held hands and talked, and talked. They skirted the heavy things, the things that mattered, the logistics of who they were and the unfolding situation with Julia. Those conversations didn't

195

come until after meals were shared and wine was indulged. Not until they were lying in Chris's bed, taking hits from his vape and kissing to pass time.

Chris was situated on top of Nathan. He trailed his lips along the grooves of Nathan's neck, and let his hands roam the skin around his hips. He pulled away after a while, staring downward, wanting to have him and know him, too.

"What happened with you and Julia today?"

Nathan had his arms around Chris's neck while he stared at him deeply.

"We decided to keep it. Is that okay? Does that scare you?"

Chris kissed his mouth and worked his way down his neck again, whispering against anxious skin, "Nothing about you scares me, Nathan."

He tilted his head back and gave Chris his neck, closing his eyes and struggling to keep some semblance of control over his breath.

"Are you sure it's okay? I can't help but feel like I'm not quite what you bargained for?"

"What do you mean?" he asked, pulling Nathan's sweater off.

They carried on for a while, Nathan unwilling to speak until he felt sated. That sensation never came, though, and he finally gave in and grabbed Chris's cheeks, holding them firmly while he answered, "I mean me. I'm going to be a parent...I don't know if I'm a dad, or a mom, or both...I don't know if I'm ready...I'm scared, I'm different, and I understand if it's too much...I wouldn't hold it against you..."

Chris grinned with confidence, and it made Nathan's stomach roll.

"Too much for what? I'm your friend, remember?"

The words didn't hurt because Nathan knew exactly what they were doing. He wasn't telling him he was his friend. He was asking him if they were more. They were flirting with the truth of what was developing between them, deepening with every kiss, every touch, and every moment spent lost in each other's eyes.

"You're a hell of a friend, Donahue," Nathan whispered.

Chris smiled wide and kissed him. They fell into each other, the sounds of their breath, their hearts, and shared souls filling up the room. Neither of them said it out loud, but while they connected and shared what they did have to offer, they knew it. This wasn't just friendship. This was so much more than that.

Still, as time passed and things shifted, they continued to hold hands and expertly navigate only waters deep enough to hide the truth. Good moments were abundant, and awkward ones were, too. Chris was there the day Nathan went to get his things from his old place. The lease had run up, and Maverick was moving out. At first, it'd been an entirely wordless affair. Jackson, thankfully, did not attend. Maverick packed his own things, and Chris helped Nathan. Just about the time they were finished, as Chris carried the very last box toward the truck he'd borrowed from his dad, Maverick approached Nathan. He asked if he could talk to him alone, and Chris nodded before making himself scarce. Nathan stood wordlessly before Maverick, his hands deep in the pockets of his coat. He was wearing one of those sweaters Chris had gotten him, as well as the boots, with his neatly cut hair. Maverick addressed the obvious first. He wasn't sure how else he could do it.

"I see you're being open about it…that's good. I'm happy for you. It suits you," he offered.

"Thanks," Nathan replied. He meant it, but also, this moment was making him shake.

Maverick cleared his throat before deciding to just come out with it. Nathan deserved as much. Their friendship had to count for something, didn't it?

"I'm going to level with you here…I'm relieved you're going to be gone. I love you…God, Nate…I care about you so much. All of those years we were close, they were some of the best of my life. But, if I'm honest, we've grown apart, and I've been struggling with the idea of you being around Jack. He says you're not a threat, and he doesn't love you, but…" he hesitated before sighing, "…I think it's a lie, and I'm glad I don't have to worry about it anymore. It's good for all of us, you know? We can all just move on and be happier without fucking up each other's lives now."

Nathan swallowed hard. It was difficult to hear, and in a way it made him angry. He drew in a sharp breath and let it out slow. What else could he do? He wasn't about to argue with Maverick. It was senseless. It wasn't worth his time. Not now, not ever.

"Well…I'm out of your way now. He's all yours."

Maverick nodded before dropping his gaze. They stood there another uncomfortable moment before Nathan looked away, scratching his cheek briefly.

"Have a nice life, Mav," he finally said with a shrug.

He walked back to the truck. Just when he was about to get in, Maverick raised his voice. He had one last thing he wanted to say and, for once, it wasn't ugly or meant to cut.

"I heard you're going to be a dad…or, well…a parent…?"

Nathan's face softened.

"I am."

"That's really great. I'm happy for you. I think you'll be good at it."

Nathan smiled, and for a fleeting moment it was genuine.

"Thank you. I think I will, too."

They eyed each other a moment before Nathan decided to budge.

"I'm happy for you, too. I am. I hope you two manage to make it work. I hope you find some happiness. Don't take him for granted, okay? Treat him good. He deserves it, and you do, too. You both deserve the very best things."

Maverick smiled even though his gut was sour. He almost wished Nathan hadn't been nice because it reminded him of who he used to be and the things they used to share. It made it hurt. Nathan always had a way of drawing out their wounds.

"Bye, Nate," he offered solemnly.

"Bye, Mav," he said, emotionless, before getting into the passenger seat and shutting the door.

Maverick watched while Chris walked over, shooting him an uncertain glance before he took the wheel and left. Maverick watched until he couldn't see them anymore, and once they were out of sight he started to cry. He broke down heavy and hard for just a few seconds then abruptly stopped. A gust of wind blew while he wiped the snot and tears from his face. He sniffled, tightened his jaw, and left. He drove with the windows down, no music on the radio. It was like that all the way home, back to the new apartment he now shared with Jackson and no one else. There were no longer roommates, no boisterous parties or hang outs. It was just the two of them in a quiet, one bedroom place that smelled like pine and echoed because they didn't have enough furniture to stop it.

Once he'd gotten there, he paused and looked in the visor mirror, making sure it wasn't obvious he'd cried. Once he was convinced he looked normal, he hurried to the apartment and left his cares behind. He stepped inside, and it was warm. Jackson was there, unpacking his things. Maverick watched, an overwhelming, painful sensation gripping his chest. Jackson stood upright, smiled at him wide, and said hello. Maverick rushed to him then. He kissed him frantically. He leapt into Jackson's arms and wrapped his wiry legs around him. Jackson held him easily. They kissed like that for a while, then Maverick pulled back, fistfuls of Jackson's short brown hair in his hands.

"I want to marry you. I know it's fast, and it's crazy, and probably pretty stupid, but…I can't help it…it's what I want," he admitted.

Jackson blinked, his eyes wide with shock. Maverick felt nauseated while he waited for a response. Just when he felt like he should probably walk that bold statement back, Jackson spoke.

"I'm not taking your last name."

Maverick laughed, entirely too relieved to bicker about it. He kissed Jackson deep. He kissed him with love. The apartment felt full of dreams and possibility while they fell to the floor. There wasn't any fighting between them that night. In a strange, freeing way, it felt like they might just be done with that now.

***

Once all ties were broken with Jackson and Maverick, things started to fall into place for Nathan, too. Life with Chris proved relatively simple. There was a lot of joy, a lot of sex, and a lot of reassurance. Nathan found himself dressing the way he wanted, even out in public. At first he was uncomfortable, but over time it just became the regular state of his life. People were kind for the most part, even with the conservative bent of the place. The people who were the kindest were his regular customers at the bakery. Outside of the surprising support of strangers, Richard and Chris were both rocks in his life, too. He talked with them about everything in the world, and over the course of time Richard started to feel like the father he'd missed out on in youth. Things still weren't budging out of the friend-zone with Chris, at least not out loud, but their relationship was growing closer every day. About a month ticked by before plans were made for a trip to the mountains with Chris's friends Melissa, David and Craig. Nathan asked if Julia could come, which was naturally welcomed. Chris drove Nathan and Julia up together, having to stop several times along the way for her to vomit. She complained about all the ailments of her pregnancy, the intensity of the smells, the nausea and the exhaustion. Chris thought it was sweet the way Nathan indulged her gripes. He was always thoughtful when he interacted with her. Chris found the closeness of their relationship beautiful.

When they arrived at the cabin, though, Chris felt nervous. Nathan did, too. It was really the first time Nathan would be in contact with his friends since they'd started spending time together, and it felt like it was a test to be passed. Julia wasn't oblivious, of course, and she resolved to do whatever she could to help. David felt like the biggest obstacle because he was Chris's lifelong best friend. Not to mention, back in high school, Nathan and David were kind of salty, and certainly not friends. That tension apparently lingered, because when they'd first arrived David barely so much as looked at Nathan, let alone spoke to him. It was uncomfortable, but Nathan did his best to be cordial. He figured he'd thaw the ice between them by throwing himself into conversation with the others. Melissa and Craig were friendly, which was a relief. It wasn't long before the cabin felt cozy, and everyone settled in, claiming their rooms for the night.

Once sleeping quarters had been selected, plans were made to hit the touristy part of town. They walked around the very same streets Nathan had roamed with Jackson on the day he'd helped him pick out the mood ring for Maverick. They went into that store, and though it hurt some, it felt more distant than Nathan thought it might. He quickly shook it off, the reminders of the part of his heart he'd never be able to give to someone else. He held onto Chris's arm and continued trying to ingratiate himself with his friends. They ate dinner and had drinks, then made their way back to the cabin when it got dark. A propane fire was lit on the patio and everyone gathered. The conversation flowed easily, and people came and went. At some point, Nathan found himself alone with David. It was terribly awkward. Nathan considered excusing himself to the restroom to escape it, but before he could David spoke to him frankly, in a flat, careless way.

"You make Chris smile. I haven't seen him happy like this in years."

Nathan's eyes were wide, "Oh, yeah? Uh...cool...thanks."

"It's not a compliment. It's just an observation."

Nathan's face flushed. David made him so nervous. A moment passed before David shrugged.

"Anyway, it's good. I give you my blessing, or whatever. Don't hurt him, though. I'll have to kick your ass if you hurt him."

Nathan couldn't help but smile.

"I won't."

"Good."

They were quiet after that, and though the discomfort lingered, it lessened. The rest of the group made their way back out, everyone except Julia with a drink. Chris handed Nathan a glass of wine, a mixed drink in the other hand for himself. He sat down, and Nathan promptly settled into his lap. He rested against him, sipping and quietly listening to conversation. He finished his drink, and Chris did, too. They started to yawn and pretend they were tired, though they weren't. They said their goodnights and excused themselves as smoothly as they could, though they were met with a great deal of protest from their friends. They laughed it off and disappeared into their room. Nathan went to the window while Chris lit up the fireplace. Once that was done, he came up behind Nathan, wrapped him in his arms, and kissed the back of his neck.

Nathan closed his eyes and tilted his head, letting Chris's familiar lips run along his skin. He turned after a moment, interlacing his fingers behind Chris's neck, looking at him intensely. Chris was still, just staring into Nathan's eyes. He couldn't help it. His emotions got the better of him while he whispered the truth of it, unable to stop despite the vulnerability.

"I'm in love with you," he confessed.

Nathan's face was serene, "I'm in love with you, too."

Chris shut his eyes, a relieved smile crossing his face. He opened them back up and touched Nathan's cheek.

"Let's do this thing for real, then. Let's go for it, okay? I'll help you with everything. I'll help you raise the baby. I'll support you while you write your book. I'll be yours, if you'll be mine. We can buy a house, with a stupid picket fence and all that noise. We can really be something. I can tell. I know it. I know you."

Nathan's stomach ached while he drank in the sight of Chris and all of his dreams.

"You really want this? You really want me?"

"God, Nathan…I do."

Nathan leapt up to his toes and planted a clumsy kiss on Chris's mouth. Chris hugged him hard, and when they parted Nathan regarded him as a wonder.

"Okay, let's do this. Let's stop pretending we're friends."

Chris kissed him again, led him to the fire, and though they'd nearly done this a hundred times over, now that they'd finally said it out loud it felt like it was more than it'd been before. It was love that they made together that night, and even though Nathan knew he couldn't give Chris every piece of his heart, the parts that belonged to Jackson alone, over time Chris had come to occupy more of it than not. Nathan did love him. He really, truly did.

Regrets

Jackson stood before the mirror, studying the small lines that were only starting to gently etch themselves upon his forehead. He looked much the same as he had six years ago, back when they'd graduated and headed off to law school. The only indication that any time had passed were found in fine lines; that and the bruise struggling to heal beneath his eye. It made him sigh, deep and long while he looked at it. He was freshly showered, a towel around his waist. His once flat belly was starting to protrude ever-so-slightly. He'd been stress eating and, at times, drinking too much. How often he'd watched these bruises go from black to a hideous mixture of green and yellow. It'd been six years now, and though many of the incidents blurred and bled over one another, the first one was simply an event he'd never forget.

He shook his head and opened up the drawer where he kept his concealer. God. Never in a million years did he think he'd have to keep something like *that* on hand. He wasn't like Nathan. He wasn't into the feminine or the soft. He was all man, no doubt about that, but if he was going to do things like go to the office, or court, or this stupid ten year high school reunion, he needed to try and hide the injuries on his face. The bodily ones could be covered up with long sleeves, so at least that was simple.

He leaned forward. He dabbed some cover-up on his finger and gently started applying around the damaged eye. He didn't feel sorry for himself. It wasn't like he was afraid of Maverick or anything like that. The first time it'd been a shock, sure. It was especially surprising because, once Nathan had drifted from their lives, things felt really easy there for a while. It was about a year or so. They got married in the interim, only two months after their friendships ended. The wedding wasn't big or fancy. It was a courthouse, rushed sort of thing. Maverick hid it from his family for ages. That was what they'd been bickering about when it happened. Jackson was tired of being kept in the shadows. Maverick was terrified to speak the truth. Jackson had reached his limit, and it was when he walked off and grabbed his keys that Maverick flipped. Jackson wanted to go to a bar and cool off. Maverick punched him in the face so hard he fell down and saw stars.

It was a real jolt for the both of them. Jackson can still recall the way he'd stared at Maverick with wide, unbelieving eyes. He'd always known Maverick was a hot-head...but hitting him? It felt like there was no way that could be true. Yet, it was. Maverick had done it, and while Jackson laid on the floor in a daze, Maverick threw himself at his feet and started begging for forgiveness. Jackson shoved him away, grabbed his keys and left that night. He drank himself sick and slept in his car. When he returned the next morning, Maverick had clearly been awake all night. He pled for forgiveness. He promised it'd never happen again. Jackson accepted it because he felt like it wasn't possible for a guy like him to be a battered husband. He was tall. He was fit, at least back then. If he'd chosen to, he could've absolutely put Maverick in his place. It was just that he didn't have it in him to hurt him. Maverick, unfortunately, very much did.

Jackson winced, trying his best to rub in the concealer without causing too much pain. It was still tender, only a few days old now. Once he was through, he leaned back and took in the sight. It was obvious he had makeup there, so he decided to dab it all over the rest of his face. He could always pretend it was a vanity thing, like he was worried about wrinkles, not the violence on his face. Despite the many times it'd transpired between them over the last six years, Jackson still felt nothing akin to a battered spouse. He still harbored that ability to beat the shit out of Maverick if he wanted. He took comfort in the fact that he was even tempered enough to restrain those urges. In a way, he felt like it made him better than his husband. It was a dynamic he'd always been familiar with when it came to them, the struggle over who was stronger, better, braver, or smarter.

"Hey...uh...how's that going?" Maverick's voice suddenly cut through the room.

He was standing behind Jackson, a look of shame on his face. They hadn't spoken much since the incident. Usually they fell into a bout of sex right after, a tantric, confused expression of the terrible things that went on between them. This last fight was different, though. They hadn't touched at all since that blow to Jackson's face. It wasn't because the violence was any different or worse. It had to do with the reason they were fighting at all, which, with no shortage of total exasperation happened to be Nathan. The fact that he might be at the reunion tonight had opened this gaping wound, festering with the threat of infection between them for weeks. It'd blown up in their faces the other night. Jackson didn't feel like thinking over the details just then, but that was what it was. Nathan somehow, incredibly, still managed to be a pressure point in their marriage.

"It's fine. I don't think it's all that noticeable," Jackson finally answered.

He finished rubbing the cover-up over his skin and strode quickly from the counter. Maverick stayed where he was, his shoulders hunched apologetically. Jackson didn't feel like forgiving him just yet. It was the only time he felt like he had power, really; these little lulls between assaults where Maverick felt like he hated himself. That was when Jackson could breathe easier because the ball felt like it was in his court during those intervals. He relished the upper hand, and he was damn well planning to use it now, because if Nathan *was* at the reunion tonight, he was going to need it.

Jackson quickly dressed in a nice outfit, a button up, blazer, jeans and dress shoes. Maverick opted for the full-on suit, never having changed after a long day of work. The two of them exchanged no words, nor glances as they left their swanky apartment and got into an SUV they'd purchased a few months prior. They still lived on the outskirts of Boise, so the reunion at the old high school wasn't far. Maverick assumed the wheel, and Jackson kept his eyes straight while they drove. The radio wasn't on. The tension was so damn thick.

Normally, they probably wouldn't have even gone to this thing. They'd had their friends and kept in touch as they pleased. It wasn't terribly common for Idahoans to leave the state, so the connections ran deep and the community was small. They'd sort of kept in touch with Greg for a while, surprised when he moved over to Seattle and got all coked-out and cocky. He was a shady finance guy now, which didn't jive with the English degree he'd gotten at all. Long gone was the friendly nerd who'd camped with their solid crew all those years ago. Neither Maverick nor Jackson were holding their breath that he'd be there tonight.

On the other hand, it felt very likely that Nathan, Chris and his little band of friends would be there. Jackson had been almost afraid to ask Maverick if they could go when the invitation magically showed up in the mail, but the urge he felt to see them…to see *him*, was overpowering. That was what planted the first seed of their altercation, weeks upon weeks before the punch was thrown. At the time when Jackson asked, he was pleasantly surprised to be met with an eager response. Maverick, apparently, wanted to go and catch up with people. So he'd said, anyway. What he most likely wanted was to go and show off how well he was doing, which he was, no doubt. That, in fact, was another string of conflict between them.

Maverick, as it turned out, had been offered a job over in New York City. He'd won this super high-profile case, even though he was only a couple of years into his already impressive career. That was all well and good, and it wasn't that Jackson wasn't proud or excited for him, it was just that it didn't exactly bode well for his own career, not to mention his wants and desires. He was doing pretty well at work, too. He was second chair already, and there were rumblings of him making first when his aged mentor retired in just a few short years. If he were to move away, he'd lose all of that and have to start from scratch. Not to mention it'd be in a colossal city with substantial competition. Plus, there was his mother to consider. She'd gotten clean a few years back and they'd reconnected. It was tough, but things were feeling better between them now. Of course, Maverick didn't like it. He said it was because he didn't trust her, but Jackson knew the truth. What he really didn't like was the fact that she loved Jackson and cared. The fact that she might one day notice the bruises and tell Jackson he ought to leave.

Jackson dropped his eyes to his lap while unpleasant thoughts ran through his head. He didn't want to think about the fights. He didn't want to think about New York. He didn't want to feel pain in his gut over seeing Nathan like he was. It felt like he was cornered, trapped in a cage. There was no winning, not on any front. He knew in the end he'd give in to Maverick, just like he always did, in the name of a peaceful marriage. He'd sacrifice his own career. He'd continue to take punches and the empty apologies they came with. He'd never hit back. He'd never experience a love like he'd brushed up against with Nate. He'd never stand up for himself because it made him 'the better man'. He knew in that moment it didn't, though. It really just made him tired. God, he felt so exhausted and done.

While Jackson nursed his anxieties, Maverick was ruminating, too. He was stressed about the situation between his husband and himself. He always felt like he was coming out of his skin after an outburst. The guilt ate at him relentlessly, and he was always fearful that in the interim, Jackson might just wise up and leave. He knew the violence was wrong, but Jackson intentionally provoked it sometimes! Sure, it was easy as hell to point the finger at Maverick, and obviously he knew he deserved some of it, but the thing was, it wasn't as simple as all that. He wasn't an outright villain who beat his helpless, weak spouse. Jackson was strong willed, and provocative, and he knew exactly how to drive Maverick to the edge. They were toxic. They fought endlessly, then they fucked with such intensity it wrapped it all up in this disgusting package of cruelty and lust, and it was so damn far from a one-sided affair. Yeah, Maverick could be vicious and stubborn, but Jackson could be, too.

Jackson wasn't some weak, timid deer in the blinding beams of Maverick's lights. He was a bull, he was a wild animal willing to charge and knock Maverick off course at any given moment. The problem wasn't steamrolling, or an imbalance of power. It was quite the opposite, really. The core of their issues was that they could both be these awful, biting men and it manifested in ways that made things abusive. Of course, up to this point at least, neither one of them had been willing to let it go because, beneath all those layers of harshness and hostility, there was love. It was fucked up, sure, but it was still, palpably there.

God, it was *always* the same. Hell, the familiarity of it had become an aphrodisiac of sorts. Jackson would push his buttons. Maverick would get uptight and pissed. Jackson would shut down and take it until he couldn't anymore. They'd both erupt, say horrible things, and sometimes Maverick would get physical. Sometimes he'd shove Jackson to the floor, straddle him, and throw blows. Those were the moments he most lost control. Jackson would stop him, of course. He was bigger and stronger, and certainly capable of defending himself. He was always so calm in those moments. He'd just grab

208

Maverick's arms and stare at him. It'd jolt Maverick from all the red he couldn't see past. Maverick would stop and fall silent. He'd think. He'd breathe. The control would come back. Very rarely they'd give each other the silent treatment, much like they were now. More often, though, it ended with sobs, apologies, and sex that made them both feel like dying in each other's arms.

Please, don't leave me. I'm so sorry. I'll never do it again, I promise...

He'd plead while they got intimate. He'd always make the same promises, and he meant them. He did! It was just that, at some point, the wheel would turn and the cycle would start to ramp up. The aggravation and resentment would grow until one day Maverick snapped and it happened again. He'd always do it again. Rinse. Wash. Repeat. The interim was always precarious, much as it was now. Most of the time Maverick would try and make up for his wrong-doings with an over-abundance of sweetness. Jackson exploited it, of course. He would hold Maverick's transgressions squarely above his head. Jackson would take that fraught kindness and make it his own. He'd take, and he'd take, and Maverick would give, and give, and give. Things would be intimate in a desperate manner until it all fell apart again. Resentment, frustration, conflict and rage always returned like thunderstorms in spring. Tensions would rise. The wheel would turn again.

Round, and round, and round they went.

Which was another reason Maverick was so worried about tonight. He knew what he was in for. They were already on the edge again, even though it'd only been a few days. They were walking that thin line along the edge of an eruption, and it was all because tonight they'd walk into that building and Jackson would see Nathan. Maverick could see it all so clearly in his mind, the way it would play out. It was going to hurt, because even though Jackson would never say as much out loud, Maverick knew. He knew Jackson had regrets about his choices. He knew Jackson felt like he'd let the wrong person go.

They didn't acknowledge each other the entire drive to the school. They didn't hold hands, or even so much as look at one another. At some point, Maverick did turn on the radio, though Jackson hardly registered it. His mind was too caught up in his worries about New York and his eagerness to see Nathan. Naturally, when they parked, that dynamic had to shift. Maverick was always really into his image, like life was this grand performance that solely took place to impress the people in his orbit. It was important to him that he looked like the essence of success in every area of life, and so, though they were hardly feeling warm and friendly, Maverick took Jackson's hand while they walked into the school. A pretty, popular girl Maverick somewhat remembered was sitting at a table upon entry, volunteering her time. She was all smiles and joy while she checked them in and briefly caught up. Jackson felt miserable, dark and exhausted as he took his sticky name tag and slapped it against his chest. He continued holding Maverick's hand until they located a makeshift bar. They headed straight for it, letting go of each other in the process. Their thoughts were too isolated for togetherness just then.

They waited in line and collected their drinks. They found a high, round table to stand around and take stock of the room.

"There's Chris," Maverick said, tilting his chin. Jackson followed his eyes, quietly looking while Maverick mused further, "No Nathan. Maybe they split?"

There was a hint of glee behind Maverick's tone that rubbed Jackson the wrong way. Why would he want that for Nate? Hadn't they been friends? Was he really still that bent out of shape over a kiss Jackson shared with him six long years ago?

Probably.

He didn't acknowledge Maverick's bitterness. He drank his beer and watched until Chris noticed them. He must've felt their eyes. He grinned and excused himself, then walked over to Maverick and Jackson with a confident expression on his face. It made Jackson feel a little nauseous. Chris looked really good. He was shorter and smaller than Jackson was, but it suited him perfectly. He was handsome, there was no way around it, and it made Jackson think of how fetching Nathan must've found him, too.

"Hey guys! Damn, I gotta be honest, I didn't think you'd show!" he laughed, leaning against the table and setting down his beer.

"And miss all this?" Jackson quipped, gesturing around the somewhat lackluster room. It looked like preppie cheerleader had thrown up in the place.

Chris grinned, "Eh, they did their best. At least there's plenty of booze, right?"

Jackson laughed and raised his glass before taking a big drink.

"Where's Nathan?" Maverick asked, another hint of that glee from before.

"He'll be here soon. He's driving up with Jules. He's been away most of the summer on his book tour. I haven't seen him in a month! But he wanted to see the girls before he came up, and he told me to go ahead and get here so I could catch up with our buds. I see David and Craig all the time, but Melissa moved away so it's been cool."

"Oh, yeah…Julia had twins, right? I think I saw something about that on Facebook…" Maverick mentioned, clearly a little let down that Chris and Nathan were just fine.

Jackson shot him a nasty glance, which Maverick most definitely caught. He ignored it. Jackson let it go and refocused on Chris.

"Yeah, they're great. Here, I'll show you some pictures. They look exactly like Nate, it's a trip…" he pulled up a family photo on his phone and handed it over.

Jackson held onto it, regarding it while he listened to Chris telling them all about how the girls, Nancy and Alicia, had just started kindergarten. He talked some about how nice it'd been co-parenting with Julia, how close they all felt in that perfect, sweet bubble of their intertwined lives. Jackson *was* listening, but also, he was staring. The girls did look exactly like Nathan, and Nathan…God…Nathan looked gorgeous. He'd clearly embraced his identity at some point along the way. His hair was cut like a pixie, he wore a dainty golden necklace with a pretty stone around his neck, and he had a flowing cardigan over his shirt in the photo. His nails looked like they were painted, too. Jackson knew he was letting his eyes linger too long, but he didn't care. It was just such a surprise to see Nathan beaming like that, holding his children, resting against his husband. Jackson was happy for him, of course, but also…damn, it hurt more than he'd thought it would.

Maverick held out his hand and Jackson reluctantly surrendered the phone. He couldn't help but wonder what he thought. He supposed he'd shit talk Nathan later. That was usually what Mav did when he felt someone was a threat. Anyone who took any morsel of Jackson's affections away from him was fair game in that regard. Neither of them commented when Maverick handed the phone back to a proud, glowing Chris. Jackson couldn't be sure, but he did know Chris was aware of the situation that unfolded between them all those years ago. Everyone did. Did he only come over to make sure Jackson knew Nathan was off limits? Perhaps it was a mixture of both the honest and the insecure. Chris was sweet, of that Jackson was fairly certain, but he didn't seem like a pushover either. It appeared he was cognizant of the subtleties of their tense relationships, too.

Jackson found himself gazing and wondering while the rest of Chris's friends approached and settled around the table. He was quiet for the most part, drinking beer, going back and forth every time it ran out. He listened while the conversation easily flowed, there was so much to catch up on, even Maverick was chiming in. Another beer was had, and then another. Jackson *almost* forgot about his troubles, and it seemed for a moment that Maverick did, too. They both softened and started to enjoy the goodness of conversation with friends past. It happened, then.

Chris's eyes lit up as he looked across the room. Jackson noticed, following his gaze. It felt like slow motion as he took in the sight of Nathan, in the flesh, for the very first time in just over six years. He was even more stunning than he'd been in the photograph. He was wearing a black sweater with some lace along the collar bones, skinny jeans and boots. He had on the same necklace from the photograph, with bright red nails and the same pretty haircut. He broke out in a charming, gorgeous smile before picking up the pace and sprinting toward Chris. They embraced and kissed with enough passion to make it obvious they'd not seen each other for some time.

When they separated, they regarded each other fondly, completely oblivious to the rest of the world.

"How was it!? A success!?" Chris asked, touching the sides of Nathan's head.

"It was amazing, I mean…like…wow, I've got *so* much to tell you…" he let out a laugh.

Chris put his arm around him and led him to the table. Julia followed and exchanged warm hellos with Chris. The two of them fell into conversation while the group situated around the table. Nathan's eyes met Jackson's then, and if Jackson wasn't mistaken, they briefly faltered. Nathan collected himself quickly, though. He offered a reserved smile before shifting his gaze toward Maverick and doing the same. Chris excused himself to get Nathan and Julia glasses of wine. It was awkward, no doubt, but having other friends there eased it some.

"Hey, guys," Nathan said, kicking off the dreaded conversation.

"Hey…so, book tour, huh?" Maverick acknowledged.

Nathan smiled with more brightness, "Yeah! Who knew people would care about the memoirs of a nobody?"

Maverick shook his head, "Well, you're somebody now! I've seen your book on the promo tables in the mall. It's pretty crazy."

"Yeah, it's wild. Have you read it?" Nathan asked, a bit nervous.

"I will when I have some time. Work's been killer. I just got offered a job over in New York. I haven' t accepted it yet, but, you know…we're considering it," Maverick shifted gears, clearly not wanting to admit he had no intention of reading his former best friend's book.

"Oh, wow! New York!" Julia commented.

Maverick grinned, conspicuously eager to brag. He carried on for a while about the case he'd won, a long shot of an ordeal. It was his favorite thing to talk about, and it left Jackson more than a little checked out. He openly stared at Nathan, in fact, while his husband droned on and on about his success. Nathan felt it, and he looked at

213

Jackson, too. They both stared and stared. Jackson couldn't help it, the words just came falling from his mouth, despite the fact that the subject had been expertly changed.

"I read it."

Chris arrived and handed Nathan and Julia their drinks. He wedged himself between Nathan and David, on the opposite side. Nathan looked anxious while he took a sip of wine. He swallowed it down and continued locking eyes with Jackson.

"What'd you think? I'm sorry, I know I wrote a little about you…"

A little?

Jackson's face was serious and forlorn while he considered it. He'd loved the book. It was beautifully written and he'd devoured it in a day. He kept it in his briefcase, tucked away where Maverick wouldn't be able to find it. It was entitled '*Becoming Me*' and it was all about the ways Nathan had come to terms with his sexuality and gender identity over the course of his life. It was pretty and conversational, and it tore at Jackson's heart. The chapters that dealt with him naturally stung. Nathan had described it painstakingly, the way it'd felt to fall for Jackson, how he grappled with his doubts about what role his gender might've played in those events. He wrote tenderly about the days he'd spent falling in love with Chris, healing his heart, moving on and being okay with who he was. There weren't really any adequate words to describe it, but Jackson did his best to respond honestly.

"Your prose was beautiful, and the story was hard to put down. It's okay. I was a part of it, there wasn't really any way you could've left that stuff out."

Nathan smiled and let out a relieved sigh. He linked his arm up with Chris's, showing his commitment and resolve to the relationship while he moved through conversation with the person who'd shattered his heart and arguably made his story compelling enough to share.

"Thanks, Jack. That means a lot."

Jackson tilted his head, raised his beer and took a swig. They regarded each other only a moment before they dropped the eye contact. Chris continued observing Jackson, though, and Maverick continued watching Nathan. David cleared his throat and shifted the conversation, though even with the change, it was painfully evident how fraught things were between this small group of people who'd once been considered friends. Everyone coped via drinks, and they all put in a notable effort to get through it. They talked about their jobs, their families, and the like. Most of them had kids by this point. Maverick and Jackson visibly did not, yet another festering point of tension between them.

The night wore on, and things remained cordial. Eventually, the music got cranked and dancing started. Chris took Nathan's hand and led him to the floor. The rest of the group paired off with their spouses or people of interest. Maverick and Jackson hung back, neither one of them really in the mood for it.

Jackson watched Nathan some more, taking note of how comfortable he looked in his skin. He danced with Chris, and his mannerisms were soft and muted, just the way Jackson remembered. Nathan smiled a lot more, though. He wasn't nearly as sad. It should've made Jackson happy, and in a way it did. It was nice to see him like that, clearly in love with the person he'd wound up with. Yet, still, it ached in ways Jackson wished it wouldn't.

"Here…" Maverick said miserably, handing over a beer.

Jackson hadn't even noticed he'd gone to get one.

"Oh, thanks."

Maverick mumbled something while he looked at Nathan, too. He was irked with how openly Jackson was staring at him. It made Maverick feel intensely jealous, and it also damaged his ego some. They were supposed to be the perfect couple at the ball. They were supposed to be the ones everyone knew were meant for each other. They were supposed to show up and dazzle everyone with just how distinctly made for each other they were. They weren't those people, though, were they? They weren't those people at all. Instead, they were two well intentioned men who did, indeed, carry a great deal of affection, but neither one knew how to love the other right. They

215

were slowly destroying each other, a daily erosion, a yearly decay. Maverick felt sickened and sad about the state of things, and it made him reach for Jackson's hand. Jackson looked at him, noticing the blatant sadness on his face.

"Can we dance?" Maverick asked, his voice more pitiful than Jackson was accustomed to.

He felt his stomach roll. He felt guilt, just the same as he remembered all those years ago. He felt remorseful for all the things he'd done, the feelings he still carried around for Nathan in the dark.

"Of course," he replied, taking his husband's hand and leading him to the floor.

He held Maverick close, resting his chin atop his head while a slow song started. Maverick didn't move away from him, not once. He simply rested against him and followed Jackson's lead, purple and blue lights shining all around them, making things look unnatural and disorienting. Jackson spotted Nathan and Chris across the room. They locked eyes again and it made Jackson want to scream. Nathan looked away. Chris said something in his ear and they smiled. They held each other's hands while they quickly left. Jackson couldn't help but wonder where they were going while he buried his face in his husband's hair.

You have to stop this. That life isn't yours. You made your decisions. You have to find a way to live with them now.

***

When Nathan's eyes met Jackson's it made his stomach hurt, too. He forced himself to look away because the tension was far too much for him to take. He didn't want this, not one bit. His life was perfect and joyful, exactly what he'd always dreamt it could be. He loved Chris, deeply, and so he tore his eyes away and focused on his husband. He touched his face lovingly while he spoke.

"I missed you."

Chris smiled wide and touched Nathan's face, too.

"And I missed you. What do you say we go make out under the bleachers? Let's have the full on high school experience, eh?"

Nathan grinned. He agreed and took Chris's hand, following him out onto the field, down beneath the bleachers. He had to admit it was fun to be pressed against the wall, fooling around like that. He'd always wanted to do something like this when he was young, but he'd never had the nerve. This was okay, though. No one was around, so the thrill of public intimacy was there without much of the risk.

"God, a month is *so* long," Chris whined.

"Entirely."

The air around them filled with the familiar sounds of love. When it was finished, they re-dressed in a hurry, giggling like teenagers. Nathan rested his back against the chilly concrete wall. It was true, a month was long. He'd missed Chris more than he could describe.

"I love you," he insisted, wrapping his arms around Chris's neck.

"Nathan, you have no idea how much I love you. Nothing compares," he grinned, and though it was playfully stated, Nathan knew it was true.

They gazed into each other's eyes, and Nathan couldn't help but notice a hint of insecurity clouding them over. His face grew sympathetic as he brushed the side of Chris's head.

"I mean it. I love you. I'm really, really happy," he reassured him, knowing all too well what was on his mind.

"You don't ever wish you'd wound up with him?" Chris asked.

It was unusual for him to be insecure like that, and it broke Nathan's heart.

"Not even for a second."

Chris broke out with his usual hearty, goofy smile.

"Thank God," he whispered, kissing Nathan again.

They carried on for some time. They felt connected, solid, and real when they took one another's hands and made their way back inside. Nathan went to the floor with Julia for a fast, silly dance. Chris grabbed a drink and somehow wound up resting against the wall watching them with Jackson. Maverick wasn't there.

"Having regrets?" Chris asked, finally addressing the elephant in the room.

The music was loud and the movement was steady all around. Jackson swallowed hard, not especially wanting to have this conversation. He was drunk and tired, though, so he found himself getting loose with his words and saying things he really knew he shouldn't.

"Yes. I am," he said, looking earnestly toward Chris. He met Jackson's gaze, a somewhat pensive expression on his face. Jackson continued, despite his obvious discomfort, "You're lucky to have someone like that. Someone who really loves you. Someone who gives a damn about what you need, not just himself, you know? Ha! Man, I fucked up so bad letting him go, and damn do I know it," he took a miserable swig of beer, staring unabashedly at Nathan.

Chris followed his eyes, resting on Nathan, too. In a way, he felt sorry for Jackson. It was true. He really did fuck up letting him go.

"Don't worry, though..." Jackson blurted, looking down at the ground. His voice was terribly sad, "I won't ever leave Mav. I'll find a way to fix it. I always do, and I have no interest in busting up your family. Your kids don't need it, and neither do you."

Chris looked back at Jackson and shrugged, "It wouldn't matter if you did, Jack."

Chris could've elaborated on it if he'd wanted. He could've rubbed it in Jackson's face, the fact that Nathan loved him and would never even consider leaving. He didn't want to pour more salt into the wound, though. He let his sympathies get the better of him, but that didn't stop the air between them from growing thick. He drank quietly beside Jackson for a moment then slipped off to the restroom. The dancing stopped and the DJ put on another slow song for the couples. Jackson scanned the room for Maverick, and when he was nowhere to be found he decided to go outside and get some fresh air.

He stepped out the front doors, the entry to the school. He felt nauseated and frustrated. The alcohol was making the world spin, and he suddenly realized how terribly he wanted to go home and get in bed. He heard the doors open up behind him as he leaned against the wall to steady himself. He took in a deep breath of cold night air, regarding the stars while they whirled around his drunken mind. He was certain Mav must've followed him, and he felt his entire body stiffen. He softened, however, when he looked beside him and saw Nathan settled against the wall instead, also gazing at the stars up above. Jackson looked upward and they stayed that way for a while, not bothering to say a word. Nathan was finally the first one to break.

"Are you okay, Jack?"

He grinned, "No. Are you?"

Nathan shifted his focus, directly looking at Jackson. He felt Nathan's eyes and forced himself to look back. They stayed like that a moment, an overt sense of pain and loss passing between them. It felt deep and endless. Nathan's voice was soft and cautious while he did his best to answer with truth.

"I am. I'm happy. I'm really sorry that you're not."

Jackson squeezed his lips together and slowly nodded.

"Yeah…me, too."

It was quiet and uncomfortable until Jackson shook it off, trying his best to lighten things. There was no need to drag Nathan down.

"You look beautiful. I know that's probably, like, the worst thing I could say to you right now, but it's true. I'm glad you're comfortable being yourself. It has to be a relief, right?"

Nathan smiled and looked at his feet.

"It feels just as good as I hoped it would back then."

Jackson let out a deep sigh, looking back at the stars with such obvious hurt on his face.

"I think about the night I kissed you all the time anymore, how it was such an important moment in both of our lives. The way everything blew apart after. When I read your book it killed me. Knowing your perspective, how different it was from mine…God, Nathan…I don't know. It hurts. I keep re-reading those passages. I keep your book in my briefcase, and I just read those paragraphs over and over, and I can't help but wonder what life might've been like if I'd made different choices…if I'd decided to share life with you."

Jackson forced himself to look at him again. Nathan did the same. There weren't any words available to make the moment feel better, or even good. It just plain hurt. Nathan looked like he had something waiting on the tip of his tongue, but before he could say anything the front doors opened and they both turned to look. Chris came out first, followed by his friends and a very drunk Maverick.

"What do you think, love?" Chris asked, walking up and interlacing his arms with Nathan's, "Should we call dad to come get us?"

He was referring to Richard, as Nathan's father was further alienated once he'd come out with who he was. His mother was tender, his brothers were understanding. It wasn't all bad or good. It was mostly just complicated, the way people are.

"Yeah, I think so. I'm getting kind of tired," Nathan agreed, contentedly resting his head on Chris's shoulder.

Chris pulled out his phone and shot off a text. Maverick stumbled over to Jackson and leaned against his chest. Jackson wrapped him up and texted Maverick's sister. She was their backup plan on the off-chance they got as drunk as they were. No one said anything else after that. Maverick simply rested against Jackson, and Nathan did the same against Chris. Maverick did eventually look at Nathan, and Nathan caught it. They eyed each other pensively, trying to figure one another out for a while. Eventually, Maverick's sister arrived to take them away. Nathan didn't look at either one of them when they left. He simply closed his eyes and waited, entirely relieved when

Richard showed up and took them both home. They went straight to their bed, plopped down and snuggled up. They relished the familiar warmth of one another's bodies. They were so very grateful to be together again.

***

When Jackson and Maverick got home they stumbled into the bedroom. Jackson helped Maverick from his shoes because he was much further gone. Jackson got himself stripped down to his boxers and settled in bed beside his husband, wrapping him in his arms and holding him. He stroked Maverick's back, just between his shoulder blades. He thought about their evening. He thought some more about Nathan.

"I know you wish you'd picked him…" Maverick whispered, drunken and lost.

Jackson didn't say anything for a while. He simply rubbed Maverick's back and thought about what he should say. He eventually pulled away and looked Maverick straight in his insecure, jealous eyes. He touched his face while he spoke in earnest.

"How about, instead of arguing about the past, we focus on the future? I'll go to New York with you, okay? Maybe it'd do us some good to get away from this place."

A look of utter shocked seized Maverick.

"You'd really do that for me? You're not just saying it?"

Jackson shook his head, "I know we've got problems. I'm not blind and I'm not daft, but I want to get through them. I love you, and I want us, so let's just get the hell out of here, okay? Idaho blows anyway. I'm over this shitty place."

Maverick kissed him happily and, for once, they didn't go through their usual routine. They didn't argue and have sloppy sex to kick off another cycle of resentment and abuse. They avoided the collision, the inevitable clash. They kissed and embraced, then started to let sleep take them.

Still, as Jackson started to fall into his dreams he felt deeply unsettled. He knew New York was just a bandage on a wound that really needed to be stitched. He also knew that he couldn't run away from his past forever, because the truth of it was, Maverick was right.

He did, indeed, wish he'd chosen Nate.

New York wasn't Jackson's scene, not by a long shot. As a boy who'd grown up in Idaho, the place felt loud, and dirty, and cramped. They'd been living there a few months now. Maverick's new employer provided them a nice place to live, and the salary he was given was more than enough to indulge in all the city had to offer. Comfort was very far from the problem. Although, truthfully, Jackson really wasn't sure what the problem was to start. Sure, he recognized some of it had to do with the way he'd blatantly given into Maverick to escape his regrets over Nathan. He wasn't too blinded by his heart to know that. The thing was, though, the time for mourning Nathan had come and gone many years ago, so why the hell was Jackson spending most of his day wallowing in bed with the shades drawn? What was making it so difficult to get out from the covers? To shower, and shave, and be the adult he knew he was more than capable of being?

Were these the fuzzy edges of depression? Jackson hadn't really known something quite like this before. He'd had days in his childhood much like this, cowering in a dark room while the ceiling fan whirred. Back then there weren't shades, but blankets tacked against the window. The light always poured through little holes in the fabric. He remembered reaching up his young, trembling hand and placing it before the light, hoping it might warm him in the winters they'd lacked heat. He never did feel warm then, and he sure as hell didn't feel warm now. New York was massive, and bustling, and disconnected. There was no rural charm in a place like this. Perhaps that was some of it. Perhaps it was all of it. He really didn't know.

He was lying in bed with melancholy when Maverick came home from work. The resentment over things was starting to boil over, no doubt. He heard the front door open, and he instinctively pulled the covers above his head. Maverick had been in on him for the last few days, putting Jackson down because he hadn't bothered to get a job. It wasn't that Jackson didn't want to. He did. He wanted to be successful, to own this town the same way Mav did. If only he could just get out of bed…

He heard Maverick's footsteps approaching. He noticed the deep, acidic pit it put into his belly. Long gone were the butterflies of the days they'd fallen in love. He felt Maverick's weight, listening while the bed creaked. He waited for an extension of comfort or understanding; a hand on the back, an 'are you okay'. But nothing like that could ever come from Maverick's thin mouth. Instead of recognizing lying in bed with the shades drawn in yesterday's clothes as something to be concerned about, Maverick only saw a bum who wouldn't budge.

"Did you get out of bed today?" he asked with a flat tone.

Jackson blinked, staring at nothing beneath the darkness of the blanket. He didn't want to say no. He didn't need to. Maverick went on to chastise him anyway.

"Did you check out the jobs I emailed you? Did you brush your teeth? Did you shower? Did you do *anything*?"

Jackson kept staring at the blanket. He didn't want to say anything because there was nothing he could say that would ever be right. If he lied, Maverick would know. If he told the truth, he'd tear him down. There was no escaping the cycle they were leaning against. He might as well save himself the energy and let it happen without all of the shouting before it. The pit in Jackson's stomach deepened as he felt Maverick's weight lift from the bed. He mentally tried to prepare himself that this was it, this was the moment Maverick would scream and shout, maybe slap or punch him if he was really in a mood. However, while Jackson tried to accept what he felt was inevitable, he was surprised when Maverick lifted the blanket. He was kneeling on the ground at eye's level and looking at him with concern. It was the first time in months, Jackson suddenly realized, that they'd actually had a moment to look in each other's eyes. It gave him some pause, and it made his heartbeat irregular and uncertain.

He drew in a small breath as Maverick sighed and ran a hand through his hair. That was it. That small, gentle gesture was enough to make Jackson crack. Up to that point, he'd just laid there, numb. At the feel of Maverick's palm against his scalp, however, he couldn't help but sob. He was horrified and embarrassed as the wails escaped. At first they were slow, but then they grew heavy and rapid. He could hardly manage to catch a breath between cries. Maverick slipped into bed with him. He held Jackson close and let him weep. Jackson clutched the fabric of Maverick's button up shirt, feeling bad that he was soaking it with tears. Maverick rubbed his back and started to talk, and Jackson did his best to listen.

"I know this isn't what you wanted. I know this has been hard, and it's been a huge sacrifice for you. I really appreciate it. I do, Jack. I couldn't have done this if you hadn't been willing to give up a hell of a lot for me. Please know that I see it. Please don't ever think I don't see you...I do."

Jackson struggled with his sobs. He wrestled with them for a while. Maverick continued rubbing his back and shushing him. With time, Jackson settled, falling into trembling breaths and unsteady hands.

"What do you see, then? Huh? Because I don't know what's going on with me. I don't know why I'm like this. I don't know why I can't just be happy with you here."

Jackson's eyes were faltering and pleading. Maverick looked surprisingly soft and in control. His voice was smooth and measured when he spoke.

"I see a person carrying a lot of loss. I'm not stupid, Jack. I know why you wanted to come here. I know you didn't only do it for me. I saw you at the reunion. I saw the way you and Nathan looked at each other. I know you came here because you needed to put more miles between you. Please, you don't have to deny it, and I'm not saying any of this to pick a fight. It's just the truth, isn't it? And I get it. You and I, we're just the same people we've always been, aren't we? I know we had all these big dreams and high hopes when all of this started, at least I know I did, but in the end you're you, and I'm me, and there's a lot of space between us. It's hard to stay close, it's hard to weather storms when you're oceans apart," he paused and his eyes faded.

Jackson felt terrified and exposed while he listened. Maverick trailed his thumb along the skin of his cheek before he swallowed and poured out the rest, his voice wavering while his emotions started to best him.

"I hate the way we fight. I hate the ways we don't understand each other, and we keep getting so much wrong. But I love you, Jack. I love you, and I love the way we keep pushing through all of these tough things. I can't imagine what it'd be like to lose you...there's just too much of you I've gotten used to in my life. I need you. Do you hear me? I *need* you. I need you like I need water, or food, or air. I don't want a life where you're not right by my side pushing me, fighting me, pulling me to all the places I could never go on my own. Life without you would be nothing, and that's simply a life I refuse to accept," he paused and eyed Jackson intently, "It's time now, okay? It's time to get out of this bed and fight for your life, for *our* lives. It's time for you to get out of this fog."

Jackson rested there a moment, letting those brutally honest words wash over him. They were wide eyed and watching each other, uncertain and terrified to say another word. Jackson eventually gave Maverick a timid kiss, then pressed his face against his chest. He let Maverick rub his back for a while, though he never did acknowledge it. He didn't say anything because, honestly, what could he? It was true. All of it. He felt exactly the same way. He felt like they were this horrible mess, fallen so short of the dream that a kiss could fizzle out their conflicts like water. Of course it didn't. They'd been young and naïve when they'd chosen one another, and they'd married so fast it left them feeling trapped, which would all be so easy to end if only they didn't still have love wedged in their stubborn hearts. It was there, though, like a knife permanently pressed between the heart and the ribs, slicing and shredding with every beat and every breath they spent tethered. As precarious as it was to hold onto what they had, what would life be if they let it all go? Would the knife fall out and leave their hearts sapped? Could they possibly go on without the steadiness of their bond? Jackson didn't know, and it was beyond clear that Maverick didn't either. While Jackson drifted into a fitful sleep that night, his eyes puffed and distressed, he couldn't help but wonder which move most threatened the rhythms of his heart: staying tangled up with Maverick's selfish, violent love, or separating from him and letting that caustic knife fall?

226

No answers came over him that night, but the following morning after Maverick had long brewed coffee and gone, Jackson got out of bed. He opened up the shades. He got onto his computer and he found himself a job.

...

Things were good for a few years after that. Time kept slipping while they got established in their careers, moving through the arduous ups and downs of their marriage. Jackson worked his way up, securing his previous position as second chair rather quickly. From there, it wasn't long before he was lead prosecutor for his district. It was a fast paced, demanding job with very long hours, but tremendous reward. He felt good about his service to the community. He wasn't entirely in control of which cases he took and did not, but for the most part he felt decent about the people they went after; the ones Jackson felt ought to be locked away.

In parallel to Jackson's success, Maverick plugged along, too. He quickly rose to prominence within the firm, and after a few demanding years he split off and founded his own. It was an exciting phase of their relationship, a time where they actually showed up for one another. It was a small, positive flash in an otherwise fraught relationship they both clung to. Though they heedlessly tried to fill up that space, to stay there and actually hold it together, their problems never managed to entirely recede. They fought long, frequently, and loudly. Maverick continued to throw tantrums and hit. Jackson never did lay a finger in response, other than sometimes holding him back, waiting for his fiery husband to stop. The cycle continued. The rises in tension, the explosions, the fallout, the pleading and the remorse. It ate at them both, slowly and insidiously. A blanket of exhaustion settled over them, and that was when another phase of their relationship moved in. Maverick got colder, and his days grew longer at work. He iced out Jackson as a method of defense at first, an escape from the rancor that stubbornly kept growing between them. It was purely accidental that beside him most nights was a beautiful assistant with a penchant for short skirts.

The nights became later. Maverick came home smelling of infidelity and perfume. Jackson grew more despondent, unable to confront Maverick because he didn't want another knock-down, drag-out fight. He knew it wasn't good, it wasn't fixing or addressing anything. He understood he likely should've brought up counseling, or at least admitted he knew what was going on. He realized this would be the totality of a relationship he'd obsessively fantasized and dreamt about in his youth. There never was a big, beautiful, celebratory wedding. There were no children in their arms. There was no house with the clichéd picket fence. All they had to show for who they were was a fancy, clean condo and the bruises on Jackson's aging body and face. It was all wrong, the way they handled one another. The ways by which they tried to protect themselves became ugly parts of who they were, widening the space they already had between them, making it that much harder to hold on. More years passed. More problems arose. Their defenses and resentments ballooned and took on a life all their own.

With age, Jackson started to yearn for the things he'd once been so certain he'd have. He wanted a family. He wanted children. He wanted that damned house with that stupid picket fence. Maverick did not. Initially, the excuse had been an establishment of their careers. Jackson accepted that because he found it prudent and fair, but eventually the time came when they were not only established, but practically stars of their own shows. It was then that Maverick was forced to outright admit he simply didn't want those things. In the wake of confession, they stayed far from the festering wounds and threatening fights, which only served to make Maverick even chillier than before. Jackson shut down, only letting himself feel anything when he was alone in the dark. He started spending too much time in the bed again. He wondered if Maverick used condoms with his girlfriend.

It was moments like that, when he was blanketed and thinking about his husband sleeping with someone else, that he was unable to avoid the crushing weight of his mistakes, his bad choices and regrets. It was times like that when thoughts of Nathan slipped in, five years, eight years, even ten years down the line. At first those thoughts and hours beneath blankets were infrequent, but eventually they came to dominate much of his time outside work. He was always alone in their posh condo anyway. It wasn't like there would be any occasion to go out. And so, ten long years after Jackson had chosen Maverick and left his opportunity with Nathan behind, he

228

found himself lying in bed all alone, wishing he'd handled every piece of his life differently. It was a painful, futile thing to indulge. He knew with all the sense he possessed it was too late, because not only was he married to an abusive, cheating, narcissistic monster, he was also thirty-eight years old, with nothing to show for the wanting of his heart. He'd squandered years upon years trying to save a love that was always doomed from the start. It crushed him, particularly on the night every piece of it fused into something both hideous and unavoidable.

It'd started out innocently enough. Maverick had returned from yet another late night at work, likely bending his assistant over a desk. Jackson was doing his best to ignore it. He ordered takeout and set it up with candlelight to try and make something pleasant of their obliterated lives. At the time, he and Maverick were fighting the same case, head to head, just like they'd joked about back when they were in college. It'd felt exciting to them then, but in real life, after all they'd been through, it only felt like another nail in a coffin that really needed to be laid to rest. The case felt really open and shut to Jackson. He knew for a fact the guy was guilty, and he was fully certain Maverick knew it, too. By that point in time, Maverick had long diverged from the idealistic dreams of his youth, the vision that he'd one day be a legal champion for the oppressed and the damned. Somewhere along the way, he'd changed course and chased after the same tired thing his father had, the very man Maverick used to rail against with nothing short of fire. Had they been younger, and things been simpler, Jackson would've teased Maverick for being such a walking, talking stereotype. However, pushing forty and on the shit end of a poorly conceived affair and unrestrained fists, he understood Maverick better than that. Jackson fully comprehended the nuance of who Maverick was. It wasn't stereotypical. Hell, it wasn't typical in any sense of the word.

No.

It was the result of a long, slow trudge from the person he'd once been into the person he now was, which Jackson did acknowledge he was an integral part of. As much as he'd wanted nothing but the best for them both, over the years they'd somehow inadvertently drawn out the worst. Long gone was the boy named Maverick who wanted to save the world. A figment of a cruel God's past was

Jackson, the charismatic youth who'd cockily attempted to push Mav into a better version of himself. All that was left now were two shells of the people that'd once been whole. Maverick was a narcissistic, self-indulgent mess. Jackson was a shadow of the confident man he knew he'd have otherwise been. It broke his heart, particularly when Maverick came home and miserably ate in silence. The tension between them practically screamed for the cut of a clichéd knife.

Jackson started it then. He prodded at Maverick. He picked that stupid fight, the one that finally drew out the truth and smashed everything they'd tried to build over the course of their stressful lives. He simply couldn't resist it, throwing the truth in Maverick's face. He just *had* to go and confront him about the case.

"You know he's guilty, right? Why the hell are you putting so much energy into his defense? A murderer like that, a fucking *child* killer, doesn't belong running loose on our streets. What happened to you, Mav? What happened to protecting the weak, defending the people in need?"

Maverick rolled his eyes.

"You don't understand, okay? You want to give him the death penalty, and yeah, okay, maybe he's a sick freak, but he doesn't deserve to die."

Jackson rolled his eyes and scoffed. He was growing so tired of this exhausting game they always played. Hell, they both were. They were both thoroughly spent. They miserably picked at their food for a while after that. Jackson wasn't exactly sure why he did it, but that was neither here nor there, because it was the thing he'd decided on that night. He wanted to push Maverick. He wanted the confrontation. He wanted to stop being so fake for once in their sorry lives.

"I know your fucking your paralegal," he said flatly, his dull eyes staring at Maverick from across a table that suddenly felt like miles.

Maverick's face barely even so much as flinched. He stared at Jackson, his eyes just as dim. It took a few tense moments before he set his fork down and responded, far more passion in his voice than his face was betraying.

"You know…you think you're better than me because you have this big 'illusion' that you're some kind of fucking savior, throwing the bad guys in prison and protecting the world, but you're not. You're just like me, don't you get that? Say what you will, but at the end of the day, we both have the same things, don't we? A decent paycheck, status, respect, people who want to wrap their legs around our waists. People know us. They wish they could be us, and I wish you'd just, for once, admit that you like it all just as much as I do. You like the person this job lets you be. You like being important. You like feeling like you matter."

Jackson shook his head with disgust, his temper finally flared, "You're kidding yourself if you think that's what I'm after!"

He rose from the table, his chair skidding violently behind him. Maverick kept sitting, watching with quiet contempt as Jackson really got drawn in.

"I'm not like you! This *isn't* what I want, it's not what I want at all! I mean, sure, yeah, okay…I wanted to be a prosecutor, and I am, and that's all fine and fuckin' dandy, but as far as this shit here between us goes!? This isn't it, Maverick! This isn't it at all! I wanted kids…I wanted a family! I wanted to stay in Idaho and be close to the land I grew up on, to my friends! But you never cared about that place, or our friends, or even me, did you!? You hardly ever visit your family, and whenever I try to see someone I care about you tell me there's no time! You don't give a fuck about anyone, Maverick! All you care about is yourself, and you know it!"

Maverick rose from his seat, tossing it back so hard it crashed and fell. Jackson could tell Maverick was about to lose it, so he braced himself. He flinched.

"Fuck you!" Maverick screamed, "Fuck you! How can you say that to me!? Do you know what it's like!?"

"What!? What, Maverick!? What's so bad about your rich, perfect life!?"

"YOU!" he finally shouted, silencing the room.

231

Jackson felt his stomach fall. Maverick did, too. They stared at each other with wide, pained eyes. Maverick's fists were balled up at his sides, but he unclenched them after a moment. Jackson watched while he stepped up close, his eyes wavering and his hands trembling.

"It's you, Jack," he said, his voice hushed and resigned.

"What are you talking about?" Jackson asked, his voice quiet now, too.

Maverick looked off to the side, blinking out tears. He wiped them away furiously before letting it all out.

"I married a person who could never love me right. I can't fault you for it, I can't…like…I'm the same. I've never been able to love you right either and I know it. Love shouldn't be violent. I shouldn't want to hit you. I shouldn't want to tear you down the way I do. It's so fucking *sick*, Jack. It's so fucked up and sick the way we are together, but we never…goddamn it, we never managed to figure it out! We've just made things worse!" he looked at Jackson pleadingly and it made his stomach hurt, "I know I'm a part of that. I know I contribute. I know I'm just as sick in this love as you are, but…the thing is…I always had eyes for you, and only you. At least…before…fuck…" he paused, unwilling to admit the fling with his assistant. Jackson quietly let it slide, unwilling to fight about it anymore, "Listen, that doesn't matter. The thing that matters is that, the way it's been for me, it was never like that for you. You regret this. You regret us. You regret *me*. Christ, Jackson, you still keep Nathan's book in your briefcase everywhere you go. I've looked at it…I see how worn the pages about you are. You loved him, and maybe it wasn't the same as the way you loved me, but I know it's true. You loved him, and you'll never be able to stop wondering what life would've been if you'd decided to spend it with him."

Jackson stood there with wide, wounded eyes. His initial instinct was to deny it, to lie. However, as he looked at Maverick's face he suddenly realized this conversation wasn't like that. This wasn't a calling to arms, a lifting of their swords. This was a dropping of their weapons. This was a sad, resigned letting go of the war they'd been waging for the bulk of their lives. This wasn't another routine bend in the road. This was the blunt, dead end of it.

"You're right," Jackson quietly said, his voice quivering.

Maverick swallowed. He was still crying some, but he didn't want to wipe his face and draw more attention to it.

"So, that's it then? We're done?" he asked.

Jackson looked down at the floor, trying to hide the tears he wasn't able to restrain, "I think we've got to be honest with ourselves for once. No matter how hard we try, no matter how much we love each other, we just don't fit. We never have, and we never will."

Maverick lowered his eyes. The room was silent while the weight of their demise started to crush them both.

"I hate that I love you," Maverick finally said, a pitiful sob escaping his lips.

"I hate that I love you, too," Jackson miserably replied.

They were quiet a while longer. Maverick put his hands on his hips and nodded before sniffling and wiping his face.

"I've got a cot in my office. We'll figure this out later. I'm tired."

Jackson kept his eyes on the ground, surprised when Maverick stepped forward and took his hands. They looked at each other. Maverick spoke, gentle and soft.

"You're free now, Jack."

Jackson stared, then shut his eyes and pressed his brows together while Maverick kissed his mouth for the very last time.

"I really did love you," Maverick futilely reminded him while he stepped back.

Jackson let out a shaky, defeated sigh, "God, Mav…did I ever love you."

A final glance was exchanged before Maverick went to their bedroom, packed up some things, and exited the condo. Jackson stood there in the quiet then started to sob. For the first time in his life, he knew for a fact that Maverick was gone. The memories of their youth flooded his brain while he cried and mourned the failures they'd wrought. All of those years spent teasing, pining and longing, the tenderness of the moments they'd shared in the early months of their relationship, the day that they'd married, the times Maverick had lifted Jackson out of his depressions and despair, the ways they'd kissed, and touched and made love…it was all gone. None of it would ever be a part of his life again.

You're free now, too, Mav. I hope you find your wings and soar.

He fell to the floor then. He cried until he had nothing left. He trudged to the bed and slid beneath the covers, acutely aware of the emptiness beside him. He touched Maverick's pillow and he wondered, *what will I do now? Who am I without you? I don't know. I don't know who I am. I don't know who I want myself to be. I don't know…I don't know…Oh, God…I don't know.*

***

The time spent between Chris and Nathan was tender and kind. The early years, just around the strange, jarring reunion, were sweet and soft. Their children were young, and the entire family's extended relationships were easy to maintain. Julia came around often, still single during that phase of their lives. She did marry later, a kind woman who folded into their family with ease. Nancy and Alicia adored their mother, and they considered their step-parents real family, too. They'd never known anything else, really. Chris and Nathan had married young, just a few short months after Julia told them about the pregnancy. The girls had a nice, warm, cozy life, exactly the kind Nathan wished he could've had growing up. He was especially grateful that he got to stay home with his daughters after the success of his book, and he made much better opportunity of it than most. There were many forts built, board games played, stuffy noses tended to and family movies watched. Chris worked relatively flexible, relaxed hours at the bakery, which brought in a decent amount of money for them, too. They were smart about their finances. They invested and saved, and what little they did spend was used on family vacations the girls could remember fondly when they were grown. There was joy. There was laughter. There was such an abundance of love.

As far as their relationship went, things were enduringly easy. Not that they didn't fight on occasion, they did. Primarily, it would happen when one or both of them got overextended. They'd been known to take out their stresses on each other when things got too tough. One particularly trying period of their lives came about when the girls got older and no longer wanted pillow fights, forts, and stories about princes and princesses falling in love. Nathan grew restless staying at home, and Chris was supportive of a career to fill the time. Nathan put out some feelers and realized he was interested in teaching. He accepted a gig at a local high school, teaching English to apathetic teens much as he'd always imagined back in the days when he was young. That, however, was when they started to clash.

Something was going on with Chris. His demeanor shifted. He was constantly exhausted. He trudged through his days as best he could, and most of the time he was able to push through and be cordial, but sometimes he snapped because he was just so run down. They bickered frequently for the better part of an entire year, mostly because Nathan was bent on the idea that Chris should see a doctor. Chris refused; it was only a bout of typical exhaustion. Perhaps he was just getting old. They were both in their thirty-fifth year of life, after all. Age was simply taking its toll on him, much as it does with everyone, so he'd said.

Until the day he collapsed at the bakery, flat upon the floor in front of everyone. An ambulance was called and he was rushed to the hospital. Nathan practically flew down the halls, thankful that his daughters were still in school. He'd been a frantic mess when they'd taken him to see Chris, and he immediately collapsed with tears of concern as he embraced his withered, worn husband. Nathan held onto his face. He kissed his cheeks and pleaded with him to let the doctors figure it out.

"It's not just getting old, Chris…it's not. Something's wrong. I know it, I *know* it," Nathan begged him through tears.

Chris wrapped him in his arms, staring at the wall and feeling sick to his stomach.

"Okay, baby...okay," he whispered while he shut his eyes, wishing so badly he could escape the harsh reality he knew was about to flatten their lives.

The diagnosis came fast after that. Stage four cancer, advanced and life threatening. It felt like an out of body experience as they sat in that office, clutching one another's hands and staring at the oncologist in disbelief. They could hardly process the information that was barreling toward them. Perhaps if he'd have come in sooner he'd have had a fighting chance, the doctor said, but he hadn't, so now they didn't. The cancer was aggressive and long progressed. It had spread to his lymph nodes and bones. It was swallowing him alive. He'd be dead within the year, and that's if they were lucky. They offered him chemo, but they practically told him it was pointless. There was no hope. They really ought to consider how they wanted to spend the rest of his time.

That night they fought. The girls were sent to stay with Julia for the night. They screamed and they sobbed. Nathan begged him to take a chance on treatment. Chris pleaded with him to try and understand. He didn't have much time left, and he didn't want to spend it sick and disabled. He wanted to be present. He wanted to be there. He wanted to experience their children. He wanted to experience Nathan while he could, too. They crashed into each other that night. They kissed and they held each other, they cried and they made love. By the time they were through the sun had started to rise, morning peaking just above the tops of the mountains they spent their lives folded inside. Nathan rested against Chris's chest and rubbed at the skin he knew he'd only get to touch for a quantified, shortened moment in time. He promised to be there for him. He promised to be supportive of his choice.

They quieted after that. They sifted through the languidly drifting ash in the air, the fallout so beautiful and calm in complicated ways. They broke the news to the girls. They held onto them while they cried. They did their best to reassure them it'd be alright. The news spread quickly to family and friends. Richard came around often to help, especially when Chris really started to deteriorate. It was fast and merciless, really. They'd hoped for this little chunk of time where they could have vacations and live their best lives, but the only thing they'd been able to manage was a weekend in the mountains over Christmas break. It was welcoming and nice, and though the sadness of Chris's death hung heavily in the air they made the best of it. The girls had fun, Nathan and Chris spent long evenings in their room, sharing their skin, their love and their need. It was the last time things felt good. After that, Chris fell apart and Richard became a fixture in the home. He, Nathan, and even the girls, who were approaching their fourteenth birthdays, stepped up. They cared for Chris around the clock, through the vomiting, the fevers, the fatigue and the searing pain. Eventually, it got to be too much. Hospice was called and pain meds were administered to help him stay comfortable on his journey to the end.

Nathan spent many hours sitting beside his bed, watching TV or reading him books. He cared for him in all the ways Chris needed, and took respite whenever the hospice nurses were there. It was like this for only three weeks, right up until the night death callously stumbled in. Nathan sat up late with him then, his girls in the room, too. They held his hands. They whispered sweet things into his ears. When Chris could really feel it, that the time was coming, he asked his daughters to step from the room. They did, and in the orange glow of beside lamps, Chris took Nathan's hand and stared at him.

"I'm so grateful for you. I'm so happy you found your way to me and took a chance on us. All those years ago, when I asked you to give us a shot, I thought for sure you'd run for the hills..." he spoke just above a whisper through the frailty of his smile.

Nathan did his best to ignore the heartbreak while he squeezed Chris's hand.

"What? Really? You thought I'd say no?"

Chris grinned, nodding slow and belabored.

"Yeah, I thought you'd say no."

Nathan looked him over, an expression of pure calamity on his face. He fussed with Chris's blankets, pulling them snug atop his chest.

"I'm glad I said yes," he whispered, running his free hand through Chris's hair.

"I'm glad you did, too."

Chris breathed a few moments before he decided to speak again.

"I love you, Nathan. Thank you for giving me a beautiful life. It's been good. It's been everything I ever wanted it to be."

A muted sob escaped Nathan's lips while he continued to run a trembling hand through Chris's hair.

"I love you, too. You were everything I ever wanted and more."

They stared a moment longer before Chris's eyes slowly closed. He released one more long, drawn out breath before his lungs completely stopped. Nathan clutched onto his now lifeless hand, struggling to wrap his head around the fact that he was empty and gone. He started to cry hard and bent forward, touching his forehead to Chris's limp hand. The girls heard and came in, crying and holding onto Nathan, hugging and kissing Chris goodbye. It felt like he was still there, and Nathan couldn't help but wonder if it was perhaps his soul lingering while they settled, shut off the lights, and left the room in a huddle.

Life felt cold to him for a while after that. The quickness of the spinning world, forgetting about Chris and forcing things to press on left Nathan feeling hollow and cracked. The body was collected. The funeral was held. People came to mourn. As genuine as it was, they all moved on so breathtakingly fast. Nathan lived in his pain, in the lonely hell that was life. The girls did, too. They struggled, they reminisced. They were wrapped up in this deep, connected, familial soreness. Years passed like that until they slowly emerged from the darkness as a trio. The girls, mature in ways they wouldn't have otherwise been, never acted out. Nathan was there for them, and they were there for him. Time marched forward, and Nathan watched with pride while his children moved into their later teen years. It felt surreal as he drew closer to forty, their sixteenth birthdays arriving so bittersweet in Chris's absence. It was there at the party, amidst cake, and music, and laughter that they told Nathan he should date. They'd told him he should be brave and look ahead, concealing the earnest message in a false wrapping of jest.

He considered it when he laid down for bed that night, his heart full of the usual blend of love and despair.

I don't know who I am without him, though. I still have no idea who I am.

He rolled over in distress and quietly let his dreams pull him in, doing his best to let go of his fears and his doubts. Chris was there. He was always waiting in Nathan's dreams. He spoke to him, updated Chris on their lives. It felt like he was whole, safe and good in those moments. When morning came, of course, the realization that it'd only been another dream hit like it always did. He trudged into the kitchen, drank his coffee without enthusiasm, and watched the snow falling outside, blanketing the world in silence and white. He opened up his phone listlessly and got onto Facebook. He typed in his name before he had much chance to think. He looked at his face, he remembered how he'd once felt as he scrolled down to see how he was, surprised when he saw he was no longer married to Maverick. His status was single. Nathan stared down at his profile while the words his daughters had playfully said echoed in his mind.

You should date, Appa. It's time for you to date.

It's Been a Long Time

Nathan resolutely pushed through another week of his life before acknowledging the idea already planted in his brain. The thought of contacting Jackson was flitting in and out of his brain consistently, yet every time he tried his best to turn it away. He'd already been hurt by him once. He was struggling enough to navigate life after loss. His emotions were complicated, and torn, and frustrated. He really just wanted the curiosity to go away.

It wouldn't, though, and by the time Friday rolled around and Julia was coming to pick up their daughters, Nathan desperately needed to talk to her about it. He asked Nancy and Alicia to hang out in their bedrooms while he spoke with their mother. They looked rattled and it dawned on him then that, in the past when he'd gotten secretive, it had been because of Chris and his illness. He was quick to promise them it was nothing like that, and with some peace of mind they went away more curious than concerned. Once the girls were out of earshot, Nathan brewed two cups of tea and sat down at the kitchen table with Julia, an inquisitive expression on her well aged face.

"What is it? Is everything alright?"

Clearly Julia was still carrying some trauma, too.

"I'm okay. No one's sick or anything like that. I've just been, well...I don't know if you overheard the girls at the party, but they really were teasing me. They told me I should date and I guess it got me thinking, yeah, it's been three years. It's probably okay to move on, right? But, you know, the thought of being with someone new is scary. I don't want to do the online dating thing again, even though it obviously worked out last time. So, anyway, I got on Facebook and, I don't know why I did this, but I looked up Jackson..."

Julia raised her eyebrows in surprise.

"Jackson Mitchell?"

He nodded.

"Yeah. I looked him up and, wouldn't you know it, he and Maverick split. He's single now, and ever since I saw that I haven't been able to put him from my mind. I really want to reach out,

240

but…I don't know, is that nuts, Jules? I mean, he just *broke* my heart when we were young. Not to mention, I have no idea what kind of person he is now. It's practically been a lifetime! Something like, what, sixteen years since we were friends? Not to mention the girls…they don't need a series of dates waltzing in and out of their lives while I try to find someone. Ugh! It just feels like so much, but I really can't stop thinking about sending him a friend request and seeing where it goes."

Julia eyed him with an unreadable expression before smiling and yanking out her phone.

"Let me take a look at him," she said, opening Facebook and searching for his name.

Nathan pulled his chair closer so he could look with her. As tempted as he'd been all week to creep a little more, he'd forced himself not to. It pulled at him too much for reliable judgment and he knew it. It felt a little better doing it with Julia, though, so he watched intently while she scrolled through Jackson's profile and properly checked him out. His bio was fairly standard. It laid out some basics, that he was the lead prosecutor for his district in New York. It listed his mother as his one and only family member, which was interesting because as far as Nathan could recall they'd never been in touch. Once they'd vetted that, they moved onto his posts. The divorce, as it turned out, was still rather fresh. They'd only been separated about six months, and the divorce itself was only finalized in recent weeks. Julia commented on that and Nathan nodded. It was definitely a check in the negative column. What if he was *still* hung up on Maverick? God, he didn't think he could take another round of that drama.

From there, they took some time perusing Jackson's photos. He hadn't yet taken down, if he ever even intended to, photos with Maverick. It was weird because, while Nathan and Julia snooped on Jackson's life, the photos really were an effective story-telling device. They moved backwards in time, so they were first encountering who Jackson was now: single, living life, and by all appearances content. There were pictures of him out with friends, though none of them were overly wild. Nathan assumed he had to demonstrate a certain level of decorum due to the nature of his job.

There were also pictures of him doing outdoorsy things, sometimes in groups, sometimes on his own. He looked like he'd put on some weight, but it was pleasant on his frame and eased the fine lines of his face.

While they kept traveling through photographic time, pictures of Maverick eventually started to show. The unhappiness was there and it was jarring. The pictures they took together looked forced, and the selfies they most often posted were after court cases they'd fought on opposing teams. There weren't hikes or outings at bars so far as Nathan could see. Not for several years. There was some happiness when he moved through the earlier phases of their relationship, but even there he detected hints of unrest. He could see there was one particular photo Jackson had posted of himself. He looked miserable with a slightly healed black eye. He didn't have a caption on it, but Nathan had a sick feeling he knew where it'd come from. He and Maverick both had such tempers, it wouldn't be surprising at all if there'd been physical abuse.

Something about the awfulness of that picture seemed to do it for them. Julia shut off the phone and looked at Nathan with uncertainty.

"So…what do you think, Jules? Am I nuts? Am I better off just leaving it alone?" he pleaded.

She sighed, "Honestly?"

He nodded, "There's no point in saying anything that isn't."

She drew in a breath, "Well…I think you're over thinking it. You're right, he did break your heart, and you definitely don't know who he is anymore, but I also know that once upon a time you told me he was the love of your life. You said he was the kind of person you don't ever get over, and look, I know, I *know* you loved Chris, but I also understand if you never fully shook off Jackson, too. I feel that way about Ginny. She was the most passionate love of my life. I don't regret any of it, Nate, don't get me wrong. I love you. I love our girls, and damn, I really love my wife…but still, sometimes when I'm sleeping I see Ginny in my dreams, and on those days…I don't know…it's like there's a cloud over my head that just won't leave. And as far as the girls go, they're sixteen. You don't have to worry about father figures or mother figures, or what-have-you. They're grown and they know who their parents are and were. Chris will always and forever be their dad. He's gone, but that doesn't mean he isn't still who he was to them, and to you. And it's okay. It's okay to move on and fall in love again, Nathan. Chris would've wanted that for you, trust me. You're still young. He wouldn't have wanted you to spend the rest of your life alone."

Nathan was quiet while he thought.

"You're right. I mean, I understand what you're saying about Ginny. It's the same for me. I hate to admit it. It makes me feel horrible, like…it sounds like I never really gave Chris my all, even though I know that's not true. I did. I gave him all of me in the best way that I could, but yeah…sometimes I would have dreams, too, and they were difficult and I felt so…*pulled*. I loved Chris. I loved him, and I still do, and I always will. I would never even think of trading the life we had together for anything, not even lost time with Jackson…but now that Chris is gone and I've been alone for so long…God, I really am thinking about him. It makes me feel guilty, though, Jules. I feel so gross and guilty."

Julia reached over and grabbed Nathan's hand.

"That's just you and your own head, hon. Chris wouldn't be upset about this. I can promise you that. Just because you're still attracted to Jackson and considering what might be possible, that doesn't make what you and Chris had any less. It's not like you secretly pined for Jackson your whole life. It wasn't like that. It was obvious you loved your husband, and it was obvious when you lost him how difficult that was. You and the girls were so broken for so long…I worried about you constantly…" she sighed, "Look, the point is, wanting Jackson now doesn't mean you wanted him when Chris was alive. There's no reason to feel guilty. It's okay to want to reach out now, and if you want my opinion, I think that if he's really on your mind that much you should. Hell, the worst thing that could happen is he'll turn you down, and would that really be so bad? Then you could finally put him to rest and move on for sure. Of course, if he says yes…who knows what you'll find? I think the benefits outweigh the risks."

Nathan pressed his lips together and looked at her.

"And you really think the girls won't mind?"

Julia laughed and sat back, taking a sip of tea before she answered.

"Nathan, they're the ones who were nagging you to date. They've talked with me about it before. They want you to be happy. They miss you having someone to laugh and share your life with. The house was warmer back when Chris was around. Don't get me wrong, they love you and they love being here, but they miss the way things felt back when you had Chris."

Nathan sat back as well, folding his arms and chewing his lip while he thought.

"Really? They feel like that? They never told *me* that."

Julia shrugged, "I'm their mother. They give me girl talk."

Nathan feigned shock, "I can have girl talk with them. Come on, I'm the parent that goes to get manicures with them!"

Julia laughed, "True! Well, maybe it's just because they're talking about you. I'm sure they worry about hurting your feelings."

"It doesn't. Actually, that really helps. Knowing they'd be okay with it makes this a lot simpler for me."

"You're going to friend request him then?"

Nathan looked at her, a wide, charming smile crossing his face.

"Yeah, I think I will."

The two of them decided to talk about other things while they finished up their tea. The girls eventually came from their rooms, groaning about being 'imprisoned' while their parents caught up. It made them laugh, realizing the time for them to wrap things up had come. Nathan said goodbye to his girls, giving them long embraces and reminding them of how much he loved them. They probably would've rolled their eyes and brushed him off, but they always accepted and said they loved him, too. Losing Chris had shaped them into rather family oriented teens. Nathan and Julia were so grateful they'd emerged from the loss intact. He hugged Julia goodbye then told her he loved her, too. He waited in the doorway, watching while they took off for the weekend. He always missed them terribly when they were gone, but the time alone also had some perks.

At first, he busied himself. He did laundry, cooked some food, and read the news on his tablet while he munched. Of course, being on his tablet meant he should probably check Facebook and see what was going on. He pretended he wasn't doing what he was, scrolling through his feed and leaving comments on friends' photographs. That occupied a good chunk of time, but once he was all caught up and out of distractions, he found himself finally looking up Jackson. He'd already scrolled through his profile with Julia, but even so, he wound up doing it again. He liked looking at the more recent pictures. He'd aged really well. His face was pleasantly lined, much like Nathan's own. He looked healthy, happy, and young for his age, but also more distinguished and refined than in youth. While he studied Jackson's photographs and life, Nathan's emotions suddenly crept up and felt stifling. It was incredible, really, the fact that merely looking at his photos could still render him breathless. His heartbeat was quickening. His stomach ached and his hands gently shook. Damn. Julia was right. He really shouldn't ignore someone who made him feel like that.

He scrolled back to the top of his profile and located the friend request button. He stared down at it for a moment, then drew in a deep breath and sent it off. He watched the screen for a moment, but quickly realized he should probably move on with his day. It could be a while before Jackson got online. He didn't want to just sit there staring with a pit in his gut.

***

The day Nathan friend requested Jackson was a busy one. It was Friday and he was on the final day of trying a very high profile case. Maverick, thank God, was not on defense this time. All that was left to accomplish were his final arguments, his ultimate, grand speech to the jury instructing them of all the reasons why this murderer belonged in prison rather than institutionalized, or worse, free. He agreed with his words, which helped, and he was a gifted man when it came to giving a convincing speech. Still, it always felt like there

245

was a lot riding on him when closing arguments came. The pressure pushed along the fringe of his nerves. He got through it, though. He gave a powerful, moving speech and then, when all was said and done, he moved out to the halls with everyone else to wait on the jury's verdict. This was when he pulled out his phone, desperate for a distraction. He saw a notification for a friend request on Facebook, and when he opened it he was shocked to see it was from none other than Nathan Donahue.

His stomach rolled and his heart raced while he stared, his mouth hanging open as a million thoughts flooded his stunned brain. So many times he'd typed in that name and attempted to look at his profile. It was private, though, and the only thing he could ever view was whatever his profile picture happened to be at the time. It'd been a few months since he'd looked, and he assumed it was still locked, but now he could accept this request and *finally* see what was really going on with Nathan. He eagerly pressed 'accept' and did just that.

The very first thing he did was check his relationship status, surprised to find it was single. He could hardly believe it! Did he and Chris divorce? He never would've thought. They'd seemed so happy at the reunion ten years ago…

He had to get to the bottom of this, so he started eagerly scrolling through posts. The photos were sweet, though he did notice selfies were more prominent in recent years. He was adorable, looking so very confident in his style and identity in a way that can only come with a good support system and age. Nathan was both masculine and feminine, sexy and cute, and he'd unsurprisingly aged beautifully. He was still one of the most stunning people Jackson had ever laid eyes on, and the little lines on his face, the ones that surrounded his eyes when he smiled, only made him hotter. It almost wasn't fair…

Jackson smiled to himself while he continued scrolling. There were lots of pictures of him with his daughters, who did still look an awful lot like him, though Jackson definitely recognized Julia in them, too. There were some pictures with Julia, and pictures of Nathan at a bakery he presumed belonged to him. The answers were pretty low about what happened with Chris until Jackson arrived at his posts from three years prior. He felt his stomach and heart sink while he read what happened:

Friends and family,

I don't even really know what to say. These last few months have been some of the most difficult of our lives, and we've kept it very private. Those who needed to know about it did, and we have had a little time to process before now. The time has come, however, to let you know that Chris has passed away. He was diagnosed with cancer a few months ago. It was aggressive and far along, and there was nothing we could do to fix it. Chris wanted to spend the time he had left living his fullest with me and the girls, so that's exactly what we did. We lived, and we loved, and we did our best to laugh when we could. It wasn't long, and we took measures to alleviate the pain. He slipped away from this world with his hand in mine, and the girls nearby, too. We got to say the things we needed to say, and I think as far as death goes, his was peaceful and he knew he was loved. If you need to ask me anything, please do. I love talking about Chris and I don't ever want to forget him.

Love you all. Thank you for your understanding and patience. Our little family is trying our best to heal.

Jackson unpredictably felt emotional while he read over the paragraph a second and third time. He couldn't believe it. Chris died? Three years ago? How did he not know this? Had he known, he would've been there for Nathan. Although, maybe that wouldn't have been the best thing. Nathan did tell Jackson he loved him. He did tell him he'd never get over him.

Jackson felt a wave of nausea while he thought about it, the poor, sorry luck of Nathan. He'd fallen in love with Jackson and been left in the coldest of ways. He'd fallen in love with Chris and then lost him to disease. How did he carry on after such things? It made Jackson feel disgusted with the nature of his own divorce. He'd made all of his choices. Everything that transpired between Maverick and himself, all of the miserable turns of his life, had been his own doing. Nathan's most painful events were entirely out of his hands. He deserved so much better than that.

Jackson bowed his head and ran a hand through his hair. He wanted to send Nathan a message right then, but before he could, it was announced that the jury had reached a verdict. He wasn't sure if that was a good thing or a bad one, but either way he needed to put the phone away and get back inside.

***

Nathan got the notification on his phone, the one letting him know that Jackson had, in fact, accepted his friend request. At first he was excited about it, but then, when no message came for hours on end, he started to second guess himself. Maybe he'd only accepted it because he didn't want to be rude? Maybe Jackson didn't want Nathan in his life? Maybe he felt awkward or uncomfortable about it?

Agh!!!

Nathan was anxiety ridden and doubtful after that. He did his best to stay distracted, though he did wish he had the girls around to help with that. Life was always a lot busier when they were around. That wasn't available to him, though, so he had to find a different way to fill the time if he was going to get through the day. He spent some more time cleaning up the house, went out to get some groceries and ran into a co-worker. They talked for thirty minutes or so. Once that was through, Nathan finished shopping, went home, and methodically put everything away before deciding to take a long, hot shower. When he got out he put on a cozy sweater and some joggers. He brewed some herbal tea and curled up on the couch to try and read a book. Normally it was one of his favorite things to do, but he was so worried about what was happening with Jackson he couldn't focus. He eventually tossed the book aside and switched on the television, settling on old sitcoms. He zoned out and watched them for a while, but then he finally heard a ding on his phone. He felt utterly ridiculous at how eagerly he picked it up, but that quickly faded when he realized he had a message waiting from Jackson.

Jackson: Hey, Nate! Sorry it took me so long to send this. I've had a hell of a day...let me tell you! Haha. Anyway, I was happy to get a friend request from you. How are you?

Nathan's stomach was instantly full of butterflies, which was absolutely unbelievable after all of this time. It felt good, though. It was nice to be excited about something, so he chose to lean into it and let his worries go.

Nathan: OMG…hi! No, it's okay! Don't be sorry :) I'm really glad you got back to me. I'm doing okay, nothing major going on. I'm alone for the weekend, my daughters are with Julia. How are you? What are you up to?

Jackson: Haha…okay, cool. Oh, same old, same old. There are always plenty of criminals to prosecute here, so I'm usually just busy with work. I had a big one today. I won, which was pretty nice lol. Anyway, I was totally creeping on your profile when I had some time earlier…looks like you work at a bakery now?

Nathan: That sounds exciting! Oh, yes. Kind of. It was Chris's. His dad bought it for him back before we got together and he took it over when we graduated college. I was teaching for a little while, but he died a few years back and I didn't want to the place torn down so I took it over. I like the work, it's pretty flexible and the money isn't bad. I'm glad I was able to keep it afloat. My father-in-law helps a lot, though. I didn't know anything about running it when everything fell apart.

Jackson: I saw that he died. I'm so sorry, Nathan. That must've been awful.

Nathan: It was. It still makes me cry sometimes, but not so much these days. It's been a few years. Time does help, at least some. What about you? I have to tell you, I creeped on your profile before I sent you a request. I saw that you're single now…?

Jackson: Oh, did you now? Lol. Yeah, I'm single. Mav and I split six months ago. Biiiiig blowout, but neither of us were all that surprised about it. The writing was on the wall. We never did get our shit together. We were always at each other's throats. I was really scared about it at first, but, honestly…? I'm happier now than I've been in more than a decade. Being single isn't so bad! Having money and power doesn't hurt in the hookup department, either! Haha. But, yeah, we're officially DIVORCED and it's one of the best things that's ever happened to me.

Nathan: Wow, well...dang! I mean, I'm sorry to hear about all that, but I'm glad you're happier now. That's a plus.

Jackson: Yeah.

Nathan sat there staring at his phone. He wasn't sure where to take the conversation from there. Jackson clearly wasn't either because the whole thing seemed to grind to a halt. Before Nathan could think of anything, however, another message came through.

Jackson: You look really good, by the way. The years have been pretty kind to you.

Nathan: You, too.

Another long pause lingered between messages. Nathan chewed his lower lip, the nerves in his stomach continuing to race.

Jackson: Well, I don't know about you, but I don't have anything going on tomorrow. Do you want to, like, video chat and have a drink? I'd love to catch up with you. I'd really like to talk.

Nathan smiled wide while he swiftly typed a response.

Nathan: Yes! I'd love that! I'll call you right now.

He quickly set down his tea. He ran to the kitchen and poured a glass of red wine. He retrieved his tablet and opened the messenger app. He clicked on the video chat icon, his stomach in knots while he waited for Jackson to pick up. When he did, Nathan's heart practically leapt up to his throat.

"Jackson...wow! Hi!" he said, a huge smile on his face.

Jackson smiled back at him, charming and confident just the way he always was, "Hey there, Nate. Damn, it's been too long!"

Content

The conversation between Nathan and Jackson had gone well. There were no awkward silences or difficult moments. Granted, they didn't exactly dive into the deep end with things, opting instead to keep it fairly light. Neither one could bring themselves to acknowledge the painful things that'd happened in the past, not so early in this fragile chance to reconnect. Even so, the conversation was nice and the door was clearly wide open for more. Both of them decided to tenuously indulge.

In the beginning, it was just the occasional message here and there. Jackson kept it going for the most part, sending memes he thought Nathan might laugh at. Eventually that blossomed into regular messages about their days. Weeks went by in that vein, until the two of them hardly ever went a day without speaking. The small, mundane moments of their regular lives became these vital things that needed to be shared. At some point Nathan requested another video chat, which naturally became a regular thing they did on the weekends the girls spent away at Julia's. All of these things were nurtured and tended, a little garden that was nourishing something beautiful beneath the surface. They were comfortable in that place, the caring and the learning, but now they were in this moment where things felt like they were wanting for something more. The holidays were already in full gear, which meant schedules were rapidly shifting and changing. Thanksgiving came and went, and Julia was spending the week with her wife's family out of state. The girls were with Nathan, and so it happened that he had them when he retreated to his bedroom for his weekend chat with Jackson. He nursed a glass of wine and spoke as quietly as he could, trying not to tip his daughters off that he was talking to someone in private.

They were nosy, though. They'd noticed it when he'd sauntered off. They'd noticed him trying to keep them at bay, and it naturally made them want to investigate. He thought he was in the clear by the time he'd gotten fifteen minutes or so into conversation, but then Nancy and Alicia opened the door and let themselves in. The twins walked over to Nathan's side and knelt down, looking at the tablet and launching into excited chatter.

"Hello, there mysterious man! Who are you that my Appa is being so secretive about!?" Nancy teased first, a look of fascination on her face.

Nathan felt his cheeks flush. Jackson looked amused, smiling and launching easily into conversation with the girls. He always had such an air of confidence about him.

"I'm Jackson…damn, you two look exactly the same! How can you tell them apart, Nathan?"

"I can tell," he insisted, looking awkwardly between his daughters and Jackson.

He felt a little busted, like a teenager trying to put one over on his parents. Since when did his daughters get so much older? Since when did he worry about what they thought of him? It was such a trip, and it definitely gave him a moment of pride.

"Jackson, like…Jackson from the book?" Alicia asked, which threw Nathan for a loop.

Jackson laughed, "Um, yes. That'd be me."

"How do you know about that?" Nathan asked with wide eyes.

"We've read your book," Nancy casually answered, as though it was the most obvious thing in the world.

"What? Who let you read that?"

"Mom," Nancy replied, refocusing her attention on Jackson, "He's cute! Look at his face, Ali!!"

Jackson laughed some more while Alicia nodded in agreement, "Very cute, not bad."

"Alright, alright…that's enough, girls. Go on, get out of here," Nathan waved his arms, shooing them away.

Jackson kept right on chuckling while they feigned irritation and listened to their parent. They left, shutting the door respectfully behind them. Jackson couldn't help but be charmed by Nathan's furiously blushing face.

"They seem spunky," he said.

"You don't know the half of it," Nathan joked before sipping his wine.

"So, uh…Appa? What is that?"

Nathan swallowed and nodded, "Oh, right…yes, that's what they call me. Um, Chris was trying to teach them to say papa and Ali came out with that. He eventually got them calling him dad, but Appa kind of stuck for me…I liked it because it felt like it was mine. It works. They've never called me anything else."

Jackson grinned, "That's sweet. I like it. I meant to ask you, sorry it took me so long, but, um…pronouns…last time I asked you were still using he…has that changed?"

Nathan's face was soft and breezy while he answered. Clearly the question was no longer new or worrisome, "Sort of. I'm pretty easy going about pronouns. The people who knew me as 'he' still call me that, but I usually introduce myself as 'they' when I meet someone knew. You can use whichever you'd like."

"What do you prefer?"

"I'd prefer they, honestly. It feels more like who I am."

Jackson nodded, "Okay then, they it is. I might slip up, I apologize in advance, but I'll get used to it."

Nathan thanked him and they shared a fond glance. They were quiet for some time before Jackson leaned forward, resting his chin in his hand. Nathan held his gaze, falling easily into the moment. They were doing this sort of thing more and more, just staring, longing and pondering.

"You know, I've got this retreat coming up. It's just a thing I go to sometimes, kind of a fancy affair. It's in San Diego. I know it's pretty last minute, but it's next weekend. Would you be interested in coming? Most of the time people bring dates to these things, and I'm not saying that necessarily, but it'd be fun to have someone to hang out with."

"Oh, yeah? That sounds interesting. Uh, I'd have to talk to Julia. She's supposed to have the girls, but I'd just need to make sure she knows I'm going out of town. But, uh, yeah…okay, yeah…I think I can do that! Why not? I haven't travelled anywhere in forever."

Jackson was practically beaming while he sat back, "Alright…great…cool."

They exchanged warm smiles and moved ahead. They wound up talking fairly late into the night. Nathan didn't come out of the room until his daughters were long asleep for some water. He stopped by the girls' bedrooms and looked in at them, marveling at his luck, before returning to his own for a pleasant night of sleep. The following day, he contacted Julia and let her know what he planned to do. She asked him about a million questions, most of which he dodged. He wanted at least *some* privacy. After all, he still wasn't sure exactly where he and Jackson stood. They were talking a lot, almost constantly in fact, but that didn't necessarily mean it was going to be anything more than the rekindling of an old friendship. He didn't want to get his hopes up for something more. He'd been through enough as it was.

Nonetheless, he made the arrangements to follow through with the trip. He bought a plane ticket and reserved a room and rental car. The week felt like one of the slowest of his life, he was so eager to actually see Jackson for the first time in more than ten years. Friday did, of course, eventually roll around. He hopped on a plane, landed in Los Angeles and proceeded to sit in traffic for an absurd amount of time before he finally reached the hotel. Despite how frayed his nerves were from travel, checking out his room more than made up for it. It was right on the beach, the door opening up just a sidewalk away from the sand. The salt in the air was nice, the sounds of the ocean were soothing, and the breeze was refreshing. He loved it right away.

Once he was settled in his room, he texted Jackson to ask how far away he was. His flight was overnight, and he'd apparently already arrived and taken a nap. Nathan's text woke him, so he asked for an hour to get ready. Nathan agreed, utilizing the time to freshen up, too. Tonight was supposed to be a bit of a soiree and he didn't want to disappoint. He showered, shaved, put on a spritz of perfume and dried his hair. He eagerly went to his suitcase and pulled out a very familiar pink sweater that thankfully still fit. He complimented it with some business slacks and nice shoes. There was one last piece he considered wearing, but decided against. He set that on the bathroom counter and walked away instead, topping off his outfit with the necklace he always wore; the one that Chris had given him shortly after their wedding day. Despite the uncertain nature of the trip, he still wanted to keep a piece of Chris close. He wanted to remember the husband he'd kept for so many years of his life, no matter the way this whole thing played out.

By the time that was through, the hour was nearly up. Nathan texted Jackson and told him he was going to be waiting in the lounge. He sat at the bar and ordered a drink, quietly sipping and doing his best to ignore the excited butterflies in his stomach. He looked around, watching all the unfamiliar people milling about. Eventually, though, his eyes landed on a memorable, carefree face. He couldn't help it as he broke out in a smile and rose to his feet, his gaze transfixed on Jackson while he approached.

"Oh my God…hi…" Nathan said with relief while the two of them embraced.

Oh, wow…

The feel of Jackson's sturdy, warm body was breathtaking. He didn't want to let him go, but out of necessity did. They separated and stepped back, surveying each other with kind, eager eyes.

"Wow, you look amazing," Jackson commented, sitting down.

"You do, too," Nathan agreed.

It was true. He did. Jackson was the definition of tall, dark and handsome, dressed in a black business suit complete with tie and watch. His hair was still thick with only a few grays sprinkled throughout.

"Do you want a drink?" Nathan asked while he took a seat, too.

"Yeah, sure."

Nathan flagged down the bartender. She approached and took Jackson's order before promptly coming back with it. He took a swig and thanked her while Nathan handed over some cash.

"Thanks," he said once she'd gone and they were alone.

"Yeah, of course."

They eyed each other, neither really sure what to say. Jackson laughed then, always one to acknowledge things.

"I guess it's a little more awkward in person, huh?"

Nathan smiled softly, "Yeah, it is."

"Well, the event starts pretty soon. Let's pregame a bit, things should get easier after that."

Nathan's grin broadened while he lifted his glass.

"So, uh...does Maverick usually come to these things?"

Jackson nodded, "Yeah, he definitely does. I'm pretty sure he'll be here."

Nathan raised his brows, "How do you think *that's* going to go? Have you seen him since you split?"

Jackson shrugged, "Who knows? I don't know. I've seen him here and there. We still cross paths on cases sometimes. We had to sign the divorce papers, too, so there was that. We don't really talk whenever we see each other. I *do* know he started dating this chick from his firm within, like, *days* of our split. I'm not an idiot, I know they had a thing going before we broke up. I knew it when it was happening, all those late nights, the way he smelled, the way he never wanted to...uh, well, you know."

"Wow...that must bother you?"

Jackson smiled and shook his head, "You know, you would think so, but it doesn't. I'm happier without him, and if he's happier without me then that's great, too. Like I said, we weren't good together."

256

Nathan eyed him, nervously messing with his fingers while he looked Jackson over.

"What is it, Nate? You look like you've got something to ask?"

Nathan hesitated before leaning in close and speaking low.

"I saw that picture of you on Facebook…the one where your eye was all black. Did he do that to you?"

"Ah…" Jackson said with a light, sad smile. He looked down at the top of the bar, using one of his hands to move a napkin back and forth, "Yeah, he did. It's not what you think, though. Well, I mean, it *is*, but it isn't. He hit me sometimes, but I wasn't like this helpless victim he wailed on all the time. I fought back…I never actually hurt him, I have enough restraint to avoid that, but he never dominated me or, you know, *abused* me like that. The physical shit happened sometimes, but it wasn't without my participation. We were toxic and we both fed it. I fucked with him, and he fucked with me…it was a cycle of retaliation and revenge all the time. So, you know, yeah, he hit me, but I hurt him in other ways. We were just a mess like that."

Nathan kept looking at him while he processed the information. He wasn't exactly sure what to say. He wasn't sure if it was some kind of victim denial, or if it truly was that mutually torturous. He supposed, frankly, it could've been both.

"I'm so sorry, Jack. I never wanted things to be that bad for you guys. I know it was really horrible when we all went our separate ways, but I never wanted that for you."

Jackson smirked like it was nothing, "Don't worry. I know."

They were silent for a while, working on their drinks while they thought.

"So, things were never like that with Chris, huh?"

Nathan looked at him, trying his best to be careful with his response.

"No…no. Neither one of us had that kind of temper. We didn't fight much."

257

Jackson swallowed and looked down at the bar, still pushing the napkin around.

"Yeah, I could tell at the reunion. You two looked really happy when you danced. He looked at you like you were the whole world."

Nathan smiled and looked down, too.

"He did look at me like that…I know."

Jackson raised his eyes to Nathan and reached over, touching his hand lightly so he'd meet his gaze.

"Did you love him like that? Were you both happy? Did you have a nice life together?"

Nathan's face betrayed the sorrow he felt in candor.

"Yeah, I did. I loved him completely. We were really happy. We had an amazing life. He was so good to my girls…well, our girls, really. He was good to me. He helped me, you know, come to terms with who I am. I know you read the book so you know that part, but, even years down the road. When I started teaching I encountered some parents who took issue with my appearance, and I told Chris I should probably just dress like a man when it came to work, and he told me to ignore it. He said I had a right to be who I was, and I had a right to exist and be seen. He told me I shouldn't censor myself just to make some crusty, conservative moms and dads feel like they'd gotten one over on me, and he was right. So, I did. I kept dressing the way I wanted and I showed up as who I am, and people calmed down after a while anyway. It worked out."

Jackson smiled and took his hand away.

"That's great, Nathan. Truly. I always wondered about you, you know?"

"I always wondered about you, too."

They regarded each other with fascination for a while. It felt tender and endless. Though, Jackson eventually snapped out of it and checked his watch.

"Welp, looks like it's about time! You ready to go mingle with a bunch of boring lawyers with me?" he asked, standing and holding out a bent arm.

Nathan laughed, stood, and laced his arm with Jackson's, "Yeah, okay, let's go."

Jackson led him away from the bar, toward the events room. They stepped inside, immediately impressed with how nice it was, decorated the way a fancy wedding might be. There were round tables with chairs and lavish table cloths. There was dim, colored lighting overhead, and a person playing live piano on stage. It was already pretty full with a cacophony of voices filling up the air.

"Come on, over here," Jackson said, leading Nathan to a makeshift bar.

They ordered some more drinks. From there, Jackson took Nathan around the room, his hand firmly pressed to the small of his back while he introduced him to people he knew along the way. Nathan was mostly quiet, listening while Jackson expertly chatted people up in the most impressively self-assured manner. He was smooth, and suave, and Nathan got the distinct feeling Jackson was showing off for him, which he didn't mind. He ate it up in fact, and once he'd gotten sufficiently liquored up he started falling into conversation, too. There were whispers he caught every so often, people leaning in and telling Jackson he'd brought a 'catch' and things of the like. It made Nathan smile, and it made Jackson do the same. After some time, there was a formal dinner served. They sat around a table full of lawyers and the conversation flowed more. Lights were dimmed and a few speeches were given. Once that was complete, they were served nice desserts and allowed to roam again.

Jackson got them each one more drink, neither of them especially interested in over doing it. They hung along the outskirts of the room, feeling like they were more alone in that space. They rested against the wall and faced one another, smiling without reserve. They were smitten and it was obvious. It gave them both warm, fuzzy feelings. It gave them both hope they hadn't felt in many years. Before they could indulge it further, however, a familiar voice caught their attention.

"Hey guys," Maverick said while he approached with a beautiful, tall brunette woman on his arm.

Nathan and Jackson straightened up, moving away from the wall.

"Oh, hey," Nathan said, looking him over, "Wow…long time no see, huh?"

Maverick nodded, "Yeah. I didn't expect to see you two here together."

Jackson didn't say anything, and Nathan found himself watching Jack's body language for cues. Was he still into Maverick? Or was it really, finally through?

"I see you and Lisa are still going strong," Jackson offered, nodding toward the brunette.

The one that he knew he'd been cheated on with.

"Yeah, uh, we're engaged actually," Maverick admitted, scratching the back of his head.

"Oh, wow…cool, congrats…" Jackson stammered.

Nathan watched Jackson before turning his attention toward Maverick, "Congratulations."

"Yeah, thanks. So, uh, you two here, like, *together* or what?"

"Uh…" Nathan looked flustered.

"We haven't talked about it," Jackson said.

Nathan let out a nervous laugh, "No, we haven't."

Maverick nodded, looking them over. His face was softer than Nathan remembered. He didn't look jealous or frustrated at all.

"Well, I'll leave you two to figure it out then. I just wanted to say hi. It felt like I'd be acting like kind of an asshole if I didn't."

Jackson smirked, "Yeah, well…you know."

Maverick rolled his eyes, but then he gazed at Jackson kindly, "You doing okay?"

Jackson nodded his head, "Yeah, I am. I'm doing just fine."

Maverick looked uncomfortable, but earnest, "Good. I'm glad. Okay, well, see you guys around. Have fun tonight."

Jackson and Nathan nodded, mumbling awkward goodbyes while Maverick took off. They looked at each other, grins slowly crossing before they burst out laughing.

"That was so uncomfortable! He didn't even introduce us to her...?" Nathan mused.

"Damn, for real. Come on, let's get out of here. I think I've had enough of all this."

Jackson took Nathan's hand and led him from the room. The two of them wandered outside to the pool. The air was a little chilly, and it made both of them fold their arms close to their chests.

"Come on, let's put our feet in the spa," Jackson suggested.

"Okay, sounds good."

They walked over and slipped from their shoes and socks. They rolled up the bottoms of their pants and sat side by side, dipping their feet and shins into the hot water.

"Aaaah, that's so nice," Nathan sighed.

Jackson nodded in agreement. The bubbles weren't on, so it wasn't loud. They could hear the ocean waves crashing in the distance. It was such a gorgeous atmosphere. It was perfect, really. They didn't say anything for quite some time, simply relishing the warmth on their feet, the salt in the air, and the rhythmic sounds of the sea. At least, they were like that until Nathan decided to talk, his voice soft and reserved.

"You broke my heart, you know."

Jackson looked down into his lap, "God, Nate...I know. I'm so sorry. It's one of the biggest regrets of my life."

Nathan smiled timidly while he looked at his lap, too. The breeze moved over them, sending little chills down their spines.

"It's okay. It worked out for me. I had a nice run with Chris. He was…" Nathan paused. Jackson looked at him, and he could see he was getting emotional. He listened quietly while Nathan tried to get his point across, whatever it was, "…He was perfect. He loved me in this really honest way. I miss it all the time. I miss *him* all the time. Losing him, it was one of the most awful moments of my entire life. I held his hand while he died…I watched the light go out of his eyes, and the breath leaving his lungs forever. His hand was still warm in mine…and it was so *strange*…"

Jackson watched while Nathan reached up and wiped his eyes.

"I've seen death, Jack. I've seen it up close. I know better than most how fleeting our time is," he looked up at Jackson then, and it made his heart skip a beat. Nathan held his gaze and leaned in, laying a hand on top of his thigh, "Life's too short, Jackson. Life is entirely too short."

Jackson reached down and took Nathan's hand, his eyes wavering while he tried to understand. Nathan gazed at him before tenderly saying, "Do you want to come to my room with me?"

There was insecurity behind those blue eyes. Jackson held them for a beat, then smiled and sighed with relief.

"I thought you'd never ask."

Nathan laughed before lacing his fingers with Jackson's.

"Come on then."

The two of them stood and grabbed their shoes. They felt butterflies at the beep of a keycard opening a roomful of possibility. The door was shut and the world was behind them. In moonlight, barely tracing outlines in the dark, they formally set their shoes on the floor. Nathan went to the window, opening it up so they could hear the ocean outside.

"Give me just a minute," Nathan said, his voice hushed while he held up a finger.

Jackson nodded and watched while Nathan headed into the bathroom. He swallowed and had a seat on the bed, trying hard to

262

ignore the steadily increasing beat of his heart. He listened to the waves crashing outside. His eyes adjusted to the dimness of the room. Within just a few moments Nathan slowly emerged. Jackson smiled as he realized what he'd done. He still had on the old pastel sweater that fell down to the middle of his thighs, but he was otherwise undressed with a familiar, floral crown decorating his head. Despite the pretty presentation it was obvious Nathan was nervous.

"Come here," Jackson quietly said, a warm, inviting expression on his face.

Nathan approached and settled in his lap, straddling him and wrapping his arms around his neck. Jackson placed his hands on Nathan's waist and stared, admiring the honest view. It was so refreshing to see Nathan owning who he was, no longer hiding or afraid as he'd been in youth.

"I never thought I'd be here with you like this," Jackson admitted.

"Neither did I."

They stayed like that another second before Jackson slid his hands beneath the sweater, along the bare skin of Nathan's back. There was hesitation in that moment. The waves of the ocean crashed to the sand and retreated. Their eyes were locked and full of uncertainty. It almost felt unreal to be there together in time and space. To be touching. To be vulnerable. To have been through so much life always wondering what could've been. Jackson moved one of his hands to caress Nathan's face. His expression grew pained as he gradually, tenuously guided his chin. They closed their eyes and kissed, slow and patient for the first time since that festival, a lifetime long past. Nathan held onto Jackson's neck with one hand and slid the other to his cheek. They parted lips and stared, both of their faces betraying how tentative it all felt.

"I'm so sorry I broke your heart," Jackson whispered.

"Just be careful with it now."

Jackson nodded and pulled him close for another kiss. They lingered in caution for some time, taking it slow with their movements. Jackson's hands eventually found the courage to roam

Nathan's very unknown body. Nathan responded, lightly grabbing fistfuls of Jackson's hair while he deepened their kiss. Their breathing picked up and urgency took over. Jackson, still worried about missteps or awkwardness, timidly grasped Nathan's hips and lovingly pressed him upon his back. Jackson settled on top and kissed him a while longer before he started to breathe out words, needing to know what was okay and what wasn't. It wasn't that Nathan was his first after Maverick. Far from it. The thing was, though, Nathan was, without a doubt, the first physical encounter that mattered. This wasn't a fling. This was someone he cared about deeply. This was someone he wanted to treat well.

"How should we do this…?"

"How do you want to?" Nathan asked, short on breath with wide, sparkling eyes.

"Well, um…I have preferences, but…Maverick rarely let me…so…you know…" he cleared his throat, feeling lost and on the spot, "I want this to be good for you…but, I definitely prefer top."

Jackson's stomach hurt, choked with insecurity. His breathing was shallow and he looked uncharacteristically vulnerable. Nathan couldn't help but be charmed. He leaned in close and started kissing Jackson's neck, speaking tantalizingly between each meeting of mouth to skin.

"Well, lucky for you, I'm not Maverick."

Jackson's confidence suddenly felt restored. He kissed Nathan with need and their bodies followed suit. They undressed, prepped, and got wrapped up intimately, faintly aware of the ocean's waves between breaths. The fervent ache in their bellies had an ebb and flow of intensity that varied throughout. They held each other tight, like they both thought they might run off. It was beautiful and fully embodied the tension that came along with sixteen years of wonder, a lifetime of boxed love. Surprising even himself, when they were finished and tangled, holding each other with belabored breaths, and salt, and understanding that can only come with hearts shared like this, Jackson buried his face into the crook of Nathan's neck and cried. It wasn't a sobbing. It wasn't sorrow. It was simply a relief to finally know this thing he'd almost obsessively wondered about for

264

year upon torturous year. *This* is what life with Nathan could be. *This* was the raw, honest sort of love he'd never known.

After a while, Nathan gently nudged Jackson away from the safe corner of his skin. He held Jackson's face in his hands and wiped the tears from his cheeks, evidence of his own shining in a trail back to his dark hair. Neither of them said a word. They didn't need to. They knew what this was. It was instinctive. It was shared. It was fully understood.

They gazed contentedly for what felt like ages, letting fingers roam the contours of each other's faces. Their breathing and hearts settled down over time. Jackson let himself fall to the side, taking his weight from Nathan and wrapping him safely in his arms. He brushed some of Nathan's hair from his face and tenderly regarded him. Nathan's eyes wavered. He didn't say anything, he just looked at him and smiled. They kissed and stayed close, resting against one another while the ocean's song came back to their attention. Jackson pulled the blankets atop them while they listened for a while.

"You're different than I remember," Jackson said.

Nathan's eyes were closed while he answered, "You are, too."

"I like this new you…it suits you, you know? Being okay with who you are."

Nathan didn't say anything, and another long silence passed. Jackson rubbed his fingers along Nathan's arm while he thought, eventually deciding to better explain what he meant.

"I always wondered and worried about you. I worried that I broke you, that you'd never be alright…but then, wouldn't you know it…I turned out to be the one who wasn't okay."

Nathan opened his eyes. He moved away, resting his head on the pillow so he could see Jackson's face. He kept his hand resting upon his chest, and Jackson grasped it, not wanting him to leave.

"What do you mean?" Nathan asked.

Jackson swallowed and gripped his hand tighter, "I mean…I was so sure of it…I was *certain* Maverick and I were this, like, written in the stars, destined to be thing. But I was wrong, Nathan. We were terrible as friends, but we were even worse as lovers. I know what I said, about me being in control or whatever when Maverick lost his mind, but…" he hesitated, glancing at Nathan anxiously, "it wasn't true. I wasn't in control. I could've hurt him…but also, I couldn't. That was never me. That's not who I am…and that's fine, but…I guess sometimes I just want to kick myself because why, *why* didn't I leave for so long? Why did I let him cheat on me for years? Why did I let him hit me? Why did I cover up the bruises, and make excuses to others and myself, you know? And then, to make it worse…I just…I always kept thinking back on that day when I kissed you and how *good* and *right* that felt…I wanted to tear the world apart when I thought about it. I wanted to tear myself apart. I meant what I said, Nathan. Walking away from you is by and large the biggest regret I've got in this life."

Nathan was full of sorrow as he reached up and rubbed his thumb along Jackson's cheek. Jackson pressed his hand over Nathan's once more, holding it firmly, not wanting the contact to retreat.

"I'm here now," Nathan whispered, not sure how else he could put it.

Jackson kept pressing his hand over Nathan's, regrettably letting another tear fall.

"I know. I think it's just going to take me a while to believe."

Nathan's face softened. He leaned in and kissed Jackson's forehead. When he pulled away he looked into his eyes and whispered, "I like this new you, too."

Jackson searched his face with confusion. Nathan smiled and explained, "You're not hiding behind your walls anymore, Jack."

He understood in an instant. He sighed and grinned, feeling a little helpless and realizing for the first time, it was okay. He pushed Nathan's hand to his lips and kissed with eyes closed. When he opened them again Nathan kissed his forehead and snuggled up close. It wasn't long before sleep started pull.

While Nathan began to drift, he couldn't help but think about the night they'd spent together, yet so very separate in the tent all those years ago. He'd been drunk and confused, and he remembered how desperately he'd wanted to lie against Jackson exactly like this. He remembered Jackson in all his false confidence and certainty about the course of the world and his life. He smiled peacefully through closed eyes while he sorted through who they were before and how they'd grown now. Nathan had been so lost, insecure and frightened in those days. It was a lifetime ago, and yet, as he laid there in Jackson's arms he couldn't help but feel like he was right back in that moment, only this time he wasn't afraid. This time, he knew who he was and what he wanted.

All of those things had somehow, miraculously, led him here to this very moment, an openly nonbinary person with a beautiful flower crown barely resting on his head; the sort of person who now had the confidence to come out of a bathroom wearing nothing but a pastel sweater and hope, offering his heart to the most elusive man he'd ever known. He was here against the steepest of odds, affectionately interwoven with Jackson, starting to make something new of a life that once felt hopelessly lost with Chris. Things were the same, and yet they were so, very different.

Jackson kissed the top of his head, and it was the last thing Nathan remembered before he fell into a deep, bewildered sleep.

When the sun rose, Jackson was the first to wake. He stirred just a bit, forgetting for a moment that he had someone keeping him company in the bed. He blinked and took stock of his surroundings, memories of the night before flooding his mind. He looked toward Nathan, listening contentedly to the waves outside while he took in the sight of his face. Though many years had passed, he was just as lovely as Jackson remembered. Perhaps even more so now that they'd gotten intimate. He felt an instant closeness, not that he hadn't before. He and Nathan were always easy going like that, naturally able to be in one another's company since the moment they'd met. It was nice to know that comfort was going to easily fold into this romantic thing it seemed they were pursuing. It was beautiful and kind, and Jackson fully relished how the kindness between them only seemed to increase with every step they carefully took. It felt so much softer with Nathan than it'd ever been with Maverick. It was quieter, yet still enthralling; it thrummed and it sang. Jackson grinned, unable to help himself as he reached out a hand and rubbed Nathan's arm. His blue eyes fluttered open and a wide, genuine smile crossed his face.

"Jack," he whispered happily.

They hugged and then kissed for a while, feeling grateful and contented to be together as they were.

"I still can't believe you're here," Jackson whispered.

"Me neither. It feels like a dream."

Jackson laughed and brushed some hair from Nathan's face. Nathan grinned with contentment before deciding to kiss him a while longer. Jackson let out a groan after some time because he really did have to get up and get ready.

"I've got a seminar thing this morning," he whined, putting his hands on Nathan's hips.

"Aw, no…really?"

Jackson nodded, looking slightly tortured, "I want to stay in bed and have another go with you so bad, but…yeah, really."

Nathan chuckled and kissed Jackson's neck, tormenting him all the more.

"What about breakfast...do you have time?"

"Yes...always! Have you seen me?" he joked, rubbing the slight belly he now sported in middle age.

Nathan bit his lip and touched Jackson's stomach, too, "I've seen you."

Jackson's face ran hot as he realized Nathan was complimenting him. It wasn't that Maverick didn't, he obviously did, but it still felt nice to hear it coming from the person he'd spent the night with.

"Alriiiiight," Nathan sighed, forcing himself to roll away, "Let's go eat."

They exchanged brief smiles before getting out of bed, both of them naked in daylight for the first time. It was a bit of a tense moment, but they moved through it. They went to the bathroom separately to kick off the day, then wound up showering together without any discussion or to do about it. They washed up, flirted, laughed and teased. It was mesmerizing how easily they were slipping into this thing together, whatever it was. They didn't want to question it. They just wanted to chase the good, so that's exactly what they did. They finished showering and dressed. Nathan got into a new outfit and Jackson got into his from the night before.

"I've got to get some clean clothes from my room," he said while they left, instantly met with the salty ocean breeze.

Nathan closed his eyes and took in a satisfying breath.

"Okay."

They took each other's hands and walked toward Jackson's room, clear on the opposite end of the hotel. It was really quiet all around because it was still relatively early, which was pleasant. Nathan followed Jackson into his room and waited while he changed. When finished, they held hands again and found their way to the restaurant. There were a few people up and at it, talking while they ate and drank juices and coffees. It was kind of a swanky little place, and Nathan felt like it was a real, proper date once they were seated beside a large window overlooking the beach. The sun was still rising and the horizon was pink and orange. It was beautiful, and while he glanced in Jackson's direction he couldn't help but think he was, too.

"This weekend's already going by too fast," Nathan lamented while they picked up their menus.

Jackson nodded, "It really is. I can't believe we've already got to go home tomorrow."

Before Nathan could respond, a waitress was beside them asking how they were and what she could get them. They ordered coffees and breakfasts, then she left them alone for a while. Nathan rested his forearms on the table and gave Jackson his full attention. Jackson leaned forward and did the same.

"What about Christmas?" he asked, trying not to sound as eager as he was.

"What do you mean?"

"I mean, could we arrange something? Can I see you?"

Nathan smiled, lifting a hand and resting his chin upon it.

"We have kind of an annual tradition. The girls and I always spend it with Julia and her wife. They come to my house and we all have a big breakfast after opening presents. We hang out in our jammies and drink hot chocolate, put on some Christmas movies, stuff like that. I can't really go anywhere, but if you want to join us I think the girls would like to meet you. They were so nosy about you on the phone…"

"You'd want that? Like…to introduce me to your daughters?" Jackson asked, a look of surprise on his face.

"Well, yeah….I mean, if you do? I don't want to, like, push this too fast or anything, but, I don't know. I mean, you and I haven't spoken in years, but I still feel like I know you. It's almost like we were never apart in a lot of ways and, you know, like I said, life is so short…what do you think? How do you feel about it?"

270

Jackson blinked and processed then broke out in a bright smile. The waitress showed up with the coffees and food, interrupting the pivotal moment. They thanked her and waited for her to leave before Nathan looked back at Jackson and waited for a response. Jackson was still smiling wide when he did.

"I would love to spend Christmas with your family. More than you know."

Nathan let out a relieved sigh and laugh, "Okay, okay…great. So, let's make it happen."

Jackson nodded before they dug into their meals. They ate quietly and somewhat rushed. They finished up and Jackson treated Nathan this time. They walked from the restaurant hand in hand, parting ways at the start of a busy hallway that led to the various conference rooms. They hugged and kissed briefly before Jackson went off for his day, groaning one last time in his reluctance to separate. Nathan blushed and laughed, watching while Jackson disappeared down the hall. Once he was out of sight, Nathan let out a shaky breath and looked around, realizing he had a good amount of time to kill.

He decided to take the morning slow and easy, starting off with a long walk on the beach. The sun had risen by then, though the air was still chilled from the perpetual breeze the ocean brought. He had a knitted cardigan on, and he wrapped it around him tighter while he wandered. He took in the sights, the sounds, and the smells. The salt of the sea stuck to his skin and made him feel centered and good. He felt exceptionally connected to the moment, taking note of the wet sand beneath his feet. His mind drifted to Chris after some time, and the familiar ache of that loss took hold. It was so physical it made him press a hand to his chest and squeeze his eyes shut. He stopped walking then, breathing through it. Things dulled out, his senses quieted down. Sound eluded him for a moment, leaving him with an intense ringing in his ears. It grew in volume then slowly faded. The sounds of his breath and his beating heart returned first, followed by the ocean's waves and the melancholy air. He opened his eyes and turned, looking out at the vast, endless sea.

He understood in that moment what was happening. He'd felt the presence of Chris before, often enough that he recognized it now. He realized Chris was getting his attention, and he supposed it must've been a letting go of sorts, perhaps even a blessing. His fingers squeezed the fabric of the cardigan while he quietly watched the waves.

"Thank you," he whispered, blinking out a tear.

He let it run down his cheek and trail the edge of his jaw to the earth. The waves crashed upon sand and shallow water surrounded his feet, carrying it away and making it a part of itself. Chris was gone. There was no bringing him back. Nathan stood there, gazing and understanding it was just a part of life and it was going to be okay. It was okay to move on. He didn't need to feel guilty or burdened anymore.

He stayed a while longer before smiling and walking the rest of the way back to his room. He felt both settled and invigorated, sitting down at the desk and pulling out his laptop. He started typing away, words flowing from him effortlessly. He had an idea for another book. He finally had some inspiration to share.

He worked on that for several hours before tiring. He video called Julia and the girls, who naturally bombarded him with questions. He brushed a lot of it off, and when the conversation drew near a close he spoke with Julia alone, sharing more of the details with her. He explained that Jackson would be joining them for Christmas, and she encouraged him with enthusiasm to do it. He felt in high spirits by the time they hung up, which was refreshing. It'd certainly been a while since he'd felt this at ease. He checked the time on his phone, realizing it was nearly lunch. He was hungry, so he wandered back to the lobby with intentions to patron the same restaurant. He was caught off guard when he spotted Maverick sitting alone, drinking coffee and eating. Instead of waiting for a seat of his own, Nathan decided to go over.

"Hey...where's your fiancée?"

Maverick looked up and smiled, "Oh! Hey! Sit down...she's not feeling good...kind of hung over."

"Oh," Nathan laughed, sitting across from his old friend.

They regarded each other hesitantly, neither one sure what to say. Maverick opened his mouth like he had something, then closed it and stared. Nathan finally drew in a deep breath and sighed.

"Oh, Mav…it's been a lot of years and a lot of…well, I won't lie, I was pissed off at you for a while there."

Maverick leaned forward, "Yeah, I know, Nathan, I know."

An awkward moment passed before Nathan leaned back and shrugged, "So, tell me, what actually happened that night? You had to have seen us…?"

Maverick nodded with a reverent expression on his face, as though he was remembering something fond, "Oh, yes…I saw you."

Before he could elaborate a waiter came up and offered to take an order for Nathan. He rattled off a quick request and thanked him before giving his attention back to Maverick.

"I thought so."

Maverick sighed before shrugging, "I really did feel bad about it, but…man, I *freaked* out when I saw you guys like that. Like, I'd been in love with Jackson for years, and I guess I took his devotion for granted. It just never even occurred to me that he could have eyes for anyone else, and when I saw that it was a real wake up call. I drove over to his place that night and jumped him. It was intense. It's still, like…even after all the shit he and I went through, and I am better-off apart, it's still this moment in my life that makes me really happy to think about. It was a relief…you have no idea what a relief it was to finally come out with it."

Nathan looked down, "I think I have a little understanding."

Maverick's face softened before growing a bit somber.

"I am sorry, though. I heard the things you said to him on the balcony. You know, how much you loved him and everything. It was weird, like, I felt so defensive and paranoid, but also, you were my best friend for so long…it was hard. I didn't want you to hurt like that, but I was way too prideful to be there for you, too. I wish

I'd have done things differently. I mean, I still would've wanted Jackson, but I should've at least tried to be your friend, too."

As much as Nathan wanted to accept the apology outright, there was a moment of hesitation. It wasn't for himself. Rather, the thing he couldn't get out of his head was the bruise on Jackson's face and the confession he'd made of his helplessness last night. It soured Nathan's stomach, and yet he could also appreciate what Maverick was trying to do. Though his feelings were guarded for what Maverick had done, how poorly he'd treated Jackson, how oblivious he was to the years of potential happiness he'd stolen from them both, he wanted to take this opportunity to be the bigger person. He wanted to forgive, even if he would never forget.

He swallowed and held Maverick's eyes while he forced a response, "It's okay, Mav. Honestly, had you tried to be my friend I definitely would've pushed you away. I wasn't in the right headspace for it. Besides, it worked out alright. I got with Chris and we had a lot of good years together."

Maverick's face darkened, "I'm so sorry about Chris, Nate. I heard what happened."

He faltered some hearing Chris's name from Maverick's mouth, "Thank you."

An uncomfortable silence slowly passed before Maverick cleared his throat. Nathan looked back up, listening while he tried to push the conversation forward.

"So, did it happen or what? You two here together now?"

Nathan fiddled with his hands and cleared his throat, "Yes, I would say so."

He felt a pit in his stomach while he waited for Maverick to respond. He was always so jealous, and for a moment there was a flicker of heat in his eyes. He was measured when he spoke, though, despite the momentary lapse.

"Well, that's good. I'm happy for you guys, I am. I mean, don't get me wrong, it's kind of a bitter pill to swallow, but it's for the best. He and I had moments of happiness, a lot of them, but overall I'd say it was a shit show. I'm happier now, and I can see he is, too. My fiancée is great, and it's more in line with the life I always pictured, frankly. And as far as you and him go, I think you could be really good for each other. You're…well, you're easier than me, and he's always been really soft for you. He'll be better with you, and you'll be good for him. It's for the best. It is."

Nathan grinned, "You sound like you're trying to convince yourself."

Maverick unexpectedly laughed, "Uh, well, I guess a part of me is. But there is a part of me that really means it."

Nathan nodded, "Well, thanks. I appreciate it."

Maverick shrugged. The waiter came back with Nathan's food and they switched to lighter conversation. Maverick talked about work, Nathan talked about his daughters and Julia. They had a decent time with surprising moments of nostalgia peppered into a larger backdrop of ambiguity. For fleeting seconds, it was almost as though they were children once again. By the time they were through, however, it was quietly understood it was nothing more than a moment in time. This was the end of the road for them, and though it'd been a softer than expected departure, that's exactly what it was at the end of the day; a final farewell to a friendship that always felt so unresolved. They hugged and said their goodbyes, both of them knowing it was over forever. They each felt lighter when they walked away from the restaurant. They both felt free to finally let it go.

While Nathan walked through the lobby, he noticed a crowd flowing from the hall where he'd left Jackson. He decided to wait, scanning and watching for Jackson to emerge. It wasn't long before he did, and as their eyes met they both smiled and started in for each other. Jackson hugged him and took his hand.

"Ah! Finally! It's over…I'm starving…"

"I just ate, but I'll keep you company."

Jackson looked at him with a playful expression on his face.

"Food would be nice, but that's not what I meant."

Nathan's cheeks reddened, "Your room or mine?"

Jackson assertively took Nathan's hand and led him to his room. As soon as they were shut inside they practically devoured each other, not bothering with the bed. It was more frantic than it'd been the first time, each of them emboldened by the familiarity gained from a shared night. Jackson felt like he was high on something good, and once they were through there was nothing short of bliss.

"God, I love the way you feel," he whispered, holding Nathan close, still sprawled out on the floor, tired and satisfied.

"I do, too."

They didn't say anything for a while. They indulged in a nice, long nap. When they woke, they showered for the hell of it. They wound up having sex again beneath the heat of the water, and then dressed and left the hotel for a fancy seafood dinner on the beach. They flirted and talked endlessly, excitedly making plans for the next time they'd be together. Their feelings were cozy, spiraling toward the elusive, intense love they'd only brushed against before. Of course, neither one of them was ready to say it out loud. It all felt rather fragile, despite how easily it was happening. They slept in Jackson's room that night, and the following morning when the time came to go, they hugged tightly in the parking lot, feeling so unwilling to let each other go. They did, but not until a long time was spent embraced.

"I'll see you over Christmas," Nathan almost asked, hovering beside his rental car.

Jackson smiled. He thought about being playful, cracking a joke or something. Instead, he found more vulnerable words kindly falling out.

"I'll see you at Christmas, Nathan. I'll be counting down the days."

Nathan felt his heart skip. He gave Jackson a final kiss and, just before he dropped into the car he answered, "So will I."

Jackson watched with hands in his pockets while Nathan drove away. It was true. He meant what he'd said. He really would be counting down the days.

The Last

Nathan was waiting anxiously in the airport with Julia and the girls for Jackson to arrive. It was Christmas Eve, so Julia and her wife, Wynona, were staying over as they did every year. Wynona decided to stay behind since she was cooking up dinner for everyone, but the girls came along because they were especially eager to see who this mysterious man was that had their Appa so enrapt. Julia tagged along out of curiosity as well. Having all of the women he loved most around only served to increase Nathan's anxiety, but he was doing his best to smile through and get to this big moment where his past and present would thoroughly, irreversibly collide.

Large swaths of people flooded out in spurts while planes landed. The baggage claim carousels went round and round in shifts. The television overhead, the one they were standing closest to, was lit up for Jackson's flight. Nathan's stomach felt fickle and light when the carousel started and people settled around. Julia touched his arm and smiled at him reassuringly, knowing the anticipation was really starting to build. He smiled back at her, nervously raising his brows. Not a moment later, he looked up and spotted Jackson. He was taller than most so he was easy to notice, and it wasn't long before Jackson clearly caught sight of Nathan, too. He picked up the pace. Nathan walked forward, quickly finding himself scooped up in Jackson's arms for a long awaited embrace. They exchanged a brief, PDA-approved kiss and took each other's hands. Nathan led him over to meet his daughters and say hello.

"Jules!" Jackson said, releasing Nathan's hand and giving her a quick hug, "Never thought I'd get to see you again!"

She laughed, "Yeah, well, that makes two of us!"

"These are our girls, Nancy and Alicia…you kind of met on Facetime," Nathan explained, gesturing toward them.

Jackson smiled with warmth, "Hello, yes! I recognize you. I know I'm not going to be able to tell you apart…"

They smiled and laughed. Nancy walked up to Jackson and hugged him, which clearly took him by surprise, but he quickly returned the affection. Alicia embraced him, too, and when all the pleasantries had been exchanged, Nathan took Jackson's hand again. They waited by the carousel for the luggage, breaking off into their own conversations for a while. Nathan was speaking low when he addressed Jackson.

"I've missed you way too much."

Jackson grinned and squeezed his hand, also doing his best to be discreet.

"Me, too. No matter how much we talk, it never feels like enough."

Not long after their small exchange, Jackson's luggage made its way out. He collected it, then the group walked out to Julia's SUV and got inside. This was when Jackson really felt like he was in the hot seat. The girls were relentless with their questions and interest.

"So, you went through college with Appa...we know a lot about you from their book," Alicia started.

"Uh-huh. Yep. Me, them and Maverick were all best friends through college," he looked at Nathan, "There was this other guy Greg we spent time with...did you keep in touch with him? Mav and I never did. He got kind of, uh...lost."

"No, I lost touch with him, too. He's on my Facebook, but he doesn't post very often."

Jackson shrugged, "Well, at least he's alive I guess."

Nathan nodded, "So it seems."

"Okay, so, we know you married Maverick. You're divorced now...how's that going? Are you happy? Are you over it?"

"Nancy!" Nathan warned.

"What? We want to make sure he's got good intentions with you, Appa!"

Nathan felt a little mortified, but Jackson chuckled and took it all in stride. It made Nathan settle down once he realized he could handle his nosy children just fine.

"Yes, we divorced. I've been really happy. I know it was a good call. He's engaged now, and I'm moving on, too. I promise, I'm not out to hurt your Appa."

"Sooo, you two *are* a thing, then? We know Appa talks to you every day, even if he tries to hide it from us," Alicia teased.

Jackson looked toward Nathan for a little guidance. It was true, they were official. They'd all but made that decision the weekend they'd spent in San Diego, but it was really true when they'd discussed it on the phone later. There was no issue when they spoke, quickly agreeing to close off the relationship and be partners, albeit long distance. Even so, it was going well. They spoke on the phone every night, and they texted every free moment they had, too. Nathan had fallen in love with him all those years ago, and so he slipped back into it easily. They hadn't said as much yet, but Nathan had a sneaking suspicion those affections were mutual.

"We're dating, yes. He's my boyfriend," Nathan clarified.

Jackson immediately looked relieved as he reached forward and gave Nathan's hand a squeeze. They exchanged smiles, and the girls took note. Nancy settled down in her seat, deciding to stop interrogating Jackson. Alicia pulled out her phone and started scrolling through her social accounts. It seemed they were satisfied, at least for the moment.

It wasn't long after when they arrived at Nathan's house. They went inside and Nathan led Jackson to his bedroom, telling him he could put his suitcase down in the closet. Jackson did before he stood before Nathan. Dinner was clearly ready because the house smelled amazing, and he still had yet to meet Julia's wife, but he wanted to take just a moment and say a proper hello, so he gathered Nathan in his arms and kissed him like he meant it. By the time he was though, Nathan felt a little weak in the knees and he wasn't able to hide it.

Nonetheless, they walked back out of the room to join everyone else. Wynona was introduced, then they all settled around the table for a roast dinner. The adults split a nice bottle of Cabernet, and the girls enjoyed some sparkling cider. The conversation flowed easily, though Jackson mostly listened. He answered when he was asked to share some stories about his exciting life as a New York prosecutor. The family seemed pretty interested in all that, which Jackson ate up. Nathan couldn't help but smile the whole time, remembering the natural entertainer Jackson was. He'd always been so good at carrying a conversation.

When dinner was through, everyone helped clean before a lengthy game of Monopoly to pass the time. It got pretty competitive, and in the end Nancy came out the winner. Everyone was exhausted after that, so they went off to bed, eager for Christmas to arrive the next morning. Julia and Wynona went to the guest bedroom, the girls went to theirs, and Jackson followed Nathan down to his. It wasn't frantic, but as soon as the door was securely shut they found one another. Jackson kissed Nathan deeply while they undressed, then lifted him and carried him to the bed.

"God, I've missed you...I can't believe how much I've missed you..." Jackson whispered, catching Nathan's lips between words.

Nathan didn't answer. He just pressed his tongue in Jackson's mouth and held onto him like he thought he might run off. This thing they had between them wasn't as simple as want or desire. It was more like need, like something they'd die without. They spent a long time just kissing, but eventually it became more. Nathan's breath and sounds were soft, yet he held onto Jackson so hard it might've hurt had he not been so focused on what they were doing. The necessity of it grew, and when it was done Nathan still clung to him like that. They briefly caught their breath before Jackson cracked a joke.

"Nathan...I'm not going anywhere..."

"Huh? Oh! I'm sorry," he laughed and released him, "I guess I do that sometimes."

Jackson chuckled and rolled off. The two of them freshened up and dressed in their pajamas before getting back in bed. It was much better actually being there together, rather than falling asleep with screens substituting a connection they constantly missed.

"I think it's hot you hold onto me like that," Jackson admitted before kissing the tip of his nose.

Nathan grinned through closed eyes. He looked so tired.

"Good, because I'm not really aware of it."

Jackson smiled and rubbed Nathan's arm, looking out the window. It was snowing and the moon was illuminating everything brilliantly.

"Your girls are really great. You're so lucky to have a family like that."

Nathan opened his eyes and Jackson gazed into them fondly.

"You and Mav never adopted or anything...why?"

"He didn't want them. I always did. I wanted them so bad."

Nathan was quiet for a moment, looking rather sorry.

"Don't feel bad. It is what it is. I made my choices, and I've lived through the consequences," Jackson quickly insisted.

Nathan briefly pressed his lips together.

"I'm not pitying you, but I do wish you'd had more of what you wanted."

Jackson shrugged, "Meh. I'm not dead yet. Who knows what'll happen, right?"

Nathan's eyes widened, "What...kids?"

Jackson instantly blushed, "I'm not saying we'll do that...I mean, I know we're still pretty fresh here. Don't get freaked out."

Nathan laughed, "I know. Although, I mean, as you know...it *is* kind of important to be on the same page at some point. Do you still want them?"

Jackson eyed him for a moment, clearly hesitant. He didn't want to screw everything up by making everything too big, too fast. Yet, this was Nathan, and Nathan was someone Jackson could always be honest with, so he decided to go out on a limb.

"I mean...maybe? I'm not sure. I'd definitely be open to it. What about you? Would you ever want to do that whole thing again?"

Nathan's smile widened, "I guess I'm not sure either? I mean, I'm definitely starting to have some of that empty nest anxiety. The girls are already researching colleges, and of course they can't do me the mercy of looking in state. They have big dreams for themselves. Nancy wants to be a lawyer, actually, you should talk to her about that while you're here. She'd love it. Alicia's always been a little softer than her. She's really into the idea of beauty school. But, uh, sorry...I got a little off track. My point is, um...I guess I'm saying maybe. I might be open to doing it all over again. Life seems like it's going to feel really quiet when they go, and that does freak me out."

Jackson was beaming by the time Nathan was finished rambling. It tugged on Nathan's heart in the best kind of way. He reached over and caressed Jackson's face.

"You look like a kid in a candy store," he joked.

"I feel like I am," he admitted, his tone more than serious.

Nathan's eyes wavered and he swallowed, the fluttering in his belly overwhelming.

"I love you, you know...I'm sorry if it's too early to say that."

Jackson placed his hand on Nathan's neck, his expression sincere when he responded.

"It's not too fast. I love you, too. I really do."

Nathan let out a sigh of relief, "God...I've wanted to hear you say that to me for so, *so* long."

Jackson smiled before kissing him tenderly. When he pulled back, he answered quietly, "I'm sorry it took me so long to say it."

Nathan pulled him close and held onto him, doing his best to contain the rush of emotions he felt. He clung to Jackson again, much as he had earlier when they'd been intimate. Jackson rested his head atop Nathan's and neither of them spoke. Nathan's grip softened as he drifted off to sleep. Jackson wasn't long after that.

When morning came, Jackson woke up and it was still dark outside. He carefully left the bed. Nathan was completely knocked out cold and snoring, which Jackson found adorable. After admiring him a brief moment, he crept to his suitcase and pulled out his wrapped gifts. He had a bag full of them, one for Nathan, each of his daughters, Richard, Julia, Wynona, and Nathan's parents and brothers, too. He tiptoed to the living room, the soft warm glow of lights on the tree giving the room a serene ambience while he carefully organized the presents beneath. He sat down on the couch and admired the view when he was done. It was so pleasant seeing all of those gifts there waiting for so many people. With Maverick, it'd always just been a handful because they never really celebrated with anyone else. Maverick didn't really care about Christmas, or family, or connection. Jackson sighed while he regarded the tree, recognizing the fact that those terrible years of his life were officially behind him.

"Hey…I woke up and you were gone," Nathan's voice suddenly interrupted his thoughts.

He looked exhausted while he walked over, rubbing his eyes when he took a seat. Jackson promptly put an arm around him and kissed the top of his head.

"Good morning, love. How'd you sleep? I just came out here to put some presents under the tree."

Nathan looked over, realizing there was a new little pile of gifts there waiting. He smiled and nestled up against Jackson.

"Mmmm…so good. I'm still tired."

Jackson rubbed his arm, "Sleep more then. I'm not planning to move."

Nathan yawned and nodded, closing his eyes and falling back asleep where they were. They stayed that way about an hour before the girls were up and at it. They were intentionally noisy because they wanted to get started on their morning. Julia and Nathan both chastised them, reminding them they had to wait for their grandparents to arrive. Ordinarily, Julia's parents would've come, but they'd done the typical thing and moved down to Florida and found the trip too much.

Jackson would've liked to have showered before seeing Nathan's parents and Richard for the first time, but he could see the tradition was lounging around in jammies all gross, at least for the morning, so he stayed as he was. Nathan got up from the couch and made coffee for everyone, pouring in some Bailey's for the adults. He distributed cups and helped Julia with a large breakfast of bacon, pancakes and eggs. Though Jackson would've liked to have gone in and helped, he was promptly cornered by Wynona and the girls. They talked his ear off about their own lives in that way teenagers do, and Jackson was truthfully interested in what they had to say. He did start getting into conversation with Nancy about what it was really like to be a lawyer, and how difficult and long the schooling had been. She didn't seem deterred by it. If anything, she only looked more resolute, now armed with some authentic information. Not long before breakfast was ready, there was a knock at the door and Wynona let everyone in.

Nancy and Alicia quickly introduced him to their grandparents and uncles. Jackson exchanged hellos, accepting a hug from Nathan's mother, siblings and Richard. His father was a bit icy, which didn't surprise him. Nathan warned him a while back he never accepted the way of things. Despite his father's frigid hello, it was otherwise clear everyone knew about the nature of their relationship. Richard was very friendly, and Jackson was grateful Nathan had that connection in lieu of what he couldn't have with his dad. At one point, his mother whispered a comment in Jackson's ear about how happy she was that Nathan was finally moving forward. After some time spent catching up and getting acquainted, the large family gathered around the table to eat, then huddled around the tree for presents. Nancy distributed gifts in little piles around each person's feet. From there it was a free-for-all. People tore into their presents and it was loud and terribly fun. Naturally, most of the gifts were for the girls. There was a moment, though, where Nathan and Jackson exchanged theirs. It was a gentle thing while Jackson watched Nathan opening his gift, looking completely moved when he realized it was a pastel blue sweater, much in the same fashion as the pink one from long ago. Beneath it, there was a floral scarf and a bottle of red wine.

"Oh, these are so nice," Nathan said with a smile, moving his fingers over the items.

"Yeah, I remembered you like colors like that, uh...pastels, right?"

"Yes...they're my favorite! Thank you!"

He hugged Jackson tightly, and Jackson returned the sentiment. When Nathan sat back he nodded, wanting Jackson to open his, too. Jackson grinned and tore into it, letting out a happy laugh when he realized what it was. The package contained a variety of things, all of which he enjoyed. There was a decorative weight for his desk in the shape of the scales of justice, a leather folio for his notes, a small sampler of high end smoked meats, fancy cheeses, and a bottle of nice, aged scotch to boot.

"Nate, this is awesome, thank you!"

Nathan bit his lip and shrugged, "I'm glad you like it."

They exchanged another hug before realizing Nancy and Alicia were watching. Nathan's cheeks flushed while he waved a dismissive hand at them, "Mind your own business, girls..." he teased.

They smiled, and before Nathan could get more insistent with them Nancy spoke up in a genuine, loving tone that caught him by surprise.

"It's just really nice to see you happy again, Appa."

Nathan practically melted while he smiled at his daughter with pride. Alicia nodded in agreement, backing her sister up. They regarded each other a moment before gently letting go, leaving everyone feeling a little lighter than before. Jackson held Nathan's hand while they watched everyone finish opening their gifts, and when it was through movies were put on and more spirited coffees were handed out. The morning wore on like that, slow and fun, until the extended family decided it was time to go. The first to leave, Richard paused in the doorway and exchanged a look with Nathan, the sort that felt like a silent, sweet blessing. It left him a little choked up before long hugs were shared with the rest over chatty goodbyes. When it was over a collective sigh of relief was had in a much quieter house. They took turns showering and the girls fussed with their gifts. Julia and Wynona hung around for dinner, then they wandered out, too. Nancy and Alicia stayed up for a while, but they were tired from waking early, and before long it was just Nathan and Jackson left to themselves, resting on the couch and gazing at the Christmas tree together. It was just like the morning, only now that the day was behind them, they felt more relaxed.

"I loved this, every minute of it. It's exactly the kind of life I always wanted," Jackson said.

Nathan looked content while he relaxed, wrapping his arms around Jackson's torso.

"I loved it, too. I loved sharing all of this with you."

The two of them quietly joked and reminisced for a while before settling down and accidentally falling asleep on the couch. It wasn't until the girls woke the following morning that they came to, launching into a quick week that would lead up to New Year's. They did a lot of things during that time. As a family, they looked at lights, ate at nice restaurants, played lots of card games and had long, involved conversations that were surprisingly deep, considering Nathan's daughters were only teens. Jackson could tell that losing Chris had been a major moment in their lives and a catalyst for maturity seldom found in girls their age. He admired them for it. They were resilient and strong, and Nathan was, too. He could see how tightly knit the three of them were, and he appreciated how open to bringing him into that intimate, safe place they were. He slipped into their family dynamic easily, and was surprised at how quickly he felt like they were cementing themselves in his heart. Time passed entirely too fast, and before he knew it, it was New Year's Eve and he was due to return to New York the following day.

Nancy and Alicia left to spend that night with Julia and Wynona. They all shared dinner over at their house, then Nathan and Jackson returned home to enjoy what little time they had left. Nathan lit up the fireplace in the living room and piled some blankets before it. They made love; deep, connected, actual love, then rested in the blankets unwilling to let go.

"Damn, I *really* don't want to leave..." Jackson complained, trying to hold onto every sensation so it'd get him through the long months they'd soon spend apart.

"I know. I hate this. But, I mean, there's Facetime, and we can plan our next visit. Maybe I'll come to New York. I've never seen it. When do you think I could? Maybe President's Day?"

Jackson felt a pang in his stomach, "Yeah, that's probably the next time I can swing anything. But it's so far away..."

Nathan felt sick to his stomach, too.

"I know."

The weight of that truth hung heavy in the air while they clung to each other. Jackson felt desperate to stay, he'd have given just about anything. Alas, it wasn't meant to be. They simply made the best of what little time they had. Despite their ages, the newness of the relationship and the weight of borrowed time made it possible for them to get physical twice more that final night. When the morning inevitably came, they kissed and held onto each other, trying their best to ignore the nausea in their guts. They begrudgingly let go, showered, and got ready. With a heavy sense of melancholy, they shared a cup of coffee and then headed for the airport. They didn't speak because it simply hurt too much. Jackson, in particular, felt awful. He wanted to stay. He wanted to stay there with beautiful Nathan. He wanted to stay and help finish raising up those smart, delightful girls. He wanted to spend some time getting to know Julia again, and even Wynona, too. He wanted that family. He wanted that belonging, and he didn't want to do it from afar.

Still. He had a job and a life that wasn't so simple to leave behind, despite the fact that none of it was ever what he'd wanted in the first place. The truth of that cut deep as he acknowledged it. It haunted his mind up until the moment they arrived at the airport. Nathan parked and walked Jackson inside, nothing but the sound of his rolling suitcase between them. It lingered when Jackson embraced Nathan, kissed him, and tearfully said goodbye. It ate at him while he waited in the security line, knowing Nathan was standing there watching him leave. His stomach lurched while he continued to do his best to hold back threatening tears and endless frustration.

What the hell are you doing, Jack? This was never the life you wanted. You never wanted New York, or to be so swamped with cases there was nothing else to live for. You always wanted that small town charm. You always wanted to be near family and friends. You wanted simple, easy, warm and down to earth, not difficult, cold pursuits of wealth and status. You never wanted to spend the bulk of your life in rooms full of people who never gave a damn who you are!

He was just about to flash his ID and ticket when he abruptly stopped and turned around. He locked eyes with Nathan, who clearly forced himself to smile while he waved. Jackson swallowed, his heart pounding while the people around him started to grow impatient. He barely registered them as he instinctively went beneath the ropes and ran around them, not toward the gate, but back toward Nathan. He sprinted, his suitcase rolling loudly behind him, before he dropped it and grabbed Nathan hard, holding him tight.

"Jack…what are you doing?" he asked, hugging him through the shock.

Jackson didn't say anything for a while. He just held him, reluctant to let go. Eventually, he pulled back and looked him sincerely in the eyes.

"What if I stayed? Could I do that? Would you want me?"

Nathan let out a breathy laugh and shook his head with disbelief. Jackson swallowed, feeling exceptionally exposed.

"Jackson…there's nothing in the world I ever wanted more."

Jackson laughed, smiled, and picked Nathan up. He spun him around, then gently placed him on the ground and gave him a kiss. They indulged a moment before releasing one another and clasping their hands.

"Let's go then, beautiful. It seems we've suddenly got nothing but time."

Nathan smiled and squeezed Jackson's hand while they started to walk off. It was true. Though they were pushing forty and still navigating the complicated intricacies of their lives, both separate and together, the fact of the matter was there was plenty of time left to do this thing all over again. For all the times they'd fallen, faltered, succeeded and flew, something about this time around felt like it was going to work. They'd lived lives together, then splintered off and fractured. Their hearts had once beat for other people entirely, but now, in the wake of all the loss and mistakes, the divorce and the death, the wondering and the unknown, there was hope for rejuvenation, a new life, a second chance at the things they both desired. The things Jackson never had, and the things Nathan still wanted more of. Though neither of them would ever want to change a single moment of it all, the truth of it remained.

Of all the times they'd fallen in love, they knew in their hearts that this one would be the last.

Printed in Great Britain
by Amazon